T0160889

ADVANCE PRAISE

"*From Away* is a complex, surprising, and haunting novel. Sutton's trademark wit lives within these pages, but here he reaches deeper, into a dark place, and finds something richer, something more human, than in any of his previous books. This is a page-turner of a different kind: mysterious, weird, and deeply affecting."
— Tod Goldberg, *New York Times*–bestselling author of *Gangster Nation, Gangsterland,* and *Living Dead Girl*

"I loved this book—it's the best take on ghosts and how they work that I've ever read. Scary and mad but real, with crackling dialogue, *From Away* is a rare creature: a proper novel and a proper ghost story. I massively enjoyed it."
— Steven Moffat, co-creator of *Sherlock* and writer/producer of *Dr. Who*

"Phoef Sutton's *From Away* is a unique trip of a book. It starts off as a family drama, then morphs into an intense ghost story. It's about finding love in the real world and finding freedom to escape into the real hereafter. It's funny, wild, and touching, and not like any other novel I've ever read."
— Robert Ward, author of *Red Baker* and *Four Kinds of Rain*

Also by Phoef Sutton

Colorado Boulevard
Heart Attack & Vine
Crush
15 Minutes to Live

By Janet Evanovich and Phoef Sutton

Curious Minds
Wicked Charms

FROM AWAY

PHOEF SUTTON

Prospect Park Books

Published by Prospect Park Books
2359 Lincoln Avenue
Altadena, California 91001
www.prospectparkbooks.com

Distributed by Consortium Book Sales & Distribution
www.cbsd.com

Library of Congress Cataloging-in-Publication Data
Names: Sutton, Phoef, author.
Title: From away / Phoef Sutton.
Description: Altadena, California : Prospect Park Books, [2018]
Identifiers: LCCN 2017040327 (print) | LCCN 2017043967 (ebook) | ISBN 9781945551116 (Ebook) | ISBN 9781945551109 (paperback)
Subjects: LCSH: Psychological fiction. | BISAC: FICTION / Psychological. | FICTION / Family Life. | FICTION / Suspense. | GSAFD: Suspense fiction.
Classification: LCC PS3569.U896 (ebook) | LCC PS3569. U896 F76 2018 (print) | DDC 813/.54--dc23
LC record available at https://lccn.loc.gov/2017040327

Cover design by David Ter-Avanesyan
Book layout and design by Amy Inouye
Printed in the United States of America

To my brother John,
who made me want to be a writer

ONE

Christmas is a time for ghost stories.

That's why I'm making this for you now, to set aside and wrap in a red and green ribbon and give to you on your twenty-first birthday.

I have to believe you'll have a twenty-first birthday. I have to believe you'll grow up tall and straight and strong and beautiful, even though believing doesn't come naturally to me.

Well, naturally or not, I'll will myself to do it; to believe that one day I'll hand this to you and you'll open it and read all about your first Christmas on Fox Island and assume you got it mixed up with childhood fairy tales and fantasies. Probably you won't even believe it after you've read it.

No, I'm wrong; you'll believe it, unless you've changed completely. Believing is easy for you, and not just because you're a child. It's a part of who you are to think that there's wonder and mystery in the world. I could never do that; that's just one of the ways you and your poor uncle are different.

So, I'm telling you a ghost story even though I never believed in ghosts. In those days, a lot of people did. Ghosts and angels and all that. I'm writing about the end of the twentieth century here, the years of the internet and

Prozac and Viagra, so it's no wonder that people wanted to believe there was a supernatural heart beating somewhere just out of sight.

The first ghost I remember ever seeing was in my seventh-grade P.E. class. I didn't buy it. I might have been convinced if it had looked anything like a ghost. Transparency would have been nice. Strands of ectoplasm streaming from a skull-like face would have helped a lot. Or a shrouded form floating above the floor; if I'd seen that, I'd have been a convert in a heartbeat. Instead, what I saw looked a lot like my junior high gym teacher.

I was policing the equipment after a vigorous game of Murder Ball (also called Dodge Ball or Kill the Queer—depends on what part of the country you're from) in which I'd received more than the usual number of stinging blows to the face from the tightly inflated ball. The resounding *ping* produced when rubber struck my cheekbone was bringing joyous merriment to the line of kids across from me. Fortunately, David Needles, four boys down, gave an even more delightful whimper when the ball hit his midsection, so the boys were distracted from me and the game turned into something like a handball match, with David Needles filling the role of the wall. A part of me felt sorry for him, but mostly I was relieved they'd found another victim. In junior high, as in war, it doesn't pay to care too much about the other guy.

So, I was left to concentrate on the throbbing pain in my head while Mr. Ingram, the new gym teacher, cheered my classmates on. What it all had to do with meeting the President's Physical Fitness Standards was a mystery to me.

When the bell rang signaling the end of class and sending new blasts of pain through my head, I remembered it was my turn as Equipment Monitor. It wasn't a job anybody loved, but at least it kept me out of the showers. So, while the rest of the boys ran off to inflict new and unconsciously homoerotic torment on David Needles, I went to collect the balls.

Bending down to pick them up made my pummeled face hurt all over again, and I had to suppress a flood of nausea as I stood up. That's when I saw Mr. Meloni, blue gym suit and all, sitting in the bleachers, his referee's whistle resting on his massive gut.

Nothing unusual about that. Mr. Meloni always sat there. Only thing was, Mr. Meloni had died of a brain aneurism three weeks before. I dropped the balls, and they pinged off the floor and rolled away.

"Pick 'em up, faggot," said the ghost of Mr. Meloni.

Instinctively, I glanced away at the rolling balls, and when I looked back to the bleachers Mr. Meloni was gone. All that was left of him was an emotion washing through me, like a sound wave broadcasting from where Meloni had been sitting; pure, unadulterated *annoyance*. Once that passed, all trace of him was gone.

And I didn't believe he'd ever been there, not for a minute. It must have been an illusion, brought on by the pain in my head and my own vivid imagination.

Why didn't I believe? I know you would have, but you have to remember, Maggie, you're not me. I'm a third child, and my mom told me there was no Santa Claus before I turned four. Marvels were never a part of my world.

So I analyzed it. I asked myself, if Mr. Meloni had traveled back from beyond the grave, wouldn't he have had more to say? Wouldn't he have delivered some pronouncement, like Marley did to Scrooge, about how life should be lived? Or, like Hamlet's father, wouldn't he have relayed some vital piece of information that was disturbing his eternal rest? Wouldn't he have returned to impart some threat or some warning, some regret or some insight? He wouldn't have come back to say, "Pick 'em up, faggot." He wouldn't have bothered to resurrect himself just to send me a psychic message that he was still annoyed with my incompetence. It wouldn't have been worth the trip.

Also, wouldn't the experience of dying, of meeting St. Peter and sitting at the right hand of the Lord, or of descending to the depths of Hell, or of floating into that bright light people were always going on about, have changed the guy in some way? Instead, the Mr. Meloni I saw on the bleachers was the same asshole he'd been in life. And if you weren't transformed in some transcendent and cosmic way, I wondered, what was the point of dying in the first place? And, most damning of all, if you were going to come back, why in hell would you appear to a nobody like me?

So, as I gathered the balls again, I dismissed the whole thing, denied it, put it out of my mind. Until the next time.

I went to get a Coke just now and to see how your mother is doing. She's sleeping in a chair beside you; she tries to slip into the bed with you, but the nurses always catch her and shoo her out. I'm back in this typically depressing hospital waiting room, sitting by a grim little aluminum Christmas tree and flipping channels on a TV mounted high on the wall. No holiday programs, even though it's Christmas Eve. Why do they run all of them two weeks early nowadays? I could really use the Grinch or Frosty to keep me company. Or even some half-assed remake of *A Christmas Carol*.

Ghosts and Christmas. Most people don't get the connection anymore, but your grandpa taught us all about it. I wish you could have known him. He was a professor of English Lit at Georgetown, and every year he had us practice the old Victorian tradition of telling spooky stories on Christmas Eve. We got really good at it, me and your mother and your Uncle George. While our friends were hanging stockings, putting out milk and cookies for Santa, and watching Charlie Brown find the true meaning of Christmas, the Kehoe kids were sitting in our dark living room, flashlights under our chins, telling tales of reclaimed limbs and family curses and premature burials.

Your grandmother, the math teacher, didn't approve of these flights of fancy, of course, but we appeased her by assuring her that we all knew it was make-believe. Ghosts were not a part of her worldview; she had little patience for Santa and none at all for a walking dead apparition like Jesus.

Going to sleep after our spooky stories, the visions that danced in our heads were white-garbed specters and headless widows, and the things we heard scampering across the roof or skittering down the chimney were not coming to give gifts. Not that they frightened us. The imaginary thrills and chills were delightful and intriguing; they gave just the right amount of spice to counter the sugary sweetness of Everybody Else's Christmas. A Kehoe Christmas was naughty *and* nice, candy *and* coal. That was as it should be, because Christmas was a magic time, and magic was never all light, but always half dark, just like the world.

So, with an upbringing like that, it didn't really surprise me two weeks ago when I was awakened on a cold December night by the voice of my lost love. All right, maybe Anne wasn't dead—maybe she'd only dumped me. But that didn't make the sound of her voice any less disturbing and heartbreaking. It still rocketed me from sleep and left me in a cold sweat to face a sleepless night in my dark apartment. You don't have to be dead to be a ghost.

I glanced at my bedside clock. 10:04. That was another way this night reminded me of childhood Christmases; I'd tried to go to bed as early as possible so as to make the morning come more quickly. Not in hopes of receiving presents or treats. The coming day held no special promise except that I wouldn't have to spend it alone in the bed I'd shared with Anne.

I turned on the lamp. All alone. The apartment seemed even more desolate in the light. My eyes fell with perverse accuracy on the traces of her still left in the room. Those books she'd loaned me—if I'd gotten around to reading them, would she still have wanted to see other people? But I'd listened to her albums, hadn't I? Sang along with her to the tuneful angst of Paula Cole and Sheryl Crow, and that hadn't stopped her from wanting more room.

I knew her bra was still in the second drawer, even though I couldn't see it. She'd forgotten it one hurried morning when she'd been late for work. I'd called her when I found it while making the bed that afternoon and we'd laughed, and I'd said I was holding it hostage and we'd laughed again. Now it would be nothing more than the embarrassing centerpiece of the always hideous returning-of-the-borrowed-stuff encounter we had yet to schedule.

It occurred to me I should just do it right then; I was up anyway. Put all her things in a box and drop it on her doorstep. How could I be expected to sleep with these reminders of her lurking about the room, ready to ambush me wherever I glanced?

And that voice. That beautiful, husky, just-about-to-break voice I'd loved so much and that I could hear so well it might have been in the room with me. How could I sleep at all when I never knew when it might call out again, saying those words I knew so well: "Anne isn't here right now, so leave a message after the beep."

It served me right for dating the girl who lived in the apartment next door.

I jumped out of bed, sending the television remote, which had been tangled in my sheets, sailing across the room, hitting the floor with a rattle and a scattering of batteries. Hell with it. I padded on my bare feet to the living room, pulling up my pajama pants as I walked. I used to sleep in the nude, but I had begun to find the sight of my own naked body just another depressing reminder of Anne.

(Suddenly, I'm thinking I can never show this to you, picturing you as the innocent girl you are now. But you'll be a woman when you read it, wise in the ways of love. Depressing thought.)

Looking out the window, I saw a nightclub cruise ship gliding down the black river, lights ablaze. I could get in my car and be in Georgetown in fifteen minutes. I could be sitting in Blues Alley, listening to jazz and drinking from a longneck bottle. I could be grabbing life and living it.

I picked up one of my many videos of Italian horror pictures, went back to my room, reassembled the remote, and fell into the bed to watch somebody else's nightmare.

Fifteen minutes later, her voice was coming through the wall again. "Anne isn't here right now, so leave a message after the beep." And then, far more horrifying than anything Baron Blood was doing on my TV screen, the message began. "Hey, honey, this is Bill—"

I turned up the volume so that Elke Sommer's screams could drown out the rest of Bill's sentence. (Dear God, what kind of nitwit would call a woman like Anne "honey" or "sweetie" or anything at all ending in a long "e"?) When it was safe and silent, I shut off the set and called your mother to ask her advice.

"Don't do it," Charlotte said.

"But she gave me a key. I could just pop in, turn the volume down on the answering machine, pop out—"

"Sammy," my sister's voice was calm, but insistent. When we were kids, she used to do that voice in imitation of our mother. Now that she was a mother herself, she did it for real. "This is a terrible idea. Don't do it."

"Why not? Just pop—"

"Don't pop, Sammy. Trust me, breaking into her

apartment is a terrible idea—"

"It's not breaking. She gave me her key."

"When you were *dating*. Now you're not. So, all key rights have been revoked."

"No, no, you're wrong there. She gave me the key *before* we were dating. So I could feed her fish when she spent that weekend in Baltimore. So, it's not a 'boyfriend key.' It's a 'good neighbor key,' and I'm still her neighbor."

"Sammy." I could hear the bedsprings squeak as Charlotte sat up, taking a more insistent pose. "When you move to the boyfriend role, that totally preempts the neighbor role. You can't go back."

"Who says?"

"And why would a good neighbor break into her apartment at eleven o'clock at night, anyway?"

"Not break, 'let.' Let myself in."

"But why?"

"Well...," I knew I was losing the debate on points. I always lost debates with my sister on points. But, ultimately, I always won them through blind persistence. "Her machine's on too loud. She doesn't want everyone in the building hearing her messages."

"You're the only one who can hear them."

"Well, she especially wouldn't want me to hear them. I'm her ex-boyfriend. Those calls are personal."

"So, to preserve her privacy, you're going to break into her apartment?"

"If I have to."

"Sammy, if it was daylight, you'd know this was a bad idea."

Another voice came over the line. Distant, but piping and clear and full of energy. "Who are you talking to, Mommy?"

Charlotte's voice sounded even sleepier as she answered, face away from the phone. "Darling, why are you up?"

"I heard you talking."

"God, it is *so* past your bedtime."

"I'm not tired. Who's on the telephant?"

"Uncle Sammy."

"Hi, Unca!" you called out. "Can I say hi?"

(Yes, that's you, appearing in the story at last. And not a moment too soon, I can hear you saying.)

"Yeah, tell him he's crazy," your mother said.

You took the phone, dropped it, then picked it up again. "Hi, Unca. Mom says you're crazy."

Even in these depths, your voice, ringing so musically, so clearly enunciating its mispronunciations, could make me laugh. "I am. Totally." And I vibrated my lips with my finger to prove it, sending you into fits of laughter. "Anne left her machine on too loud. Should I go turn it down?"

"Sure," you said.

"That's right," Charlotte called from the background, "listen to her. She's four."

"Four and a half," you snapped. You dropped the phone, and I jumped as it clattered on the floor. "I wanna watch a movie!"

"No, it's bedtime." Charlotte picked up the phone. "I have to put the little creep to bed. You want to come over?"

A tempting thought. The warmth of Charlotte's house. Her lumpy pull-out sofa. The homey clutter of your toys underfoot. The fragmented remains of our family.

"No, I should sleep."

"And you're not going to do anything stupid?"

"Don't be stupid, Unca!" you hollered.

"I won't be stupid."

"By stupid, I mean don't break into her apartment," Charlotte said.

"I know what you mean."

"Can I tell Unca my joke?"

"We're going to bed."

"Not till I tell my joke!" You could always go from zero to furious in two seconds flat.

Charlotte sighed and handed over the phone. She might occasionally match our mother's firmness of tone, but Charlotte can never really stand up to you, Maggie. She values your friendship too much.

"Unca?"

"Hey, Maggie."

"Okay. Well, okay, well, here's my joke, okay? Okay?"

"Okay."

"Knock-knock."

"Who's there?"

"Banana. Knock-knock."

"Who's there?"

"Banana. Knock-knock."

"Who's there?"

"Banana. Knock-knock."

"Who's there?"

"Banana. Knock-knock."

"Who's there?"

A long pause. "I forget the rest."

I laughed.

"That's not the joke, Unca!" you cried out, affronted.

"Do you want me to tell it?" Charlotte asked.

"No! It's my joke!"

"Tell it tomorrow."

"I'll tell you tomorrow, Unca."

"Night, Sam—" Charlotte started to say, but you hung up before she could finish, leaving me alone in an apartment that felt darker and emptier than before I'd called.

The phone beeped and whined and told me that if I wanted to make a call I should hang up and dial again. I pressed the button to summon the dial tone again, dialed four digits of Anne's number, then hung up. Was that what I was going to be reduced to? The masochism of calling her machine just so I could torture myself with the sound of her smoky voice in its cheerfully welcoming tone?

Anne wasn't one of those people who changed her outgoing message frequently. I redid mine once a month, with different selections from movie soundtracks playing in the background—Bernard Herrmann's score for *Vertigo* seemed to fit the mood this month. Not Anne. She had the same recording on her machine that she'd had when I'd first called her last spring, when she was still just a neighbor, to tell her that I'd gotten some of her mail by mistake. (It wasn't quite true that I'd fallen in love with her voice right then, but I'd sure as hell felt it resonate somewhere deep and low inside myself.) And that was the same message I'd gotten when I nervously called to ask her out the first time, to see Susan Werner sing at the Birchmere in Alexandria. And when we were first dating, I'd hear that greeting when I would call to leave messages of playful, erotic promise. And once that stage had passed and the messages had transformed to simple logistical plans for the weekend, that was still the greeting that welcomed me. And now, with it all over and done with, that same outgoing message still answered her calls, unaffected by any of this, as if I'd never been in her life at all.

Her key was hanging on the hook in the kitchen where I kept all my keys. It was there in plain sight, and she could have taken it last Friday when she had responded to my marriage proposal, so she had nobody to blame but herself.

Walk out my door, five steps to hers, key in the lock, open it, and step in. I'd done it many times, but now my heart was pounding and the familiar ground of her apartment was transformed into a foreign landscape, enemy territory.

Well, I wasn't doing anything bizarre there. I wasn't going to rifle her drawers and search for evidence of an infidelity she'd assured me didn't exist.

She hadn't left me for someone else, she'd told me. She'd just felt that things were going too fast, that I was trying to take the relationship to a level she wasn't ready to go to yet. So, fine, I'd said, let's go back three steps, whatever you want. But she'd said no, love wasn't like a board game. What the hell did that mean? If she'd just said she'd been cheating on me it would have been easier to take. Better to be left for another man than for some metaphorical bullshit I couldn't even follow, much less argue with.

(Have you been through all this yet, Maggie? Have you been lied to, or had to lie to someone? I've always prayed you'd be spared that kind of pain; now I hope to God you have the chance to feel it.)

Well, I wasn't here to snoop or take any petty revenge. All I was going to do was turn the volume down.

There it was. Loudness up to ten. What sort of sadistic move was that? I set it down to zero, realized she'd notice that and turned it up to four. Over and done with. Five messages on the machine. She'd get home and listen and I wouldn't have to hear a word of it. And I didn't want to. Her life was her own now, and pressing playback, easy as it was, would be a clear invasion of her privacy.

I pressed playback.

"First new message, sent today at 8:04 a.m." And after the computer voice, Bill's voice came on. "I'm watching you walk out to your car and I'm just feeling, like, so incredibly sad that you're not with me, but so happy I can feel this sad, do you know what I mean? I mean, it's like this whole stupid house of mine was like *altered* while you were here. You know, like the holodeck on the *Enterprise*; it's an empty room and then, *voosh,* you're here, and it's, like, Paris or Arabia or something. But now you're gone and it's just back to being my house again and I can't believe I'll be able to get up the energy to go get dressed and go to work and watch you there all day without being able

to talk to you or touch you. I'm not going to make it till you come back here tonight. Bye."

"Second new message, sent today at 8:17 a.m. 'I found your red scarf under the sofa. Bye again.'"

I hit stop and the tape started to rewind itself.

Hand on the table to support my suddenly heavy weight, I knew how wrong I'd been. This was worse, much worse, than any intellectual reasons she could come up with for dumping me. This was real. This was primal. This hit me way down in some pre-evolutionary level. You didn't even have to be human to feel this pain. This was the pain the smaller mountain goat felt after it clashed horns with the larger one and lost and went tumbling down the hill. This was the pain the loser bull elephant felt when it had to stand aside and watch the victor mount the beautiful gray round rump of his beloved.

As the pain passed from the primitive parts of my brain to the more civilized ones, it only got worse. Personal insult. That she should choose this one, Bill Zacharias, the computer nerd at work, a man who would use *Star Trek* references in love talk. How was Bill superior to me? Was Bill better looking? A better lover? Was she fucking crazy? Or were her evolutionary instincts instructing her to pick the man whose offspring would thrive best in the twenty-first century?

I squeezed my eyes shut, not crying, but feeling the pressure of tears behind my eyes and a throb of pain in my head, because this *hurt*, this physically hurt. I opened them and blinked the watery distortion away.

That's when I saw the old woman. I hadn't turned the lights on, so I couldn't see too clearly, but I knew I wouldn't have seen this image clearly even in broad daylight. She was on the sofa, her flesh a topography map of crinkled lines. She twisted on the cushions, and the cushion did not move under her, not one bit. Her bloodshot eyes stared up at the ceiling in a look of such agonized want that I felt my own pain well up again. But it was a stronger pain now; a biting, bitter, lonely agony that could only be built up after years, decades, a lifetime.

Shut your eyes, boyo, she's not there and you know it, I told myself. *She doesn't match her surroundings; she floats above that sofa like a bad computer special effect in a B-movie. Clench your eyelids shut until you get the light show and open them and she'll be gone, you'll see.*

I looked again and she was staring right at me. Watery gray eyes with pupils shaped like keyholes. Dry skin turning moist now. Wrinkles smoothing, skin being pulled taut. Thin gray hair turning red, turning gold. Eyes focusing, rounding, turning green as the ocean. Turning into beauty. The agonized loneliness was turning to yearning, to hope that flowed from her now-lovely, now-youthful eyes into mine.

The overhead light flared on, and another woman screamed.

I felt my knees buckle. I pushed off from the table, out of breath, sweat soaking my body. The answering machine was beeping and clicking and finishing its rewind. Mere seconds had passed.

"Sammy?"

Anne was in the doorway, going from anger to relief and back to anger. I turned to face her, but I kept feeling those wanting green eyes on my back.

"Did you let yourself in?" Anne demanded.

I swallowed, trying to bring some saliva to my parched throat.

"Why are you here?" Anne wasn't beautiful when she was angry.

"You left your machine on too loud. I turned it down."

Anne stared at me in disbelief. "You used my key? Do I have to take it back? Can't I even trust you?"

"Trust?" I tried to get indignant, but I was too drained.

She glanced at the machine. "You listened to my messages."

Well, I was making this much too easy for her, wasn't I? Now I was a creepy stalker, and she was lucky to be rid of me.

"I'm sorry." I wasn't sure if I would hate myself more for trying or not trying. "I know I moved things along too fast, I know I scared you off, but I'll give you room, I'll give you all the room you need. I just think we should give it another chance."

No change in her face. She wasn't letting herself listen. "Go home, Sam."

"You won't even talk to me?"

"You're lucky I don't call the police."

"Come on. You can't tell me you're afraid of me; you can't tell me that."

She looked away, conceding the point. But any ground I gained I immediately lost by exclaiming, "Bill Zacharias?"

"You don't even know him," she said, coldly.

"What's to know?"

She sighed. "He's smart. He's got a future. He's got a *job*. I'm thirty years old, Sam. I have to start thinking about that stuff. I've got to start thinking about kids and—"

"That's what *I* wanted!" I sounded as affronted as you always do, Maggie, when you're threatened with bedtime.

"Yes, but there's a difference." And the difference was me. She ticked off the high points of my life: twenty-eight years old, part-time substitute teacher, part-time clerk in a video store, a man who spent his off-hours running a fanzine website about Italian Gothic cinema. "This is not a husband. This is not the father of children," she said. "This is a fifteen-year-old boy."

So, it *was* all about reproduction in the end. The larger mountain goat *had* clobbered me.

She could have run through that descriptive list in a fond way, even an affectionate or amused way. She might at least have criticized me with hope, like my mother always had, as if she thought I might listen and improve. Instead, she said it all with cool disinterest. When she dumped me the week before, she'd said she still wanted to be friends. A friend was the last thing she was now.

Didn't she remember that I was the same man who'd held her when she'd awakened from nightmares, weeping? That she'd once spent nine hours straight sitting on a bed with me, doing nothing but talking—about the wine shop she wanted to open one day, about how her uncle touched her once when she was nine—pouring out secrets she swore she'd never told anyone else? We'd built up habits; we had a favorite song; we had private jokes no one got but us. No one would ever laugh at those jokes again.

I turned and trudged to the door, muttering under my breath. "Italian horror movies are a hell of a lot better than *Star Trek*."

"What?" she asked.

"The guy's a Trekker, Anne. He said you were like the holodeck."

"What possible difference could that make?"

Well, if she couldn't see that, had we ever had anything in common at all?

Out of the corner of my eye (and only out of the corner, because when looking straight on there was nothing there), I saw the woman on the sofa, old again and weeping with her face in her hands, her hope turned to ash that I could taste in my mouth.

"I can't just stop loving you," I said to Anne.

"Sure, you can," she answered, and shut the door.

TWO

didn't sleep at all that night, but I didn't think about the old woman, either. Call it denial, call it willful blindness, call it what you want, but those visions hadn't been a part of my life for a long time, and I wasn't about to admit to myself that they were starting again. Besides, I had enough pain of my own to keep me occupied without letting some spook's sorrow add to it.

I resisted the temptation to lash back at Anne in some childish way. Instead, I put on a bootlegged video of *Lo Spettro* (Panda Films, Italy, 1963; four and a half stars on the Kehoe Scale, docked half a point for being a sequel). I drifted off to sleep just before my favorite part, where Barbara Steele's murderously insane husband accidentally drinks the poison she'd intended for herself.

My eyelids had just fallen shut when all at once it was broad daylight and the gothic black and white romanticism on the TV had been replaced by smeary color and a man screaming about an amazing new car wax polymer. I dug through the covers for the remote and started to channel surf. With my illegal cable hookup (do those words even mean anything to you, in your distant future?) I had the proverbial "fifty-seven channels and nothin' on" to choose from, and I could spend hours flipping through them, never landing on any show for more than a second, always hopeful that something wonderful was about to turn up. You know, the same way I lived my life.

On mornings like that, getting out of bed feels impossible. I can picture doing it, but I can picture flying, too—that doesn't mean I know how to get started. I could have spent the whole day stretched out on that bed, flipping channels, eating Krispy Kreme donuts. These lethargic moods don't hit me too often, but when they do, they make all the sense in the world. "Just stay in bed," they say. "You have everything you want here. You don't need the rest of the world; it sure as hell doesn't need you. Just watch the glimpses of the sportscasters and TV chefs and news pundits and old dead sitcom stars as they flash by like passengers on a train speeding past you. Let them hurry, the idiots. You have four pillows and a dozen donuts. Do they have anything better to offer?"

Your mother hates it when I get that way. She starts calling me the Krispy Kreme Donut Man and worrying that I'll turn into one of those agoraphobic types who are afraid to leave their house. Shows how much she knows. It's the people who go out all the time who are the scared ones—you can see it on their faces as they flip by on the TV. They're afraid to be alone with themselves, afraid to be still. They keep in motion to hold the fear at bay. At times like this, I think about those freaks you hear about on the news now and then—you know, the four-hundred-pound men who have to be taken to the hospital on a forklift and buried in a piano case—and they seem to me like the bravest people on Earth. They have taken the time to face their demons. And eat them.

Okay, I know that sounds crazy to you. But when the Krispy Kreme Donut Man mood is on me, it makes perfect sense. That's the dangerous thing about moods. They convert you to their cause at the same time they attack you.

The phone rang. I had just taken a bite of a glazed, and

I cursed the gods of timing as I muted the volume on the TV and answered.

"Hello?"

"Is this Samuel Kehoe?"

I only had to think for a second. "Yeah."

"This is Cara Brendel at Willoughby Preschool." Willoughby was your preschool in those days.

"Is Maggie okay?" I sat up, all alert. Nothing banished the Donut Man like danger to my Maggie.

"We've been trying to reach her mother—"

"She's working. Is Maggie okay?"

"Perhaps Maggie should tell you herself."

You came on the line, your voice very small and solemn and grown-up. "Unca, I have bad news."

"We take physical displays very seriously here at Willoughby."

The chair I was struggling to sit in had been built to support kindergartners, so I looked at Cara Brendel framed between my bony knees—a difficult position from which to maintain dignity. "Physical displays of what?" I asked.

The principal looked disappointed at my lack of familiarity with the current jargon. "Of anger," she said. "Of violence."

"Just tell me what happened, Cara." Everyone called each other by first names at Willoughby Preschool.

"I'll get to that. I'm trying to put the incident into the proper context. You can't just look at these events in a vacuum."

I glanced over my left knee to you, sitting across the room amidst a pile of neglected building blocks, looking tiny and forlorn, your chocolate eyes staring out from your wild, dark ringlets. A papier-mâché whale hung from the ceiling above your head like the sword of judgment.

Outside the window, a gaggle of kids played and screamed in the crisp winter air.

"Can't she go outside and play while we talk about this?"

"That's what we're here to discuss," Cara said. "Her notion of play."

"Oh, for Christ's sake, will you just tell me what's going on?" I tried to recover my composure by adding, "I understand your difficulty. I'm a teacher myself."

Cara looked up in some surprise. Her loose-fitting cotton dress and pressed-tin half-moon earrings tried hard to give off a funky, "I'd-like-to-buy-the-world-a-Coke," ex-hippie air, but her cold eyes just couldn't carry it off.

"Really?" she said.

"Absolutely." I didn't think it was politic to add the word *substitute*. "So, really, I understand the, you know, context."

She nodded, as if unconvinced. "Maggie assaulted a boy in class."

Well, I didn't answer at first. I gave you a glance over my shoulder. You were scribbling with a purple crayon and didn't look at all like a juvenile offender. "Assaulted? You mean she pulled a knife on him?"

"This isn't something to joke about."

"She's four years old."

"Four and a half!" you objected, looking up from your crayons, wavy hair not obscuring the fire in your eyes.

Cara called to you in sugary tones. "Just keep working, Maggie. We can't wait to see your picture."

"Okay, Cara," you answered, going back to work.

I hated the hypocrisy of Cara's friendly tone; hated having to talk about you as if you weren't there. "Just tell me what she did to this kid. And what the kid did first."

Cara's round face crinkled in a sad and patronizing smile. "You see, we find that kind of blame assignment to be very counter-productive in these cases."

"Really? 'Cause I always thought finding out the truth was very productive."

"I should really be discussing this with her primary caregiver. Why don't you take her home, and I'll talk to her mother on Monday?"

"I have to take her home?"

"I think that would be best."

"You're kicking her out of kindergarten?"

"It's a policy decision," she said, smiling pleasantly. She had that wonderful combination of liberalism and fascism that only American educational training can produce.

"What did she do?"

She frowned at the thought of having to actually impart information. "She was kicking and spitting on a child in the playground."

Well, to be honest, that did sound like something you'd do. "Okay, sometimes she does have a temper."

"She pushed the child's face into the mud."

"Which child?"

She hesitated, as if this were a national-security issue. "Bobby Neumuller."

"She likes Bobby Neumuller."

"They've always been friendly, yes."

"So, they got into a little tussle, that's nothing to—"

"Mr. Kehoe, Maggie also violated our sexual harassment policy."

"Excuse me?"

She leaned forward, crescent moons bobbing. "She was angry with Bobby Neumuller because he wouldn't take his pants off in front of her."

Which, I decided later, was probably the worst time in the world for your mother to walk in. She had her junior executive outfit on, and she flung the jacket onto one of the mini-chairs, knocking it to the floor as she hurried to you.

"I'm in trouble, Mom," you said.

Charlotte turned to Cara, relief quickly changing to suppressed anger. She'd checked her machine at work and heard the message that something was wrong. Like any mother would, she'd assumed the worst, left work, and hurried here.

"I'm sorry, I should have clarified," Cara said. "It's a disciplinary problem."

Charlotte's potential for fury was a match for yours any day, but since she was a grown-up, she'd learned to channel it into withering glances and intestinal disorders. "You made me leave my job because of a disciplinary problem?"

Cara demurred. She hadn't made anyone leave anything. She had informed Charlotte of the problem and then called her secondary contact, which I remembered was me. Charlotte glanced at me, and I felt a little guilty just being in the same room with Cara Brendel.

"Is anybody going to tell me what's going on?" Charlotte leaned forward on a bookshelf, shooting down the cuff of her Anne Klein II blouse to cover the dragon tattoo on her wrist. Body art didn't fit the righteously indignant image she was trying to convey.

Cara didn't notice it; she just fell comfortably back onto her catechism. "As you know, we take physical displays very seriously here at Willoughby."

This is where I came in, I thought, and I took you by the hand to lead you to the door. "I'm going to take Maggie for a walk."

We walked away from the playground and the screaming kids and sat on the curb by the water fountain. You still looked very solemn.

I suppose this is as good a time as any to introduce you to your four-year-old self. A perfectly enchanting child, if a doting uncle's opinion counts for anything. Dark, almost gypsy in complexion; not at all like the rest of us pale, apple-cheeked Irish Kehoes. You'd had long, black, curly hair from the day you were born; a howling, wild-eyed banshee squirming like a slimy eel in my arms in the delivery room. Mine were the first arms to hold you (we don't count the doctor, that's his job). I cut your cord and eased you into your mother's arms, and you started nursing, precocious thing that you are, without the least prompting.

Your eyes were shining and bright from the get go; none of those dull, wandering, glassy stares for my Margaret. You looked so unlike our side of the family that we used to laugh and make jokes about changelings and cuckoos, but you were one of us from the beginning. I know we spoiled you. You were the only solid feature of our lives. We focused on you to keep us steady.

You walked early and talked early, but showed little interest in reading or playing the piano or tying your shoe-laces or anything that involved being taught. If you didn't already know how to do it, it didn't seem worth doing.

There were things going on in your mind, I sensed then and know now, that the rest of the world couldn't guess at. I caught glimpses of it in some of the things you said. At night, you never asked for the lights to be turned off, but for us to "turn the dark on," as if dark was a positive thing, not just the absence of light. Once we took you to the Natural History Museum, and you were entranced by a skeleton of a caveman in a glass case. Through some trick with mirrors, the caveman would change from a skeleton to a mannequin of a live caveman, then back to a skeleton. Back and forth, skin and bone, you watched, totally enthralled. Then you turned to me, eyes shining, and said, "You do it!"

I would have, if I could. I will, in time.

Now you sat on the curb at Willoughby Preschool, your old-soul eyes wide and sad, your olive face speckled with birthmarks like a wild bird's egg, and asked, "Is Mommy going to get in trouble, too?"

"Of course not." *Only if Mommy decides to choke the life out of your teacher*, I thought. "Nobody's in trouble. This is just silly stuff."

You shrugged. "I like silly stuff better when it's funny."

I agreed, comforted by the absence of screams coming from the classroom. "So, why did you want Bobby Neumuller to take his pants off?"

"I wanted to see his penis," you said.

I didn't ask any more questions for a while. Then, "Why did you want to see Bobby Neumuller's penis?"

(It just occurred to me how much this is going to embarrass you. Maybe writing this is a mistake. Maybe I'll never show it to you at all.)

"'Cause it's fair. How if I said I was going to do something and didun' do it? That wouldn' be fair."

"So Bobby Neumuller said he was going to show you his penis."

"And he didun'," you said, emphatically. "I said I was going to show him my bagina."

"And you did?"

"O' course. I'm fair."

I shifted on the curb, uncomfortable. "Look, that's kind of a private thing. Remember how you talked with Mommy about private things?"

"But I love Bobby Neumuller."

"I know you do. But still, there's a lot of people *I* love, and I—"

"You don't show them your penis?"

"Right."

You thought that over. "But when you marry 'em, then you show it, right? After the wedding?"

"Uh, yes, yes, sometime after the wedding."

"Why if I married Bobby Neumuller?" You always said *what* instead of *why* and *why* instead of *what*. I assume you've grown out of that.

"Okay, well, you might do that. But, remember, you have to be a grown-up to marry somebody."

"Was Mommy a grown-up when she married Daddy?"

"You bet she was." The curb was getting more uncomfortable by the minute.

"And then Daddy died."

I shifted a pebble from under my right buttock. I had enough trouble lying to you about the Easter Bunny; this lie always killed me. "That's right."

"How if he didn' die, and he just left?"

This struck me as a pretty deep thought for a four year old. I looked into your big eyes and gave you a hug. "Well, he'd be crazy to do that, 'cause he'd be missing out on knowing you, and you're such a great kid."

You didn't look like you were buying it, but we were interrupted by a pudgy boy with stubble-short hair and an *X-Files* T-shirt who trundled over and sat next to you.

"Did you get in trouble?" the boy asked. I'd forgotten that about childhood—the constant struggle to avoid "trouble" in the form of the adult world's mysterious and arbitrary justice.

"Yep," you said, then added, "I'm sorry I kicked you and spit on you."

He nodded. "Okay."

You looked like you were waiting for something. "Now you say you're sorry."

"Why? I didn't do anything," Bobby Neumuller said.

"Just 'cause it's fair."

"Okay. I'm sorry."

You asked if you could go play with him and I said yes and you ran off, all fences mended. Things back in the classroom were more complex. Your mother was confronting Cara in her lioness-defending-her-cubs mode. "Christ, didn't you ever play doctor when you were a kid? *Were* you ever a kid?"

But she couldn't seem to get a rise out of Cara. Irony and sarcasm had been institutionally removed from her worldview. "Sexual curiosity can be perfectly normal. When it's coupled with violence, we have concerns."

"Oh, God, you make her sound like a serial rapist." Charlotte picked up her jacket, and I picked up her purse. We both knew she had better leave now.

But Cara wouldn't shut up. "I think it's time to consider that Willoughby Preschool may not be the best environment for Maggie."

Charlotte groaned. "Oh, don't do this."

"I'm recommending that she be tested for Attention Deficit Disorder."

"Christ. Do you people hate children, is that it?"

"Charlotte—" Cara was patient, always patient.

"No, really. If a kid's jumpy, you call her Hyperactive, you give her a pill. If she daydreams, you say it's ADD, you give her a pill. You treat childhood like it's a disease."

Once again, Cara went on as if none of this had been said. Maggie had difficulty concentrating, Cara said. This was disruptive, Cara said, not only to her own learning process but to the learning of her classmates.

"So, her mind wanders sometimes," Charlotte said. "She's creative. That's why we sent her to a hippie school."

Cara hated that the mothers called Willoughby a "hippie school," and Charlotte knew that. "These are not daydreams, Charlotte. These are..." And for the first time, I saw real emotion in Cara's eyes. She stifled it quickly. "...disruptive to the learning process," she finished, her old self again.

"What are you talking about?"

Cara took off her glasses and composed herself, as if fearful of letting honesty slip out again. "Yesterday she spent all of recess sitting next to a puddle. She said she was talking to the water."

"So, she's got an imagination."

Cara continued, with mounting intensity. "She said she *saw* things in the water. She brought the other children over. She said she saw Jake." Her voice broke for a second, and she pressed her lips tight.

Jake had been the school's unofficial mascot, Cara's big Labrador. The kids had loved him. Cara had loved him. He'd been hit by a car in front of the school last month, and the kids had seen him die. The mourning had gone on for weeks.

Cara shoved her glasses back on, as if they might hide the tears welling in her eyes. "She said he was in pain. She said she could feel the pain. She said he was crying. That he wanted to come home. All the kids started crying then. They'd just gotten over it, and now she had them all crying again." She wiped tears and snot from her face in sharp, violent swipes.

Charlotte looked chagrined. Even I had heard how much the dog had meant to this woman. "God, Cara, I'm sorry. But she was probably just expressing her feelings about—"

"Bullshit!" The outburst shocked both of them. Cara's face was red and mottled and she was spitting tears like venom. "She was just trying to get attention! It was cruel!" The anger of her words cut straight through me.

Charlotte moved forward, not even looking angered by that statement, just sad and full of compassion. "Oh, she'd never do that." But Cara backed off, moving behind the gerbil cage. Charlotte hesitated, to and fro, not knowing where to move or what to say. "Jesus, Cara, you can't kick her out of school just 'cause you don't like her."

Cara tried to pull together the remnants of her patronizing smile. "Don't be ridiculous. Maggie's a wonderful child, very special—"

"Don't give me that 'special' crap!" Charlotte circled the

gerbil cage, crowding her. "Are you doing this because you think it's what's best, or because you're scared of her?"

Cara pushed past Charlotte and ran from the room, sobbing. The kids on the playground looked up in surprise as they saw their crying teacher running past them and into the haven of the teacher's lounge. Then they went back to playing.

The tiny fireplace in your house on Quander Road was not meant to contain actual flames, but the short winter day had ended so soon and the temperature had dropped so suddenly, we threw a Duraflame log in and hoped for the best.

Charlotte hadn't gone back to work; she called in a personal emergency. They probably wouldn't ask her back at that office, but that was one of the best things about being a temp. If you burned your bridges, there were plenty more to cross over.

"I can't get Maggie into another school. Not in the middle of the year." She dropped her head back on the sofa. "Willoughby's the only place I can afford."

Well, it was time for me to make a decision. For the past five years Charlotte had always had to be the responsible one, the one who shouldered the burden while I went off on my crazy tangents. It wasn't fair to her, and it was going to stop now. "I'll help. I'll get a real job."

Charlotte laughed fondly and patted my leg. "That's sweet, Sammy, but you're like Maggie. You've got ADD. Adulthood Deficit Disorder."

I laughed along with her, trying to ignore how uncomfortably similar Charlotte's joke was to Anne's rant of the night before. She took my hand, and we stared into the fire, and I knew we were both thinking the same thing. There should be other people with us to shoulder these troubles. But no. There were just the two of us, clinging to the wreckage.

"I'm really ready to do it, Charlie," I said. "I mean, you've done enough."

Her hand in mine felt tense, and she gave me her big-sister-pity smile. "You have no idea the things I've done."

Now, every now and then your mother would do this. She'd hint, darkly, about some terrible secret from her past that no one could ever know but that she was clearly dying to tell me about in great detail. Once she'd dropped her teasing clue, though, she'd always pull back, and no amount of cajoling could get the real story out of her. One time, curiosity got the better of me, and I invested forty dollars in margarita mix, tequila, and a video of *The Breakfast Club*, figuring if that didn't soften her up, nothing would. All I got from my effort was a sledgehammer hangover and the sense that the world wasn't ready to know The Truth About Charlotte Kehoe. Fair enough. We all have our secrets. But considering what I *did* know about your mother's past, this unspeakable thing must have been pretty impressive.

I smiled back at her, knowing there was no point in going down this road, not tonight. We sat in silence for a while, then I got up and found you in your little bedroom trying to put the head back on a Barbie.

"Hey."

"Hey."

I sat yoga-style on the floor next to you and helped re-capitate the doll. You thanked me.

"Maggie, did you really see Jake the other day?"

You looked up at me, your wild hair—which no twisty or scrunchy could ever tame—falling in your eyes. The shadows of your hair always made your face look smudged so that, no matter how clean Charlotte kept you, you looked like a Dickensian street urchin. "I really did," you said.

I patted your curls. "Do you know how we were talking about private things? Things we don't share?"

You nodded.

"That's one of them," I whispered to you.

THREE

On Sunday I decided to get a career.

Since I was on the downslope to thirty, I figured I didn't have time to start from scratch, so I looked for things already in my life I could build on.

I was a clerk in a video store. Not terribly promising on the surface, but it was a good video store, maybe a great one. Video Vista on Washington Street was an old brownstone just barely converted into a retail outlet by lining the walls of the rooms, all three stories' worth, with shelves. And that rabbit warren of shelves had it all: classics, foreign films (Satyajit Ray emphasized), action films, cult films (Italian *giallo* emphasized), Blaxploitation films (Rudy Ray Moore emphasized), fine porn, and art house films. They had a mail-order business that went all over the country and a website I had personally designed. Hugh, the manager, loved me and had often tried to talk me into running a second store he was planning in the District. But I'd always turned him down, not wanting the headache, and Hugh hadn't brought it up for quite a while. Besides, everyone knew video rental was on its last legs, about to be replaced by satellites and cable and God knew what. You couldn't plan your future on a transitional technology.

There was my movie website, *The Horrible Dr. Kehoe,* but even I knew that was little more than a time-consuming hobby. Even if I achieved my ultimate goal of writing that book I was always researching on Italian Trash Cinema, I didn't harbor illusions that anyone but me would want to buy it. I couldn't send my niece through school on a vanity project.

That left teaching. Well, I loved substituting. I loved talking to the kids, listening to them, making them laugh. Even if teaching didn't pay much, it was a noble profession. The profession of both of my parents. I'd only have to take a semester at NoVaCoCo, the local community college, to finish my degree and get certified. Hard to say why I hadn't done that long ago, except that it was what Mom had wanted, so it had seemed pretty pointless. Now it felt like the greatest idea I'd ever had.

It was settled. I was going to become a teacher.

I got up and had two Krispy Kreme donuts to commemorate the occasion.

As if sensing my resolve, the automated phone service called me Monday morning and informed me that a history teacher was needed at Washington Irving High School. W. I. was one of my favorite venues; the kids were hip without being delinquent and the principal, Mr. Manning, had often encouraged me to think about a teaching career. Fate seemed to be leading the way.

Of course, I knew being a real teacher would be different from substituting. For one thing, kids were always happy to see a substitute. They meant a break in the routine, no real work, a holiday. Facing those kids every day, following a real curriculum, well, that would be an awful lot like work. But I was up for it, I had no doubt of that.

The absent teacher at W.I. had left a summary of the material I was supposed to cover—the economic boom of the twenties and how it paved the way for the Great

Depression. It was just the sort of statistical droning I always hated—a surefire way to make history boring—so I decided to tell a story instead.

Since it was Christmastime, I told my favorite Yuletide history story, the one about the English and German soldiers in World War I climbing out of the trenches in Flanders on Christmas Eve 1914 and celebrating together, singing songs, and playing soccer, then climbing back in and resuming killing each other the next day.

I told it to every class that day, and I got better at it every time, so that even the kids who acted bored and superior were spellbound by the end, feeling the cold and the mud and the warmth of good will and the bitterness of the violent aftermath. I told it without moralizing, so that the rest of the hour was filled with kids discussing it and coming to their own conclusions, not ones a textbook told them to make.

I had never felt more certain about my future.

It all fell apart at lunchtime. I was walking down the hall when I heard sobbing. A freshman ahead of me heard it, too, pushed open the door to the boys' rest room to check it out, spun on his heels, and hurried down the hall.

I caught the bathroom door still swinging and stepped in. A girl was squatting on the floor by the sink weeping soggy, sloppy tears. Standing in front of her was a lanky boy in enormous jeans, greasy brown hair falling about his eyes.

"Will you shut the fuck up?" There wasn't any charity in his voice. He looked up to see who had walked in on them. "The fuck are you staring at?" the boy asked.

And right then I knew why I would never become a teacher. Oddly, it was the same reason I wanted to be a teacher in the first place. I liked the kids. I identified with them. I was one of them. And because of that, I didn't respond as a teacher; I didn't say any of the things Cara

Brendel would have said, like, "Is there a problem here?" or "Isn't this a discussion you should be having off-campus?" I didn't even come out with an old-fashioned, hard-ass teacher remark like, "Don't you use that language with me, young man."

What I said was, "I'm staring at you, asshole."

The girl, as if suddenly embarrassed by her situation, struggled to stand up and cracked her head on the porcelain sink.

The boy barked a laugh. "Stupid bitch doesn't even know how to stand up."

I went over to help her. "Is he bothering you?"

She shook her head rapidly, her short hair vibrating with shame. Another barking laugh from the boy. "Yeah, tell him how *I'm* bothering *you*! You're the one sucking Nelson Duey's dick."

The girl started her howling, gooey crying again, her humiliation increased by the fact that the freshman was standing in the doorway again with an audience of half a dozen other students.

"Tell them all about it, jizz monkey!" The boy was playing to the bleachers now, getting gasps and laughs from the crowd.

I tried to hustle the spectators out the door. "This isn't any of your business, okay?"

"She was doin' me too, J.J.," someone in the back of the clump hollered as I closed the door on them, and the girl sobbed even louder. Now, I'm not the kind of guy who gets mad easily, but when I looked at that girl and knew she was going to be "jizz monkey" to the whole school until the day she graduated, I just lost it; I spun around and pinned the boy to the greasy bathroom mirror with my forearm.

"You cruel little fuck. How dare you humiliate her like that? I ought to shove your head in the toilet and flush it till you drown." J.J. looked at me in wide-eyed shock.

Teachers weren't supposed to go this postal.

I backed off, shaking the cramped muscles of my arm loose. J.J. looked scared and rattled and meaner than ever. I offered to lead the girl out, but she shook her head again. "No. I gotta explain to him. It's not what he thinks. I love him."

What could I say to that? I just looked at her drowned cat eyes and wished her luck.

Stepping out into the hall I saw a crowd gathered, buzzing with gossip. They stopped, dead silent when they saw me, so I could hear it clear as a bell when J.J. started hitting her.

What I did next was pretty much the same thing you'd do. But then, you're four.

"You struck a student in the face?"

Mr. Manning wasn't encouraging me to think about a teaching career now.

"Once. One time. Not hard. There was no bleeding. It was an educational thing. I wanted him to know what it felt like."

Manning sighed and shook his head. He looked like he hated this more than I did.

"He was hitting that girl, Alec," I told him, not defending myself, no hope for that, but just so Manning would know.

"She says he wasn't."

"You know she's lying."

"Yeah, I know she's lying. But what we *know* isn't the issue here."

"What is the issue?"

Manning tried to pace around his office, but it was too damn small. "Sam, do you really think that was the proper response for a teacher to have to a situation like that?"

I let my head drop back on the masking tape that held the sofa together and told him, no, I didn't.

"Why'd you do it?"

"Alec, this kid is *such* an asshole."

"That's not our job. Our job is not to police the assholes of the world." Manning sat on the edge of his desk, his big face heavy with sorrow. I wished he was being an officious jerk, but he wasn't, and I was just sorry I'd made a good man feel this rotten. "Did you even think about what kind of lawsuit that kid's family could bring against this school?"

I hadn't. I hadn't thought anything, actually. Now I remembered a line in the Substitute Services Handbook: "Touching a student in any way to control or modify behavior is an unacceptable form of discipline." I supposed a punch in the jaw fell into that category.

"I like you," Manning said. "The kids like you. But...I don't think this job is a good match for you."

I saw it coming. He was going to put a "Do Not Send" request in my file, and I was about to be discontinued as a substitute teacher for Fairfax County Public Schools. Doing that would show good faith on the school's part and maybe deflect the lawsuit. One substitute wasn't a big sacrifice, and Manning had no idea I'd picked education as my career twelve hours ago. I nodded, prepared to fall on my sword, then asked, "What should I have done, Alec?"

"Reported the incident. Sent the girl to a counselor. There are responsible ways to deal with these things."

"I guess that's the problem. I didn't want to deal with it. I wanted to punch that kid in the face."

Thing is, I'm not really a violent guy. I've only been in a couple of fights my whole life, if you don't count getting beat up daily during junior high. One of them you might remember. It was on the occasion of your first visit to the National Zoo. You'd only just learned to walk, in the stumbling gait of a toddler, like a drunk just catching himself from falling on his face, over and over.

There were grizzly bears, Siberian tigers, and zebras by the truckload, but what fascinated you were the sprinkler heads poking out of the grass next to the sidewalk. You would trundle up to one, drop with a thud onto your padded Oshkosh-covered bottom, and stare at the star-shaped metal apparatus with enraptured delight, completely ignoring the giraffe towering over your head. Beauty is a subjective thing.

We were particularly close that week, you and I. Your mother had gone off to visit a friend in California for five whole days, her first time away since you were born... no, since long before that. You and I had bonded with rapturous abandon while she was gone. Watching marathon sessions of Felix the Cat, Betty Boop, Little Lulu, and Casper the Friendly Ghost cartoons I'd spirited home from the shop, you laughing at them as if they'd been made just for you, and not for a generation fast fading into the twilight. We went on fast bike rides, you strapped in a seat behind me, through the wilds of Rock Creek Park, and you squealed with delight as flocks of pigeons scattered before our rocketship trajectory. It was all so carefree and so blissful that I sometimes remember it as a time from my own childhood, not yours. But no, I don't think I ever had that much fun as a kid.

That trip to the zoo, we took the day after your mother came back from LA (well, actually, she'd been to a place called Sherman Oaks, but she said it was right *near* LA), and you were still taking your revenge on her for leaving you by ignoring her completely and occasionally calling me "Mommy." ("Bommy," actually, was as close as you could get, but she knew what you were getting at.) Charlotte was depressed, as one usually is after deliberate attempts to go somewhere and have fun, and she refused to say even a word about her trip West. I was sulking, too, partially because your mom hadn't gotten me a picture of that famous sidewalk staircase in Hollywood that Laurel and Hardy carried the piano up, over and over, in *The Music Box* like she'd promised she would, and partially because the rest of you were sulking and I didn't want to feel left out.

To make matters worse, on the night of your mom's homecoming, when everyone was in mid-sulk, our old family cat Henry got out and somehow drank anti-freeze that was leaking from one of our redneck neighbor's cars. We didn't find him until the morning, panting and foaming at the mouth, curled up in our window well. Charlotte cradled his body in an old towel, and I drove through red lights all the way to the vet's, but it was too late for the old guy, and we had to have him put to sleep to finish the job the poison had started. Your mother stayed with you in the waiting room, and I stroked the smoky old cat's matted fur as he purred through the pain, looking up at me with a milky, uncomprehending eye. I watched the life go out of that eye and cried harder and more painfully than I ever did for my parents. The nurse technicians kept a respectful distance and watched as I shuddered and shook. I think they understand that when we mourn for a pet we mourn for more than just the animal itself; we mourn for the time it marked in our lives, the time that will never be regained. Henry had been the last link with the Kehoe family intact, and it was gut-wrenching to watch him leave us.

We drove away from the animal hospital, and you watched with fascination as your mother and uncle bawled like babies. It wasn't a sight you had ever seen, so you laughed at us at first, thinking we were making faces. Then you started crying, too, not out of sorrow for the noble cat who had known my brother and my mother and father, who'd slept with me every night through high school, who had sat on the bed and watched with a contented purr during my first make-out session with Julie Haley, who had slept beneath your crib like a watch-cat during the first nights of your life, who had painfully clambered up onto your grown-up bed when that transition came and always stayed at your feet through the long nights, eyes aglow, a warm, vibrating nightlight. You didn't understand yet that he was gone, that you'd have to sleep alone for years to come. You only cried because we were crying so hard, and it must have scared the hell out of you to see the people who kept you alive and fed falling to pieces like that.

We couldn't go straight home to a house so empty of prowling, so we decided to take you to the zoo, walk around in the tropic heat of a DC summer and sweat the sorrow out of ourselves. Once your little Velcro running shoes hit the steaming asphalt, the thrill of being bipedal took the sadness right out of you, and even your mother and I found ourselves laughing as we chased you past the flamingos and elephants, past the hippos and rhinos as you raced from sprinkler head to sprinkler head like a misguided bumblebee trying to pollinate those metal blossoms.

What it was you found so fascinating about the irrigation system I never learned. It wasn't an obsession that stayed with you, thankfully; I'll be very surprised if you've grown up to become a landscape gardener. I suppose it was that the animals were too big and too far away from your ankle-biter perspective for you to comprehend them, so you opted instead to focus on something you could grasp in your hand. Or with your mouth. Your mother and I took turns bending down to stop you from wrapping your lips around a sprinkler—we didn't have much faith in the sanitary qualities of the District of Columbia Department of Water and Power.

It was Charlotte's turn to crouch and keep you from kissing the rusty metal star when I noticed the laughter of a group of high school kids over by the alligator pit. The big kid in the middle (and wouldn't it always be the big kid in the middle?) was tossing something into the pit. Tossing repeatedly, like a farmer sowing crops. And with every toss came a gale of encouragement and laughter from the boys and girls around him. I strolled over to the rail to see what worthwhile endeavor this young man was engaged in that garnered such support from his peers.

A great metallic blue 'gator sat in the reeds beneath them. Hooded eyes sunk into its monster-movie skull reflected just a hinted glint of the marshy Washington sun. And, *kerplunk*, a penny landed on the steak-knife ridges of its massive back. A back already covered with copper disks. Heads and tails. Lincoln and the Memorial. The girls laughed the loudest.

Do I have to tell you how much this pissed me off? You're my Maggie; you're thinking all the same things now as you read this. Seeing this magnificent creature being treated like a sight gag by this Neanderthal football player, knowing that if the world were a just place, Bubba there would be occupying his rightful place in the food chain as this alligator's chew toy. If the walls of this pit were to miraculously fall away, Godzilla would lift his massive trunk onto his powerful legs and bolt with startling speed toward that fool. Would the girls be laughing then?

Of course, none of that would happen. Bubba was safe and superior, and the animal powerless and at his will. Had this numbskull seen that grotesque photograph that was posted by the sea lion pool—a graphic autopsy picture of a dead female, its guts stuffed with shiny coins that idiot tourists had thrown to it, as if it were a living wishing well? Did the asshole know he might be killing this great beast to get a laugh? Did he care?

"Don't do that," I said.

Bubba looked surprised, as if he was shocked to see anyone else at the zoo.

"What's your problem?" he said, and the girls laughed. I still haven't figured out why that was clever.

"Don't throw pennies on the alligator." It was exactly what I meant to say, which didn't make it sound any less foolish.

"Why? Is this your own personal alligator? Does it belong to you?" Another laugh from his fans.

Ordinarily, I would have just frowned and walked off, but today I saw before me the face of Henry being put to sleep, and I couldn't let it go.

"Yes, it does," I said. "This is the National Zoo. This alligator belongs to all of us." I suppose I could have come up with a dorkier thing to say if I'd had the time.

The girls laughed again, but it sounded meaner when it was directed at me.

"Go fuck yourself," he replied. Another laugh. Bubba knew his audience.

But then, I swear it was as if I heard a voice in my head—or felt the urgency of an unseen person standing at my side. And this person was pissed off, fed up and just not willing to take crap from anybody "Fuck *your*self," I said and this time there was no laugh, for the words sounded much uglier coming from me. The girls gasped, and Bubba swung at me. Instinctively, I raised my arm and blocked his punch—I think I was more surprised by this than he was. The Other's anger was still fueling me, so I swung and landed a useless blow on his right pec, but my next punch hit him right in the face.

You see it all the time in the movies, the right-cross to the chin, but I'd never done it before. I was shocked at how powerful the impact felt and how dull the sound was—just the opposite of the way it plays on the screen.

I had a moment of deep and abiding satisfaction before Bubba began to pound me into ground beef.

It was my own fault, of course, and if he'd picked me up and dropped me into the pit to be eaten alive by the alligator, there would have at least been some poetic injustice to it. But, no, in a few blurred moments, he knocked me down and then, mercifully, allowed the girls to pull him off me and lead him away while they muttered to each other about the crazies they let run loose these days.

I felt blood on my lip and a spectacular pain in my nose. You were next to me, bawling wildly at the sight of me. Charlotte was there, too, offering comfort while calling me an idiot. I heard no word of thanks from the alligator.

So, there I am, Maggie. Your dear uncle, Defender of the Meek and Mild. Protector of Jizz Monkeys and Man-Eating 'Gators. Funny thing is, I never get mad for my own sake. People can push me around, insult me to my face, and chances are I'll just nod in agreement and move on. But when I see those things happen to other people, that Other always shows up at my shoulder, slapping me like Bud Abbott used to slap Lou Costello and telling me, "You're not just going to stand by and let that happen, are you? Do something!" So, I'd dive in as if I thought this Bud Abbott guy would back me up. But, true to form, once the fighting started, he was long gone, and there was nobody there but me.

Okay, that's not quite true. And we're writing this to get to the truth, aren't we? We're telling the truth, the whole truth, and so much truth that I'll probably toss this out before I even finish it. So, the truth is, I'm not entirely alone in those fights. There's another guy who shows up—a guy who fucking loves it. A guy who loves the whole messy mix-up of a fight, who loves seeing the moment of fear in the face of the one I'm going at, who even loves it when the fight turns around, as it always does, and I start getting my ass whupped. Who loves the danger, and the blood, and the give and take of pain.

Now, who this guy is, I have no idea. Once the fight is over, he's long gone, too, hiding in a dark corner of shame, and I never think about him or admit even to myself that he's there.

Do I sound crazy to you? Talking about this guy and that guy, as if I had multiple personalities, or as if these aspects of my own personality weren't a part of me? I guess I've always thought that there was within me this whole cast of characters, like the supporting players in a good Howard Hawks movie. The Bud Abbott guy. The Fight Guy. The Krispy Kreme Donut Man. The Good Mother, who somehow knew how to change your diapers, bandage your boo-boos, and soothe your tears without ever being taught. These have always seemed more like friends and enemies who visit me than parts of myself.

Trains of thought like this are just a few of the reasons I've never done well in therapy.

FOUR

'd like a refund on this." Mid-twenties and just out of law school, I guessed. The guy's suit was too expensive to put on a body that hadn't quite finished growing yet. I figured him for an intern at one of those lobbying firms that littered Alexandria. Spent his days playing gopher for a bunch of tobacco-pushing fat cats and his nights hounding secretaries in Old Town.

The unkind nature of this assessment was colored by the fact that the yuppie scum was pushing an un-rewound copy of *Black Sunday* (Galatea Films, Italy, 1960, Italian title *La Maschera del Demonio*, five stars on the Kehoe Scale) over the counter at me.

"Why's that?" I asked.

"It was boring. You said it was exciting, but it was just slow. And it was in black and white; you didn't tell me it was in black and white. I can't watch that."

I controlled my breathing and laid a hand on the tape. I'd already lost my temper and one job today. "This is the greatest vampire movie ever made."

"I thought it was stupid."

"No, I think what's confusing you is that *you're* stupid. This is poetry, this is beauty."

"Look, I just want my $2.99 back."

"No. You don't deserve it. Go rent *Con Air*. Go rent

fucking *Armageddon*. As a matter of fact, no, you don't rent anything. You're not a member here anymore." I clicked through the computer. "Look, I'm erasing you from our membership list."

"You can't do that!"

"Then you get one more chance. Rent this." I slapped a copy of *Les Yeux Sans Visage* on the counter. *"Eyes Without a Face,* aka *The Horror Chamber of Dr. Faustus,* France, 1959. A fucking masterpiece."

"It's black and white, I don't—"

"You'll like this."

"Is it gross?"

"It's *very* gross. All that face-removing stuff from *Face/ Off?* They stole it from this."

"Cool. Can I get *Big Daddy* too?"

What do you do with people like that? "Yeah, you can get *Big* goddamn *Daddy,* too. I don't know why I bother."

Hugh, the owner and manager, sidled up to me after I checked the guy out. "Did I ever mention to you that the customer's always right?"

"Not that guy. That guy was so wrong."

He laughed, so I thought this might be the proper moment to tell him that I'd been doing a lot of thinking about that second store in Dupont Circle and I'd decided I was ready to open it. "I'm ready to dedicate myself to running a video store," I said. "I mean, I've been thinking it over and it's really what I want to do with my life."

Hugh just laughed and waddled off to the stock room. I didn't take that as a good sign.

So, it wasn't shaping up to be the best Christmas ever.

I drove home on the George Washington Parkway, singing along with the car radio. Dwight Yoakam and a heartbreak song that fit my mood so dead-on perfect it was like

I wrote it myself. A moaning yodel caught in my throat, but when I tried to choke it down I felt a bubble of panic in my chest. I gripped the wheel to steady myself, to stifle the sense that the bottom was falling out of my life.

But who was I kidding? It had fallen out long ago. What terrified me now was the sudden awareness that the new supports I had painstakingly built for myself over the past five years had proven false, nothing but paper simulations that were tearing loose, threatening me with another dreadful free fall.

No Anne. No career. Barely a job. No school for Maggie. Charlotte alone and drifting. And that old woman in Anne's apartment.

As I said before, I hadn't let myself think about the apparition I'd seen on Anne's sofa; there was enough other unpleasantness for me to focus on. But I couldn't ignore it forever. It kept flickering around in the corners of my vision like an annoying floater. Now, it forced itself to the top of the garbage heap in my mind; I wondered for the millionth time just how crazy I was.

It had been years since I'd seen a "spook." Five. No need to count, I knew the time exactly. As the years had passed, I'd assumed I'd grown out of it or that the tumor, or whatever it was that made me see these things, had dissolved in my brain and left me like everybody else. Could it all be beginning again?

Maybe not. Maybe that image in the apartment had been a one-shot deal. I'd been upset; heartbroken, in fact. So, maybe it was some ordinary, stress-linked delusion. Comforting thoughts. But I'd had those thoughts before.

After the first incident in the gym, I'd never seen Mr. Meloni again. Not a trace, not a shadow. I didn't feel icy fingers down my spine any of the hundreds of times I walked into the gym after that. Sure, I hated the place, but I hated it for all the normal reasons teenage kids hate gyms. Once, I found myself sitting in that very spot in the bleachers where the gym teacher's phantom had appeared, and I didn't even realize it until the game was half over. No eerie sensations, no spectral visions, no big deal.

I never kept a journal (this is as close as I've ever come to that), so I might have forgotten the whole business if it hadn't been for Charlotte's seventeenth birthday slumber party. It was the evening of Senior Skip Day, the end of Charlotte's last year at Henry James High School. She'd spent the day with four of her friends, all beautiful, grown-up women—at least that's how sixteen and seventeen year olds looked to my fourteen-year-old eyes—cruising up to Great Falls in Melody Fleming's Buick Skylark. They came thundering back that night, rushing through the kitchen door, a flash of legs and hair and pure clear skin that I caught just a glimpse of as I looked up from a game of Stratego I was playing with my brother, George. They were gone in a second, but my head stayed turned in their direction, like Wile E. Coyote when he realizes he's about to hit a mesa. Feminine beauty hit me hard in those days, leaving me flattened and fluttering to the ground like a Kleenex in the wind.

George grabbed my head and turned it back toward the board. "Don't start that, Sammy; you'll never stop." But words of wisdom, even from a revered older brother, often backfire. In this case, they captured perfectly the feeling swelling in my lungs; something had just happened that was going to keep on happening to me until the day I die.

Melody was the redhead of that blurred mass of beauty. The oldest, of course, the most ridiculously unattainable of that unattainable group. The worldly one. The one whose eyes looked out from a place of deep sorrow. The one whose laugh was music from deep in her throat. The one who could drive.

I'd had crushes before, but good God, never one I felt

in every cell of my body. Never one that made me feel like there was a balloon being inflated in my chest that was going to keep on expanding until my ribs shattered and flew across the room like confetti.

George knew what was going on. He tried to get my mind off the whole deal. Offered to play Trivial Pursuit with me, which he only ever did on rainy summer days on the island when there wasn't a blessed other thing to do. I said I wasn't in the mood. He tried to talk me into joining the Parents as they watched *The Jewel in the Crown* on Masterpiece Theatre. The Raj would have to fall without me; I was tired, and I was going to bed. At nine o'clock.

But how could I sleep, my mother wondered, with Charlotte's room right next to mine and them blaring her stereo at full volume? Pat Benatar and Bruce Springsteen, with the bass up so high it made the bed frame vibrate.

Not just the bed frame, either, but my bones as well, as I lay in my bed, hand under the covers, half-dreaming, half-fantasizing about Melody and the whole adult world of love. There was no way to make out their conversation under the pulsing beat of "Love Is a Battlefield," but I could hear the rhythm of their voices, their laughter like rainfall on the other side of the wall.

I couldn't hear footsteps, though, so I was taken entirely by surprise when the door opened and light from the hall fell onto my bed. I snatched my hand from under the covers, guiltily, and looked up at Charlotte and Melody.

"What the hell are you doing here?" Of course, the way Charlotte meant it, the question was about why I was in bed at this early hour, but I didn't take it that way.

"Nothing," I said.

Melody's laugh rumbled. "I think he's busy, Charlie."

A blush, a warm blend of humiliation and excitement that set the stage for hundreds of bad moments in my love-life to come, rushed to my face.

(Look what I'm writing. I can't possibly ever show this to you, my little niece. But I can't stop writing it either.)

"Shut up." Your mother defended me in her off-handed way, and even with all I was feeling I had time to note it and be grateful.

The girls were searching for something in the corner of my room, where the board games were kept. So, that was why they had come in, I realized, and surprised myself by feeling disappointed. But had I really thought sixteen year olds would leave a party to visit me?

"Well, fuck, it's not here."

Swearing, like drinking too much and driving the Parkway at night with the headlights off, was reckless youth's idea of acting like a grown-up, and it always thrilled me to be in the presence of it. I sat up, turning on my bedside lamp and illuminating the wall display of old Vincent Price posters; I wondered if I should start opting for more mature decor. I wonder that still. "What are you looking for?"

"The Ouija board."

"We took it to Maine."

"Shit."

I adjusted my pajamas to make sure all was concealed and threw off the covers. "You don't need one."

I leapt from the bed and, with a boldness that amazed me even as I did it, walked down the hall and into Charlotte's room. Well, the girls were still in their day clothes, which exploded my fantasy of them all rolling around in their jammies like Olivia Newton-John in *Grease*. Probably just as well, considering my own state of comparative undress.

I stumbled over the towel that had been crammed under the door and breathed in a roomful of smoke. The window was open on the hot night, and Jamie Butler stood by it with a pillow case, trying to fan the smoke into 9the backyard.

Seeing it was just harmless me, they all laughed, and Lyn Adams appeared from the closet, joint still smoldering in her hand. Charlotte's homemade cassette tape cut to an end in the middle of "Darkness on the Edge of Town," and the room was suddenly silent and waiting for me to say something.

Charlotte saved the day again, speaking up from behind me. "What's the plan, Sammy?" Well, that was Charlotte all over. Most big sisters would have thrown a fit at the invasion of a little brother into a scene like this.

"I can make a Ouija board. All we need is a table and masking tape and a wine glass." It was a trick I'd seen in a sixties British horror picture from Hammer Studios. Even then my knowledge of trash cinema bordered on the obsessive.

A scavenger hunt ensued, and I cleared Charlotte's desk of its usual rubble. They were an odd group, your mother's high school friends, neither in the "in" crowd nor the "out" crowd. An unnameable clique that really didn't give a damn what anyone called them. Ten years earlier, they might have been hippies, but our generation missed that opportunity, as they would continue to miss so many others.

Charlotte was their den mother, or gang leader, depending on your opinion of the group. Even when she led them astray into the world of recreational drugs and casual sex, she did it with maternal concern and a warm heart. (Now I can't show this to you until after Charlotte's dead, too. Maybe I'll never show it to you at all.) That unhappy mix of good impulses and terrible choices would plague her all her life, but for now it looked like nothing more than youthful exuberance.

Our mom and dad approved of all this, or as much of it as they cared to be aware of, seeing something almost Victorian in the passionate nature of Charlotte's friendships. More than anything, they were thrilled to see her refusing to conform to the new conservatism of the eighties. "She's just plain ornery," Dad would say with pride. "She doesn't cut her conscience to fit this year's fashions," Mom would say, placing the whole burden of Lillian Hellman's martyrdom on Charlotte's deceptively broad shoulders. For the Kehoes, nonconformity was a birthright, a responsibility. A heritage that went far deeper than the crabgrass that sprouted on their front lawn.

My parents thought of their children as more than just family. We were friends; we were entertainment. Supporting players in their *You Can't Take It With You* style of living. So, they loved Charlotte for her untamable character. They loved George for his piercing intelligence. And me? Well, I was the baby of the family, and I'm sure they came up with something.

I watched this group of girls in my sister's room, filled with fascination; an astronomer studying a newly discovered planet. I loved them as pals and lusted after them as women. At fourteen, I couldn't distinguish one feeling from the other. (Oh, why kid yourself, Sammy, do you think you can now?) Melody found the masking tape, and they tore off twenty-eight pieces at my instruction and stuck them in a big circle on Charlotte's desk. On each piece, Lyn wrote a letter of the alphabet and on the last two the words *yes* and *no*. The wine glass was placed in the middle of the circle, upside down.

"Are we ready?" Charlotte asked.

"This is stupid," Angela Gray said, filling the vital "this is stupid" role every group needs so much. "Nobody believes this crap."

"Give it a try." That was Melody, placing her slender fingertip on the base of the glass. The six of them all reached out, placing one finger on the glass; Melody was next to me, so that our fingertips touched, and I thought, *This is it, this is all I need for the rest of my life.*

I had started out loving all of them, in sort of a mad, indiscriminate lump, simply infatuated with the whole notion of females being in the world. In the past year, my crush had narrowed its focus onto Melody, and not because she was the most beautiful one of the group, but because she was the saddest. Sorrow seemed to pour out of her deep-set eyes; sorrow over a father who died last year following a long bout with cancer; sorrow over a known scumbag of a boyfriend who cheated on her and slapped her around; sorrow over an alcoholic and heartbroken mother. She needed rescuing, and I knew that my love, untried and untested as it was, could save her if she'd just give me a chance.

Now, here we were, fingers touching, me already in my pajamas. Could true love be far behind? I'd have killed myself for her right then, if I thought it would bring us together.

Angela Gray still scoffed. Nobody believed in ghosts, she said. "Has anybody even seen one?"

Now, I'd never told a soul about seeing Mr. Meloni in the gym; I figured I'd have been laughed at, at best. But here was a chance to make myself stand out, to center all attention on me, to possibly impress the woman whose fingerprint was currently in contact with mine. I couldn't pass it up.

"I did."

All eyes were on me now, and Melody's seemed particularly engaged. I could only go forward. So, I told them about that day in the gym and, when I'd reached the end of the tale and sensed the impending let-down of the anti-climactic truth, I knew I had to embellish. "Then he reached out a bony finger," I said, visualizing Meloni's pudgy digits as I lied, "and he said 'Forgive me.'" It was the best I could come up with on short notice, but the wide eyes around me told me it had been enough.

"Gawd," said Melody, "that's amazing."

"What did he want you to forgive him for?" Angela asked, still skeptical.

"That's the mystery," I said.

They asked if I'd ever seen anything else like that, and I shrugged, as if in modest reluctance to tell all my marvelous stories.

"What if you're, like, a medium?" Melody asked. "What if you have a real gift?"

She was praising me, and her finger was still touching mine, and I was tingling all over with rapture. I caught Charlotte's eye, and even she seemed intrigued. They were all treating me like I was something special. I wasn't used to being special; the sensation was intoxicating.

"You're not shitting us, little brother?"

"I saw him," I said.

"Well, let's see what else you can come up with," Angela said.

"Yeah, little brother, show us some spooks," Charlotte said with a laugh; we called them "spooks" from then on.

I swallowed nervously. Were they expecting me to perform now? Was I going to have to follow this up with some new apparition? Was I going to have to live a lie for the rest of my life just to keep that look of admiration in Melody's eyes? It seemed worth it.

The first half-hour went like any teenage Ouija-board session. The glass slid from letter to letter, with everyone laughing and denying that they were the one doing the pushing. I knew only that I wasn't doing the leading, but I imagine no one thought they were; they were all following little gestures from the others and pushing the glass together. You see, I've always been a skeptic, too.

So, we communicated through the board with the usual cast of Shakespeare and Amelia Earhart and Abe Lincoln, and it all seemed like harmless fun until Angela reminded them that they had a real medium on their hands and couldn't they do much better? There was some laughing now and some teasing, and just when it looked like it was going to die down and be forgotten, Melody had to speak up for me. "I bet he could do it if he really tried."

Was she mocking me or defending me or a little of both? It didn't matter; there was only one way to save my dignity either way.

I closed my eyes and tried to get in touch with the Other Side, ignoring the fact that I didn't believe there was another side. I summoned all my energy to contact some-one, anyone, over there. No use. It was like trying to make myself cry or force a sneeze.

I looked and saw all those beautiful eyes staring at me. I was going to end up humiliated, a laughingstock. How could a good night have gone this wrong? But I could still save myself. They were all half-kidding anyway, weren't they? Why couldn't I kid along? Why couldn't I loll my head back and start speaking in voices and do the whole routine, like I'd seen in a hundred movies from *Blithe Spirit* to *The Legend of Hell House*?

I closed my eyes tight, till the blood pounded and my head started to throb. I moaned once, just to see if I could do it without bursting out laughing. The girls giggled; I didn't. I kept going.

"Who has disturbed my rest?" I asked, in as deep a James Earl Jones voice as I could muster.

The girls really cracked up now. If I could keep playing this angle, somewhere between reality and camp, I just might get out of this.

"Who are you?" Charlotte asked.

"Vincent Kehoe." A dead ancestor from the Ould Sod seemed a good bet. "Dead these many years."

"What's it like?" Lyn asked, laughing.

I gave another moan. "Some things are just not meant

to be known."

"Your brother's a nutcase," Angela said. The other girls poo-pooed her for spoiling the fun, and I peeked enough to see her slump back in her chair, muttering, "This is stupid," her mantra.

"Who did you wish to speak with?" I said, wishing I hadn't sounded so much like a switchboard operator.

"Elvis," said Jamie. "I want to know if he's really dead."

"Or Jim Morrison!" Lyn said.

"Or Marilyn Monroe!" Jamie said.

"Or President Kennedy!" Charlotte said.

"Or Melody's father!" This was Angela. The room gasped. Melody snatched her hand away from the glass. My eyes flew open just enough to see the look of glittering satisfaction in Angela's eyes. I shut my eyes, hoping no one had seen me cheat.

"Angela, you are such a cunt," Charlotte said.

"What?" Angela protested in mock innocence. "If he can really do it..."

"Let's stop this," Lyn said.

"No," said Charlotte. "We were having fun. There's no reason to stop having fun just because of Angela. Vincent, are you still here?"

I had an easy way out; I could say the circle had been broken. But, like Charlotte, I wanted to get back to the fun.

"Yes. To whom do you wish to speak?"

"How 'bout John Lennon?"

"I will see if I can contact him." I let my head drop. The pounding in my skull was much worse, not helped by the tension of the last few moments. I tried to clear my head, tried to remember what a Liverpool accent sounded like, but I was distracted by the awareness that someone was standing behind me. Watching me. I wondered which of the girls had left the circle, what prank they were trying to pull. I felt the figure move away from me, move toward

Melody. Then I asked myself—how did I know where it was moving if it didn't make a sound?

My eyes flew open. Melody's father stood over her, in the cardigan sweater and flannel shirt I'd seen him wear the one time we'd met, when I stopped by her house and saw him watching a football game and dying by inches. My breath stopped in my throat. Melody's father looked at me with pleading eyes. My hand was shaking; the glass was clattering on the table.

The girls were laughing again, but in a tight nervous way, as if the joke was going sour.

"Are you okay?" Charlotte asked.

Melody's father stared at me. I felt anguish rush through my body. Deep, powerful, aching. Like no pain I had ever felt before. His lips trembled and he spoke, with a voice full of yearning. "Tell her I'm here."

I blinked, my eyes feeling as dry as my throat. Melody was looking at me, too, with fear and concern.

"Why won't you tell her?" Melody's father moaned.

But every muscle was frozen, and I couldn't make a sound. The man raised a bony finger and pointed it at me. "I want a kiss from my little angel," he said.

I came out with a low whisper barely audible to anyone but Melody sitting right next to me. "He wants a kiss from his little angel."

Melody flinched as if struck. She bolted to her feet and spit angry words at me. "You sick little jerk!" I knew she meant it, because she didn't even bother to swear. She ran out the door, never to come back again.

The party was over, and from then on, to all of Charlotte's friends, indeed to the whole school, I was a "sick little jerk," either crazy or ghoulishly cruel or in touch with the devil or some combination of the three.

Whatever I had, it was not a gift.

And again, Maggie, I did not, could not, let myself

believe it. I'd been asked to produce Melody's father, so I had, out of my own memories and my own twisted brain. After all, why should this ghost be wearing the outfit he was wearing the one time I'd seen him in life?

And the delusions kept coming after that. Visions of spirits known and unknown, yelling at me, nagging at me, pleading with me. Not all the time. Usually only during periods of extreme emotional stress. Analysis didn't help. CAT scans didn't help. So, I bottled it all in, ignored the spooks when they came, and felt myself grow more and more isolated from the world around me.

Until they stopped coming.

I had gone without them for five years. That's about the only positive thing I could say about the last five years. If they started coming back, it would be more than I could bear.

I turned away from the river and drove my loyal Mustang up the hill to Charlotte's place. I parked in front of her little house. Two bedrooms, a kitchen, a living room, three baths, and a full basement. They didn't make houses that small anymore. All the new ones they were building along the river and in the few patches of farmland that survived were huge $500,000 jobbies that nobody I knew could ever afford, certainly not the kids who'd grown up here. They had all moved into condos and townhouses, if they were lucky. And guys like the "I don't like black and white movies" jerk-off from the video store would be the ones who would ultimately inherit these neighborhoods.

Them and the guy who owned the BMW parked in front of Charlotte's house. I checked my watch, but it was a useless gesture, since I didn't know when he'd gotten here and I didn't know when he'd be leaving.

If I'd had a car phone, I'd have called her house just to hear her not answer. But I couldn't afford a car phone, and if I could have afforded a car phone, I probably could have afforded a life, so I wouldn't be spending my evenings spying on my sister.

No, not spying. Just coming to talk to her and politely waiting for her gentleman caller to leave. Politely waiting, since I didn't have a high-powered rifle to take the asshole's head off as he stepped out the door.

I fell asleep, then awoke with a start as Charlotte climbed in and slammed the door. "Are you spying on me?"

I shifted around and saw that the Beemer was gone. "Did Mr. Right leave?"

"Fuck you, okay? Let's go pick up Maggie. She's at her friend Jordan's house."

The radio blared as I started the car; I switched it off. "I thought you weren't seeing the asshole anymore."

"I am not seeing him, and he's not an asshole. When will you see that he's done the right thing through all of this?"

"The right thing? The right thing is not fucking around when you're married."

"I knew he was married."

"The right thing is not fathering a child and then not even acknowledging her."

"He always gives me money for Maggie when I need it. And besides, would you rather he *hadn't* fathered her?"

Cheap shot. "No, of course not."

"Well, he was never going to leave his wife; that was never in the cards. So, what was he supposed to do?"

"I don't know. Something decent. Commit suicide?"

Charlotte laughed with surprising kindness. "I love it when you try to protect me, little brother, but some things just aren't perfect."

She's a beautiful woman, your mother—is, was, will always be. Not that I could really see her beauty (what brother sees that in a sister?), but I could see it in the way men acted around her. Her blond hair, long legs, dazzling smile, and creamy white skin attracted men with disastrous enthusiasm. Ever since she began to bud at the cruelly young age of nine and a half, boys had phoned, followed, courted, and stalked her, lied to her in act and word, all in hope of gaining access to her beauty. The arbitrary fact of her appearance had affected the way the world treated her and the way she saw the world, so that now, at thirty, she was tired of the whole ride.

I drove on a block. "I don't like it when you ask him for money."

"I don't like it either. Neither does he."

"There's something seedy about it. It's like you're blackmailing him or he's—"

She turned to me. "Or he's what? I don't sleep with him for the money, if that's what you're worried about."

"But you do sleep with him?"

"Sometimes. We're both lonely."

"Well, if he's so fucking lonely, why doesn't he leave his wife?"

"It's complicated."

"It's complicated, fine. Just tell me this, does he *know* you're not sleeping with him for the money? Because if he thinks you are, that's just as bad, isn't it?"

"Shall I call him up and ask him?"

I sighed and turned onto Jordan's street. What the hell gave me the right to tell her how to live her life? "We're both a couple of freaks, Charlie."

"Speak for yourself," she said.

"I think we should go to the island," I said.

Charlotte blinked at me, patronizingly. "The island?"

"For Christmas. We always talked about that."

"You know how long it's been since we were there?"

"I know exactly."

A somber look came into Charlotte's eyes; she banished it at once. "I got jobs lined up."

"Come on, it'll be good for us. Like going home. That was always the one place where we could think. Where we could figure things out. We need it now."

"Maybe you do."

I stopped the car. "Face it, our lives have been screwed up ever since Mom and Dad died."

"My life is perfectly on track, thank you."

"Did you call the asshole, or did he call you?"

"I called him. I wanted to ask his advice about Maggie's school situation."

"How long has it been since you've seen him?"

"About a year."

"Was it nice to see each other?"

"He's really a very charming guy, if you'd get to know him."

"Damn it, Charlie, you're letting him back into your life, can't you see that? You're like an alcoholic with this guy. One taste and you're hooked again, letting him string you along, convince you this time is gonna be different. He's gonna fuck up your life all over again."

(Maybe I'm being too hard on the guy I hate to call your father. Maybe you've tracked him down and gotten to know him and you think he's a real decent guy. God, I hope not.)

She gave me a hurt look, climbed out of the car, and slammed the door.

Fuck. I hurried after her. "I'm sorry. I didn't even mean to bring up all this Big Picture stuff. I'm just talking about Christmas. The island. Maggie's never been to Maine. She deserves a Christmas on the island."

Charlotte stopped and turned to me, her face blotchy with tears. "You don't really think he thought he could sleep with me because he gave me a check, do you?"

"God, of course not. Anybody who could think that about you would have to be such an asshole."

"Which he is," she laughed once, then started to cry harder. I grabbed her and hugged her tight, and she whispered to me, "We're not really freaks, are we, Sammy?"

"No," I told her, thinking they could open a carnival sideshow with me alone. "Of course we're not."

We left for Maine late that night, during the first snowfall of the year.

FIVE

It's a mercy that school kids don't realize that summer vacation is a cruel tease; that a morning will come when they are adults and they are rudely told that those blissful, unproductive months of idleness are to be no more; that they are expected to work year-round, with maybe a week or two off, until the day they retire or die or both.

It's even worse for the children of university professors. Their parents have every summer off, even though they are at least technically grown-ups, so there is no reason to ever suspect the vicious switcheroo that lies in wait. Because of this, the Kehoe kids were able to go to paradise for two months out of every year, and we had no idea that one day we would be cast out for the simple sin of having to make a living.

Every summer, the Monday after the spring semester ended, Dad would wake us up before the first light, already nattily dressed in his knit tie with its always perfect four-in-hand knot, and tell us it was time to hit the road. My mother would already be out in the driveway, packing the car with mathematical precision, filling the station wagon to its maximum volume.

(I still can't reconcile myself to the fact that you never met Mom and Dad; will never meet them. You'd have laughed just to see them. Dad, short and round, with gray hair and a tiny mustache. Mom, tall and thin, with gray hair and no mustache. They looked like the king and queen from *Alice in Wonderland*.) We'd all help cramming in the last of the luggage, books, toys, and whatever pet had survived the winter, and start the drive up to Maine. Since summer days were precious, we would make it without stopping, driving all night, Mom and Dad taking shifts behind the wheel. Later on, Charlotte would drive, too, and George, and finally even me, with my learner's permit sweaty in my shirt pocket and Mom nervous and wide-eyed beside me.

Bleary-eyed, reeking of sweat and fast food, we would climb out at the ferry landing in Rockland, make a mad dash for the bathroom, and buy our round-trip tickets for the ferry boat to Fox Island. To rolling meadows of wild-flowers, to rocky beaches strewn with lost buoys and star-fish and the occasional carcass of a dead seal, to twisting broken roads just made for a swiftly cruising bicycle, to old men perfumed of fish sitting on bustling docks and telling lies, to summer personified.

All of this I wanted to give to you, Maggie. And to give back to your mother and to myself.

We picked up 95 from the Beltway, following the old route north, knowing it so well that glances at the map were a formality. We'd always been Summer People, so we'd never made the trip in winter before, on icy roads and snow. December in Virginia that year had been mild, chilly but clear—jacket weather. With every hour we traveled further into winter so that by nightfall we were in the thick of it, wheels gliding over ice or spinning in gray slush, wipers fighting a losing battle to clear the windshield of splattered freezing rain, headlights illuminating the twirling ice drops and reflecting them back into my eyes.

"We ought to stop," Charlotte said.

You were snoring in the back, strapped into that car

seat you always hated, your head rolling back on the belly
of Mr. Tee, your soft Gund teddy bear. Nothing on the
radio but talk shows, so I plugged in a tape I'd made back
in college expressly for this drive, filled with incongruous
summer songs. "Folks come driftin' round the bend, why
must summer ever end?" Louis Armstrong sang to Dave
Brubeck's piano, while the windows fogged up and I tried
to punch the defroster back to life.

Once we'd grown up, what with summer jobs and college and all, it had been harder and harder to make the
trips to the island and the house on the Thorofare. But
we were an unusually close family and always made it together for at least a week or so. The yearly reunion on the
island was the beacon in our lives, the one steady element
in the roiling sea of young adulthood.

The summers were full of comings and goings then,
since our schedules never coincided exactly. So, there
would be a lobster feast on Charlotte's arrival and another
when I left. And George, the only one of the three of us
who'd been able to get a real degree and a real job, would
always make it for the shortest time. He'd try to get there
at the end of summer so he could help Mom and Dad drive
back to Virginia. That was why he died in the accident, too.

They were pulling another all-nighter—well, you know
the story by now. Dad was a good driver; it wasn't his
fault. They were in Maryland, only a couple hours from
home, when a trucker in an eighteen-wheeler fell asleep
and plowed into them.

In an instant your mother and I were alone. The Kehoe
family had exploded like a firework, and we were remnants of ash floating to the ground.

Charlotte was twenty-five, out of college, and living in
our parents' house between jobs. She was waiting for them
to get home, coffee on the perk, a carrot cake in the oven,
so she was awake when the call came. I was in my dorm

room at Georgetown, and the instant she called I rushed to her. I never went back to that dorm.

We sat alone in the house that morning, watching the sunrise, not knowing what to do next, where to go, who to see. Things haven't changed much since then.

The bright beat of Jonathan Richman's "That Summer Feeling" came over the car stereo, clashing rudely with these memories. I switched it off. A single headlight glared in the rearview mirror. I flicked it to the night setting. The light still seemed unnaturally bright.

As it came closer, it glowed brighter. Brighter and more phosphorescent than any headlight had any business being. I felt the muscles of my stomach tighten.

"You okay?" Charlotte asked.

"Just, that's very weird."

"What is?"

She didn't see it.

The light grew brighter still. It seemed to flood the car, to attach itself to every surface, till everything seemed lit from within, about to burst into flame. I gripped the wheel, trying to keep the car on a road I couldn't even see anymore. In an instant the light passed on, flying through us and shooting ahead, like a guided missile on its way to a target.

I swerved onto the shoulder and hit the brakes. The wheels locked and hydroplaned on the slush; we slid sideways to a halt.

"Jesus!" Charlotte cried. "What happened?"

"You better drive. I think I fell asleep."

"Well, Jesus. Jesus, Sammy. God."

I opened the door and felt the cold rain on my head like a blessing. I opened the back door and climbed in next to you.

"Hi, Unca," you said.

"Is she okay?" Charlotte asked from behind the wheel.

"That was fun, Momma."

I snuggled up to the hard plastic of your car seat as Charlotte pulled back out onto the road.

"Sorry I woke you up, kid," I said.

"I was already waked up. The light waked me up."

I looked toward Charlotte; she had the music up louder, she hadn't heard. "You saw the light?"

"Yeah. Wasn't it pretty?"

I took your tiny hand in mine and whispered, "It was, wasn't it?"

I laid my head on the side of the car seat, and you shifted around so I could share your pillow-bear.

The snow stopped with the sunrise so that by noon, when we finally reached Rockland, the weather felt almost balmy, even though it was fifteen degrees colder than it had been in Virginia.

The state of Maine only ran one ferry in the winter months, so we had a two-hour wait after I put the car in line. Nothing much had changed in the five years since I'd been to Rockland, except for the big new ferry terminal. It was typical of Maine to replace the terminal but not the rusted old ferry boats, which had been making the circuit among the islands of Penobscot Bay for thirty years and more.

We killed time eating candy bars and reading you Dr. Seuss books until you had to go to the bathroom and discovered the wonders of modern technology in the form of an automatic toilet that flushed itself when you stood up. This enchanted you so much that you had to go potty fifteen times in the next hour.

The boat, when it finally arrived, was an old friend, the *Capt. Ethan Showalter*, the smallest of the ferries, only used on the frequent occasions when the larger boats broke down. We climbed into the Mustang and waited, feeling the usual suspense about whether we'd make it on board this trip. There were fifteen cars in line and a big freezer truck besides, but the ferry boys are as skilled as my mother ever was at squeezing the most out of limited space. They whistled and waved and cajoled, and we finally found ourselves nestled so tight against the freezer truck that I couldn't open my door. But we were on board, and that was all that mattered. We were leaving the mainland behind.

Extruding ourselves from the car on the passenger side, we raced up to the pedestrian deck, breathing in the bracing mixture of salt air and diesel fumes I remembered so well. We cleared the cabin just in time to see the old Owls Head lighthouse go by, reaching out to us from its long spit of sand, the last contact with the continent.

The breeze was cold and cutting, so I held you on my lap, wrapped in my jacket, and sat on the wet metal deck watching the sailboats float by us. The sea was rough, with cruel gray chops that made the ferry bob and twist in ways I'd never experienced before; I exchanged green glances with Charlotte, but you just laughed and cheered as you saw a seal pop its doggy head out of the water. Leaping from my lap, you ran to the rail, attached yourself to a clump of other racing children and dashed down the stairs. Your mother and I shifted over to where we could watch the kids darting between the parked cars; strangers playing an impromptu game of tag. We watched, but we weren't worried or concerned, as we would have been if you'd run off at a park or a mall back home. That was one of the blessings of the island. It was a place out of the past, where kids could run and play without fear of Stranger Danger, since everyone knew everyone else and watched out for everyone else. A place where a kid could ride a bike to a friend's house on his own. Where a woman could go for a walk after dark. It was like Home Base in a game of tag; there, you were always safe.

I squinted into the wind, the cold bringing tears to my eyes, and took Charlotte's hand. With a nod of my head, I indicated familiar faces on the deck. Earlene Gillis's grandmother was on the bench. The incredibly old man we always used to see marching in the Labor Day parade was standing by the rail. A lobsterman crony of our old friend Neil Amudsen, name of Carl or Ken or something, was sitting on the top step. No one we knew well, but recognizable just the same, and comforting.

Charlotte, always friendly, always good with people, went over to chat with them. I was going to follow her when you ran back up the stairs, at full steam, and butted smack into my crotch. I twisted in time to avoid a painful impact.

"Carry me!"

I hoisted you up onto my hip, brushing your wild hair out of your eyes.

"I saw a witch," you said.

"You did? Did she fly on her broomstick?"

"Not that kinda witch. The Hansel and Gretel kind. She cooks kids in a pot. Wanna see?"

You pointed over the rail, and I saw a fat, pimply-faced, mustached middle-aged woman leaning against a pick-up, biting a cigarette out of a pack of Kools.

"It's not polite to stare, honey."

"Not in a pot, in an oven, I mean. She keeps 'em in a cage first. Then she makes 'em in a pie."

"Who told you that?"

"I dunno."

"Well, don't you believe it."

"You know what I'd do, if she tried to cook me in a pie, I'd cook *her* in a pie!"

"That sounds fair."

"But I wouldn't eat it, 'cause that'ud be gross."

The bell clanged as we passed the boathouse on Fisher's Island, and the ageless Yankee couple that always sat out there waved as we went by. I taught you the Fox Island Wave, a big arcing sweep of the arm from side to side, visible at long distances, so you could wave back.

We were in the Channel now, a corridor between populated islands that ended with Fox and Hog and Brown's Head Islands. Houses big and small were scattered among the heavy green trees and granite rock of the coastline. American flags whipped in the frigid breeze. Dories and punts and Boston whalers bobbed in the choppy water, hanging onto the few splintery gray floats that hadn't been pulled up for the winter.

I'd never seen so few boats in the water here. I'd never seen so few of the brightly colored lobster buoys on the surface. I was used to the bustle and industry of the summer months, but I knew only the most industrious lobsterman was still hauling this late in the year. Winter was mostly for the big shrimp boats, not the one- or two-man lobster boats that stayed close to shore, hauling traps from sun up to sun down.

Familiar rocks and roof lines began to roll past us, and I felt a flood of memory; it was a progression, a ceremony that brought me back to youth, to when I was your age, Maggie, to before that, to before I could even remember, since my folks had been bringing me here since I was a baby, and I couldn't remember the first time I'd seen these sights. They had been with me always, like the faces of my parents. No matter where I am, I can close my eyes and see the view from that ferry.

Fox Island was on the port side now, its coastline squiggled with hundreds of tiny inlets and waterways. I saw it from above once, in a small plane, an island the size of Manhattan but with an outline so wrinkled you'd go through a whole pencil trying to trace it. It has a population of around a thousand in the winter and two thousand after Memorial Day. When the Summer Jerks come.

Only the natives would be here this time of year; fishermen mostly, and a half dozen lawyers to handle their lawsuits. And now the Kehoes.

I was surprised to see one lobster boat on the water after all. It was just ahead of us, hauling a full trap up with its hydraulic. Charlotte was with me again, and I asked her if she recognized the boat; a remarkably clean craft, made of fiberglass, shiny and brilliant white on the gray sea. Charlotte said she didn't, and she couldn't imagine who would be ambitious enough to still be at it this close to Christmas.

"Not making himself any friends," she added. Lobstermen were a close-knit community, and it didn't pay to be conspicuously more or conspicuously less hardworking than average. To be accused of trying to show the others up was a fairly serious breach of etiquette.

But it was nothing compared to what we saw next. As the fisherman dropped the trap back into the water and looked up at the passing ferry, I saw that she was a woman. Well, I'd never seen a woman lobsterman—I didn't even know the word for such a thing. Some men took their wives out as sternmen, but they usually found the subsequent ribbing so humiliating they never kept it up for long.

This woman was out on her own with no man at the wheel. In her thirties, I guessed, wearing a gray cable-knit sweater, her long, dirty-blond hair swept back in a ponytail, her pale face turned red by the chafing of the wind, her eyes...could I really see that they were a piercing sea green from this distance? She didn't smile at the boat as it passed, just waited for it to go by.

My hand tightened on the rail. The boats were parallel now, and our eyes met. I smiled broadly, and she gave me a look of surprise and laughed once before she turned back to the wheel and drove her boat to the next buoy.

"I think I'm over Anne," I said.

Charlotte laughed. "Jesus, you're a piece of work."

Well, I knew you would be more sympathetic. "Did you see the pretty lady, Maggie?"

"I wanna boat," you said.

"Do you know who she is?" I asked your mother.

"Nope. Maybe she's from away."

"Come on. It's weird enough they let a woman haul. They'd never let an off-islander do it."

We were interrupted by a sudden rush of activity as people hurried to the rail and pointed. The ferry landing was in sight now. On shore, the parking lot was crowded with on-lookers; waiting to see who got off the boat was the social event of the day during the long winter months.

"Izzat where we're going?" you asked.

An elderly couple, white-haired retirees from Connecticut, I would guess, stood next to us and beamed at you. You're such a beautiful child, you produce smiles like that wherever you go. I knew people usually assumed you were my child and, I hope you don't mind my saying, it was a misunderstanding that secretly pleased me every time.

"Yep, that's where we're going," I said.

"We used to come here with Grandma and Grandpa every year," Charlotte said.

"And dead Uncle George?" you asked.

"And Uncle George," I said, noticing curious looks from the elderly couple next to us.

"He's dead, though," you went on, sounding as cheerful as ever. "And Grandma and Grandpa are dead too!"

"Yes."

"And one day I'm gonna be dead!" you hollered.

"She's a realist," I tried to explain to the elderly couple as they moved quickly away.

Then there was the dash to the car deck, with everyone wedging themselves back into their cars and waiting while the ferry settled itself between the barnacle-encrusted pylons and the metal ramp was lowered in place. The cars drove off, leaving the ferry riding a little higher as each one reached the broken asphalt of the parking lot.

I followed the big truck off, waving to the ferry watchers and seeing the startled smiles on their faces as they recognized us. The gossip would begin as soon as we passed. Word that we were back would hit town before we did.

"Should we stop and chat?" Charlotte asked. It was very important for Summer People to observe proper decorum with the townspeople and never give offense. Otherwise, broken windows and suspicious fires had a way of occurring in their homes during the winter months.

"Let's settle into the house first," I said. "Then, we'll go calling."

"One problem with that," Charlotte said, passing the last juice box back to you. "I don't have a key, do you?"

Here. Exhausted. Locked out. Mom and Dad never made mistakes like that.

SIX

I felt my heart lift with every spin of the tires that brought us closer to town. We passed the boatyard. The old ice cream stand. The sheriff's trailer. The fire department. Everything looked just as we'd left it, as if it had been stored away and had just been unpacked and dusted off for our arrival. A Christmas present forgotten long enough that it seemed like new again.

It was a good ten degrees warmer this far off the coast than it had been on the mainland, and the hardy souls we saw on the streets were wearing only jackets, keeping their fingers warm with cigarettes rather than gloves. I lifted my hand from the wheel and waved at each car as it passed. The people in the cars always waved back. Small-town courtesy at its purest.

Main Street on Fox Island is a block of wood-frame houses on one side and the harbor on the other, buildings mostly two stories high with gabled Victorian roofs, their wooden shingles turned steely gray from the salt air. A few were now painted a vivid yellow or red in a show of garish enthusiasm that was new to the island. The harbor was crowded with all manner of boats, from pleasure crafts to working boats to Boston whalers to big fishing trawlers.

We remembered we'd need food, so we parked in the harbor parking lot below the great stone eagle, a monument to the days when this island had been one of the nation's centers for granite quarrying. The sea air hit us with renewed freshness as we stepped out of the car, and you rushed to the water's edge, balancing on the end of a pylon and calling to a group of seagulls who looked down on you with the indulgent interest of a superior life-form.

We saw Neil a half-hour later as we were steering the fully stocked shopping cart out of the town's only grocery store. He was sitting with a pack of friends in front of the hardware store. Fishermen sat there every day, as they had sat for a hundred years or more, only exchanging a wooden bench for plastic lawn chairs and floppy oilskin hats for colorful baseball caps with boat manufacturers' logos.

"Sammy Kehoe!" Neil climbed out of his chair and moved to me with his always slow, rolling gait. "Where the fuck have you been?"

I smiled and thumped my old friend on the shoulder, remembering that social hugs hadn't quite reached this part of the country. "Just around, you know."

"Stayin' for Christmas?"

Before I had a chance to answer, Neil's attention was caught by Charlotte, and his face lit up as he hurried to give her a bear hug. Times change, I thought.

Neil backed off, smiling his lopsided smile, and noticed you, sound asleep in your car seat.

"Who's the little one?"

Well, I thought, there's a detail we forgot to tell people about.

"That's Maggie, my daughter," your mother said, proud as always.

Neil's face fell, just for a second, but he rallied courageously. "Didn't know you were married Charlie, congratulations."

"I'm not."

We might have left it at that, if you hadn't spoken up.

"My daddy's dead. So's my grandma and my grandpa and my Unca George."

Neil didn't seem sure what to say to that.

"We were only married for a short while," Charlotte said, as we pushed the shopping cart across the street. "He died in the war."

"Oh, God, I'm sorry," Neil said. Then, "Which war?"

She barely missed a beat. "Bosnia. He was with the, you know, U.N. peacekeeping forces."

"Jesus," Neil said, loading the groceries into the trunk. "I didn't know about any of this. I'm sorry. Don't know what the fuck we were doing over there anyway."

Neil offered further condolences for three or four uncomfortable minutes, after which we climbed into the Mustang and followed Neil's pick-up truck to his place, where he had the spare key Mom and Dad had given him so that he could check on our house during the winter.

"Bosnia?" I said to Charlotte as we drove.

"It was the first thing I could think of."

I told her I didn't see why she had to think of anything. Neil was a friend, he wouldn't judge her.

"Maybe Neil wouldn't, but word would get around. This is a small town; I don't want to get a reputation."

I pointed out that un-wed parenthood was the second-favorite pastime on Fox Island, but Charlotte wasn't amused.

"Look, one of the best things about coming here when we were kids was that no one really knew much about us, right?" she said. "I mean, pardon me, but back home we were just nerdy kids who never fit in, but here we were exotic children from the mainland. We could make up any stories about ourselves we wanted, right?"

I admitted that I might have fibbed about a few track and field medals.

"So, what's the difference?" she asked.

"The difference is, you're supposed to be a grown-up now. And also, I don't think we ever invented a whole person and killed him off back then."

"Speak for yourself," she said.

I followed the pick-up past the town museum and the old cemetery, up the hill to Neil's house. "I think you like him," I said.

"We always liked Neil," she replied, noncommittal.

"I think he likes you."

"Neil always liked us," she replied, noncommittal.

Neil was my age, exactly. We even shared the same birthday, as we discovered one afternoon some twenty years ago while we were swimming in the quarry. We'd grown up together one summer at a time. When I would arrive on the island, the first thing I would do was force Dad up the stairs to the attic to pull down my old bike and inflate the tires so I could speed off to Neil's house. Together, we covered every inch of the island, learning to sail in Percy's Cove, catching frogs in Biggin's Pond, learning to drink beer under the Brown's Head Channel pier.

I never had a friendship that lasted so long or so faithfully, perhaps because it thrived only two months out of every year and went into hibernation for the rest, perhaps because we simply trusted each other so much. Whatever the reason, it had always been the way it had been just then outside the market; when we saw each other, we picked up where we'd left off, as if no time had passed.

Perhaps in our hearts, we Kehoes had always felt a little sorry for Neil, a bright, imaginative boy trapped on a picturesque but back-water small town. What kind of future did he have on Fox Island? Now Neil was grown up, a successful lobster fisherman, with his own boat and his own house and a thriving winter business making and selling wire lobster traps. And me and your mother, what had we done with all the opportunities offered by the fabulous mainland?

Neil ran into his house, got the keys, and told us to follow him to the Thorofare. The dirt road was barely intact, and we were bumped and jarred around in the car until we reached the crest of the hill and heard it scrape the bottom of the car. We skidded down out of the woods into the meadow. I felt a lump in my throat as the sky opened up before us. A part of me couldn't believe the house would still be there.

It was there.

But this winter it looked a bit forlorn. The meadow hadn't been cut for a long time, and the dead grass was long and tangled and exhausted, with sapling trees growing here and there. The white paint was peeling, and the screen door had fallen off its hinges. But the windows were all intact. Neil had made sure of that. No local vandals would mess with anything under his watchful eye.

We slid onto the gravel driveway and climbed out. You immediately dashed from the car and ran into the meadow, rushing toward the freezing water. Danger always attracted you like a magnet.

We followed, the wind whipping our hair and snatching Neil's "Jones Boat Company" cap off his head. We sat down on the rocky beach while you played with a neon orange buoy that had washed onto one of the stone ledges.

"Who lives there?" you asked, pointing to Brown's Head Island across the Thorofare.

"Nobody much," Neil said.

"C'mon! In the house with the green roof." I squinted and could just make out a house with green shingles on the shore. Man, you had good eyes. "It looks like th'Emrald City! Can I go there?"

"Sure, I'll take you in my boat."

"You have a boat?" you asked Neil, as if he'd claimed to have his own spaceship.

"Yep. I'm the captain. And the crew. You can be my sternman."

"Yeah! What do I do?"

"Scoop dead fish into a nylon bag."

"Gross," you said, laughing at this absurdity.

Charlotte was standing in the meadow looking back at the house. I knew we were both holding back from actually going in.

We walked up the meadow, barely able to find the old footpath, tripping over the well with its tar-paper cover. You ran ahead of us all, and your mother hurried to keep up. I stayed with Neil, who never hurried in his life.

"Good to see you, Sammy," Neil said.

"Good to see you."

"How you holding up?"

"Eh. So-so."

"Mmm."

That was going to be the extent of our soul searching about the past five years. But before you start rolling your eyes and making jokes about insensitive, uncommunicative men, try to understand how eloquent shared silence can be.

"Charlotte's looking good," Neil said.

I agreed that she was.

"Seeing anybody?"

I said she wasn't. "How 'bout you? You get married?"

"Not that I noticed."

He pulled out his keys and sprinted (yes, sprinted) to the porch to open the door for you and your mother.

Stepping in was like tripping back in time. The house didn't look deserted; it looked like it did at the beginning of every summer. Empty and waiting for us. I half expected to see Dad's short, roly-poly figure come strolling in, chuckling over some witticism from *The Mill on the Floss* and demanding that we sit and listen.

Something about the sea air keeps things remarkably clean on the island, so there wasn't even a layer of dust on the counters of the kitchen. The plates and pots were all stacked and waiting for us. The only sign of abandonment was a family of field mice that had made itself at home in the downstairs bedroom, but we didn't discover them until the next morning.

As you know, it's a terribly old house; the middle section dates back to before the Revolution, and it's been added onto in a haphazard fashion ever since so that it sprawls out sideways, with low doorways and uneven stairs so steep that they are almost ladders. When Mom and Dad bought it for almost nothing (he was only a university professor, remember) way back in the sixties, it had been a dilapidated wreck, and we'd been fixing it up in our own incompetent fashion ever since. It was never finished, and I assume it never will be.

Any solemn feelings we had on walking in were fortunately spoiled by your yelps and laughs as you dashed from room to room, opening every door, jumping on every bed.

Neil said he had to go repair the fuel line on his boat if he wanted to go hauling tomorrow.

"Jesus, Neil, you're going out in wintertime?" I said.

"It's my business. I got to take it seriously," Neil said. I wondered who he was trying to impress and knew it wasn't me. Before he left he asked me, as he always did, if I wanted to go out hauling with him tomorrow. In a weak moment, I said I did. He reminded me that the day started early for fishermen, and then he was gone.

You ran in with an old Chinese kite made of flimsy plastic and painted like Pegasus. You whipped it around the room and wanted to know what it was, so I took you out to fly it. With a strong breeze like that, all I had to do was unwind the string from the spool and it took off like an eagle. We unwound it further and further, until the kite was just a tiny speck in the gray sky. You wanted to hold it yourself, and I let you, though I was half-afraid the kite would lift you off and carry you over the trees. You held on tight, though, racing back and forth across the meadow as if it was you flying and not the kite.

I glanced back into the house and saw your mother standing in front of the fridge, head down. You seemed to be having enough fun without me, so I went in to check on her.

The refrigerator was covered with pictures held in place by magnets. A big metal family photo album. Charlotte was looking at them and crying.

You know the pictures, I'm sure. They're probably still up there, covered, I hope, with a new layer of photos of you growing up, becoming a woman. Your mother was looking at decades of summers; us as kids playing ball in the meadow, swimming in the quarries, learning to sail, having food fights by the stove, playing games at the kitchen table—backgammon, Scrabble, gin, Oh Hell, all the games in Hoyle, and a few we made up ourselves. And sunsets. Dozens of sunsets, out there in the meadow, with us blurred and poorly lit in the foreground. A massive, out of focus, collage of memories.

This was why we hadn't come back, of course. Facing these memories was overpowering. This island, this house, had come to be the concrete embodiment of our family life. Being here pointed out more than anything else how shattered our family was.

"How can there just be the two of us?" Charlotte asked. I put my hand on her shoulder and felt just as helpless as she did. Two people couldn't be the Kehoes.

Then you called out to us from the meadow, and I

remembered that we were three now. Maybe that's why we'd had the strength to come back.

I walked out in time to see you let go of the string and watch the kite fly away into the clouds.

"You're supposed to hang onto it, Maggie."

But you just laughed and said how pretty it was and danced as it disappeared.

We picked out rooms next. You got my old bedroom upstairs. Charlotte kept hers next door; the walls were still covered with pictures from fashion magazines and old art books she'd cut out and pasted up. I took Mom and Dad's room downstairs just to show that we were making the place our own again.

While you fought against taking a nap, I went into town and bought you a new kite at the hardware store. The fishermen still sat there; I even joined them for a while, discussing the weather and reactionary politics. Then I dropped by the electric co-op to see about getting our power turned on and found Mike Jensen, the family plumber, and asked him to come out and get the pipes running and the heat turned on. These were all things Dad used to take care of, and it almost made me feel grown-up to do it myself—that'll give you an indication of just how not grown-up I am.

By mid-afternoon, with the sun setting in its usual spectacular way, the water was running and the steam heat was rattling in the radiators. I sat on the porch, bundled in two sweaters, watching you fly your new kite, listening to fish bubbling in a fry pan on the stove, feeling safer than I had in years. The house always had that effect on me, as if it held me in kind and protective hands. Our family was never more of a family than when we were there. It was the house, more than any person, who taught me how to take care of you. To be the Good Mother. Like I said, I never believed in guardian angels, but if I ever had one, it was that house.

I walked into the kitchen, where your mother was making fish and chips. We could see you through the glass doors, running like a wood sprite across the lawn. It was all too perfect.

"I think we should stay here," I said.

Charlotte laughed. "You mean for the rest of our lives?"

"Why not?" I asked.

"What would we do for a living?"

"I could fish. I've gone out with Neil lots of times. I'm going out with him tomorrow. I could start out as his sternman, then after I've saved up enough, I could get my own boat. And I can still sell articles to Filmfax and Fangoria and Video Watchdog. That'll supplement things." After all, I reasoned, we owned the house free and clear, so we wouldn't need that much money. There'd be no problem paying for your schooling; the public schools on the island were safe and drug free—unless you counted beer.

"What about me?" Charlotte asked.

"I don't know. Be creative. You could go back to giving massages."

"I'm not ready to see a bunch of fishermen naked."

"C'mon, Charlie, think about it."

She scooped a piece of fish out of the pan and let it drain on a paper towel. "You know, you've got a real commitment problem."

"I commit," I protested. "I commit all over the place."

"Yeah, that's your problem. Don't you see that's the same as not committing at all?"

If she wanted to get off the point, I was willing to go with her. "Hey, I'm the one who asked Anne to marry me."

"When you knew it would scare her off."

"I didn't know it would scare her off."

"You knew."

"You're saying I maneuvered her into dumping me?"

"All I'm saying is, it's a pattern, isn't it? You get yourself rejected so you don't have to commit to things. And do you think it's a coincidence that the *day* you decide on a teaching career is the same day you punch out your first student?"

"Now you're saying I didn't want to be a teacher?"

Charlotte sighed. "I'm not saying anything. Get Maggie, dinner's ready."

"And I don't really love Anne?"

"Maybe you do. Maybe that's why you scared her off."

Your mother reads too many self-help books. I don't read enough.

"Look," I said, coming to my feet, "I admit I have self-destructed a few times, but this is different. This place has always felt like home to me. And to you, too, I think. We can make it work. Just think about it, okay?"

Charlotte smiled, a little too fondly. "It'll be a nice thing to think about."

"Lookit, lookit, lookit!" you cried from outside.

We turned to see you, laughing and twirling little Gypsy arabesques as your new kite sailed off, string dangling, over Brown's Head Island and out of sight.

SEVEN

alling asleep is not my best thing. I hear for other people it's this simple matter of closing the eyes and relaxing and drifting off. I figure they've got to be lying, but that's what they say. For me, it's work. Like digging a ditch; I have to physically make a hole in the dark and throw myself in. Sometimes the dark is awfully hard to plow through.

It was particularly difficult that first night on the island because with you and your mother there I couldn't listen to music or watch TV, my usual sleep aids. It was just me and a whole lot of silence.

I know that's why you always have to have stories and songs before you go to sleep, Maggie—so you can drift off before the quiet comes. Because as any kid will tell you, when all the noise is gone, that's when the monsters come out. All those thoughts you've been avoiding, the ones that have been waiting through the hurly-burly of the day, building up strength; when the lights are out and the lullabies are sung, that's when they pounce.

But I did it. I went straight to sleep with none of the expected depressing funk about my hopeless love life and bleak future. And I'd probably have slept through the night if Anne hadn't come in.

She walked right up to me and sat on the edge of my

bed. She was wearing that lace teddy I'd bought her as a joke on her birthday. The fact that she was wearing it said she was sorry before she said she was sorry.

Sorry for putting me through all this. Sorry for making such a horrible mistake. Bill Zacharias was a jerk. He was dull. He was boring. A total nerd. What's more, he was a sexual deviant. He beat her and made her wear rubber panties. He also stole from her bank account and seduced her sister. How could she have been such a fool?

She wanted to know if there was any way I'd take her back.

I was a big man. A forgiving man. I took her into my arms and told her it was all forgotten. I was even generous enough to say some of it was my fault, since I was sure we both knew it wasn't.

She stretched out in bed next to me and grew large enough to encompass my whole body in warmth, in softness, in love.

Even before I woke up, I could feel reality coming and tried to shoo it away. It was going to be so damned depressing to wake up alone in that bed. I asked Anne if she could stay just a little longer, and she said I was crowding her and moving too fast and she needed more room.

Awake, I looked at my watch. 11:31. I'd been asleep for twenty-five whole minutes. I tried to think of other things. Happy things. That girl on the passing lobster boat, for instance. Instead, I kept wondering if Anne had noticed I was gone yet. Was she wondering about me? Worried? Maybe she was missing me. Maybe that dream had been her soul crying out to me.

Well, if I didn't believe in ghosts, I sure as hell couldn't believe in shit like that.

But I could call her, just to make sure. Just to let her know I was okay. Just in case she was worried.

"Oh, you've been gone?" I could hear her answer in my

imagination. I couldn't call her.

But she could call me. She might have already called. At least to apologize for being such a cosmic bitch the other night.

I should check my messages. I leapt onto the icy cold floor and tiptoed into the living room, quiet as a shadow. There was enough moonlight for me to find the phone without turning a light on. I didn't want to be caught; I knew in my heart it was a stupid enough thing to do that I didn't want to have to explain it to Charlotte.

I grabbed the receiver, ready to punch in my number and my PIN code, then stopped, dumbfounded, staring at the wheel on the phone. A rotary phone. Mom and Dad had never gotten around to putting a touch-tone phone in here. I suddenly felt cut off from my century, isolated from the technology that made my world work. With no touch-tone pad, I couldn't check my messages. I was lost. Adrift.

Unable to check them, I was suddenly sure that there *had* to be messages. Vitally important messages. Anne *must* have called. Dozens of times. Weeping, probably. Begging forgiveness. Then calling again, angry at me for not calling back, for leaving her to stew in her agony. Then calling to tell me off and letting me know she was going back to Bill Zacharias, even though he was a nerdy pervert. And all that without my being able to lift a finger, without my even being aware.

And who knew who else might have been calling? Hugh, offering me my own store. Publishers dying for my book. Barbara Steele finally agreeing to give me that interview. Ed McMahon telling me I'd won millions.

I tried to imagine things so ridiculous that they'd turn the whole thing into a joke, but I couldn't shake the feeling that something marvelous was happening just out of sight and I was missing it.

Then something marvelous did happen. Something so unusual that I can feel it now, while I write this. I started to relax. To feel calm. Actual peace and restfulness enveloped me. I could feel my pulse rate slow, my blood pressure drop.

And there was no reason for it. Nothing I was doing or thinking. No happy news had come my way. It just was. I felt as though my mother's hand was stroking my hair and she was singing one of her oddly chosen lullabies like "The Look of Love" or "What the World Needs Now." Peaceful. Content.

I drifted off right there in the chair and slept the whole night through.

Four o'clock the next morning (if you can call four o'clock "morning") I was jolted awake by the ringing of the phone at my elbow.

"Rise and shine, sternman," Neil said with cold-blooded enthusiasm. "We got traps to haul."

By 4:30, I was sitting in Monty's, the fisherman's diner that overhangs the harbor, eating scrambled eggs and Tabasco sauce with Neil. I'd used the pay phone to check my messages, and, of course, there weren't any. I banished my regrets of the night before and prepared to plunge into my new life as a lobsterman.

"And another reason this'll never work," Neil was saying, "is that you're from away. The only way an off-islander can fish here is if he's born here."

"Then he wouldn't be from away."

"That's my point."

But I told him I wasn't going to be dissuaded. I had some money saved up, I was going to invest in his business, become his partner.

"I'm not a law firm," Neil said. "It's just me and my boat. I don't need a partner. If you want to help out, fine, but I won't say more than that." You never "worked for" somebody on the island; you only "helped them out."

"Call it whatever you want," I said. "I'm going to make this work."

The door opened, bringing in a blast of freezing night air and a new customer who sat at the counter.

"I quit," I said to Neil.

"You lasted longer than I expected," he said.

I pointed to the newcomer at the counter—the woman I'd seen from the ferry. She was wearing the same sweater, and her face looked even fresher now in the middle of this cold winter night.

"I want to go hauling with her," I said.

Neil leaned over to take a look and gave me a sympathetic smile. "Kathleen Milland. Good luck to you."

"Where'd she come from?"

Neil shrugged. "She's from away."

"I thought your gang didn't let off-islanders haul?"

Neil smiled over his coffee. "Well, when we see her sailing by, we don't mind so much." He glanced over at her again with a hopeless but amused look in his eye. "Is there anything prettier than a beautiful, sad woman?" We were soul-mates, Neil and I.

"You in love with her?"

"The whole island's in love with her."

"So, is she married? In a relationship? A lesbian?"

"Well, she lives alone, and the island lesbians haven't gotten anywhere with her either."

"There are island lesbians?"

"There's not a lot to do here in the wintertime."

Neil told me her story, or as much of it as was known. She'd come over on the ferry four years ago, driving a Saturn with New York plates, and put herself up at Marcy Swensen's bed and breakfast. She got a job as a grocery clerk, then took over as butcher in Raymond's Market when old man Orville died. The second year, she started hauling for lobsters part-time. They should have stopped her then, Neil said, but she kept to herself and didn't make any missteps (poaching in somebody else's territory or fouling somebody's line, etc.), so nobody could find an excuse. Also, everybody had a crush on her, and since she never dated anyone, everybody kept holding out hope they'd be the one, so nobody wanted to offend her.

Oh, there was the usual harassment any new man gets: pots cut loose, buoys defaced, you know the kind of crap the lobster gangs get up to. But she never retaliated, just took it in stride, so the perpetrators ended up feeling sorry for her and defending her from any new pranks. Before you knew it, highliners were giving her tips on the best places to haul and she was at it full-time, fishing with seven hundred traps.

"She's a damn fine fisherman," Neil said, the highest praise he could offer anyone. He said he knew she could bring in twice as many lobsters as she did, but she was smart enough not to push it.

As I heard all this, I was liking her more and more. I asked if she had a sternman.

"Weren't you going to be my partner?" Neil asked, amused.

"Come on."

"Well, she used to use Jimmy Norvag, but he got drunk and fell overboard, so he says. Now she hauls on her own."

"Talk to her. Put in a word for me."

Neil laughed. "Jesus, you haven't changed a bit. When are you going to stop all this flitting around and settle down?"

"Right now. With her. Go talk."

So Neil slid off his chair and strolled over to her, and I sipped some of the worst coffee I'd ever tasted while he engaged her in a long, drawn-out discussion, which was pretty much the only kind you could have on the island, where it was considered bad form to get to your point in less than ten minutes.

Now and then they'd look over at me, and I'd have to decide what kind of expression to put on—smiling and friendly? serious and professional? brooding and sexually magnetic? I tried them all and probably came across as a manic depressive with multiple personalities.

Neil ambled back over to me, just as he had left—he'd mastered the island trait of making his body language a bland cipher, so you never knew if he was crossing to you with news that you'd won the lottery or with a death sentence from the chemo ward. He sat down and sipped his coffee. "It ain't any better when it's cold, is it?"

"So, what did she say?"

He shook his head with that why-are-these-tourists-always-in-such-a-hurry expression. "She'll give you a shot."

"Really? When?"

"Now."

I felt suddenly ridiculous. "Jesus, now?"

Immediately, I started looking for a way out. "But you were counting on me today."

Neil laughed, snorting back his coffee. "I think I'll get by."

"What'd you tell her about me?"

"Enough to get you on her boat."

This was starting to feel like a stupider idea by the minute. "What's enough to get me on her boat?"

"Just that you've been hauling for years and you used to have your own boat off Matinicus, but you're a drunk and you lost everything and now you've joined AA and you're trying to start over."

I stared at him in numb disbelief. He came up with that story while strolling over to the counter? No wonder he walked so slow. "Why did you tell her that?"

He shrugged. "She goes to the AA meetings in the

Union Church, and you know how they all stick together; it's like a cult."

"You could have just told her I needed a job."

He slid his coffee back with his elbow and leaned into me with a wise smile. "She wasn't going to hire you because she needs a sternman, because nobody really needs a sternman. The only reason you bring one on is because you think he might have some good stories to pass the time. I gave you a good story. Now, it's up to you."

I stood up and crossed over to her, ready to set her straight, to tell the truth, to make a devastatingly bad first impression. I hesitated, hands in my back pockets, unsure how to start.

"Hey. I'm Sam Kehoe." She didn't look up. Close to her, looking at her in profile, she seemed even more beautiful than she had from the boat. She was a little older than I'd thought, past thirty, I guessed, and the wind and sun had left their mark on her face. But they were all marks of experience, and they'd been drawn on with loving grace, like the pen strokes of elegant handwriting, and I wanted to kiss the salt out of them and blend them smooth with my tongue.

"Let's go," she said, tossing change onto the counter and heading out the door.

I hurried back to Neil, paying him for my breakfast. "What'll she do if she finds out I'm a fake?"

Neil smiled again. "Probably throw you overboard like she did Jimmy Norvag."

Now, I don't want to make it sound like I don't know my way around a lobster boat. I worked three summers as sternman on Neil's father's boat when I was a teenager. (The sternman does all the shit jobs—loading the bait, banding the lobsters, hauling the crates off the winches.) I knew the job and could do it efficiently and with good humor.

What I didn't know was the lingo. I could never remember what a following sea was or what the difference
between a reef and a shoal was. I couldn't make head
nor tails of the high-tech navigational equipment—GPS,
Loran-C, and God knew what-all satellite tracking sys-
tems—that beeped and blipped on flickering green screens
in the wheelhouse. Of course, Neil had tried to teach it all
to me, and I tried to learn it, but as soon as he launched
into the jargon, my eyes would just glaze over and my mind
would wander, just like it did those long winter evenings
when Mom tried to tutor me in algebra.

I could do the job I was supposed to just fine, but I
could never have engaged in the tiniest bit of small talk
that would have convinced her I was a former lobsterman.

Fortunately, I didn't have to. She didn't talk. I don't
mean to say that she was shy or a woman of few words.
I mean, she really did not talk. There wasn't a word exchanged between us that wasn't absolutely necessary for
the running of the boat.

At first, this was a great relief to me. Through the
hours of early morning I scooped bait and unloaded traps
in a state of constant anxiety that at least distracted me
from the unpleasantness of the job; when would she start
chatting and ask one of the million simple questions that
would unveil me as a fraud? But she didn't chat, she didn't
ask questions, she didn't even gab on the radio like every
other fisherman I've ever known. All she did was work.

She worked with thoroughgoing intensity, like a sur-
geon doing an organ transplant. Her eyes were forever re-
garding the sea around her or checking the GPS or reading
her charts; whatever she looked at seemed to claim her
attention to the exclusion of all else. I worried for a while
that there might be a specific reason for this. That maybe
the weather was worse than it looked or that we were

going through a particularly dangerous patch of ocean. The more time passed, the more I sensed that there was nothing unusual about her behavior today. This was simply the way she lived. Everything she did, she did totally and with a purpose.

And what's more, despite the rain slicker and wool sweater and clunky rubber boots, she was beautiful while she did it. I'll maintain till the day I die that there is nothing more attractive than watching someone do something really well.

She kept her boat spotless. She measured each lobster with scrupulous care and threw back any that were even slightly below or above legal standard. She instructed me to do the same, not with words but by example and a curt nod of her head. She was a lobstering machine.

Now, as I said, I appreciated all this. I admire good workmanship as much as the next person and lament its disappearance from the American scene and all that, but still, after three or four hours, this professionalism was starting to grate on me. For one thing, there was nothing to take my mind off what I was now realizing to my disappointment was a singularly unpleasant job. Handling stinking bait fish and strapping rubber bands onto the claws of angry crustaceans while trying to stave off seasickness was feeling less and less like a route to fulfillment.

My disappointment with the job was only matched by my disappointment with myself. Why couldn't I find simple fulfillment in doing a job well, like Kathleen did? Dear God, this wasn't going to turn out to be another one of my fifteen-minute whims, was it? I think you can answer that one for yourself, but to get my mind off it, I started focusing more and more on Kathleen and getting her to talk.

I dragged a trap off the winch, unhooked the bungee cord to open the cage, and pulled out a pissed-off crab. I held it out to her as it snapped and swore at us in crab.

"You want to keep this?" I said.

"Nope."

"You sure?" I asked, perversely putting on a heavy Down Easter accent. "Crab sandwiches. Good eatin'."

She looked at me as if I was just slightly nuts. "I'm not fishing for crab."

And that was that for the next hour.

The sea grew rougher as the day went on. The surface turned darker and angrier; white caps popped up all around us. The boat started bobbing and leaping in a nauseating, corkscrew motion that made it harder and harder to hook the lines and pull the traps up.

I was reaching out to grab one of the wire crates, all green and dripping with slime, when the deck gave a sudden lurch, and I felt myself toppling over the side. I grabbed hold of the rail, felt my feet fly out from under me, and landed on my ass, seawater and bait juice soaking my pants.

Kathleen looked down at me, puzzled; apparently, I didn't cut a very seaman-like figure. Just as she reached down with a ragged work glove and pulled me up, the boat obliged by bucking the other way, and I fell into her, stumbling like a drunken man and pushing her against the wheelhouse. I could feel the swell of her breasts through our layers of clothing and had just time enough to think what a ridiculous way this was to cop a feel before the boat threw me back against the bait barrel.

I shifted on my feet, trying to keep my balance, doing a little dance I knew I was going to be doing for the rest of the day. Kathleen stood on her two feet, moving with the boat and not against it, a true seafarer.

"Been awhile since you were out?" she asked.

This was a huge speech coming from her, so I hardly minded that it meant she was getting suspicious.

"Yeah, it has," I said. In the dozen or so words I'd

exchanged with her over the course of the day, I'd been careful not to say anything that wasn't perfectly true. If I hadn't corrected the lies Neil had told her, I'd made a point of not adding to them myself.

She went to grab the trap I'd left swinging on the snatch block, and I tried to think of something to say to keep this lengthy conversation going. "Why'd you call her the *Portland Queen?*"

She looked back at me with patient annoyance, as if I were some dumb foreigner who just didn't understand the ways of her country. "What was that?"

"Your boat. Why'd you name her the *Portland Queen?*"

She went back to work, methodically extracting two lobsters from the nylon mesh in the trap. "I didn't. That's what the guy I bought it from called it."

I tried to stroll over to her and bumped back against the rail. "Really? Most fishermen like to name their boats. You know, after their mother or their dog or something. It's kind of sentimental, you know."

She stood on the deck, lobster in one hand, the mean, scissor-like tool used to clip rubber bands on its claws in the other, and looked like she was trying to figure out what to do with me. To her credit, she made an effort at small talk. "What'd you call your boat?"

Well, I stepped right into that one, didn't I? It's not that I wasn't quick enough to come up with a fake name (the *Betty Lou* sprang to mind), but rather that I couldn't decide whether to take the plunge and start lying or tell her the whole stupid truth.

So, I hesitated for one guilty second. Then, the sea saved me by lifting the boat with a mad punch and slamming it back down. I fell one way and then the other, and then I kept falling. Right off the side of the boat until I hit water.

Hit it hard, like it was covered with a sheet of glass that I had to break through before I even got to the freezing, sinking, drowning part. I don't suppose there are too many good ways to die (maybe sleeping or doing something else in bed), but drowning must be one of the very worst. It hurts in so many ways; the sharp needles of the cold, the exploding panic in the lungs, the red fog that fills your brain as every cell of your body fights for the little bit of oxygen left to go around. There was no time for watching my life flash in front of me; I was too busy dying for that kind of shit.

I broke the surface for a moment, just time enough to suck in a frothy mouthful of sea water that filled my aching lungs. Squinting my burning eyes, I saw the white bow of the boat in front of me. I allowed myself a moment of hope before a swell threw me into the side of it, cracking my head against the fiberglass hull.

I never passed out, though I almost wanted to, so I was aware of a hand grabbing the neck of my sweater and pulling me up. I grasped the side of the boat, swung my leg up, and caught the rail. Kathleen grabbed my ass with her other hand, and together we hauled me onto the trap skids. I rolled over and dropped onto the deck, gulping air and spitting up water like a landed fish.

Opening my streaming eyes, I saw a little black patent leather shoe about six inches from my face.

I looked up, following the frilly white socks and the flowered dress to a bright pair of blue eyes and head of short-cropped blond hair. A little girl about your age, smiling with a missing tooth in front, giggling and reaching for Kathleen's hand. Kathleen stood next to her, looking at me and acting like the little girl wasn't even there.

Which, of course, she wasn't.

"Are you all right?" Kathleen's eyes were wide and full of concern. It made her look younger and softer, and I wondered what had happened to her to make it take a drowning man to bring this out in her.

The little girl crouched down and looked at me, her head cocked to one side. "I'm Jellica," she said. "Play with me?"

Then I passed out.

EIGHT

I wasn't sure if it was me or the blanket wrapped around me that was stinking up the cab as Kathleen drove me home in her Ford truck. Probably both; the bait barrel had tipped over in the swell, so everything on the boat had been given a pretty healthy stench.

Once it was clear that I wasn't going to be dead any time soon, the soft, feminine side of Kathleen vanished, and she was back to her taciturn self. I don't think I'd impressed her much as a sternman.

She pulled the truck up in front of the house, and I saw you running through the grass, yelling to your mother, who sat on the porch wearing three sweaters and reading a Douglas Adams book. You kept saying you'd found a snake.

"Snakes go to sleep in the winter," Charlotte told you. She glanced at me as I climbed, soaking and freezing, out of the truck with an angry woman she'd never met before. It was disturbing how unsurprised Charlotte looked. "How was your day?" she asked.

"I'd rather not talk about it," I said, trudging into the house.

Kathleen handed my sopping raincoat to Charlotte. "Your brother doesn't function too well on his own, does he?"

"Not really," Charlotte said.

She asked Kathleen in for coffee, and I was a little surprised when she agreed. So, we sat warming our hands on the stoneware mugs while Charlotte went to get me some dry clothes.

"You're not really a lobsterman, are you?" Kathleen asked me.

"Not technically, no." My Down Easter accent was long gone.

"Why did Neil tell me all that?"

"I needed the job," I said, and it was only partly a lie.

"Well, I lost a half day's work and a trap. Not really what I look for in a sternman." She pulled a Velcro wallet out of her coat, peeled off some bills and laid them on the table. "We'll call it even."

She set the mug down and started to walk out. I knew I had to say something to salvage the situation. Or make it much worse.

"Who's Jellica?" I asked.

She turned to me, sharply. "What?" As I said, I make it a rule never to talk about it with anyone when I see a spook; this is a good example of why. She was as angry as I've ever seen anyone.

I tried to backpedal. "Didn't you say that? When you pulled me out of the water? Something about Jericho, or Jello, or something?"

I don't know if she believed me (looking back, I guess she had no choice), but the anger cooled to resentment, she said a simple "No," and walked out. I went to look through the window over the sink. She was standing on the lawn talking to you. You *had* found a snake somehow, even in winter. A little green garden snake, which you were displaying to Kathleen proudly. Kathleen didn't flinch; I knew she wouldn't. She petted it and said it was a pretty snake and that you should let it go back home.

Charlotte came in with fresh clothes as I watched Kathleen's truck drive up the hill.

"I think she likes me," I said.

Winter came to the island the night after my debacle on Kathleen's boat. The temperature dropped like a brick, without wind or rain, without even clouds in the sky, so the next morning looked bright and clear and shining. Apparently, the whole town had been waiting for the freeze. Neil called at six in the morning (sleeping-in time for a fisherman), and the eagerness in his voice made him sound like a kid on his birthday.

"You coming down to the Mill Race?"

I'd stubbed my toe half a dozen times on the way to the phone so my eagerness, to say the least, did not match his. "Why?"

"It's frozen over."

The Mill Race was a large pond behind Main Street. It was frozen over. I'd seen ice before. "So?" I asked.

"Ice boats, Sammy. We're ice sailing."

By noon the whole town was on the sloping hill above the Mill Race, bundled in heavy coats and blankets, smiling and laughing as if it were the first day of spring.

The Race was scattered with a jaunty armada of ice boats, elegantly handmade from spare parts, daubed with bright colors, adorned with rigging and sails cannibalized from summer boats. On blades made from sharpened bedframes, they etched the ice at breakneck speed, skittering across the frozen pond.

Children ran along the frosted shore trying to keep up with racing waterbug boats, while old men placed bets on who was the fastest and teenagers on ice skates sped around the racing craft with daredevil cunning and their parents screamed for them to get the hell out of the way.

Ice boating was an old tradition on the island, recently revived by Neil and his cronies. They'd seen some photos from the turn of the last century in the museum Mrs. Day ran in the barn behind her house, and during the idle months of a freezing winter four years ago they had decided to see if they could build such contraptions on their own. The Fox Island Ice Boat Armada had been born and had since become a winter institution.

Neil's boat was the most beautiful. Made of blond wood, its four blades painted with red enamel, it was a sleek bullet of a boat. He rode it stretched out on his belly on the narrow cab, rudder under his arm, the crossbars spreading away from him like wings or the arms of Jesus on the cross. His sister, Dora, had embroidered a golden sun on the sail that billowed above him, so that the boat looked like the bastard child of a drag racer and a Viking galley. He saw us and skidded it to a stop, then leapt to his feet and skated across the ice to where you and your mother were waving and laughing.

I'd never seen Neil look more handsome or more full of life. His husky body seemed as graceful as a gymnast's as the ice sprayed from his skates. A movie star smile spread across his face. He scooped you up in his arms, and you laughed gleefully as he slipped you under his arm like a football and skated back to his boat, you screaming and giggling the whole way.

I scanned the crowd every few seconds, expecting to see Kathleen in the mob, planning things to say to her that would make up for the disaster of the previous day. No sign of her. A weathered fisherman's wife next to the bonfire was chuckling and pointing at Maggie.

"Wicked cute, isn't she? Gonna break a lot of hearts, that one."

"That's an odd compliment, isn't it?" This from a man stretched on his belly on the frigid grass—a strange-looking fellow with long, yellow-white hair and prominent cheek-bones, whose broad smile somehow gave a handsome, swashbuckling cast to his skull-like face. He spoke with a faint Eastern European lilt. "'When you grow up, you're going to hurt men.' Is that the best you can wish for her?"

I laughed at this, but the fisherman's wife edged away. I remembered the man. Joe something. A Hungarian or Czech or something. An artist. There were quite a few of them on the island, or used to be. Back in the days when real estate prices were low, this place had been a haven for starving artists and poor college professors. Now that the prices had gone up, more and more doctors from Connecticut were moving in. There went the neighborhood.

I had encountered this man once before, while I was kayaking in one of the coves over on Brown's Head Island. He'd been stretched out in the bottom of a canoe, smoking a joint and looking like Klaus Kinski gone to seed, if such a thing were possible.

At first I'd been a little irritated to see him—to see any-one at all in the lonely place. Brown's Head Island was almost unpopulated except for a few dozen inbred Mainers on the west side who kept aggressively to themselves. Solitude was what I'd been searching for after one of those inconclusive fights with my mother about why I didn't want to go to graduate school. She refused to see how a person could be worthwhile without a series of initials af-ter his name. I maintained that all that was superficial in-tellectual tripe and that there were a million other things I wanted to do with my life than sit in a classroom for another four or six or eight years. Not that I could come up with any examples, but fortunately I stormed out before it came to that.

So, all I wanted to do was be alone and float in my boat and watch for seals and ospreys. I'd even heard bald eagles had started to roost here. Wouldn't it be a thrill to see one of those? I sure wasn't in the mood to share my cove with this obviously decadent left-wing pinko-type. (Not that I was conservative, but when you're rebelling against liberal parents you're forced to take some strange positions.)

I heard the oddly small peeping cry of an osprey and searched the sky. There, hovering over the water. I could watch them for hours, gliding through the air. Waiting, waiting. Then, down it plummeted, striking the water with a silver splash not far from me, seizing a wriggling fish in its talons and zooming off. Glorious.

"Hey, you got a match?" The idyllic mood was shattered. I glanced over to Joe's canoe and saw him sitting up and patting his shirt. "Fucking, whaddayacallit, ember fell off my joint. You got a match?"

I tried shaking my head, but we were a little too far apart for him to see, so I yelled, breaking the mood even further. "I don't smoke."

"Well, shit." He shifted around in his canoe, looking at the water. "I dropped my lighter. You don't see it, do you?"

I decided to paddle over so we wouldn't have to keep yelling. It didn't seem right for this crystal paradise to be echoing news of drug paraphernalia. "Do lighters float?" I asked when I got closer to him.

He shrugged, rocking his boat back and forth. "Fuck it," he said, slipping the remnants of his joint into an empty plastic film canister and putting it in his shirt pocket. "You're Gordon Kehoe's son, right? From the Thorofare house?"

Father and house. That was how one was identified on the island. "Yep," I said.

"I'm Joe Kelan." He extended a hand. I reached over the water and shook hands, each of our boats tipping unstably.

He didn't say anything else, so we sat in uneasy silence for a moment until I opened my mouth to tell him I was heading off. He lifted a finger to his lips and pointed at the skyline.

There on the top of a tall pine sat a mature male bald eagle. What a sight. It took my breath away. Like the first time I saw the Northern Lights. There are things that you see represented so often, in pictures and posters, on coins and stamps, that when you see them in real life you have to keep reminding yourself that what you're seeing is real. That this glorious beast, huge and regal, a bear with feathers, was actually up there, occupying the same air I was breathing.

We watched in silence, Joe and I, for I don't know how many minutes. Didn't even bother to look away when an osprey splashed down and caught another fish in the middle of the cove. The eagle mesmerized us.

All at once, like a dragon from a children's book, the eagle spread its huge wings. I couldn't breathe, couldn't blink. Effortlessly, it lifted off, riding the wet air. Its grandeur brought tears to my eyes.

It headed straight for the osprey. I frowned slightly, not understanding. The eagle dive-bombed the smaller bird, who screamed out in protest, twirling away, doing evasive maneuvers. The eagle circled back, diving again, not striking the osprey, just strafing it, scaring it. Again the osprey evaded. Again the eagle attacked. Finally, as the osprey screamed in protest, the glistening fish dropped from its talons and smacked the surface of the water. In an instant, the bald eagle was down, snatching it up, flying off, grand as ever.

I was appalled. The bald eagle had mugged the osprey. Stolen his fish. I felt ashamed for my whole country.

"That's terrible," I said, involuntarily.

"Why?" Joe said. "The fish is just as dead either way."

"I wasn't thinking about the fish. What about the poor osprey? He did all the work."

"Let that be a lesson to him," Joe said, lying back in his canoe and pulling his cap over his eyes for a nap.

Now, here he was again, a few years older and even more dissolute. I smiled and Joe nodded back, but I don't think he recognized me. Charlotte was with me now, laughing and directing my attention to Neil's ice boat. You stood up, arms spread in your best *Titanic* pose, while Neil lined the boat up with others for the race.

"I think you've got a rival for Maggie's affection," Charlotte said, watching Neil.

"I don't think she's the one he's after."

I meant it as a joke, but somehow it took the smile right off your mother's face. "You think he's trying to get to me?"

"Don't be a cynic, Charlie. He likes Maggie. He also likes you."

She withdrew into herself. "Yeah. He likes everybody, I guess."

I never could recall the moment your mother stopped believing people could like her without wanting something from her. It was the curse of being beautiful too young, I suppose. Of hearing compliments too often, assuming they were honest, then learning they were tactics.

I directed Charlotte's attention back to the race. The ice boats were ready to go. There was no consistency to their design—some had three and some had four blades; some were made of wood, some of fiberglass or metal; some wide, most teardrop thin; some elegant, some awkward, all beautiful. They lined up in soapbox derby formation, and old Byron from the fire department fired a flare gun to set them off. Maggie's piercing yelps almost drowned out the roar of the crowd as the sails billowed and Neil's boat flew into the lead.

Halfway across the pond, the wind died and the boats drifted to a standstill. The men got out and pushed.

Teenagers pelted them with snowballs. The whole thing degenerated into a free-for-all that was more fun than the race ever would have been.

After it was over, all of us soaked through with sweat and slush so that we were shivering like mountain climbers after a hard ascent, Neil invited us to a friend's house for "beer," a word that encompassed all socializing on the island.

It was something like a college kegger—wall-to-wall people smelling of steamed wool and Budweiser. Somebody dug up some sparklers from last Fourth of July, and you ran across the dark lawn with half a dozen other urchins, trailing sparks like comets.

I kept darting to my tiptoes to see over heads. To spot Kathleen if she should walk in. It seemed like everyone on the island was there but her. Was she holed up in her room, watching *Ally McBeal*? A sad life. Couldn't I make it better?

"Oh, God! Did I burn you with my cigarette?" a woman asked. There were sparks on my pants leg. A very young, very thin woman was standing next to me, waving a cigarette and apologizing profusely. "God, I'm sooo sorry, I don't even know how to smoke these things, I should never have started." She dropped the half-finished smoke into a Pete's Wicked Ale bottle on the arm of the sofa.

"It's okay," I said. Smiling. Friendly.

Joe Kelan was next to her now, arm around her waist in that proprietary gesture all males recognize; this is mine, keep away. "She almost burned you, why is that okay?"

I looked around for help just in time to see somebody pick up the ale bottle, bring it to his lips and blend into the crowd.

"Because she didn't," I said.

Joe laughed like this was the funniest thing he'd ever heard and pulled me out onto the porch, where it was too cold but at least you had room to breathe. "You're Gordon Kehoe's son, right? The Thorofare house?"

I nodded.

"I was sorry to hear about that. I liked him."

I nodded. So did I.

It turned out this was Joe's house, but he didn't tell me who his father was. The girl who didn't know how to smoke was named Shara, and she was from Denver and was staying with Joe for a while. With all important information conveyed, we stood in silence, watching you children run and play. Neil and Charlotte were sitting on the step below us, not arm in arm, but close to each other, very close.

We didn't talk. Just sipped beer. That's how friendships are formed on the island. The rest of the country could take a lesson.

The girl in front of you stumbled and fell and you tripped over her and the boy behind you tripped over you and it turned into a sparkler-lit, ten-kid pileup. Charlotte and a couple of other parents ran to help, but it didn't look like anyone was seriously hurt, so I hung back. Joe had his hand all the way around Shara's waist now and was diddling her tattooed belly button with his middle finger, so I moved down to sit on the stoop with Neil and give them some semi-privacy. "How's it going?" I asked Neil.

"How's what going?" Neil asked, defensively. "Nothing's going. What do you mean?"

I smiled. "Nothing, nothing at all."

It was a perfect night. Or would have been if Kathleen had walked up.

"You haven't seen Kathleen, have you?" I asked, nervous.

"She here?"

"Is she?"

"I'm asking you."

"Well, I haven't seen her," I said.

"Neither have I."

"I mean," I said, "you haven't seen her since I went out on the boat with her?"

"Just to say hello."

"She didn't...she didn't say anything about me, did she?"

"Can't say she did, 'cause she didn't."

"I kinda fucked that up."

"I kinda gathered," Neil said.

"I don't mean just falling off the boat."

"That wasn't enough?"

"It think I scared her, Neil. I think she thinks I'm crazy."

"Well, she's not a stupid woman."

I laughed. But only a little. "You don't think I'm crazy, do you?"

"Do you think you're crazy?"

"Sometimes I wonder."

"You could go see Dr. Hopley. He'll give you some of that Prozac shit." There was only one doctor on the island, and he was a firm believer in Prozac. Half the island was on Prozac. It was a very relaxed place.

"No, not like that," I said. I'd never talked to Neil about the spooks. Partly because I thought he was too down-to-earth to understand it. "Did you ever see visions, Neil?"

He gave me a sideways glance. "You mean like saints? Joan of Arc, all that shit?"

"Sort of."

"Can't say I have, 'cause I haven't."

I was immediately sorry I'd brought it up. I didn't want Neil to think I wasn't every bit as down-to-earth as he was. I figured if I dropped the subject now it would all be okay. Neil wouldn't pry. Prying was anti-Maine.

"Do you have visions?" Shara asked. I'd forgotten about Joe and Shara, thinking they were still busy feeling each other up. Instead they were sitting next to me, all ears. "What do you see?" Shara went on.

I blushed with embarrassment. "I don't see anything."

"Don't tell me they're angels. The angel thing is getting so old," Joe said.

I don't know whether Neil sensed my discomfort or just wanted to be with Charlotte again, but he got up and walked out to the yard to help the now upright kids light new sparklers. That left me alone to try to end this conversation as quickly as possible. Shara was looking at me expectantly; I knew the type. She believed without proof, without even hearing the whole story. It was an attitude that made me feel far more uncomfortable than when people said I was a nutcase. "I just see people, okay? Ordinary people."

"Who aren't there?" Joe asked. I wasn't sure if he was making fun or not. Couldn't blame him if he was.

"Who aren't there," I confirmed.

He gave a soft whistle of envy. "I wish I could do that."

"You can have it."

Shara was really in my face now, eyes wide with annoying wonder. "You see spirits, you mean?"

I nodded. *Spirits* was classier than *spooks*.

"It must be a great responsibility," she said.

I didn't know what the hell she meant. "They're just hallucinations, okay?"

Joe shook his head emphatically. "You're not crazy." He'd had two and a half conversations with me and obviously considered himself an expert.

"I think there are other explanations," I said.

"Like what?" Joe asked.

Well, if I knew that....

Fortunately, Joe was on a roll and didn't wait for an answer. He looked up at the sky. "A lot of stars we're looking at aren't really where we see them, because of the

curvature of space, you know? Maybe you see people who
aren't there on account of the curvature of time, what do
you think?" I guess he'd found his lighter since I saw him
in the canoe; his words were smoky with dope.

I don't know why I didn't just shut up. But despite all
my discomfort, it did feel good to talk to someone about
all this. I'd held it in for so long. "I don't just see them,"
I said. "They talk to me."

"They *talk* to you!?" Joe looked almost heartbroken.
"Why does this happen to other people and not me?"

"What do they say?" Shara asked.

"Just...different things. I don't know."

"Don't you listen?" Shara went on, breathless.

"Not if I can avoid it."

Joe suddenly hollered out to the crowd, "Hey, is Emily
Day here!?" Noncommittal grunts came in reply.

"She called," Shara said, "I forgot to tell you. Said she
couldn't make it."

Joe sat down, looking hurt. "Why is it the person you
respect most never comes to your parties? Do you know
Mrs. Day?"

I knew her slightly; one of the familiar faces on the
island. I would see her, I would smile, I would wave, she
would do the same, maybe a little more enthusiastically
than most. Word was, she ran the little town museum and
raised three kids on her own. Arlo Ransom's daughter,
she lived in the Green House. A good woman. I tried to
remember why I had such a positive impression of her
but couldn't recall any details. Just a general sense that
she was one of the people who held the town together.
Your average neat middle-aged woman with the weight of
the world on her shoulders. Certainly not the type who
would seem likely to impress a Bohemian nightcrawler
like Joe Kelan.

"She's a Wise Woman," Shara said. I could hear the

capitals. Dear Lord, had sweet old Mrs. Day suddenly gone all Goddess and Gnostic and Wicca?

"She straightened me out," Joe said, gravely. What could he have been like before?

"A very sensitive woman. Very in tune," Shara said. "She has the Gift too."

"It's not a gift!" I couldn't help myself; their complacent attitude was really pissing me off.

Joe gave me a stern look. The skull-like qualities of his face shone through. "Maybe not for you. But it's a gift for them."

"For who?" I asked.

"For the ones who are trying to talk through you. While you're too chicken-shit scared to even listen."

I bolted to my feet, hands clenched. His counter-culture abrasiveness was charming to a point, but he'd stepped over the line. "This is not some fucking parlor game," I said, stalking off.

"That's what I'm telling you," Joe called after me.

From then on, the evening was spoiled. I found you, tried to join in with the fun, but the night had turned so dark even the sparklers couldn't light it up.

NINE

Your mother and I were both restless that night, but you were completely wasted. Fell asleep on the way home and stayed limp in my arms when I laid you in your bed.

"She never sleeps through the night when she conks out like this," Charlotte said, tucking you in. You like to know you're falling asleep; to go through your ritual of stories and songs. If sleep hits you by accident, you wake up in the middle of the night, disoriented, cheated, howling for help. Getting you back to sleep after that is a tough proposition.

Charlotte dug a baby monitor out of her luggage and set it up on your night table. A plastic pink Fisher-Price model that worked like a walkie-talkie. She turned it on and we took the receiver downstairs. Reception was weak, so I had to rummage through the closet for batteries. While we were looking, we found another rogue field mouse, and that kept us busy for an hour or so, until I trapped it in the lint tray from the dryer and released it into the meadow. No doubt it found a crack and ran right back into the house.

Charlotte made popcorn. The cable was working and, miracle of miracles, Cinemax was showing *Black Sabbath* (Galatea Films, 1963, Italian title *I Tre Volte della Paura*, five stars on the Kehoe Scale). We settled down and watched together, the gorgeous glistening Italian colors and the eerie disconnectedness of the badly dubbed dialog transporting us to our childhood, to the times we used to sneak downstairs on Saturday nights and watch the local horror movie host "Count Gore DeVol" (there was a literary reference guaranteed to go over the head of his target audience of twelve year olds) as he made bad jokes and broadcast Mexican wrestling films and Hammer Horrors and whatever else Channel 20 could afford.

Nothing soothes the unquiet mind like a familiar movie at one o'clock in the morning. So comforting, to know the rhythm of the edits in your blood, to hum along with the score, to see the obvious shocks coming, like old friends dropping by for a visit. Your steady, musical breathing coming over the baby monitor completed the meditative mood.

Unlike you, I never slept better than when sleep crept up on me unawares; I love being able to drift off without having to reflect on the missed opportunities of the day. To head the monsters off at the pass. My head dropped onto my chest, and I jerked awake. On the screen, a hideous mannequin, apparently mounted on roller skates, was supposed to be a reanimated corpse trying to retrieve her stolen ring from Jacqueline Soussard. I glanced out the window at the night sky. Moonlit clouds. The flashing green light of the channel marker a thumping pulse on the water. The dark mass of Brown's Head Island a giant seal's head breaking the surface. The green roof of the house on the shore glowed momentarily, like a phosphorescent fungus.

Charlotte put her book down and reached for more popcorn. "I can't believe this used to scare us. It's so fakey."

"Of course it's fakey," I said. "That's the point. That's what makes it poetry."

Charlotte shrugged. She'd outgrown the charm of these movies. "What do you think of Neil?" she asked.

"What do you mean?" We'd only known the guy all our lives.

"We were sitting on the stoop talking. You know, while you were on the porch hitting on that skinny girl with the tattoo."

"I wasn't hitting—"

"We talked for a long time, and he kept helping the kids with the sparklers. He's really good with kids, and we had a nice talk and...." Her voice dropped off, gloomy tone contrasting strangely with her words.

"So, what's wrong with that?"

"I think he's trying to impress me." She sounded so tired.

"Well, maybe he is."

"But why? What's he up to?"

"Look, I said it before. I think he likes you."

She pushed the popcorn bowl aside. "I think we should go back home."

"Why?"

"It's just...this makes me uncomfortable."

"Did he do anything?"

"No. I wouldn't even be suspicious if I didn't know him so well. But it's like he's trying to be...charming."

"And is he succeeding?"

"A little. A little charming."

"And that's bad?"

"Well, you don't bother to be charming unless, you know, you expect to get something."

"Look, if you're not interested, just tell him."

She shook her head. "No, no. See, that already messes things up. I haven't even done anything and already I'm having to shoot down a friend. See? It just spoils everything. Things won't be the same."

"I don't think he'll be mad."

"He'll be hurt. That's worse. And I'll feel guilty and we'll walk by each other on Main Street and we won't know what to say and it's all spoiled."

"But he was charming?"

"Yeah, yeah."

"And you had a good time."

"For now."

"And Maggie likes him."

"Yeah. God. That makes it even worse."

"So, there's another alternative."

A slant-eyed look my way. "I'm not ready."

"For anybody, or for him?"

Shaking her head again. "Neil. Neil is not my type."

"Because he's charming? Because he likes kids? Because you have a nice time with him? What are his other bad points?"

"You just, you don't think of Neil that way."

"Maybe you could."

"Like it's that easy." She curled up around the popcorn bowl; end of discussion.

Now, on the screen, Michèle Mercier was getting phone calls from the dead while wearing a puffy pink negligee. All my life, I've never once seen a woman actually wear a negligee like that. Was I born in the wrong decade or just the wrong country?

We heard the squeaking of bedsprings through the baby monitor. You sounded restless. Kicking at your covers. Making short, unhappy gasps. Then a bleat of crying. Strained and confused, but not strong yet; no howling. I muted the TV and started to get up.

"Give her a minute," your mom said, "she might drift off again."

We waited, trying to will you back to sleep.

Then, we heard the singing.

A woman's voice, soft and lilting, drifting from the baby monitor. Charlotte and I looked at each other, eyes wide, sharing shivers.

I couldn't make out words. Just a lullaby of wistful nonsense syllables coming out of the tinny speaker.

"Shool shool shoolah roon, shool go sakeera na shool ka kewn."

We ran for the stairs. The rest of the house was dark, and we didn't stop to flip on the lights, so we stumbled on chairs in the dining room, clattering them to the floor, knocking against the kitchen table, skidding on linoleum. I flung open the door to the stairs and took the steep steps two at a time, cracking my head on the low doorframe.

What did we expect to find? An escaped maniac with a butcher's knife at your throat? A burglar trying to quiet you so she could get on with her crime? A kidnapper? A molester bending over your bed? Any one of the menagerie of monsters that live in a parent's mind.

The blackness of the upstairs hall was heavy, pushing me back. I forced through it, reached a hand into your room, flipped on the light before stumbling in. Charlotte was right beside me.

You were asleep. The room was empty.

We were both panting like we'd run a marathon.

"She's not even awake," Charlotte said.

I crossed to the baby monitor. The red indicator light wasn't on. I shook it. It wasn't working. "The battery must have died."

"Then, what the fuck?"

"The receiver must have been picking up somebody else's monitor. From one of the houses on the shore."

Charlotte laughed. I laughed. It was really wonderfully funny.

"Gawd. That was so freaky. I don't know *what* I expected to see up here."

We laughed some more and then shushed each other when we saw you roll over. Charlotte went down to get some new batteries. I found Mr. Tee on the floor and put him back in your arms, tucking you in again. You snuggled him and your big eyes rolled open. A happy, secure smile. "Hi, Unca."

I touched your forehead and whispered. "Back to sleep, honey."

You shut your eyes, not really awake at all. "I like that babysitter," you murmured. "Can I have her again?"

TEN

"Of course the house is haunted. Every house on the island is haunted."

Neil pried another boulder loose, and we rolled it out of the Old Well. The New Well ("new" in that it had been dug in 1937) had fed the faucets of the Thorofare house for decades, but its water had a bluish tint and tasted unwholesome. Good enough for washing, but water for drinking had to be carted from the springs along the Quarry Road. Reclaiming the Old Well on the meadow was one of a thousand projects Dad had never gotten around to. I figured this was as good a time as any to at least see if it was possible. And also a good excuse to get Neil and Charlotte together again.

"But we've lived here for years," I said. "Wouldn't we have heard something or seen something before?" Especially me, I thought but didn't say. Me with the Gift.

Neil shrugged. "Who's to say you didn't?"

No, I explained. I never saw anything spooky here at all; never even had a nightmare. Not even during my periods of frequent childhood night terrors.

"Why should it be a nightmare?" Neil asked. "Maggie wasn't scared by it, why should you be?"

He shined a flashlight down through the boulders that filled the well. We'd made enough of a gap that we could see something shining down there, reflecting back the light.

"Yep, there's water. You get a backhoe and clear out these boulders you might have something here."

We discussed how to test the water for drinkability, and I pretended to understand. It took us about ten minutes of struggling with the plywood and tarpaper lid to get it back over the well.

Walking through the brambles, cold scratches glowing white on my numb fingers, I looked at the house sitting alone on the meadow. I'd never noticed how isolated it was. How it stood out by itself. Like the sapling trees the woods had cast out into the meadow, trying to reclaim it.

"Do people tell stories about the house?"

"Ghost stories?"

I nodded.

"It's an old, empty house. 'Course they do."

"Like what?"

"Spooky lights in the windows. Ladies in white. Phantom pirates. The usual shit."

I stopped and gave him a serious look, which we both found quite uncomfortable. "Do you believe in that sort of thing?"

"Folks are always telling stories."

"No, not just the stories. The whole thing. Do you believe in...." Well, fuck, what was the word for it? Spooks? Ghosts? Spirits? Life after death? It all sounded too foolish.

But Neil knew what I meant. "Sammy," he said, "the way I figure it, at this point, my life is about making a living, falling in and out of love occasionally, and getting sick twice a year. If I didn't think there was another world, I'd probably blow my brains out."

Which maybe wasn't an answer, but was at least a point of view. More than I had.

It was time for lunch, so I cooked up some fried egg and onion sandwiches. Charlotte was making herself scarce;

I supposed that she'd seen through my brilliant plan to keep her close to Neil. She came in, just as we were finishing up.

"Where's Maggie?"

The last she'd seen of you, you were flying your kite by the side of the house. We went out and looked. Kite number three was whipping at the top of a tall pine, but you were nowhere around. You were gone.

Now, grown-ups have to play moments like this carefully; everyone searching, but smiling, joking, trying not to let the panic in. The panic that's always dancing on the sidelines when a child is in your life. Because the worst thing can always happen, and it only takes a second, and you always know that.

Neil searched the shore. Charlotte called through the woods. I checked the well, of course. Imagining you slipping in when our backs were turned, getting wedged down in the cold, staring up as we dropped the lid in place. When you raise a kid you get real good at elaborate horror stories like that. Children turn everybody into Edgar Allan Poe.

You weren't down there. You weren't in the woods. You weren't around.

We reconnoitered at the house. We danced around the fear, not sure if we were trying to protect the others or ourselves. Neil showed the most concern, but then he had the least practice.

"You want to get in the truck? She mighta gone down the road."

You might have, you might not have. For an adult, the road was the obvious choice. For a four year old, it was just one of many.

Charlotte hurried to Neil, grabbing her down coat with one hand, taking his arm with the other. Going to him. Instinctive. Grateful.

"I'll follow you in the Mustang," she said. "That way we can split up and cover more ground."

I stayed, because odds were you'd pop your head out of the woods as soon as they were gone.

I hate waiting more than anything. Time hanging heavy. Knowing that a second is coming that will change everything or put it right back the way it was. I couldn't sit, couldn't perch anywhere. Couldn't stand still, couldn't keep walking. Just milled around the meadow, aimless, eyes scanning the horizon like a sandpiper.

But I really couldn't believe that anything bad had happened. Not here. Not on Home Base. I thought again about my lack of night terrors here. I'd had doozies as a child. Big, bearded, masculine monsters, half-man, half-Muppet, shaggy and wooly, snorting in my closet all night. But only back in Virginia, never here. Nightmares were banished by the ferry ride or by the warm embrace of these walls. Was there something odd in that? I wondered for the first time. Was it normal that a worried child should feel that secure?

The phone rang. I bounded up the hill, over the rail of the porch, skidded open the sliding screen door, dodged a kitchen chair, grabbed the phone.

"Hello?" All out of breath. The Good Mother on overdrive.

"Is this Sam Kehoe?"

"Yep."

"This is Kathleen Milland." This was another call I'd been waiting for, but it hardly seemed to matter now.

"Hi."

"Your niece is here."

You feel the fear after everything's okay; when you can afford to. "Thank God."

I didn't even have to ask Kathleen to put you on; she handed you the phone right away. I liked her for that.

"Hi, Unca," you said, bright as ever, "I went for walks."

❈

Kathleen's truck was in the shop (a bigger deal than it sounds when "the shop" is across eighteen miles of choppy salt water), so she couldn't bring you back. I would have to wait for your mother or Neil to get back and send them for you. It was either that or walk.

I put a big note on the fridge and walked.

It took me about forty minutes, trudging the twisting, unnamed roads, taking wrong turns and doubling back, to find her house. If you'd walked along the shore, climbing over boulders and racing across the stony beaches, it probably took you half that.

My body wasn't used to spending that much time in the cold. Tears thickened, glistening on my eyes. Cheeks and fingertips sang with vibrating pain. I walked fast, to warm myself, to get there quicker, so I sweated, and the sweat chilled on my skin. I felt like a bucket of ice cream when it gets that scummy layer of cream frost on the top.

Only two roads on the island have names, and they aren't marked. Kathleen lived on the fourth road that branches off the road that branches off Old Quarry Road. People who live on it call it Eyre's Cove road, but I didn't know that until I asked a guy who was working on his car in the front yard of a mobile home. He pointed down the dirt track, sloping to the cove.

"White house with blue trim," he said, then went back to work.

White-house-with-blue-trim was down the hill, sitting on stilts at the edge of the water like a crane. Somebody's old boathouse, I supposed, tiny and tidy. Freshly painted, with a garden lying fallow in the winter. It reminded me of Kathleen's boat—too clean. Like she had too much time on her hands. And small. Aggressively small. Not intended as a living space for more than one—probably not intended as a living space at all.

I hurried down and hammered on the door. The closer

I came to the warm inside, the fiercer the cold outside felt. Kathleen opened the door. I hadn't been mistaken. She really was beautiful. Hair swept back, trailing little fiery wisps along her slender neck.

"I thought maybe you got lost," she said.

"Only once or twice."

"Hi, Unca!" You didn't run to me; you just danced from leg to leg while you played with an old Rock'em Sock'em Robot set. "Lookit. Lookit!" You bopped one of the robot's heads off and screamed with ecstasy.

"Haven't seen one of those in years," I said to Kathleen, pointing at the plastic game.

"Yeah, well, I don't really have any toys. Had to borrow that from the Angstroms up the road."

She cleared a space on the kitchen table. Or the dining room table. There was only one room, and I didn't know what she called it. Kitchenette to one side; pull-out sofa bed against the window; no TV; a boombox playing some cool *Peanuts* jazz. It was a studio apartment that somebody had slipped out of its building and stuck on the Maine shore.

"How'd you find her?"

She raised a laconic eyebrow. "I looked out the window and saw her walking up from the shore." It really was a nice eyebrow.

"Thank God," I said. But it was amazing that you would turn up here, of all the places on the island. Like something out of one of those *Incredible Journey* movies. "What are the odds of her coming here?" I said.

"That's what I wondered." Her smile was odd. Did she think I'd sent you here, to give me an excuse to pay a visit? If so, she didn't seem angry.

I moved to you, as you bopped your head to the music and pushed the buttons to keep the boxers punching. "You shouldn't have wandered off like that."

"I sorry. I was playin' hide-and-seek, but I couldn't find her, and I found this lady instead."

"Who were you playing with?"

"Ida know. Some girl."

I looked over at Kathleen. It didn't sound too convincing. "What was the girl's name?"

"I don't bemember." The gray robot lost again. You shoved his head back in place.

I shrugged, feeling like the featured display in an Irresponsible Parent exhibit. "It's hard to keep an eye on her. She likes to run wild."

"Kids should be able to do that," Kathleen said.

"You like kids?" I asked, then immediately wanted it back. Why didn't I just ask if she was seeing someone; if she believed in marriage; how many children she wanted?

But she didn't seem to mind. "I love 'em," she said, simply.

"I don't know if I do," I said. "But I love her."

"She's a good kid." It sounded like she meant it. Her lips were full and grapefruit pink. It was going to be hard not to say something stupid.

You came to my rescue. "I wanna go home."

"We'll have to walk. It's cold out."

"I know the way!" you said, proudly. "The girl, she showed me."

I hesitated, not wanting to brave the cold and certainly not wanting to leave Kathleen. Kathleen stood up and grabbed a down vest. "I'll come with you. I could use the walk."

This couldn't have worked out better for me if you'd planned it. Did you plan it?

We walked along the shore. The tide was low and the rocks were slippery with cold sea. The sun was bright and the sky was blisteringly clear. A wispy fog prowled low on the water. If heaven doesn't look like that I'm going to want my money back.

You dashed ahead, sure-footed as a mountain goat, examining shells and broken sea urchins. Kathleen and I strolled behind, placing our feet carefully on the unpredictable stones. Every few yards the patterns beneath us changed; rolling smooth boulders to sharp, jagged flagstones to flat gray expanses with currents of white quartz running through them like ripple fudge ice cream.

"You can never learn this coastline, no matter how many times you come here," I said.

"You've been here a lot?" Small talk. I knew I was making progress.

"Every year since I was a kid. How did you find the place?"

"Oh. I just ended up here," she said.

I wasn't sure whether to push it. I pushed it. "It's funny for somebody from away to decide to come here and start fishing. Is that something you always wanted to do?"

She shrugged. "Like I said, it just happened."

Okay, so she didn't like to talk about herself. That just made her more unusual.

"Well, it's a perfect place to be a kid." I gestured to you, standing on a great boulder, looking out to sea, wind whipping your hair, looking like a selkie about to dive in and swim for home.

"When I first saw her, I thought you were her father," Kathleen said.

I nodded. "Yeah. A lot of people think that."

"And you are, kind of, aren't you?"

Well, if she wanted to talk about me, that was fine. "Kind of. She's my sister's kid and the father...he isn't really in the picture. So, I kind of stepped in. I was there when she was born. When she took her first steps. I'm always there. I just don't live with her."

"So you're *better* than a real father."

I laughed, even though I wasn't sure what she meant. "Do you want to have kids?" My God, did I really ask her that?

She stood squinting into the wind, looking at you from very far away. "I can't imagine being that brave."

I laughed again. "Yeah, well, you do spend a lot of time worrying. And the rest of the time actively terrified. But things have a way of working out."

She looked at me, surprised. "You don't really believe that, do you?"

"Well, they don't work out *always*, but most of the time. Or a lot of the time. Some of the time."

She kept looking at me, like she was testing me. "You have to tell them there are no monsters, just so they'll sleep at night. But how can you lie like that?"

We connected in that moment, one sadness to another. "Sure, I know," I said. "Terrible things happen. But you can't live that way. You have to go ahead and take the risk."

She shook her head and walked on. "No, people just say that 'cause they have to. Trying to make the best of a bad deal. If I'm going to take risks, I'll take them on my own."

If I wasn't in love with her before, it happened right then. I knew why her boat was so clean and her house was so small. Something had hurt her and made her retreat to a world small enough for her to control. I wanted to take her in my arms and make it all better, even though I was too old to think such things.

The way got too steep, so we had to go inland a little. You played hide-and-seek in the pine trees until we found an old dirt road with a sheriff's car parked on it. Kathleen rapped on the window and the barely post-teen cop sleeping in the driver's seat sat up with a jolt. He grabbed the wheel and tried to look official for a Barney Fife moment; then he saw it was Kathleen and blushed.

"Catch any perps, Donny?" she asked.

"Jesus, Kathy, you're going to give me a heart attack."

"This a stakeout?"

"No, I just, I thought I'd take a tour of the outskirts and I started getting sleepy."

"This town is nothing but outskirts, Donny."

This joshing, good-natured side of Kathleen was something I hadn't seen before.

Donny got out of the car to stretch his long legs. Deputy Sheriff Donald Beirko, face red with acne scars, shoulders sloping from his neck like the sides of a teepee. I'd never envied a cop's lot on the island. There were no police permanently posted to the town. Just some loser of a deputy sent out from Rockland three days a week. The town resented him; no one here believed in state-enforced justice. If a crime happened on Fox Island it was a personal matter. Somebody stole something of yours, you just went and stole it back. Why get all official about it?

"I hate this place," he said, "it's boring."

"You could try doing your job," she said. "That might keep you occupied."

"They won't let me. If I pull somebody over for speeding, they act like I'm infringing on their civil rights. They send letters to the Rockland office telling them what an asshole I am. They already think I'm an asshole in Rockland, that's why they send me here. It just keeps getting worse. I don't know what to do."

"You could try solving some crimes," I said, trying to be funny.

"They don't have crime here," he said, plaintively.

"There's plenty of crime," Kathleen said. "Domestic violence, drug abuse—"

"Oh, I don't like to get mixed up in that kind of stuff," he said.

Kathleen bundled him back into his car and sent him

back into town, watching him drive off with a fond smile.

"How do you know him?" I asked.

"I don't really, I just feel sorry for him," she said, taking you by the hand and heading back toward the shore. "He starts out wanting to do good and winds up doing nothing. That's the way of the world, isn't it?"

We were almost home when the Mustang and Neil's pick-up came down the hill behind us. Charlotte was out of the car almost before she'd stopped it, rushing to pick you up. Scolding and kissing you, all with the same breath. I don't think you realized you'd done anything wrong till then, but when your mother started crying, you started crying, too. The both of you howled as she carried you to the house.

Kathleen and I stood by the Mustang, motor still running. Neil waved as he passed us on the way to the house. I paused by the open driver's door, not sure what to do next.

"I could take you home," I said. "Or you could come in to warm up. Have some coffee?"

"I'll have some coffee."

Yes.

Your mother sent you up to your room as punishment. We could hear you talking to yourself up there, as if to prove you could have a perfectly good time without us.

Neil and Charlotte sat in the dining room. She was just over her tears and Neil was patting her hand and saying kids did stuff like that, it was perfectly natural, and Charlotte was saying she didn't know what she'd do if anything happened to you, it would be too much, more than she could stand, and Neil patted her hand some more. This had clearly been a bonding experience for them, as well as for me and Kathleen. When was the last time one child running off had done so much good for so many people?

Kathleen watched them from the kitchen, sensing the intimacy of the moment. "Are they together?" she asked, sipping her coffee.

"I'm hoping," I said.

She nodded her approval. "Neil's a nice guy."

"Yeah. Are you seeing anybody?" Yes, I was ticking through my list of stupid questions.

She didn't seem put off. "No," she said, simply.

"Too much of a risk?" I asked, figuring I might as well go for broke.

She laughed and shook her head. "No, no. That's a risk I can handle. How 'bout you?"

I shrugged and uttered a series of nonsense syllables that were intended to be a cool dismissal.

"Is the lady with the robots downstairs?" you yelled from up in your room.

Kathleen laughed and called up, "My name's Kathleen!"

"Katleen, I wanna show you my bed."

"She loves to show people her bed," I explained. "We hope she grows out of it by the time she's eighteen."

Kathleen laughed again. I liked making her laugh; I made a mental note to keep doing it. She called to you that she was coming.

"An' my drawring," you said. "I wanna show you my drawring."

"I can't wait to see it."

I let her go up first so I could check on Charlotte, who gave me her significant look.

"What?" I asked.

"She *is* pretty," Charlotte said.

I shushed your mother and told her to be quiet. And she *was* quiet, which was why we could hear it so clearly when Kathleen started screaming.

ELEVEN

It wasn't one of those high-pitched, operatic screams like they do in the horror pictures. This was deep and rock-and-roll; appalled and offended and heartbroken. It wasn't loud, but it spoke such injury, such bone-deep woundedness, that I was up the stairs before I could think, knowing only that something dreadful had happened.

You were sitting at your little drawing table looking up at Kathleen with wide, teary eyes. Kathleen was staring at you as if you had 666 tattooed on your forehead.

She jerked her head around when I came in. "What the fuck is this!?"

You ran and hid under the bed. Kathleen flinched; crouched down and called to you. "I'm sorry. I didn't mean to scare you."

I moved to her side, and she straightened and backed away. "Why are you doing this?" Bizarre as she was behaving, she wasn't acting crazy. Something had truly appalled her.

"I don't know what you're talking about."

She snatched your drawing off the table and held it up to me with a shaking hand. All I could see was a vibrating mass of black and green. "Where did you find this?"

"She drew it."

She dropped it onto the table. "I know she drew it. Don't play fucking games with me!"

I tried to take her shoulders. "I swear, Kathleen, I don't know what you're talking about."

She twisted away. "You know! On the boat. *I never said her name.*"

She shoved past me and ran down the stairs. I followed and heard her slam the front door.

I had to go back and check on you. Crawling out from under the bed, you looked totally freaked out.

"She got real mad," you said.

"Yeah. Not at you. I don't know why."

I looked down at the picture on the table. You had a very particular style of drawing—tiny scratch marks that carefully linked together and made up your images of dragons and stick people—but this wasn't done in that style. This was drawn in bold, dark lines. Two figures, a stick-woman with a skirt and long yellow hair in a blue suit. Next to her, a tiny figure, with short squiggly yellow hair, holding the first figure's hand. The little figure was surrounded by vivid yellow lines, like the bars of a cage. Surrounding both of them was a dark mass of black and green, scribbled with ferocious intensity, crowding them in. Crushing them. Punctuating the scrabbled darkness around the two figures were dozens of white blobs with three black circles on them; staring eyes and open mouths. These bodiless faces filled the dark picture with almost audible moans.

The effect of the drawing was disturbing; like looking at an Edvard Munch kindergarten finger painting. It looked for all the world like one of those sketches psychologists use as evidence to prove that a child has been abused.

You were back at the table now, looking up at me, eyes wide and wounded.

"Is it bad?"

"No, it's a fine picture."

"I don't think she liked it."

"It's not really like your pictures, is it?"

"I guess not."

"Why did you draw it?"

"That little girl said, like, 'that'll be a good idea.' I don' think it was a good idea."

I sat down in the little chair next to you. "That little girl was here?"

You looked around the room. "Well, sorta. You know the way they are."

I felt something settle heavy in my chest. "Yeah, I know the way they are. Did she tell you her name?"

"Jellica. I told her it was a silly name, but I think I hurt her feelings."

Kathleen was almost to the Quarry Road by the time I caught up with her. She wouldn't get in the car. I drove alongside her and called out the window, saying anything I could think of to get her to listen.

No go. She cut off into the woods where the car couldn't follow. I left the Mustang and went after her. The cold wasn't bothering me now.

"Listen to me. You want to know what's going on, don't you? Talk to me!"

She turned and faced me, challenging. "All right. What's going on?"

"I have no idea."

She started to turn again; I took her hand. She fixed her eyes on me. It was a tough stare; the kind inner-city teachers learn when they want to scare the shit out of their students.

"Who sent you here?"

"Nobody. Nobody at all. It's cold out here. Let's talk in the car."

I swear it took a full minute of looking at me for her to

decide. She walked straight to the car and got in.

"How do you know her name?" she asked as I drove onto a section of paved road.

"All right, I'm going to have to give you a little background before I tell you that—"

"I don't want any damned background. How do you know her name?"

"She told me."

She softened a little. "When did you meet her?"

"The other day. I saw her on your boat."

She shook her head. "Great. I finally meet somebody I like, and he turns out to be a fucking nutcase."

At least she said she liked me. "I saw her. When you fished me out of the water. A little girl. About Maggie's age. With short blond hair. Shiny black shoes. She said, 'My name's Jellica.'"

Kathleen was bobbing her head up and down, a bottle of contained fury. "That's her all right. Do you get off on this? Are you one of these sick fucks who goes through the obituaries and makes obscene phone calls to widows?"

"No. I did not ask for this, okay? All my life I have seen things. People. But before this, whenever I've seen one of these," I still couldn't bring myself to use the *g* word, "it was always somebody I remembered or somebody I figured I made up. This is the first time I've seen somebody I didn't know who turned out to be real. And that's different, that's real different."

"Yeah, that's what it is."

I sped up a little; I didn't want her to think about making a jump from the car.

"Maggie sees them too," I went on. "I never wanted to admit it to myself, but she does. She's seen...this girl. The girl is the one who led her to your house. She told her to make that drawing. Who is she, Kathleen?" No answer. "Is she your daughter?"

She shook her head, rapidly. "No, no. She's just someone I met." I think she almost believed me for a moment,
then forced it away. "And you know that. You know all this.
You're not telling me anything you couldn't have found
out in the papers or the court records. You're playing some
sick mind game."

"I'm not." I pulled up in front of her house. "I swear.
I mean, I know me swearing doesn't mean a thing to you,
but I swear."

Her eyes examined me again. "Even if it was true. Even
if it was true. Why would she be here?"

"I don't know."

She looked around the car, checking the air around her.
"Is she here now? Can you see her?"

"I can't do it when I want to." I ground my teeth at the
thought. "Especially when I want to."

Turning away, she seemed to pull into herself, to block
me out. "She can't be here," she muttered, to herself, not
to me. "She couldn't be with me." She was looking at me
again now, demanding, interrogating. "What does she
want?"

I shrugged. "She just said she wanted to play."

She bolted out of the car and was through her front
door before I could follow.

"Kathleen!"

"I don't want to see you!"

She slammed the door.

My mind was reeling. It couldn't contain all this.
I mean, you go for weeks, months, years at a time with
nothing really coming inside, nothing new, nothing you
have to compute and then, pow, a couple of truckloads are
crammed into your skull all at once and you can't even
come close to hearing it, looking at it, much less making
sense of it; it's just a swarm of bees buzzing behind your
eyes. And, what's more, you don't want the buzzing to

stop, to resolve itself into thoughts and words, because you aren't at all sure you want those thoughts and words in your head, in your life.

I floored it, kicking up cold dust, speeding up the hill. Cranked the radio, even though I couldn't find a station. Static was just fine.

I went as far as you can go on the island, slamming the brakes and skidding to a stop at the end of Long Haven Road. I got out and walked to the end of the jetty, looking at Long Haven Island across the water. Vast wealthy houses dotted the shore. All empty. Windows boarded up for the season. Almost no one lived on that island but rich Summer People, so in winter it was a ghost town.

I laughed out loud at the term. Ghost town.

You and I should move there, Maggie.

The sky turned an uncountable number of blues as I sat there watching the sun set and the lights flicker on the far island.

The thoughts kept whipping back at me like a live electrical wire. Was it all true? Were the spooks real?

No. I tried to crowd my mind with noise, with vivid images and compelling sexual fantasies, anything to take up room, to squeeze out the obvious.

Reflections of the town lights glittered on the black water, and I imagined a ghost ship, a Flying Dutchman, flowing through those floating stars. I tried to picture it just as powerfully as I could, to convince myself that Jellica and all the others had been imagined, too. It was useless. Try as I might, I couldn't project that mere thought onto the real water; couldn't make it into a solid, staring, speaking thing.

The car door swung open. I jumped in surprise as Neil slid in next to me.

"Hey, little buddy."

"Hey, Skipper."

That was all we said for a while. The moon rose over Long Haven.

"Long Haven gets damn empty in the wintertime. I think I'd go crazy if I lived there."

I laughed, since I knew that was exactly what all the Summer People said about Fox Island. The grass is always browner on the other side.

"Charlotte and Maggie were a little worried. Sent me out looking for you."

I didn't have to ask how he found me. There were only so many places you could go on the island. "I just went for a drive."

"Yeah. After the screaming lady ran out of the house. What's that about?"

I didn't answer. Neil pulled two beers out of his coat. Handed one over to me. We drank.

"She's okay, though?"

I shrugged and nodded and shook my head all at the same time.

"You wanna talk about it?"

Now, don't go all touchy-feely on me, Neil. "Can't say I do, 'cause I don't."

"Okay."

A few more sips. A little more silence.

I figured it was my turn. "So, what do you think of Maggie?"

"Great kid. Real pepperpot."

"What do you think of Charlotte?"

"What do you mean, what do I think of Charlotte? I've known her all my life."

"Okay."

Silence. Sips.

"Tell me about the husband," Neil said.

Dear God, he didn't really believe there was a husband, did he? Well, why should he think we'd lie to him?

I was faced with a moral dilemma, and to be honest I was grateful for the distraction. "I gotta tell you, I didn't really like the guy."

Neil grunted. "How long were they together?"

"Not long. I mean, long enough, but not long. She met him right after, you know, Mom and Dad and George died. I don't think she'd have done it if she hadn't been in such a state. I think he kind of took advantage of the situation."

"How so?"

"Well, he ran the funeral home where we sent Mom and Dad and George. And, I don't know, I think that's un-ethical. Like a psychiatrist and a patient, you know? Or a teacher and a student. Know what I mean?"

"Not really."

"I mean, he took advantage of her vulnerable condi-tion. He let her cry on his shoulder and then he saw his moment, he just moved right in and...." This much of what I said was true.

"Married her?"

"Exactly." Let the lies begin. I took a swig. "A real sleazeball."

"And then he went into the army?"

I'd forgotten about that ridiculous part of the ridicu-lous story. "Yeah. Well, National Guard, I think it was."

"They use undertakers?"

"Why not? I guess they got a whole division of them. You know, for afterward."

Neil grunted again. Did he have doubts? Maybe. But he was giving me every opportunity to tell the truth. And in the end, he trusted us. So, why didn't I set him straight? I didn't think it was my place, for one. And for another, I guess I was starting to prefer the lie myself. A rotten thing to say, I know, but I never claimed to be perfect—though I always hoped you thought I was.

"Do you think she's..." Neil paused, shifting around

uncomfortably, "...think she's over him?"

That was the question that was really troubling him. The rest was just background. "Yeah, I think she's over him. I mean, a person would have to take it slow, but...I think she's almost ready to move on."

Another grunt. Another sip. "Well, I wish her luck."

"So do I, Neil."

TWELVE

The next morning, we realized it was a week before Christmas and all through the house there was nothing particularly Christmas-y anywhere. We'd never spent a winter on the island, after all, so the only decorations in the attic were red, white, and blue bunting for the Fourth of July. You offered to color the white stripes green, but we decided that would be anti-American.

Buying holiday decorations might be easy in other places, but on the island it was a matter of either settling for the one string of lights and can of spray snow they had at the hardware store or getting on the ferry and driving up to the Wal-Mart on the mainland.

We stood on Main Street, weighing the pros and cons of taking that journey; the mainland seemed an impossibly far distance away, and the water looked nauseatingly choppy. Still, we couldn't very well let you have a Christmas without all the bells and whistles.

Neil came to the rescue. He was making a habit of hovering on the periphery of our lives to sail in when needed. Swinging his big shiny pick-up around, he swooped us up like Batman and drove us out to Indian Point. There, ax in hand, he led us through the woods to an orchard of perfect Christmas trees. You spent an hour wandering among them, talking to them, picking one, then falling for another, on and on while we grown-ups sang carols and stomped our feet and froze our balls off. In the end, you picked one that looked far too big for our living room. You wouldn't be dissuaded. This is was the tree of your dreams.

"Finest kind," Neil said, and wasn't that the truth?

Neil whacked it down; we dragged it to the truck and tossed it in. Back home, it fit perfectly, leaving just enough room between top needles and ceiling for Charlotte to fit the star you'd made out of tin foil. None of us had ever made a Christmas from scratch, as it were, and we felt very pleased with ourselves.

You set to work making a chain out of red and green construction paper, while I poured popcorn into the air popper. Neil and your mother reviewed the placement of the tree for the hundredth time and decided that it was, after all, on just the right side of the room in front of just the right window, in just the right house, on just the right island, on just the right planet.

There was nothing particularly romantic about what we did that morning, but there was a glow about it, a warmth of family and friendship that brought a shine to your mother's eyes that I hadn't seen for a long time. She certainly didn't embrace Neil or hang on his every word; she paid him no more attention than she paid the two of us. But she knew, as we all knew, that this day had started out troubled and annoying and had been transformed into something glittering and hilarious and memorable, and that transformation was all due to Neil. So, even if she didn't look at him more often than she used to, when she did there was something in her eyes that hadn't been there before. She was seeing him in a new way.

I kept my fingers crossed.

"You need lights," Neil was saying.

"No, we don't," Charlotte answered.

"Fuck, you don't. What's a Christmas tree without the lights?"

"We'll use candles, like they used to in the old days."

"In the old days when they burned their houses down?"

"Well, we don't have lights, and where are we going to get them?" Charlotte asked.

"My old man's got a bunch at his house."

"We're not going to steal your father's Christmas decorations."

"He won't know; he's almost blind these days."

Which struck us all as the funniest Christmas sentiment ever.

Neil assured us that his Old Man hated putting the damned things up and would consider it a favor if we took them off his hands, so off he went to get them. Charlotte volunteered to help.

I waved them good-bye from the driveway, and you laughed and danced in the driveway as they sped off. I'd been happy as hell to see the two of them hitting it off, but as they drove out of sight, self-pity started to set in. There was my sister finding happiness in love, or at least a chance at it. And here was me, having scared off yet another prospect with my freakish qualities. I felt myself sinking into that blackest of depressions, the Christmas Blues. Try as I might, I couldn't shake it.

I'm back in your hospital room now.

Neil grabbed me around noon and forced me out to have lunch. I wasn't his first choice, of course, but your mom wasn't about to leave your room.

I wasn't too willing either, but we didn't have a change of clothes with us on the mainland, so Neil persuaded me to go with him to Wal-Mart and buy some things. I weakened and went.

I blinked and twitched like a vampire as I stumbled out into the cold daylight. Inexplicably, Rockland looked the same as always. Didn't it know what was going on? Even the water in the bay was coughing up those same brutal whitecaps from its battleship metal surface that it had the night before last, when we'd flown over, cold and nauseated in the paramedic's helicopter.

I choked down a greasy hamburger at Reedy's and then wandered the endless aisles of Wal-Mart, absentmindedly picking out cheap, ugly clothes.

Driving back to the hospital in the old Buick Neil kept on the mainland, I prayed for him to hurry, cursing myself for hoping that when I got there I'd find you sitting up in bed, slurping down Jell-O and watching the Cartoon Network.

When we got here there was no change.

I went into the bathroom to put on my new clothes and give myself a whore's bath. Gagging on four Excedrin, I vomited into the bowl.

So, now I'm hungry all over again, and my new clothes already feel like they've been slept in. I won't be tempted to leave here again. Not until you do.

There are a million board games crammed into cupboards and closets in the Thorofare house. Classics like Monopoly and Hi Ho! Cheery-O. Obscure ones like Ubi or Eddie Cantor's singalong game. Your favorite was always Quicksand.

You loved it because there was very little reading involved and you got to throw two sets of dice. Also, the game piece was a cunningly crafted little pith helmet–wearing British explorer with a handlebar mustache, and I used to do a cheesy C. Aubrey Smith imitation when I moved him that made you laugh so hard you couldn't breathe. The game board was Darkest Africa, teeming with quicksand, wild animals, and dangerous savages (needless to say, it dated from the pre–politically correct days). The plastic explorer could be divided into four segments: legs, torso, head, and helmet. If you made an unlucky roll with the quicksand dice, you had to remove a piece of your man from the bottom up, so that he appeared to be sinking into the board. Once you got down to just your helmet, you were in serious trouble.

I played that game with you the same afternoon we put up the Christmas tree with Neil, while we waited for them to come back with the lights. Sitting across from you at the kitchen table, up to my helmet in quicksand, I thought, *Well, that about sums it up.* I remembered my dad talking literary shop around the house, expounding on something called the "pathetic fallacy"; that's where a character's mood in a book is mirrored by the weather. You know how it goes, Heathcliff is brooding so the moors get all storming and bleak. Well, I sat there wondering if there could be a pathetic fallacy for board games, 'cause that helmet floating on the cardboard quicksand looked a whole hell of a lot like me.

You could always tell when I was depressed, Maggie. I guess a lot of kids are supposed to be good at that; ultra-sensitive to the moods of adults, the way dogs and cats are supposed to predict earthquakes and hurricanes. But unlike most kids in my experience, you usually wanted to make things better instead of worse. This time, sensing my funk, you stopped dancing in the driveway, led me inside, and sat me in front of the TV.

Well, despite your good intentions, being an object of pity from a four-and-a-half-year-old only made me feel worse. I watched the antics of a cartoon superhero as his powers failed him at the worst possible time and saw only myself. A pathetic fallacy for cartoons.

The live electrical wire that had been dancing around in my head last night was back; the thoughts whipping at me again.

It was all true. The spooks were real.

This thing I'd been evading my whole life was back. It had made an end run around me and was staring me in the face.

And Maggie, sweet Maggie, it had come to include you too. Why did you seem to handle it so much better than I did? To take it in stride. "You know the way they are," you'd said, so casually. Was it because you were smarter than me or more ignorant?

You caught me looking at you instead of the TV and turned it off. "Sorry I made your girlfriend mad at you," you said.

"Is that what you think?" I hugged you. "It wasn't your fault."

I banished thoughts of myself and worked to cheer you up. That's the great gift child-rearing gives a person. The constant reminder that you are not the center of the universe, whatever your self-pity may tell you.

So, I dug out the board game and sat at the table, steaming cups of Fifth Sun Cocoa at our elbows, trying to save our little men from sinking.

There was a knock at the door.

It was still broad daylight, so you wouldn't think that would have startled me. That it did was partly on account of my mood and partly on account of the fact that this was the island. People didn't tend to knock around here. It was considered rude to make somebody get up and answer the door. If you knew a person well, you just opened their door, announced yourself, and walked on in. If you didn't know them well, what were you going to their house for, anyway? Knocking was a thing only someone from away would do.

I yelled "Come in," since getting up and going to the door was also a mainland formality. My heart beat a little faster, but I controlled it. I knew it couldn't be Kathleen.

It was Kathleen.

The first thing she did when she came in was go over to talk to you. "I didn't mean to scare you, Maggie. Did I scare you?"

"No." You'd never admit to being scared. "Want me to draw you a different picture?"

Kathleen laughed. "Maybe later. Can I talk to your uncle for a minute?"

You frowned. "We're kinda playin'."

"It'll only take a minute." It had been a long time since I'd been fought over.

We went out onto the porch. The sun was starting to set. There were the usual spectacular explosions of color over Brown's Head Island that any special effects artist in Hollywood would give his left arm for. God just dashed these off in His spare time.

Kathleen didn't say anything for the first few moments. I didn't know if she was going to start screaming at me or grab me and kiss me. Not much chance for the latter, given the situation, but a man can't help but hope.

"This is no good," she said, finally.

No kissing, I thought.

"I came here to be alone," she went on, "and now you've got me thinking I'm not. And even if it's not true, even if it's just crazy, it's in my head now. I couldn't shake it all last night. I'm not alone in the house anymore."

Well, the way I was feeling now, I wasn't sure any of us was alone ever, anywhere. But I didn't think that was what she wanted to hear. "I'm sorry."

"I was running away when I came here, I won't deny it. If she's been with me all the time, that would be..." she gave a mirthless laugh. "...that would be very funny."

I was pretty sure it wasn't the sort of laugh I was supposed to join in with, but I felt the need to say something.
I remembered Neil's wisdom earlier in the day. "It might
not be a scary thing, Kathleen. I mean, she might not mean
any harm."

She looked at me with an expression I can only call horrified pity. "Jesus, is *that* what you think I'm worried about?"

"I don't know." You could write a book about what I
don't know. "What are you afraid of?"

Her expression hardened. I realized I'd asked a much
more difficult question than I'd meant to. But she didn't
storm off. She just took a long time to start talking.

"I don't believe...hell, I don't know what I don't believe. I used to believe in God, but that was when I was a
little girl."

She braced herself. "Okay, if you see her...if you can
really see her...that means she's dead, doesn't it? I mean,
you couldn't be seeing a telepathic image of her alive,
but—Jesus, I can't believe I'm asking this like there's going
to be an answer that means anything."

"No, it's good to ask. And the answer, I think, though
I don't know, the answer, I think, is she must be...
not alive...."

She nodded once and looked up at the sky. "I don't
know what happens after someone dies. I've seen people die and I've always thought, well, at least it's over for
them. The pain. Whatever they're trapped in. They can
rest now. Sometimes I even hope my mother was right and
they go and sit on a cloud and play a harp. But one thing I
do know. They're not supposed to be still hanging around
here. Hanging around me. If that happens, then something
is seriously wrong."

She stopped, and I knew it was time for me to
say something. The blank look on my face must have
been eloquent.

"Haven't you thought about all this?" she asked.

"Of course, I have. But I don't really know the answer to the question you asked me. I mean—even if it's true that we saw this—that Maggie and I saw this girl, it doesn't necessarily follow that she's a...ghost." I knew I was acting like a drug addict in full denial, but I just couldn't accept it. "Maybe we were somehow catching images from your mind. You know, like you said, like telepathy. Or reading traces of her left in the atmosphere or something...maybe she is alive." I was babbling and I hated myself for it, but I couldn't stop.

"How long have you been seeing these things?" she asked me.

"Fifteen years."

"And this is as far as you've gotten? You've never even tried to figure out what they are?"

"Of course, I've tried!" I was surprised by my own anger. "Jesus, whaddayathink? I've been to psychiatrists, and they give me whatever the drug of the day happens to be. I've been to priests, and they just get embarrassed and tell me to go back to the psychiatrists. I've been to spiritualists, and they tell me to come back and please bring my checkbook next time.

"The only thing I know is...it doesn't make sense. I am not a conduit to the Hereafter. I'm just me. Nothing special. The third kid in the family. The dumb one. Charlotte was the pretty one. George was the smart one. And I was the one who sat in front of the TV and watched stupid movies while my mother said, 'Well, two out of three ain't bad.'" I shut up, mouth gaping, horrified by my own outburst. This was no way to impress a girl.

She touched my arm with embarrassed pity. "I didn't think about how hard this is for you. I should go."

"No." Not wanting her to leave was the only thing I was sure of in this whole mess. The afternoon cold cut through me, but I resisted the temptation to go inside or grab a blanket off a deck chair or do anything that might break the mood of communication between us. "You said you were running away. I was, too. But whatever we're running from, it looks like it's following us. Maybe it's time to face it."

She nodded. "Do you have any way of controlling these...images?"

"God, no. They control me." I couldn't believe I was saying this. I felt like I was standing up at some freakish AA meeting, declaring to the group, "My name is Samuel and I am a Medium."

"And you never met anybody who believed you? Anybody who could teach you how to handle this?"

"No, you see, there's a Catch-22 here, isn't there? If they're honest and sane, they tell me I'm crazy. If they're nuts or frauds, then they say they believe me."

"Okay," she said, "I've dealt with Gypsies and con artists, too. But every now and then I've met one that made me wonder. Let's just say all this is true, all this is real. You and your niece can't be the only two people who see these things."

This made sense. Like I said, I wasn't that special. Maybe you were; not me.

I racked my brain to think of one normal, well-balanced person I'd ever talked to or even heard of who had experienced what we experienced. I only came up with one thin straw to grasp at.

Suddenly, there was a banging sound and a piping voice behind us. "You promised you'd play with me!"

Kathleen gasped, going white. We turned to see you at the screen door, the mesh still vibrating from you slamming it aside. Kathleen relaxed, laughing nervously. Who had she thought you were?

You held the helmet of my explorer in the palm of

your hand.

"Yeah. Okay. But just one game. Then Kathleen and I have to go visit somebody." I turned to Kathleen. "Mind if we finish the game?"

Kathleen smiled, breathing cold smoke. "No. It's important to keep promises."

THIRTEEN

I can't remember the last time I played a board game."
Kathleen laughed as she fiddled with the car radio.
A hopeless effort; you could only get two stations on
the island, and they both came in on the same wavelength.
She had joined us in a fast game of Quicksand, which
had turned into three games after Charlotte and Neil
rolled in, laughing, arms full of tiny lights, eyes bright
with suggestive and knowing looks directed at me and
Kathleen. It had been a long time since that kitchen had
been filled with so much chatter and so much hilarity.
I liked it. Now, we were on our way to Joe's house, just
the two of us.

"Board games are a Kehoe family tradition," I was
telling her. "My folks and my brother and my sister, that
was how we spent our nights every summer. Sitting at
that kitchen table. Playing everything. Parcheesi, Sorry,
Life, Mouse Trap, bridge, Trivial Pursuit, Careers, poker,
Canasta, you name it. Man, they were cutthroat games.
We'd get so caught up, we'd look at the clock and all of a
sudden it was two in the morning."

I laughed as I told her about the way Dad used to hold
his playing cards close to his chest, like W.C. Fields; how
Mom used to half-forget-the-rules/half-cheat her way to
victory; how Charlotte always deliberately let somebody

else win if she was ahead; how George used to pout when he lost and gloat when he won; how I used to beg for another game even after everyone else was dead tired and dragging up to bed. She laughed along with me, saying she'd always dreamed of having a family like that and wondering if she could join in the next time we all played.

Well, that brought things to a grinding halt. Much as I hated to tell the tale yet again, here it came. Dead. Dead. Dead. And yes, it was awful.

"But," she said (I could tell she wished she hadn't brought it up), "at least you *had* that. It must be wonderful to come from a close family."

Well, it wasn't all perfect, I told her. We used to fight like hell.

"Physically?" she asked.

"No," I said, a little surprised. "But real verbal battles. I mean, screaming and yelling. Throwing things, occasionally. Never *at* anybody, but still."

"What about?"

"Oh, God. Well, Mom was always riding me for not making anything of myself and not getting better grades and just sitting around, watching trashy movies and all. And what else? Well, everybody always hated Charlotte's boyfriends, so that was at least one guaranteed blowup every summer. Then George went all conservative after college, so all you had to do was bring up politics or the environment and blood would flow. Metaphorical blood, I mean. No, it wasn't all roses."

"But that's because you were close. You should try being in a family where everybody just stares at each other and doesn't say a word all night."

"There were times when that might have been a relief."

"Don't believe it. Don't believe it for a second." She didn't say it in a solemn way. Actually, she was quite cheerful again, bopping along with the radio, which was simultaneously picking up a John Anderson country tune and Beethoven's "Ode to Joy." But saying them happily only made her words sound more heartfelt.

Joe's house was a slip of a thing, a narrow, two-story sliver of wood, gone all fish-scale gray from the sea air. There must have been another half a house attached to it at one time, because it sure didn't look like someone would build a place that thin on purpose. Smoke was pouring out of the chimney, and there was one light on in the living room. I remembered how I'd left them the night of the ice boat party and was suddenly unsure of our reception.

Shara opened the door. She had on short jeans and a white tank top that didn't cover her bellybutton and its little sunburst tattoo. Billie Holiday was singing "Your Mother's Son-in-Law" on the stereo. Some things never stop being cool.

She smiled, no hard feelings, evidently, and let us in. Joe was bent over at the woodstove, shoving in a couple of pieces of wood. He stood up when he heard us, clapping his hands together in a hearty gesture that couldn't distract us from the fact that he was buck naked and sporting a squat purple erection.

"Gordon Kehoe's son! You've got to go see Dr. Hopley this week. He's giving Viagra to everyone. I've had this stinger going since two o'clock in the afternoon."

Shara nodded in agreement. "He has."

We persuaded him to put on a pair of jeans, which couldn't have been easy, and I told him I wanted him to take us to see Mrs. Day. Of course, that meant I had to tell him all (or all I knew) about Kathleen and Jellica. I felt uncomfortable relating the story in front of Kathleen, even more so since she sat there not saying a word, not even giving out any confirming grunts or nods.

"Jellica is an interesting name," Shara said. "Who is she?"

This was directed at Kathleen; I half expected her to deny any knowledge and ask them to call the men in the white coats to come get me. Instead she spoke quietly. "I don't want to say anything about this. I don't want to give out any information that might compromise what Sam might come up with next."

Shara clucked her tongue; the metal stud in it made that quite effective. "Don't you think that kind of skeptical attitude might offend Jellica?"

Kathleen just smiled. "I need something like proof before I'm going to believe any of this."

Joe poured coffee and flipped cigarette ash into a potted plant. "Shara's right. The child might not like that. How would you feel if I asked you to prove that you existed?"

Kathleen didn't rise to the bait, just smiled again. "I *know* I exist."

"That's probably how Jellica feels," Joe said. "She knows she's real; why don't you? Maybe that's why nobody's been able to 'prove' ghosts exist. As soon as you cop that 'show me' attitude, they get offended and leave. What do you think?"

Joe turned to me now. I searched my mind for an actual opinion on the matter, but there didn't seem to be any at home. When in doubt, I always talk about movies. "Come on. That's saying spirits of the dead are like Michigan J. Frog in that old Warner Brothers cartoon. Remember? It would sing 'Hello, my baby' if the guy was alone, but whenever he asked it to perform in front of people it just sat there and croaked."

Shara made a face. "I hate that cartoon. It's frustrating."

"When you think about it, though," Joe said, "it's a very profound piece of film. Asking the question, why did that man need other people to validate his own experience … of, you know, singing frogs?"

"But he wasn't trying to validate his experience,"

Kathleen said. "He was trying to get rich by selling tickets to a singing frog show."

"Well, money is one of the main ways we look for validation in this society," Shara said.

"When you think about it, though, how much would you really pay to see a singing frog?" I asked.

"A fair bit," Joe said. I believed him.

Joe started collecting coats from around the house, handing them to us, saying it was time to visit Emily Day.

"Should we call first?" I asked.

They all looked at me with puzzled expressions. I'd forgotten; you didn't call first on the island.

Emily Day's house is called the Green House, even though it's yellow, on account of the fact that a family named Green lived there in the 1880s. People have long memories on the island.

I don't know what I expected to notice first on walking into the house of someone who was supposed to set me on the path to spiritual enlightenment, but I don't think it was the overwhelming smell of pie.

The atmosphere was heavy with cinnamon, hot sugar, and flour.

Aroma-wise, I felt totally at ease. If there was anyone on Earth I'd listen to spiritualist bullshit from, it was the person who could create this glorious perfume.

My ears were less certain. The place rocked with the cacophony of a late-twentieth-century American family. The bleeping and canned music of a Nintendo game. A *Home Improvement* rerun turned up too loud in another room. Rap music from somebody's stereo upstairs.

The Nintendo player greeted us with a grunt as we walked in—without knocking, of course. He looked about fourteen, wearing the obligatory surly expression and *South Park* T-shirt. The house had a Victorian elegance on the outside, but within, it was like most houses on the island.

Remodeled during the worst, paneling-and-orange-shag-carpet period of the seventies, it seemed to pay no respect to its own age and history. Only off-islanders thought of these places as architectural gems. To the natives they were big drafty white elephants, and you just had to make the best of them.

Two kids banged a door open and ran in from the room where the TV blared. They pelted each other with Beanie Babies and collapsed in a tangle behind the sofa before I had a chance to see what age or sex they were.

On the whole, pies excepted, the house gave off the usual aura of barely controlled desperation and budding chaos you find in suburban homes throughout this country. Normal, even amusing, but hardly a place to go for an answer to the meaning of life, I thought.

Then June Cleaver walked in.

Or Harriet Nelson. Or Florence Henderson. Pick the perfect TV mother of your choice. Not that she was wearing a pleated housedress, exactly. Actually, she was in a blue chambray shirt and pair of Back to Basics Gap jeans. But being June Cleaver is all in the attitude.

She scooped the two wriggling kids up from behind the sofa, one in each arm. I saw now that they were a boy and girl, around three; they weren't identical twins, though they were the same age and were, at the moment, co-joined at the hands and throat.

"Why you don't you take all your Beanie Babies and tuck them in bed and sing them a song?"

They leapt to their feet, gathered the dolls until they overflowed in their arms, and raced up the stairs. From chaos, order. Mrs. Day switched off the TV in the other room, a door slammed upstairs, and all at once, peace, harmony, and the blessed smell of pies ruled supreme.

Okay, she could teach me the meaning of life.

FOURTEEN

Keep your mind a total blank."

Never been a problem for me, as the joke goes. Funny thing was, for once I actually knew what she meant. My mind felt clear, open, empty. The clutter and feedback that always buzzed in the background—unpaid bills, unwritten letters, snatches of half-forgotten songs— were silenced. The inside of my head felt swept clean and receptive. I was not creating static. I was tuned to receive.

If I was ever going to pick up any messages, it was going to be now. I took deep, steady, cleansing breaths and let myself fly.

It hadn't started well.

"So, what makes you think you're a medium?"

This annoyed me. For one thing, there was that silly word, *medium*, conjuring up images of a fussy Margaret Rutherford in *Blithe Spirit* or a hysterical Julie Harris in *The Haunting*. For another, there was the question itself. I wasn't here to justify myself; I was here to learn.

"I don't know if I do think that."

"Then why are you here?"

We were sitting at the kitchen table, like a happy family around the coffee cups and pie. Mrs. Day had a benignly pretty face. Up close, she wasn't as old as I'd thought; late thirties, tops.

"Well, Joe brought me—"

"Yes," patient, but stern, "I know Joe brought you, but you asked him to bring you. So?"

"Well, he thought—"

"Joe's not the one I'm talking to. What do *you* think?" There was nothing harsh in her voice, but she broadcast a beam of motherly authority.

"Look, I don't know what to think. That's why I'm here." I glanced over at Kathleen and wished I wasn't sounding so ineffectual.

Mrs. Day nodded. "Not knowing what to think can be a very intelligent position. But only as a beginning."

She stood up and started clearing the table. Kathleen and Shara immediately moved to help. I made a few piles with the plates, and Joe kept looking for beer in the fridge.

"Now," she said, when the table was all neat and tidy again, "you have to understand that the ability you claim to have—"

"I don't 'claim' anything." This whole thing had gotten off on the wrong foot altogether. One thing I'd never been, the beginning of that Ouija board session aside, was a faker. "To tell you the truth, I don't believe any of this myself."

"Then I'm stumped, Mr. Kehoe. Stumped and bewildered. If you don't think you're a medium, what do you think you are?"

Well, that's everybody's sixty-four dollar question, isn't it? "I just, I think I see things—"

"You *think* you see things?"

"Well, it appears to me that I see things—"

"You either see things or you don't see things, Mr. Kehoe. If we're not talking about concrete reality, I don't want to talk at all."

Well, this was hardly the approach I'd expected from my spiritual mentor. "But...so you don't believe either?"

"I believe in what I see, Mr. Kehoe. What I see and what I hear and what I touch and taste and feel. But that doesn't mean that what I see, hear, touch, taste, and feel are the same things everyone else sees, hears, touches, tastes, and feels. Now, I ask you again, what do you see?"

"Sometimes, usually in periods of stress, I seem to see things that don't appear to be there."

She looked at me, lips pursed, eyes squinting. "Sometimes? Seem? Appear? Why do you leave yourself so many escape routes?"

"Look, maybe I'm not using the words you like, but—"

"Words are things, Mr. Kehoe. They mean what they mean. I'm not disapproving of what you're saying. I'm just trying to understand what it is." She picked up an orange Fiestaware tea pot. "Do you see this?"

"Yes."

"That was easy, wasn't it? Now, these things you sometimes seem to appear to see, do they look as real as this?"

You know how it is when the mere act of putting things into words makes you think of them in a new way? "More real," I said.

"How is that?"

"Just clearer. Too clear. You know, like those paintings that are supposed to be like photographs but somehow the lines are too sharp and reflections are too hard? It's like that. So real, it doesn't look real. Do you know what I mean?"

Her face softened. "Yes, I do know what you mean. Why don't you?"

"I'm sorry?"

"Why isn't seeing believing for you?"

"Why should it be? I mean, why should I see something nobody else sees? I'm not so special."

"Aren't you?"

"Come on. The obvious explanation is that I'm hallucinating. That's what I've always believed. Until now. Now something new has come up, and that's what I'm here to talk to you about."

"That's what we *are* talking about, Sam." What had I done to be promoted to first-name basis? "I'm interested in why you don't think you're special."

"Let me count the ways." I was trying to make a joke, but you don't joke with people like Mrs. Day. They do that annoying thing of believing what you say.

"Why do you have such a low opinion of yourself, Sam?"

Good Christ, this was turning into Amateur Hour at the Group Therapy Coffee House. "Actually, I have a very high opinion of myself. I'm constantly frustrated that no one else shares it."

"Most people *like* to think they're special."

"Yeah, well, most people like to fool themselves, don't they? You know what I always hated? My mom and dad were both teachers, okay, and they always hated that whole *Mr. Roger's Neighborhood* thing about every kid is special. 'You're special just because you're you.' That makes no sense."

"You hated it, or your parents hated it?"

"We *all* hated it. I mean, think about it. If everybody's special, then nobody's special. Somebody has to be below average to make the special ones stand out."

"And that someone is you?" Mrs. Day asked.

"According to Mom." This I said with my charming, self-deprecating laugh that always melted hearts and showed people I was just joking. No one laughed. "That's a joke. You know what a joke is?"

"A defense mechanism, usually."

"No. Come on. You know what I can't stand about people like you?"

"I didn't know you couldn't stand me."

"You know what I mean."

"I'm not a mind-reader, Sam, I'm a medium."

"Now *you're* joking. What are you feeling defensive about?"

"So you agree that jokes are a defense mechanism?" she countered.

She didn't move at all. I, on the other hand, was squirming like a kid in church. "No, I think they're jokes. Wit. A form of entertainment. Something exaggerated to get a laugh."

"But what are you exaggerating, Sam, when you say your mother didn't think you were special?"

"I didn't say that. Did I say that?" I turned to the others for support. They said that I'd said that. "Why are we doing this? What does this have to do with me being a medium? Or a regular or an extra-large?" No one laughed at that either, but I couldn't blame them.

"Actually, I like that joke," Mrs. Day said with her gummy smile, "because it makes you think about the word. *Medium*. What does it mean?"

"Average. Small, medium, large."

"And?"

"Uh, rare, medium, well-done. You know, something in between two other things."

"And?"

"I guess it's something that something is *in*, right? Fish swim in the medium of water."

"And?"

"That's it. Oh, I guess there's like TV is a medium, or radio. Right? A way of communicating something?"

"Exactly. If you are a medium, you are all of that. Both the one in between two things *and* the medium of communication between them. And you are also the medium of the message, the thing it is *in*, so you yourself become a part of any communication that passes through you. You can't help but distort the message in some way because you are a part of the message.

"But if you clear your mind, you can hear them. If you don't listen, if you deny it and try to stifle it, they'll still work their way through. Burst in on you like bad dreams. You can't shut them out, Sam. You don't have an off switch."

I didn't reply. I didn't like what she was saying and, most of all, didn't like that it was making sense to me.

"Did you ever tell your parents, your mother, about your experiences?"

"Can we talk about why we came here?"

"We are. Did you?"

"Yes. Not at first, but...." I gave them a brief recap of my Ouija board fiasco with dear Melody, leaving out anything that would make me look bad in Kathleen's eyes, of course. "Charlotte wanted to know what the hell happened, so I told her. She believed me. She was thrilled, actually. Thought it was very exciting. Like having 'Carrie' for a brother. She wanted me to tell Mom and Dad. Like I was a gifted child and they could put me in a special class or something."

"Did you know anyone who was in a special class?"

"My brother, George. But that's because he was a math whiz. And, of course, I hated him for it and it warped me for life. I'm joking again."

"I know."

"Anyway, I knew it was a terrible idea, but I went and told Mom and Dad."

"And they weren't happy?"

"They're educators, okay? My mother's a math teacher; she didn't believe in spooks. She just blew up. She couldn't believe I'd done that to Melody. She said it was the cruelest trick she'd ever heard of, and she was so disappointed in me. I told her it wasn't a trick, but that just made things worse. I got sent to every psychiatrist in the Washington area, and that's a *lot* of psychiatrists. Had every test and scan and, God, you name it."

"Did they find anything?"

"No."

"Did you keep seeing 'spooks'?"

"Sometimes. I couldn't help it."

"But you didn't tell anyone?"

"No."

"You never told your mother again?"

"No, but it didn't help. There was distance after that. Like she didn't trust me."

"Had you ever really talked with her about this sort of thing before?"

"No."

"But you knew it was a terrible idea to tell her. How did you know that if you'd never brought up the subject before?"

I glanced at the others in room. They were trying not to listen. Or trying not to look like they were listening.

"You just, you knew my mother, okay?" I said. "Even when I was really little and I'd wake up yelling 'cause, I don't know, 'cause the Bogey Man was in my closet or something, she'd just come in, slam open the closet, switch on the light, and *show* me there was nothing there, and that was that. She didn't have any patience for that crap."

"Did you find that comforting?"

"Well, yeah, I guess. I mean, she showed me the closet was empty," I said, sitting on the edge of my seat. "And if there *had* been anything in there, she'd have whupped its ass."

"And she proved that you'd been wrong? About the Bogey Man."

"Yeah," I said.

"And that's pretty much how she reacted when you told her you'd seen Melody's father?"

"Sure. Mom was always consistent."

"Why do you think it bothered her?"

"What do you mean, 'why?' Because it's crazy. Seeing visions? Come on. That's for saints and psychotics and con men and old Gypsy fortune-tellers like Maria Ouspenskaya in *The Wolf Man*. It isn't real."

"And what's real matters that much to her?"

"Not just that. Look, she was always disappointed in me, okay? If you want to get to the whole blame-it-on-my-childhood-it's-all-my-parents'-fault bullshit. I was a below-average student in an above-average household. I didn't like great art or the symphony. I liked scary movies and country music. My brother had science fair trophies on his shelf; I had an autographed picture of Jamie Lee Curtis. I think she thought the whole ghost thing was just my way of trying to get attention and, well, she hated that more than anything. She hated lies."

"Do you think that's really what she hated?" Mrs. Day asked, smiling.

"Do I think she hated me? Is that what you mean?"

"Not at all."

"Well, she loved me, okay? She took care of me when I was sick, she liked my girlfriends, she laughed at my jokes, which is more than I can say about some people. It's just that she expected more. Can you blame her for that?"

"I don't know."

God, I knew the familiar pattern of those non-committal answers. "Are you a shrink? Is there a degree on the wall I'm not seeing?"

She smiled. "No."

"See, this is the basic con man approach. You do a little cheap psychoanalyzing, then you tell people what they've already told you. Just like Frank Morgan in *The Wizard of Oz*."

Mrs. Day wasn't offended. "Sam, I can't tell you why you've resisted this for so long. But if you're willing, if you're ready to accept it now, I can help you listen to what they have to say."

"What *who* has to say? Spooks? Ghosts? That's ludicrous!"

She took my hand in hers. Her fingers were squat and thick, her nails blunted from housework. But the flesh was soft and warm, and her touch was the gentlest I'd ever felt. "Sam, you don't have to fight it anymore. Whether they're real or not, they can't hurt you. And there's no one here who'll disapprove of you."

"Maybe I will."

She smiled. "Maybe you will. Are you willing to risk that?"

I shrugged. "Sure."

"Mean it, Sam. This ability you have, if you have it, it doesn't come along every day. It *does* make you special. Are you willing to find out the answer to the question you've been afraid to ask all these years?"

Put it that way and I had no doubt.

"Yes," I said.

The Town Museum is a barn behind Mrs. Day's that had been expanded by volunteers to twice its original size and four times its original ugliness. It's filled to the rafters with the debris of three centuries or more of life on the island. Old sleighs and carriages; broken bookcases and dinner tables; ancient stone axes and arrowheads; fading photographs of grim-faced Civil War soldiers and the equally grim-faced women they left behind; letters and legal forms and yellowed maps; splintered, flaking, rusting, threadbare, shattered toys and eyeless dolls. Whenever an old man or an old woman finally died on the island, surviving relatives would swoop down to sell and disburse all his or her belongings and the belongings of their shared ancestors. Off it would all go to antique stores and auction houses in New York or Boston. Only what was too busted or too unappreciated to garner a profit would stay on the island, would make it here, into Mrs. Day's loving hands.

She'd take these fragments and mount them over finely lettered parchment labels: "Boy's tin toy 'The Dancing Jigger' found at Indian's Head Cove, circa 1840"; "Second page of letter sent from the Battle of the Wilderness, 1864, found in top drawer of desk at the Dump, author and addressee unknown"; "Lace doily, made by Millicent Ainslie, 1912." This was the heritage and history of the island, kept by one of the few natives who seemed to care. I hope to God that when Emily Day dies it doesn't all show up on an auction block at Christie's or in an antique shop in Soho. Or in the Dump off the Quarry Road.

Mrs. Day led us into the dark, freezing room, switched on the fluorescent tubes Ticket Costello had fixed to the high rafters, and, as they flickered reluctantly to life, she turned up the thermostat. The furnace kicked in, and I figured the place would be warm and comfortable come April.

"You okay?" Kathleen whispered to me privately, her breath smoky in the cold.

"I guess. I mean, it's all pretty crazy. We can leave if you want."

She glanced to where Mrs. Day and Shara were setting up chairs at a circular dinner table in the middle of the room. "No, I want to see this through. It's not like she's crazy or asking for money or anything."

"You think she's legit?"

Kathleen crossed her arms beneath her breasts to keep warm, and I tried not to notice what the cold was doing to her nipples. "I think she believes what she says."

Not the same thing at all.

"We're ready!" Mrs. Day called out, as if tea were being served.

Mrs. Day sat us around the table, fingers touching. Déjà vu all over again. An old Tiffany lamp was our centerpiece; the light diffused by the multicolored leaded glass shade was gentle and soft once she'd turned off those unforgiving fluorescents.

"Are we all comfortable?"

We were all comfortable.

"Now, we're all here for the same reason. We're here to help Sam find out what's going on in his heart. Some of us may think we know what that is," she was looking at Joe and Shara as she said this. "Others may not be so sure," this was directed at Kathleen. "It doesn't matter what we believe right now. All that matters is that we want to help Sam. That we send out positive thoughts."

I flinched inwardly at the preciousness of the sentiment, but felt comforted by it all the same.

Like a yoga teacher, she took us on a tour of our bodies, using her voice to help us relax every muscle, every joint. Our breathing slowed, calmed, deepened; the dragon's smoke coming out of our nostrils took on a steady, even pace. She told us to let our brains relax and drop away from the top our heads and settle like a glop of Jell-O on the top our spines.

She counted and told us to picture each number as a soft cushion, a velvet pillow, and to imagine ourselves falling deeper and deeper into softness. I rolled and dropped from one to ten, feeling like Mickey in *The Night Kitchen* descending into the warm batter.

"Sam, there's a part of your mind you've closed off. Separated from the rest. You've been afraid of that part of your mind. Ashamed of it. But now you don't need to be. It's just another part of you, and you know that. I want you to picture it as something cupped in your hand. Something fragile and delicate. Something that would never hurt you. Now, I want you to open those hands. I want you to let it out. To welcome it. Do you feel those hands opening, those hands in your mind?"

My eyes were closed now and damned if I didn't feel a sensation of opening, as if a distance had suddenly appeared before me. And with it came that dizzying sensation of losing touch with ground that you get when you're drifting off to sleep, when you're halfway into a dream.

I didn't jerk myself awake or pull back. I let myself soar through the space behind my eyes.

"Sam, can you still hear me?"

I nodded, even though her voice sounded farther off.

"There are no barriers now, Sam. You have brought down the walls. You are complete now. This is what you've been running from. This is who you are."

I felt exhilarated. Swooping like a firefly. Doing giddy pirouettes in my own head, just like you were doing in the backyard as you watched your kites fly away.

"Are you alone, Sam?"

My kite started to fall.

"Is there someone with you?"

Damn it. I was becoming aware of my own breathing, of the hard seat under my butt.

"Try not to resist. There is someone there, but it isn't a stranger. This is someone you've known for a long time."

I tried to feel the enormity of space again, to lift myself from the ground.

"This is a friend. Someone who has been trying to talk to you for a long time. Someone who *has* been talking. But you haven't been listening."

I tried, but only felt myself trying.

"That person is with you. Let them be with you."

There. I felt the ground release its hold. I felt myself lifting in my mind, I heard Mrs. Day's voice growing fainter, felt the great emptiness around me again.

"It's someone who only wishes you well. Who only wishes to help you. Let this person come to you, Sam. And through this person, let the others come to you. All those ones who have been clamoring to speak. Feel their loneliness and their love, Sam."

Again, I felt freedom. The pressure of the barrier I'd held up for so long was gone. Come to me, I said to whoever might be there. I am ready for you now. Walk out of the shadows and show your face. Where are you? I twirled and twisted and looked into every corner of myself with no sense of apprehension.

And I was totally alone.

My mind was clear and open and receptive.

And there was no one on the line.

"Is she there, Sam?"

But I could barely hear her. There was too much joy rushing through my head, like blood pumping in my ears. I was alone. There was no one here but me.

The rushing in my head turned to laughter. Laughter at my own foolishness, at my wasted effort, at years spent barring the door when there was no one knocking. I know nothing when I see it, and I was surrounded by a wonderful, comforting sea of nothing.

I leapt back to consciousness, bounding up the velvet numbers again, like a child jumping from bed to bed.

I opened my eyes and saw them staring at me. That's when I realized I'd been laughing out loud.

"You were wrong, Emily," I said, smiling broadly. All those muscles she'd relaxed with her soothing words were still relaxed, and I was sure they'd stay relaxed for the rest of my life since the knot of tension I'd carried my whole life was gone, evaporated, proven false. "I'm not special after all."

FIFTEEN

I don't know if you can imagine what it's like—no, I'm afraid you can—to feel all your life that you are different, set apart, that your experiences are unshareable. But then to suddenly have that weight lifted from your heart, to feel connected to the wonderful, dull, ordinary normalness of life. It's like a stay of execution from the governor. Like having the doctor call and tell you there's been a mix-up at the lab and you don't have HIV after all, it's just the flu.

I walked out of that place with my heart still light and flying, still feeling that wonderful openness in my mind, knowing that there was no reason to clamp it shut again.

There was no Bogey Man in my closet after all.

(I know what you're thinking, Maggie. What was it about this one incident that made me so sure I was normal after a lifetime of conspicuous weirdness? I guess it's a thing called hope. There's nothing more persuasive than the sound of what you want to hear.)

Joe and Shara were palpably disappointed, but I was too ecstatic to care that I'd let them down. They'd have to find some other freak show to watch.

Kathleen, on the other hand, seemed every bit as happy as I was. She'd come here out of curiosity, out of a determination to find the truth, and she was thrilled to find that the truth was this simple, that the man she liked (and I don't think I'm fooling myself there) was normal after all. That no spirit was haunting her after all.

Yes, yes, I know, there were a million unanswered questions to spoil our mood of mutual contentment. But we were too damned relieved to think of them just then.

Mrs. Day did her best to bring me back down to earth. This was just a beginning, she said. After a lifetime of blocking myself off, I shouldn't expect the doors to open all at once. Just because you don't hear a ring, that doesn't mean the phone isn't there.

I didn't listen. I figured, yes, well, blah, blah, she has to justify herself, she can't admit there's nothing to all this. So, I thanked her nicely, probably not nicely enough, and said I hoped I'd see her around.

She said I would.

Kathleen and I decided to walk back to Joe's house to get my Mustang. Neither of us wanted be cooped up in a car with Joe and Shara, hearing whatever platitudes and justifications they'd come up with. I wanted to walk through the cold night air, looking at the stars, looking at the moon shadows and knowing for damn well certain they were nothing but shadows.

We walked together, not holding hands, but moving in step, laughing together, weaving in drunken, happy zig-zags, like two people leaving a really wonderful party.

"You know what I think," she said, babbling happily, "I bet I *did* say Jellica's name when you fell off the boat."

"That's the only explanation."

"Let's face it, she's on my mind. I think I'm running away, but you can't really run away from stuff like that."

"I bet you *did* say it."

"And so your niece drew a picture that looked like Jellica's picture? Kids draw pictures all the time."

"They do! And so she has an imaginary playmate? All

kids have imaginary playmates."

"They do!"

She stopped, her smile fading to a look of blissful relief. "God, I was scared. Not for me, but for her. For Jellica."

I took her hand. "I'm sorry."

"Don't be. You showed me I'm not over her. I needed to know that. Thank you."

"Thank you."

I could have kissed her then. She would have welcomed it. In the time it took me to realize it, the moment was gone. We walked on, holding hands, and I told myself the moment would come again.

But you saw that child, a voice said in the back of my newly opened mind. *You didn't just hear her name; you saw that little girl standing on the deck of the boat.* Shut up, I told my mind, that means nothing. I'd just almost drowned, for Christ's sake, my mind wasn't all there. *Your mind wasn't all there, so you saw a hallucination of a child from Kathleen's past?* I don't care if it makes sense. I'm happy, so shut your trap.

Before my mood was totally shattered and all the old tensions started creeping into my muscles, I heard Kathleen say a quiet, "Oh shit."

She was looking up the road. A cop's patrol car was pulled up, slantwise, at the curb, and two people were standing in the front lawn of the Neesons' house.

"Goddamn it, Cheryl, you know you don't want to do that."

I recognized the reedy, ineffectual tones of Deputy Beirko and made his figure out in the glow of the porch lamp. He was keeping a good two yards away from Cheryl Neeson. Cheryl, a muscular woman who ran the duckpin bowling alley with her husband, Jay, was standing astride a big dark, worm-like object on the ground and holding a golf club over her head.

"You are so wrong about that." She swung the club (I don't know golf; I'll call it a nine iron) down onto the worm-thing on the ground between her legs with a dull thud. The worm squirmed and gave out a litany of muffled, indecipherable cries.

"Goddamn it, Cheryl, don't make me pull my gun out on you."

Cheryl brayed. "I'd love to see that! I'd love to see you pull out your gun, Donny Beirko!"

The worm-thing sat up, and I recognized it as a human figure, wrapped burrito-style in a woolen blanket.

"Listen to the man, Cheryl!" the blanket said.

Cheryl swung the club again and the worm-thing hit the ground, moaning.

With clumsy haste, Deputy Beirko unsnapped his holster and yanked out his gun. "Goddamn it, Cheryl, now, I warned you!"

Cheryl stepped forward and swung again (beautiful form, she had) and clipped the black gun right out of Beirko's hand. The policeman scrambled for it on the dark lawn.

"Goddamn it, Cheryl, you are fucking assaulting a fucking officer in the fucking line of fucking duty!"

Kathleen plucked the gun up off the grass. "This what you're looking for, Donny?"

"Whoozat?" asked the blanket.

The golf club swung down again, this time on the blanket's midriff. It 'oof'ed and rolled backward.

"Sweet swing you got there, Cheryl," Kathleen said, very casual.

"Who the hell are you?" Cheryl's tone was challenging, but she stayed behind the blanket, using it as both shield and victim.

I wanted to pull her back, but Kathleen moved forward, holding the gun loosely in her limp hand. "I'm Kathleen

Milland."

"Are you that whore from away?"

Kathleen just laughed. "Don't call somebody a whore when they're holding a gun on you, Cheryl."

The blanket spoke up again. "Does the whole fucking town have to be here for this?"

Once again, Cheryl swung, once, twice, and the blanket dropped and was quiet.

"That's one way to keep a man quiet, Cheryl," Kathleen said.

"The only fucking way with him."

Deputy Beirko tried to regain a place in the conversation. "Gimme my gun, Kate, I'm handling this."

Cheryl brayed again; I'd moved closer myself, and now I could see how drunk she was. "Yeah, you're handling it! You like how he's handling it, Jay?" She nudged the blanket with her foot, and it moaned once.

Now that it was still, I could see the rough stitching on the blanket; someone was sewn up in it, like a caterpillar in a cocoon.

Kathleen didn't give Beirko the gun. "Just a minute, Donny."

Cheryl grinned. "She doesn't trust you, Donny."

"Is that Jay in there?" Kathleen asked. "How you doing, Jay?"

"Not so good," said the man in the blanket.

Cheryl gave him a little shove with her foot—she was gentler when she wasn't using the club. "That one of your *friends*, Jay?" She looked up at Kathleen now, weaving a little as she stood. "You're one of his AA friends, aren't you?"

"We go to meetings," Kathleen said.

"Listen to Miss Prissy! 'We go to meetings.' He spends all his time at those fucking meetings! I wanna know what goes on there. Do all the guys drink beer and play cards and then you start pulling a train, is that what's so fucking

great about it!?" Another club swing down on Jay; another
gasp, softer now and woozier.

Deputy Beirko was furious. "Goddamn it, Cheryl you
are under a-fucking-rrest!"

She leapt over the cocoon and took a vicious swing at
Beirko. He backed off, tripped over a stump and sprawled
on the ground. She turned on Kathleen next, who held the
gun in the open palm of her hand.

"We just talk, Cheryl," Kathleen said. "It's just a bunch
of old drunks sitting around and talking."

She stumbled back to her husband, stepping on him,
accidentally, I think. "I don't feel so good, baby," the
blanket said.

"Why's Jay in the blanket, Cheryl?" Kathleen asked.

"He wouldn't *talk* to me! He come home late, like he
always does nowadays, but I waited up. I wanted to *talk*.
But he wouldn't talk. He wouldn't listen! He's too fucking good for that. He just rolls over and goes to sleep. So,
I folded him up like a fucking pig in a fucking blanket,
which is what he is! And I sewed him up and dragged him
out here, and now he's listening! Aincha listening, Jay!?"
She poked him with the club, but he made no answer.

"He *is* listening," Kathleen said, "so why don't you tell
him? Tell him what you want him to hear."

Cheryl looked at her, slack-jawed and mistrustful.
"What do you care?"

"I'm just saying, you went through all this trouble. Say
what you have to say."

She leaned on the golf club and looked down at her
husband. "You awake, Jay?"

Jay groaned.

Her hair hung lank in her face and her skin started
turning red in the moonlight. "What the fuck's the matter
with you, Jay?!" There was a sob in her voice. "You got no
time for me! It's like all of a sudden you're too fucking good

for me. Too fucking *superior* for fat old Cheryl. Well, fuck that!" She was weeping now, speaking in short, breathless gasps. "You won't even drink with me anymore."

The club dropped from her hand, and in a graceful move Kathleen snatched it before it hit the ground and tossed it off into the darkness.

Cheryl twisted upright, back to her old fury, ready to spring at Kathleen. But Beirko was on her from behind, twisting her arms back.

"Donny, let her go," Kathleen yelled, over Cheryl's mad howls of protest.

In all the noise, I don't know how I heard it; the grotesque strained retching sound from within the blanket.

"Shut up!" I hollered at the top of my lungs. "Shut up, everybody!"

The three of them turned to me, shocked; I don't think Cheryl or Beirko even realized I was there till then.

"I think he's sick."

The coughing, choking sounds from the blanket were loud and clear now. Kathleen was down next to him in a heartbeat. "Get him out of this, he's going to choke on his own puke."

Suddenly, Cheryl was on her knees, tugging at the seams she'd made, trying to pry them loose. "Jesus, Jay! Hold on, Jay!" The sound from the blanket was the liquid gurgling of someone drowning.

Cheryl was keening about how sorry she was, and Kathleen was yelling for a knife, and Deputy Beirko was standing there staring. I sprinted up the porch and into the house, found the kitchen (a wretched pile of dirty dishes and spoiled food), and yanked open drawers until I found a big carving knife.

I flew out the door onto the lawn and skidded over the grass, passing the knife to Kathleen. She split the seam open and Jay Neeson burst out, spewing vomit.

We carried him into the house, Cheryl hanging onto his hand or his arm or his leg or whatever she could grab, sobbing and bleating for forgiveness.

A half hour later she was sitting solemn over a mug of coffee while her husband took the longest shower I ever heard and Beirko and Kathleen argued in the hall.

"Why shouldn't I arrest the bitch? She almost killed him."

"And she knows that, Donny. Give her time to think it over. Do a follow-up in a couple of days."

We hadn't noticed the shower stopping, so we were surprised to see Jay standing next to us, toweling his hair.

"You wanna press charges, Jay?" Beirko asked.

He just shook his head. There was a cartoon lump on his forehead and a bursting black mouse swelling under his right eye. I'd helped him undress so I knew that the damage under his bathrobe was even worse. "Jesus, Donny, I don't want everybody to know about this."

I only knew Jay to say hello to (we'd played together some as kids), but I felt I ought to offer. "You want to stay at my house?"

Again he shook his head, this time looking into the kitchen. "Naw, I don't want to leave her alone."

Cheryl Neeson stared at her coffee, silent, sullen. Once she'd realized her husband wasn't going to die, she'd fallen into a mute funk.

Jay went in and sat with her. We took that as our exit cue. Saying goodnight and thanks for everything didn't seem appropriate, so we just eased our way out.

I was the last one out, so I heard Jay tell Cheryl that if she was so nervous about the AA meetings, maybe she ought to go to one, just to see what it's like.

"No way," she said. "Just 'cause you can't handle your liquor doesn't mean I have to humiliate myself in front of the whole town."

SIXTEEN

The night air was bracing after the warmth of the Neesons' kitchen. Kathleen gave Deputy Beirko back his gun.

"I wouldn't have used this, Kathleen, you know that."

"I know that."

He was silent for a moment. "Thanks."

We walked him to his patrol car.

"Kate," he said, stopping suddenly, "I'm no good at my job."

"You will be, Donny."

"When?"

"When you remember not to let them get you mad."

All this time I'd been feeling superior to Donny Beirko, seeing him as an incompetent boob. But as she said this, I remembered punching out that kid in the bathroom of Washington Irving High and taking a swing at Bubba by the gator pit, and I realized I was the same boob.

Beirko offered us a ride, Kathleen declined, and he gave me a dirty look and drove off. We strolled on a while in silence.

"You handled all that real well. Did you used to be a social worker or something?"

"God, no," she said. "I used to be a cop."

I'd guessed as much, but I tried to look suitably

impressed.

"In New York I'd have had to file a report and make an arrest," she went on. "A place like this, you get to use your own judgment."

"Does that make it easier?"

"Not easier. But I'd rather make my own mistakes than somebody else's."

We picked up my car without calling on Joe and Shara, and I asked Kathleen if she wanted to stop in at the Thorofare for some coffee. As we topped the hill, the house flashed out at us like a firework display. Christmas lights lined the windows, the door frames, the peak and triangle of the roof, the corners, the rafters, the rain spouts, the chimney. Out there in the dark the flickering dime-store lights were blinding, piercing laser beams.

Laughing and singing half-made-up words to "Silver Bells," we tumbled out of the car and dashed into the house, ready to congratulate one and all on their festive display. But inside, the bright house was dark and empty. There was a note on the kitchen table saying that Neil had taken you and your mother over to the mainland to buy more Christmas decorations and you wouldn't be back until morning. I remembered their smiles and winks when Neil and Charlotte came in to find Kathleen in the house. This was their stupid idea, I supposed, to give me some time alone with her. Bless them.

Kathleen and I bundled up around our coffee mugs and sat on the porch, watching the moonlight gleam off the chunks of ice in the channel.

"I've never been here in the winter," I said. "It's so beautiful."

"And too cold for mosquitoes," she said.

"Hallelujah."

She looked over at me from within the two coats and sleeping bag that were piled on top of her. No place on earth had ever looked so cozy as the chair she was sitting in.

"So, I suppose this is when we're supposed to ask each other what our favorite album and favorite movie is," she said, smiling.

"Is it?"

"Isn't that what you do on a first date?"

"Is that what this is?"

"Isn't it?"

"Well," I said, "I wish you'd told me beforehand. I'd'a been a lot more nervous and screwed this up more."

"I'll remember that next time."

"There can't be a next first date."

"Not with you, no."

"If this is a *first* date, does that mean there's going to be a second?"

"Now you're screwing things up."

"Good, I'm making up for lost time."

I laughed. She laughed.

"What was the question again?" I asked.

"Favorite album."

"You first," I said.

"*Kind of Blue*, Miles Davis. My mom loved that record. And you?"

"*Wrecking Ball*, Emmylou Harris. Or Bernard Herrmann's score for *The Ghost and Mrs. Muir*."

"That's two, that's cheating."

"Then *Kind of Blue*."

"Very smooth."

"Thank you."

"I don't know either of your records," she admitted.

"I'll have to play them for you."

"I'd like that."

"Does *that* mean there's going to be a second date?"

She laughed. But didn't answer, I noticed.

"Okay. Movies next," she said. "I know it's corny, but *Sleepless in Seattle.*"

I winced inside, but reminded myself that nobody's perfect. "A lot of people like that movie."

She looked over at me, amused. "Are you trying to be diplomatic?"

"No, I just, I guess I'm a little harder on movies than most people. I'm kind of a movie critic. That's my job. Or it would be if I had a job. I write articles for magazines sometimes."

"Really?" I wished she'd sounded more impressed. "So, what's your favorite, Expert?"

"*The Long Hair of Death.* With Barbara Steele. It's an Italian horror movie from the sixties. You probably never heard of it."

She gave me a longer amused look. "Can't say that I have."

"Well, I'm not surprised."

"And it's better than *Casablanca* or *Gone with the Wind* or *Titanic?*"

"Well, I didn't say better, although it beats that *Titanic* piece of shit. And you said *favorite*, not best. Also, Italian horror movies, they're kind of my field."

"Why?"

"Well, they're underrated, so I kind of champion them. Also, if you're going to write about a genre, you have to pick something kind of obscure, because everything else has been written to death. And these movies are not mainstream. Nobody's heard of them."

She was smiling broadly. "And you like that?"

"Sure."

"'Cause you have them all to yourself?"

"I guess."

"They're like your own private treasures?"

"Exactly." My God, I thought, she understands me. Can

I marry her now?

I looked at her fingers holding her coffee mug. Rugged and calloused; nails blunt and broken. I'd never seen such beautiful fingers in my life. (I'm not one for physical types; I fall in love first and adapt my taste accordingly. So, I've loved skinny women when I loved an anorexic woman and chubby women when I loved a zaftig girl. Right then I was developing a heavy fetish for broken fingernails.)

"Why did you stop being a cop?" I asked her.

She sighed as if she knew the question had been coming. "Well, not because of the drinking. I started that at fifteen, and I was always very good at it. I guess it was the judgment-call stuff I was talking about before. Other people who don't know what they're talking about make bad decisions, and you have to enforce them. I got tired of that."

She wanted to leave it at that, and I suppose I could have let her, but I didn't.

"Did it have to do with Jellica?"

She sighed again. "You know, my dad's a cop, my brother's a cop. It's not like I'm not used to nasty shit. I grew up on it. So, I don't know why this one got to me. I try to figure it out, and I cannot say. I've seen worse, I know I have, but...."

"Her name, actually, was Jessica Delecourt, but she was four years old so she ran it all together into *Jellica*. It was a domestic abuse call. The way it works is, some pain in the ass neighbor decides the crack-whore-mom next door isn't taking care of her kids, so he puts in an anonymous call to Social Services, and they send some scared twenty-year-old psych major, who's had, like, four hours of training, out to the worst hellblock in the Bronx to go teach this mainlining streetwalker proper child-rearing techniques. Or to take her kid away.

"Now, if the social worker has any brains at all, he's pissing his pants just looking at one of these neighborhoods, so he calls for backup. Which in this case was me. I always hated getting calls like that. I wanted to be out catching 'real criminals.' And they deny it, but they always send a woman cop on kiddie cases if they can. They think we're more nurturing or some kind of shit.

"Worst thing about it is, I'm just there for window dressing. To look like a cop in the background while the idiot psych major from Iowa makes all the decisions. And if he decides to take the kid, well, I gotta take the kid. That's a trip—walking a child down ten flights of dark, urine-stinking stairs in a building full of homeboys who'd shoot you for no reason at all. Only now they've got a reason. Best reason in the world. I'm taking their baby out of there, and even if they have been beating her or fucking her or whatever, she's still their kid and what right do I have to take her? You feel that bullet about to go into the back of your head all the way down the stairs."

She set her mug down on the arm of the Adirondack.

"This was a pretty typical deal. A social named George puts in a call, and my partner Dennehy and I meet him in front of this building that no one in his right mind would go into. You know, one of those projects that look like they're made out of one piece of molded concrete; one big soulless block of rock. Busted, boarded-up windows, stairs that look like somebody takes a sledgehammer to 'em every night. You walk in and there are no lights in the hall and things are scurrying away, and you don't know if they're bugs or animals or people or all three.

"This is a Mrs. Delecourt we're going to see. Lives up on the seventh floor. Usual profile from the usual anonymous source. Possible drug use, possible prostitution. Child observed undernourished, filthy. Heard screaming at night. Now nobody's seen her for a week. Fun stuff. But you don't know if it's true. Could be made up. Some prick of an ex -boyfriend trying to get even. I've known that to happen.

"So we make it up the stairs; we knock on the door...."

Kathleen paused and sipped her coffee which must have been as cold as mine. She didn't seem to notice.

"The mother opened the door. She wasn't what I expected. I don't know what the hell she was doing in that building, or how she survived. She was roly-poly and washed out and pasty looking. But more than that, she was...she didn't belong there. She was what they call here 'from away.' You know? Totally out of place. A country girl, for God's sake. She had a Maine accent. I'd never even heard one before, except for that Pepperidge Farm guy on the commercials. She took us in, real friendly. Said everything was fine. Finest kind.

"The place gave me the creeps. Maybe two pieces of furniture and about twenty crosses on the walls and those pictures of Jesus where the eyes follow you. But no sign of any daughter. So, George asks about her, and the mother hems and haws, and George wimps his way around her, and, finally, I just started opening doors...."

Another sip of cold coffee.

"The girl was in the bedroom. It was black, painted all black, even the floor, even the windows. The only thing in it was a playpen, turned upside down with a big cinder block on top to hold it in place. Jellica was inside. I turned on the light, and she had to cover her eyes—she'd been in the dark a long time. Mrs. Delecourt burst right in, just laughing. I asked about the windows; she said the windows were black because it was so ugly outside. I asked her why her daughter was in a cage; she said Jellica liked to pretend it was her fort. I said that didn't explain all the shit and piss on the floor."

She turned to me. "Is this too heavy for you?"

It was. I told her to go on.

"I asked if there was a father on the scene. Jellica said her daddy was in the 'fort' with her. Her mom told her shut her mouth, then laughed, like that could somehow be a joke. She said her husband had died a few months ago. He was a martyr, she said, to his beliefs. Whatever that means."

"Well, Social Services George was getting ticked because I was talking too much, so he tried to take over the interview while I got Jellica out of her 'fort.' Mom started getting more and more irrational, especially once she realized we could take the kid away.

"She started telling us that we didn't understand the situation. Jellica wasn't an ordinary child. There was something wrong with her. Something in her soul. Demons came and talked with her. And walked with her. Satan was trying to make a home in her, and it was up to her mother to keep him out. Real, full-blown psycho stuff, I'm talking, you could see it in her eyes.

"But old psych major George, he's talking to her, wussy as ever, trying to reason with her, trying to remind her about hygiene and proper nutrition when this lady is ready to burn her daughter at the stake and tell her it's for her own good.

"So, I finally pulled George aside and...*persuaded* him to get the kid the fuck out of there and ask questions later. Which wasn't my place, I know, but that woman was dangerous, I could feel it. If we left the child with her she was going to make her suffer, I knew it.

"So, we removed Jellica. Her mother screamed curses at us all the way down to the street. And I don't mean bad words, I mean real curses, like calling the Angel of Death down to take our loved ones and strike us with cancer and blindness and God knows what all. I've never been so scared in my life."

The moon was setting behind Brown's Head Island, leaving us in darkness.

"Dennehy, my partner, he drove us back. George sat

in the front and kept whining about whether we'd done the right thing. Whether there had been a 'compelling reason' to take the kid. And I sat in the back and talked with Jellica."

Kathleen smiled. "I was making fun of that nurturing bullshit before, but I guess I had it in me after all, 'cause I kind of fell for her. I don't know why. She was just a regular kid. Maybe that was part of it. Coming from that environment, I couldn't believe how normal she was. Good-natured. Happy, if you can believe that. I mean it; once we got her out of there, she just brightened. Kept saying she wanted to play. How it had been a long time since anybody played with her. So, I played with her. You know, finger games—'Here's the church, here's the steeple, open the door, see all the people.' She loved that. She laughed and laughed.

"And I thought, 'She's okay. She's young, she's strong, she's going to be all right. As long as we keep her away from that fucking maniac of a mother of hers.'"

She tried to take a sip but the mug was empty.

"But when the doctors checked her out...there was no evidence of abuse. No marks, no bruises. No obvious malnutrition. No 'compelling reason.'

"By then Jellica had gotten to me. I mean, I'd talked to her. Without saying anything bad about her mother exactly, she'd told me what she'd been living through. How the 'scary people' came and visited her at bedtime. How they talked to her and touched her. How they sat on top of her and made it so she couldn't breathe. How they took her by the hand and led her places.... How if someone would just come in and be with her, even just yell her name, then the scary people would go away. But no one ever did.

"She tried to tell her mother about it, and her mother screamed at her and spanked her and locked her in her room. Kept her in the dark, and the scary people came, and Jellica had to tell them to stay away herself. She told her it was her own fault the scary people came to her. Because she was bad and she'd invited them in. But Jellica said she hadn't; they just came on in anyway. They kept coming. She screamed and screamed, but her mother just left her there, alone. When she cried, when she tried to get out, her mother put her in the cage. Told her she couldn't run away from it because they'd follow her everywhere because she was bad and they liked that she was bad.

"I dug up some crayons and paper and she drew while she talked. She drew that picture, the one I thought looked like the one your niece drew. I cried when I saw it. It didn't look like the sort of the thing a kid like her should be imagining.

"I didn't understand half of what she was saying, of course. I'm no psych major. I wasn't sure if the scary people were real people or if they were just bad dreams. But you know what? I didn't care. All I cared about was that she was scared to death of her own mother. And she was right to be; I'd seen the look in that woman's eyes. I knew if she went back there, this kid was going to end up dead or crazy. I wasn't going to let that happen.

"So Dennehy and I, we got together with George and did some more persuading. We decided to juice up the report a little. George was reluctant, but in the end he agreed that, uh, 'a purely objective summary of the facts didn't do justice to subjective experience of the child's home life' or some such shit. Fine; whatever it takes. Whatever would keep her out of that apartment.

"Of course, this was wrong. Unethical. A gross violation of policy. An abuse of power." She smiled, "You know, a judgment call.

"Jellica got sent to a foster home, temporarily. She lucked out there. She got a good one; nice people. I went to visit her a few times, which was also against policy, but I'd already crossed the line with her, so I didn't care.

"The lady taking care of her, she said Jellica still had bad dreams. Night terrors. Real screamers. I tucked her in one time, and I'm telling you, she wanted *all* the lights on. She never wanted to be in the dark again. She said there were 'people in the dark.' But if you held her, if you talked to her, if you sang to her, if you just cared about her and showed it, she was okay. She was going to be all right.

"I told her everything would work out. She wasn't ever going to have to go back to that room. I was going to make sure of that. I don't think she even believed me; she wasn't stupid. She just asked if I'd play with her, and I said I always would."

There was a tenderness in Kathleen's voice; I could hear her trying to hide it.

"I guess maybe it would have worked out if I'd left it at that, but then I did something really stupid. I decided I had to adopt her. I know, I know, but I didn't want to see her shuttled from foster home to foster home. She deserved better. And I guess I loved her by then, and love makes you do stupid things.

"Of course, her mother contested it. Took it to court. You should have seen her in that courtroom. The most decent, respectable country girl you've ever seen. Just an innocent hick who'd made the mistake of moving to the big city and had done the best she could. No talk about Satan or demons. Just how much she loved and missed her little girl. And how she'd maybe been a little overprotective after her husband passed away, but she'd learned her lesson. She was going to take her girl back to Maine and give her the home life she deserved.

"And me? Well, I was a drunk-power-mad-cop-child-abductor. Using the power of the State to break up a home and steal myself a daughter. They got George up on the stand and, of course, he cracked. Picture of guilt, telling everybody how I'd coerced him into falsifying reports. Even Dennehy, my partner, they got him by the balls and he caved. I was fucked after that. The painted windows, the little girl sleeping in her own shit, none of that mattered because I'd lied on a fucking official document. I was lucky just to lose the case, just to lose my job. I was lucky they didn't send me to jail.

"They took her away. Gave her back to her mother. I didn't even get to say good-bye. Not that I wanted to. What the hell could I have said to the kid? 'Sorry. I tried. Make the best of it....'"

She chewed on one of those broken nails for a moment.

"I started my serious drinking then. Of course, I tried to find her, but her mom left town, and the court sealed the records. I finally talked my brother into taking a look at them, and he brought me the mother's home address. Some hick town in the middle of buttfuck Maine. She'd gone there after the trial. I went up there—just missed them, actually. I tracked them all over New England, always missing them. Then the trail went cold. I felt pretty useless. I wasn't even a good enough cop to keep up with an inbred yokel.

"I locked myself in an Econo Lodge and tried to drink myself to death, tried not to think about what every day of Jellica's miserable life must be like. But drinking yourself to death, that isn't as easy as it sounds. One day I got in my car and just drove. No highways, no route, no plan. When I reached a corner I'd turn or I wouldn't; it didn't matter, so long as I kept moving. Ended up in Rockland, saw the ferry, took it, ended up here. Here, I couldn't go any further. Not unless I drove into the ocean. So, I stayed. And here I am."

She turned to me with a sad smile. "Aren't you sorry you asked?"

"No. No. That's a terrible story, Kathleen, but you know

it's not your fault, don't you?"

"Sure, it is. If I'd been smarter I'd have found a way to get her out of there. But I was just like Donny Beirko; I let them get me mad. And I guess she died because of that."

She shifted toward me in her chair. "So, you see why the idea of her haunting me...it would just be too much, wouldn't it? The thought of her hanging around, forever, reproaching me. Wondering why I'm not playing with her. I couldn't live with that."

"Jesus, Kathleen. Why have you been taking all this on alone? Where's your family?"

"Well, they were sympathetic and all at first, but after a while I think they thought I was over-reacting. Big sin in my family."

I got up and moved over to her. "You ought to give them another chance. You should see them. Patch things up. Don't put it off. Things can happen. I know. You should do it now. I mean, it's Christmas, after all."

She laughed a little and touched my face. "Yeah, it's Christmas. You're a sweet guy, you know that?"

I think I blushed.

"Okay, your turn," she said.

"For what?" I asked, sitting on the broad arm of her chair.

"Tell me your saddest story."

I brushed the hair from her face. "I already have."

"Okay, tell me your second saddest."

I breathed a laugh. "I don't want to."

"Come on, you can't leave me out on my own like this. I told you mine, now you tell me yours."

"I guess that would be fair."

"Right."

I sat up straight, inhaling the night air.

"Okay, I used to think I could see ghosts. Then one day, I couldn't anymore."

"That's it?"

"Back when I used to think I could see them...well, most of the time I used to fight it and sometimes maybe I'd play with the idea to try to impress people. But I never really *tried* to see them. I never tried to make it happen, you know? So, I never saw one when I wanted to.... *That's* it."

She nodded quietly. "When did you want to?"

"After the accident, after my...family died, when they were all on display there at the funeral home. God, that was a bad idea. I don't know how we let Walter talk us into that. Walter was the funeral director. He talked us into a lot of things. So, they were all laid out there, and the cousins and uncles were there staring at them. We didn't like the cousins and the uncles. Mom and Dad hadn't liked the cousins and the uncles. George hadn't liked them. But, you know, it's a funeral, so people have to come. Other than them, it was just me and Charlotte. Just me and Charlotte.

"So, I shut my eyes and said, 'All right. This is it. This is why God gave me this stupid, pain-in-the-ass gift. For this moment. So I can see them again. So I can joke with them and laugh with them. And say good-bye. Or, fuck that, fuck saying good-bye. So I can keep them with me forever.'

"So I tried. And I tried. I went up and looked at their faces. I called out for them in my mind. I slipped off into an empty—what do you call them— 'show room' and meditated and concentrated and prayed...and nothing happened. Nobody came to me. Not George. Not Dad. Not even Mom. Nothing. I was all alone. Charlotte found me a couple of hours later, crying. But she didn't know why I was crying, not really. She didn't know how foolish I was.

"Maybe Mom had been right. Maybe the whole medium thing *had* just been a way of getting attention. Maybe that's why I never believed in it myself. But that one time I did believe.... And that's my saddest story."

She took my hand. "It's pretty sad."

"Not as sad as yours. I didn't want to top you," I laughed. "Oh, and also, the funeral director knocked up Charlotte. But she had Maggie, so that part's not really sad."

She laughed. "And you never saw any—what is it you call them—spooks again? Not until you were on the boat with me?"

"No, that's not exactly right. I saw one just before I left DC. To be honest, I think that's why I came here. Running away from it. And there was one on the road, too. Maybe they were leading me here. But if they brought me to meet you, I guess they're not all bad."

She leaned her face toward me. I leaned toward her. I couldn't tell you who was leading; it was like the Ouija board; we moved as one. We kissed. A sweet kiss, filled with friendship and sympathy and tenderness. Not at all like a first kiss. Like we'd been kissing for a long time and had decided we liked it.

She smiled then, not sadly, but broadly, her teeth gleaming in the starlight. "You know how long it's been since I kissed anybody?" she asked.

"No."

"Neither do I," she said. We kissed again.

SEVENTEEN

Fade out on the kiss.

Fade in on the tender aftermath; both of us fully clothed, but tastefully mussed. Her body stretched out on the bed; me sitting by her side, my feet on the floor.

That's the Old Hollywood way of telling the story, and I'm still enough your uncle to want to leave it at that.

No worries, no depression, no demons came rushing in on me in the aftermath. We drifted off to sleep together. Innocent. Baptized. The single most perfect moment of my life.

Then the nightmare came.

There are all kinds of nightmares, of course. There are the surreal ones that terrify you even as you know they are illusions; all you can do with those is wait to wake up. Then there are the dreadfully real ones where you have no idea you're dreaming; when you wake up from those, you're still terrified until the slow, happy understanding comes that it was all a dream. Then there are the nightmares that come when you are already awake. There's no escape from those at all.

I was nestled against the white slope of Kathleen's throat, breathing in the scent of her hair. I didn't know the time or how long I'd been sleeping. I didn't care. Didn't care if morning ever came, just so long as I could keep breathing her in, listening to the drumbeat of her heart.

I felt the fear before I heard the sounds. A rapid, inexplicable quickening of my pulse and a tightening of my gut. There was a crash from down the hall, the sound of laughter and the tramping of feet. I jumped from the bed, and only then did I notice that it wasn't my bed. Or rather, it was my bed *and* it was another bed. An old bed made of wooden slats and covered with a down comforter. A bed that I'd made with my own two hands although I'd never seen it before.

Oh, I can't explain what I saw. Or rather, I can explain *what* I saw, but not the way I saw it. It was as if I was seeing two worlds at the same time. Before me there were two beds occupying the same space. One was mine with beautiful Kathleen slumbering in it. But the other was mine as well. I could see both beds completely as if I had two sets of eyes to see with and two minds to receive their images.

The moon gleamed off Kathleen's ivory skin in Sam Kehoe's bed. And in that other bed, with her—or next to her—or top of her—or simultaneous with her—were two other figures. Two girls. A baby and a blond girl of your age, Maggie.

The noise from the hall was getting louder. Raucous, mocking, full of masculine threat. Crashing. Breaking. The sounds were familiar even though I'd never heard them before. I could feel the fear they brought with them. I could sense the danger even though I had no *information* about what I was hearing.

I turned back to the children. The older girl's eyes flew open wide and she spoke to me. "Mother?" she said.

I gathered my children from the bed without disturbing Kathleen in her other world. Cradling the baby in my arms, I moved to the trapdoor I somehow knew I would find in the floor by the corner. We would hide in the cellar, I thought, like we did the last time. Everything would be fine.

I felt around on the floor with growing alarm. Where was the handle? Where was the latch? It seemed impossible but the trapdoor was gone.

"Sweet Jesus, don't desert us," I whispered. The sounds in the house were louder. Footsteps pounded down the hall.

I moved to the window and slid it open. *Should I wake Kathleen and take her with us?* I wondered. There wasn't time. I pushed Mary out into the grass and, clutching the baby to my breast, I climbed out. As I dropped to the ground my head jerked back with a wrenching jolt, and I thought one of the men had reached out and caught me by the hair. But it was only an old loose nail on the windowsill. Mary reached back and tore my hair free. Sweet girl. We lay on the wet grass together, out of breath, the baby just starting to whimper. *Dear God*, I thought, *don't let her start crying*.

If we could make it to the woods, then we could hide, then we'd be safe. But as I looked around, I felt my heart sink in my chest; there were no woods. Where there had been a forest of pine yesterday, there was only open pasture. It was impossible, but it was true. I gathered my babies to me, and we crept around the walls of my house, keeping in the shadows, trying to block out the sounds of laughter and destruction, of the crashing and tearing and breaking of things I held dear but couldn't name.

We found the cellar door and I slowly lifted it, letting Mary squeeze her way in first. She used all her child's strength to hold it open for me as I rolled in, baby under my arm, and dropped down the stone steps. We slunk into the corner, hiding in the wet dark earth like animals in a den.

They were above us now. Feet tramping bare inches from our heads. Light flared through the wide chinks in the floorboards, streaming down on us. Light from a lamp.

From many lamps. There was the sound of breaking glass, and now the light was brighter, bright as daylight and bringing with it a withering heat and the rending sound of flames.

The doors of the house flew open, and the men streamed outside. I was filled with a blind hatred for them as I watched their legs dancing past the chink in the cellar door, and I asked myself for the hundredth time how my husband could ever have joined his fortune with men like that.

The sorrow, the anger, the pain filled me up with an unbearable pressure. The baby squirmed in my arms, and Mary looked at me with panic all over her pink face. Keep them safe. I had to keep them safe. The baby whimpered again; then the first full-lunged cry escaped from her dry, cracked lips, and I was filled with blind terror. Fear like I'd never experienced in my life paralyzed me. The baby cried on—a piercing, seabird's scream. So loud. Louder than the drunken laughter of the men. Louder than the flames in the burning house over my head.

I tried to hush the child, to cradle her, to quiet her. I whispered her favorite lullaby into her tiny ear, the old Irish words drowned out by the fire and the laughter and the howling. *"Shoolah roon..."* I covered her purple face with my hand and prayed for deliverance.

Then the fear grew too big for my body and left me. It spread out from me and filled the dark cellar. It sank into the earth floor like rainwater and was gone.

I was myself again, huddled into a ball on the cellar floor, struggling for breath. There was no fear, no child, no baby, no men laughing cruelly outside.

But I was not alone. She sat across from me in the dirt.

So young, it surprised me. Younger than me. Twenty or so at most, though her face was worn with care. Her long auburn hair was stuck to her face with tears, but she smiled at me with pure love. The most beautiful face I've ever seen. It almost made me weep just to look at her.

"Who are you?" I asked.

"Don't you know?" Her voice was a soft Irish whisper, and when I heard it, I did weep. Because, of course I knew her. I'd known her all my life. She was the spirit of this house. The one who'd protected me and made me feel safe all these years. The one Mrs. Day had tried to help me reach; the one she'd called my friend. The Good Mother. I wasn't used to crying; I gasped, sucking in the dank air.

"How come I can see you?" I asked, finally.

She smiled again. "You always could."

I shook my head.

She leaned toward me—she was totally there, totally real. As if she were a real part of my world. Or I was a part of hers. "Who else d'you see? Do you see my babbies?"

I heard the yearning in her voice and wanted so much to help her. I looked around. "I'm sorry."

"Do you know where they are?"

"I'm sorry, I don't. What happened to them?"

Weary sorrow disfigured her beautiful face. "I don't remember. They've been alone for a long time now."

I reached out and took her hand. I could do that. I could feel the warmth of her touch rush up my arm. "I'm sorry," I said. I looked over her shoulder, into the darkness of the far corner. "I do see a child," I said, "but she isn't yours."

The woman turned and looked back at Jellica, who was staring sullenly at us.

"Ah, that one," she said. "She's a lost one, Sammy. Watch out for her."

"What do you mean?"

"She don't mean to be bad. No one ever taught her any better."

I felt her start to slip away and tried to hold her hand as it slipped from my world. "Don't go."

"I won't. I can't."

"I love you," I said.

She reached out to touch my cheek, but by then I couldn't feel her flesh anymore. "I love you," she said, and was gone. I cried again, watching them both fade away. Big, lung-bursting sobs. Weeping out every sorrow I'd ever felt and all the sorrows of all the spooks who'd tried to reach me and had been ignored. I wept for my own silly life, which I felt fall to pieces around me. I wept till there wasn't a drop of water in me or a breath of air.

I heard a sound and opened my eyes, panting like a sick dog. The morning light was streaming down on me, and Kathleen was standing on the cellar stairs, looking down at me with a slack-jawed expression, as if I were a totally gibbering madman. Which was a pretty apt description of my appearance, curled up in the dark corner of the cellar, face muddy with dirt and tears.

I didn't want her to see me like this, let me tell you. Of all the pathetic-freak moments of my life, this seemed the purest, the most sideshow of all. A few hours ago I'd been congratulating myself on being normal and here I was, a freak on display.

I couldn't think of a word to say to her. I'd been a man for her just hours ago; someone she could touch and hold, someone who could bring her joy and pleasure. Now what was I? I couldn't stand the thought of her pity; the thought of her kneeling next to me, holding my shivering body and asking what was wrong. It would be too humiliating. Better for her to leave. Better for her to turn tail and run.

Before I could gesture for her to stay away, she was taking the stairs two at a time, running for daylight.

EIGHTEEN

I didn't go after her. I should have, of course. I wanted to, but I couldn't move, couldn't even raise my head enough to watch her disappear over the top step. I just lay there in the dirt, not asleep, not awake, but in some in-between place until I found the energy to reach up to the rafters and pull myself to my feet. To stumble, hunched over and twisted, out of the cellar and onto the cool grass of the lawn.

I blundered into the house and two or three cups of coffee later I was blinking at the rude light of the sun as it reared over the lobster pound. I picked up the phone.

Kathleen answered on the first ring.

"I can't," she said.

"I haven't said anything."

"Whatever it is you called to say, whatever it is you want to ask, I can't."

"Kathleen—"

"I know you're a wonderful person in a lot of ways but... I'm just not equipped to handle...someone with emotional problems right now. I'm sorry. I know that makes me a terrible person, but there it is. I'm just not strong enough. Bye."

Click. Gone. No room to maneuver. Me sitting there listening to a dial tone. How many times had that happened?

Yellow light filled the kitchen as I looked around, seeing it with new eyes. She was here, I knew. The Good Mother. She was always here; had always been here. Comforting me. Let her comfort me now, I thought. Let her show herself and tell me what to do.

Of course, she didn't show herself. Of course, I felt no reassurance.

I looked at the clock. Almost 6:30. Mrs. Day would just be getting up, I thought. Without conscious thought, I knew she was the only one who could offer me any help.

I took the time to make myself a scrambled egg for breakfast, somehow sensing that I was going to need my strength for what lay ahead. Seven-thirty was as long as I could make myself wait. I grabbed a coat and headed out the door just as Neil's truck pulled up and you and your mother bounded out, all laughter and sleepy smiles.

"We stayed in a motel with room service!" you cried, a four-year-old convert to the high life.

Charlotte took my arm with a conspiratorial grin. "How did things go?"

"You mean before or after I scared the hell out of her and made her think I was a total lunatic?"

"Before."

"Before that it was great. I think I'm in love."

I socked Neil one in the arm for good luck, climbed into my Mustang, and pulled away, leaving you all staring at me.

Mrs. Day was putting her older kid on the school bus when I drove up. I let the bus pull away before I pulled up to the curb.

She finished waving good-bye before she glanced down through my window. "The little ones are with my sister, so we have some time. I'm thinking you need some pie," she said.

❋

"Why me?"

"Why not you?"

"I didn't ask for this."

"Maybe you did."

Mrs. Day sat back, the smell of flour and buttered toast surrounding her like the perfect perfume. "I'm going to throw a lot of ideas at you. If you don't believe any of them, that's okay. What's true for me might not be true for you. Okay?"

I thought about that. "Is this going to be, like, cosmology, meaning of life, nature of the universe stuff?"

She smiled. "Yeah, that stuff."

"Then, no, it's not okay. I mean, something like that, you can't just shop around for it. You can't just pick and choose. My universal truth can't be different from your universal truth."

"Why not?"

"Because my universe can't be different from your universe."

"Why not?"

"Because there can't be more than one universe."

"Why not?"

"Well, fine, you can just say 'why not' to everything like that means something, like that's profound, but it doesn't answer the question. I mean, last time I was here you were the one who was talking about only believing in what you can see. Now you're getting all vague and fuzzy on me."

She dropped her wise smile, and I think she took my objections seriously for the first time. "Oh, I never want to be that. Before I was talking about what you can see, but now I'm talking about what it means, and that's a lot harder to pin down." She thought for a moment. "All right, maybe there is only one truth, if that's what you want to call it. But there are many paths to that truth. And your path might be different from mine. Does that way of putting it suit you better?"

I thought it over. "I don't know. I was brought up agnostic, you know? To believe all Ways lead to folly."

She nodded. "I'm just saying this is a system of life that works for me. And it might help you. Do you want me to go on?"

"Sure. Shoot."

"I believe our souls experience many lifetimes in many different bodies."

"Okay."

"What does that mean?"

"It means I believe you believe that. Go on."

She smiled again, letting me know I hadn't offended her. "I believe this soul never stops growing, never stops learning. It never stops striving for perfection."

"And when it succeeds?"

"I don't think it ever does."

"That I do believe."

"I don't mean that cynically. Growth is a constant state. It's what being is all about."

"Okay."

"Now, every time we come into a new life it's in order to learn. To grow in some new way. That's the purpose of life."

"Oh, is *that* it?"

"This seems funny to you?"

"I don't know, it's just that people have been looking for the meaning of life forever, and I think it's a little funny for me to find it in a kitchen in Fox Island."

"Where else? And I said *purpose*, not meaning."

"You did. Go on."

"Now, in order to learn what we need to learn, each life presents us with certain tasks, certain obstacles, certain ordeals. That's why we are the way we are. That's why what happens to us happens to us."

"So, it's all laid out in advance?"

"Not at all. A path is open to us, but we don't have to take it. We may go off another way altogether."

"But then we don't learn what we're supposed to learn?"

"Maybe not. Then we just try again in another lifetime."

"Sounds easy."

"If you let it be. Usually, it's anything but."

"So, according to this theory, it's a part of my life's plan to see spooks?"

"Spooks. I like that. It's so much friendlier than ghosts." She smiled as if we were discussing kittens. "You want to know why you can see spirits when other people can't— is that what you're asking?"

"That's what I'm asking, yeah."

"I believe that before we come into a new incarnation, we agree to take on certain things. Some of these are burdens. Some of these are talents. Some of them are both. Either way, we take them on to help us accomplish what we need to in this life."

"And I agreed to be a medium?"

"That's what I believe."

"Why would I be such a schmuck as to agree to that?"

She chuckled. "I don't know if it makes you a smuck," she couldn't quite pronounce the word; not a lot of Yiddish slang was used in Maine. "Can I speak from my own experience?"

"Please do."

"I have some awareness of my previous incarnations."

"I'm sure you do."

"Because I'm a crackpot?"

"I didn't say that. Were you, uh, Cleopatra? Queen Elizabeth? Empress Josephine? Why is it no one was ever a nobody in their past life?"

"I was. Just peasants and poor people. No one who mattered much. Not in the way you mean, anyway. One of them was a boy who died in the Civil War. I was running away during the Battle of the Wilderness and got shot in the back. I felt so guilty, so bad about dying that way, I couldn't let go of my life. I became trapped between worlds. That's what a ghost is. Someone so caught up in the unfinished business of life that they can't cross over. They cling desperately to all the same hates, all the same worries. The same patterns and prejudices."

I thought of Mr. Meloni and his 'pick 'em up, faggot' and felt a new sense of sympathy for the guy.

"Of course, you can't grow in that state," she went on. "You can't learn. You're stuck, which is the worst thing that can happen to anyone. It's like being in that horrible place at the end of a bad dream when you can't move, can't scream, can't make yourself wake up. And it's like being there forever."

The pain in her expression was so real, I couldn't help but feel she was speaking from personal experience, and I didn't even notice that I was believing her.

"How did you get out of it?" I asked.

"Someone helped me. Someone like me. Someone like you. A medium listened to my pain and helped me pass to the other side. So, when I came to this life, I agreed to help other...spooks. It's a part of my path. I'm here to be of service."

"And that's why I'm here, too?"

"I wouldn't presume to say. But *one* of the reasons you're here must be to help those poor lost ones."

Lost ones. I thought of Jellica.

"So, what do I do? How do I help them cross over? Buy a Junior Exorcist Kit?"

"No," she didn't even laugh. "You work through what they're working through. That's why you can feel what they're feeling. If you let it in, if you allow yourself to know whatever is trapping them, if you face that and take it into your heart, then they can do the same. And once you face something, you understand it. And then you can let it go."

"I have to say, on the one hand this kind of makes sense, but on the other hand it sounds like the biggest load of bullshit I've ever heard."

"Of course. Because it's absurd. It's the meaning of life in a kitchen on Fox Island. Take it or leave it." Her smile was open and full of love. It made my heart weak.

"I'm sorry, I just can't believe this," I said.

"I know you can't. I think not believing is one of the main things you have to work through in this life." She took my hand. "You've been in turmoil for a long time, haven't you?"

I rolled my eyes. "I wouldn't say turmoil."

"Wouldn't you?"

"Okay."

"Okay, what?"

"Turmoil, okay."

"Because you've been trying to be something you're not. Or worse, you're trying not to be something you are. You've been on the wrong path, and it's led you nowhere. When that happens, sometimes, if you're lucky, your path reaches out to you. It sends you a jolt, a shock, to wake you up, to bring you back in line. That's what's been happening to you now. You can ignore it if you want; you can just go on the way you're going. But if you do, all this will just happen again. And it'll keep happening until you listen."

"To what?"

"To yourself."

Fair enough. I tried to listen to the voices in my head. Problem was, as always, there was more than one voice. The first one believed everything she said and felt a wild sense of exhilaration at having my whole life explained. The other voice said it was all wish-fulfill-ment and cheap New Age claptrap. How was I to know which voice spoke for my true self? I decided to bring this down to specifics.

"All right, Mrs. Day, let's just say this is true. Let's just say I have this power and I'm supposed to put these spirits to rest. What do I do about it? I can only see them when I'm sick or heartbroken. "

"They come to you at those times because that's when you're most distracted; that's when your defenses are down. But that's not an issue now. Your defenses are gone."

"That's a scary thought."

She touched my face gently. "Don't worry. You're equipped to handle this."

I felt a rush of adrenaline, a powerful sense of elation and happiness. I think they call it an epiphany; a sense that the truth was right there waiting to be grasped. Well, can you blame me? If you're a wanderer like me (and I hope that's one way, at least, we are not alike), if you've felt lost and without direction most of your life, to hear someone say in calm gentle tones 'this is who you were meant to be' is a powerful thing. Almost like a dream or a drug. Like winning the lottery. One feels for a frightened heartbeat that this could be it—the answer, the end to the anxiety, the key to peace of mind.

But, of course, the feeling was gone as soon as I felt it, replaced by my usual state of disappointment and distrust. How could it be so easy as this? How could it be in front of me for the taking?

Still, Mrs. Day was a kind, lovely person, and I didn't want to disappoint her. I came to my feet, ready to at least go through the motions. "All right, I guess I'll give it a try."

She gave me a quizzical look, and I realized she was one of those annoying women you couldn't get anything by. "What are you afraid will happen if you allow yourself to hope, Sam?"

It stumped me. I hadn't thought of it quite that way, which I suppose was why she'd asked it that way. "I guess I'm afraid I'll be disappointed."

"So, what's new in that?"

It made me laugh, though I'm not sure she meant it as a joke. It relaxed me enough to carry me with her out to the barn and to wonder as I walked if keeping hope out of my life was really such a sound strategy.

In the winter daylight, with the bleak sun making diagonal slashes of swirling dust around us, the museum looked far more haunted than it had the night before.

"How many spooks do you see here?" I asked Emily.

"None. I've cleared them all."

"Then what am I supposed to see here?"

"Oh, I've cleared *my* spooks. I don't know about yours."

"I have my own?"

"Of course. You see, in my experience, spirits don't haunt places. They haunt people. They attach themselves to people with similar weaknesses to their own. As if they believe, by connecting themselves to you, they can continue to live. By latching on to your weakness, maybe they can learn the lesson they meant to learn in their own lives.

"The danger to you is, they can also end up amplifying your weaknesses. If a spook attaches itself to, say, a quality of indecisiveness about you, if it clings to it stubbornly, then you end up even more indecisive. Indecisive for two, as it were. Have you ever sensed anything like that?"

I laughed, and the sound startled something scrabbling in some dry papers off in the corner—a shivery sound in a cold room.

"I should ask Maggie how she does it. Does this thing run in families?"

"It can."

"Well, it must have skipped a few generations before me and Maggie, that's all I can say."

"Why's that?"

"The Kehoes are a very rational family. On both sides. No Salem witches in the family tree."

"Are you sure?"

"Absolutely. My mother would never have allowed it."

Mrs. Day sat down in an old bent willow chair that looked like some thorny torture device. "Tell me about your first ghost, Sam."

So, I settled onto an old, monstrously uncomfortable horsehair sofa and started to tell her the story of Mr. Meloni and the Dodge Ball game.

"No, your *first*," she said.

"That's it. That's the first one I remember."

"Maybe that's just the first one you've *chosen* to remember."

I hate it when people presume to tell me things about myself that I know perfectly well aren't true. "Same difference."

"There wasn't an incident when you were very young? When you were Maggie's age?"

"Ask me all you want, the answer's not going to change."

"You said you used to have night terrors. That your mother used to open the door and show you there was nothing there. Was there nothing there?"

"Absolutely. I was just a kid afraid of the dark."

"But what was in the closet *before* your mother opened the door?"

"I don't know. Whatever all kids have in their closets, you know? Monsters. The Bogey Man."

"What does the Bogey Man look like?"

"I don't know. He's big with a scratchy beard and a red face and a big weird laugh."

"Sounds like Santa Claus."

"Well, Santa Claus is scary enough, isn't he?"

"Is he?"

"Man, I wish you'd stop that."

"Why is that?"

"All right, okay, when I was a kid I was afraid of Santa Claus, okay? It just struck me as very troubling, this fat old man breaking into my house and sneaking around at night. And my family were all terrible liars, too, so when they told me the story, I knew they were holding something out on me. This St. Nick character was not all he was cracked up to be. Maybe that's why I liked ghost stories at Christmas; they weren't nearly as scary as that damned jolly old elf.

"Also, when I was really little, my weird Uncle Willie used to dress up as Santa and just creep all us kids out. He was this smelly, fat old drunk, and my mother *hated* him."

"Was he her brother or your father's?"

"Hers. That's the only reason she put up with him. God, he used to *stink* of this awful mix of, I don't know, whiskey and male sweat and whatever *chemical* he kept that moth-eaten red suit packed up in the rest of the year. He'd grab us kids and throw us around—why do grownups think kids like being manhandled like that?—and hold us in his lap a little *too* long, if you know what I mean? I used to just bolt out of the room as soon as he let me go, and I'd hide down in the rec room behind the heater. I mean, I didn't know what was wrong with this guy, but I knew something was wrong with him."

"And when did your mother tell him to stop coming?"

"She didn't."

"But you said he only came when you were really little."

"Well, he died. When I was about four. I'm surprised I even remember him."

"Did he die before the Bogey Man started showing up?"

I gave her a look. "So, you're saying that was Uncle

Willie in the closet?"

"I don't know. I just want to know what you saw when your mother opened the door. I want to know what *she* saw."

I don't have revelations very often. It's not every day I get that feeling of revealed truth knocking my feet out from under me and sending me pratfalling to the floor. I felt it then. An obvious, simple thought that rang through my head and echoed back through all the years of my life.

She saw him. She saw the Bogey Man.

I sat up in bed, hollering in stupid fear at what I knew was behind that door, and my mother stormed in, snapped on the light, wrenched open the door, and *he was there*. She saw him. And she stared him down. Stared into his wandering, rheumy eyes until they blinked and turned away, until his big shape cowed and shrank. Then she turned to me and said, "See, there's nothing there."

And Uncle Willie just faded away into nothing.

So, I nodded to my mother, the woman who'd vanquished the Bogey Man while telling me he didn't exist. You had to believe in a woman who could do that.

And she came to me and sat on the edge of my bed and told me that things like this didn't happen and the sooner I learned that the better. That seeing Bogey Men and monsters was stupid and silly and childish, and if I didn't chase them off now they'd follow me everywhere. And the key to chasing them off was so simple, so simple. "Don't believe in them. They can't fight back if you don't even see them. They don't have the power to fight that."

I nodded again, half-scared, half-comforted, half-humiliated (I know, Maggie, there can't be three halves of anything—that's just an indication of how screwed up this left me). When she saw how frightened I still was, my mother gathered me up into her arms and told me her favorite bedtime story, because she wasn't a cold person, or an unloving person. I never want you to think that. She told me that old

Ogden Nash poem that always made me laugh.

"Isabel met an enormous bear.

Isabel, Isabel didn't care;

The bear was hungry, the bear was ravenous.

The bear's big mouth was cruel and cavernous.

The bear said, 'Isabel, glad to meet you.

How do, Isabel, now I'll eat you!'

Isabel, Isabel didn't worry.

Isabel didn't scream or scurry.

She washed her hands and straightened her hair up,

Then Isabel quietly ate the bear up."

The barn was cold. A spring from that cruel old horsehair sofa worked its way into the numb flesh of my ass, but I didn't bother to shift position.

"My poor mother," I said, though I don't know if I spoke aloud or if Mrs. Day could hear me or even if she was still in the room with me, I was so lost in the recoil of this realization. My mother was just like me. She could see Uncle Willie, too.

I thought of all the years my mother must have spent fighting those spooks, pushing them back, blocking them out. No one knew better than I the price they made you pay for ignoring them. And then to have me come along, this last child, carrying the same gift, the same curse. What a nightmare I must have been to her. A squalling, whining confirmation of all that she'd been denying. A child who didn't possess her strength—who couldn't keep the spooks at bay.

And yet she'd succeeded in teaching me to block them out. She'd trained me through all of those dark nights of terror and visitations to *not* believe, to never let the visitors in. To make me forget they ever were. To forget all too well, so that at thirteen, when my hormones kicked in and the spooks came back again, I'd forgotten all my defenses other than that of simple disbelief. And that wasn't enough.

Mom must have felt so betrayed that night when Charlotte told her about the séance. I could see her reaction now in a whole new light. In seeing the ghost of Melody's father, I'd rejected *her*, rejected her teaching and cajoling, rejected those close nights of coaching and comforting, rejected the role model of Isabel. I had let the bear in instead of eating him up.

I had become weak and foolish in her eyes. A drunkard back on the bottle. A masturbator caught with his meat in his hand. A worshiper of false idols kneeling before the Golden Calf. No wonder she'd found it so hard, impossible really, to forgive me. I had committed the sin she herself most feared committing.

And even in death, I wondered with silent tears coursing down my cheeks, did she hold herself back? Did she hold my father back, did she hold George back from coming to me in that funeral home, from answering my pleas? Did she tell them they were foolish to answer me, since they didn't exist? And they were stupid and silly and childish to think that they did.

Mrs. Day sat still across the room from me, somehow seeming an impossible distance away. I wanted to talk to her and tell her what I'd been thinking and remembering, but it seemed too hard to make myself heard across that gulf. Was she moving at all? Was she breathing? Was she frozen in time? Or was it me?

I lost sight of her as I thought again of my mother and felt a sudden rush of anger. Why all the effort? Why all those years of concentration and anger? Of pure focus and blind will? Why all that, when one damned moment of relaxation and acceptance, one smile of understanding, one whispered second of sharing the burden, of simply saying "It's hard, isn't it?" would have brought us together, would have given us rest, would have let us laugh together at the absurdity of our mutual struggle to deny the obvious?

It would never happen, I thought, my anger dissolving into sadness. That one look of understanding would never be shared. Not unless all that bullshit Mrs. Day was spewing about the Other Side was true and our divine sparks were going to sit down for a beer at the Happy Hour After Death and mull over the whole sorry story. "Sorry about the misunderstanding," Mom's eternal spirit would say. "You were right and I was wrong. I didn't have the courage to follow my path."

And would I be able to answer that I had?

I opened my eyes again, ready to see any spook the world had to offer.

At first, I thought there was one right in front of me, but it was only Mrs. Day again, still sitting, unmoving. But an odd, distorted Mrs. Day, who seemed to float, unconnected, above her surroundings as if she were a spook after all. I wanted to ask her why she looked that way, but I couldn't even remember how to speak. I wanted to stand up, but that also seemed to be a forgotten skill.

Flares of light were darting on the periphery of my vision—if I could have moved my head, I might have been able to focus on them and see what they were, but I needed someone to remind me how my spine and neck muscles worked. I could shift my eyes toward them, but the flares were too fast for me, flitting off like a fly evading a swatter.

I breathed in deep, but it wasn't air I sucked in. It was a miasma of emotions, a wild noise of them, like a thousand radio stations coming in on the same frequency. Grief. Anger. Hate. Resentment. Loneliness. Confusion. Envy. Jealousy. Sorrow. All swimming in a sea of regret. Whose emotions these were, I couldn't say. Mine? Someone else's? I wasn't sure there was a difference either way.

I opened my eyes wider, like I did when I was a kid lying on the grass of the Thorofare at night, trying to spot shooting stars. Charlotte and George would always see them, always in the part of the sky I wasn't looking at. So, I'd open my eyes as wide as I could, trying to take in all the stars, the whole bowl of the night. It didn't work then; it wasn't working now.

The lights flared again and vanished, and I was left alone. Frustrated. Receptive but not receiving. If this was something I was supposed to be able to do, why was I so damned bad at it? What sort of joke was this? What teasing God gives a man a gift but not the power to use it?

These thoughts weren't helping, of course. Whatever presence I had sensed a moment before had slipped away, leaving me wondering if I'd just imagined those lights, those emotions. I tried to bring back the sensations, but it was useless. This was like learning a golf swing or trying to get an erection after having too much to drink—the more you thought about it, the more elusive it became.

I shut my eyes, ready to give up. Give up the ghost, I thought with an inward laugh. Opening my eyes again, I saw an indistinct world, as if I were looking through Vaseline-smeared contact lenses. The unpopulated room was now as full as a cocktail party, buzzing with conversation. But no, it wasn't conversation; the voices, muddled and unclear, never connected or replied with one another. Each was a monologue on its own, as if this were a waiting room for a mass audition, crowded with actors rehearsing their speeches.

The faces and forms were hazy but familiar—character actors I'd seen many times but couldn't hang a name on. I found myself moving through them with no effort, nervous but happy, waiting to come up with a name, to say hello, to connect.

I bumped into an old brass bed, big, broad, and tarnished. I was in a strange room now. A cramped, cluttered room. Looking down, I saw a huge man, massively fat, grotesque. His body took up the entire bed, and the deep folds of his rolling flesh seeped with unhealthy moisture.

"Sorry," I said.

He looked up at me with big, kind eyes, peering out from mounds of dough.

"That's okay," he said.

Now, where did I know him from? Had I seen him on a TV talk show? A movie? Had I known him, perhaps, in more slender days? For whatever reason, I felt totally at home with him. An old friend. I sat on what little edge of the bed I could find.

"You know," he said, "I don't think I'm going to get up today. I mean, I'm fine right here. I have everything I need."

I smiled in happy recognition. It was the Krispy Kreme Donut Man himself. In the flesh. And so much of it.

"When was the last time you did get up?" I asked.

He frowned. "Now, don't you start. That's what Mom and Dad are always saying."

"What is?"

"You know. Get up. Go out. Like it's so great out there."

"Isn't it?"

"Not for me, it isn't. When you look like this, it's just embarrassing."

"They're probably just worried about your health."

"I know, I know." He unwrapped his shirt, revealing pendulous man-breasts resting on rolls of fat. "My heart doesn't sound so good. Want to listen?" He lifted up a huge pap; mushrooms were sprouting in the dark recesses of his flesh.

I looked away, hiding my gag reflex. "No, thanks."

He rolled his eyes and wrapped the shirt over himself again. "It's pretty gross, isn't it?"

"How'd you die?" I asked.

"See, that's a perfect example. It was so embarrassing.

My heart starts to give out, so they call the doctor. I'm all passed out or something, and I can't talk, but I can hear what they're saying. The doctor, he says I need to go to the hospital. But I don't *fit* through the *door*. So they have to take out the wall to my bedroom. And Dad's, like, watching, and he's *so* upset about *that*, like who's going to pay for that? And they have to use this forklift thing to get me outside, and it's *so bright* out there. And there are people, *everywhere*. Pointing and staring. And they're laughing and talking, and they take, like, *forever* getting me into the ambulance. I was really fat and, man, if it had been a *month* earlier I was down ten pounds, not that that made any difference, but at least I didn't look *so*...and my robe fell open and I heard everybody gasp and I said I was sorry. They got me in and the driver made a joke about the shock absorbers and the paramedics laughed and I...I just died. Before they even got me to the hospital. So, at least I didn't have to be there when they took me out. Man, I don't want to go through that again. I'd rather just stay here."

I took his huge, moist hand in mine. "You don't have to, Paul." I don't know when I knew his name.

"That's good."

I knew what I had to do, but I had no idea how to start. I glanced back at Mrs. Day. She was all gauzy and transparent and far away. A ghost compared to Paul. No help there.

"When you were dying, did you see any kind of bright light...or anything?" I asked.

"Nope. I had my eyes shut."

"You didn't hear a voice? Some old dead friend or relative? An angel?"

"Nope." He tilted his head to look at me. "You're wondering why I didn't cross over?"

"Yeah."

"I can't. Looking like this. Better just to stay here.

I have everything I need."

"Paul. I really don't think you'll be fat on the Other Side."

"I've always been fat."

I nodded. "How'd you find me?"

"You used to like to stay in your room. Even when you were a kid. I figured you'd understand."

"I do. But, you know, I go outside all the time."

"Come on, stop it, okay? I'm fine, really. I can read. I can watch TV. I can jerk off if Mom and Dad aren't home. It's fine."

I laid my head on the pillow next to his. "How long have you been in bed?"

He frowned. "Not sure. I remember watching Nixon beat McGovern on TV."

"That's an awfully long time, Paul."

"I know." He let his head fall toward mine; his big yellow eyes were full of tears. "Would I really not be fat over there?"

"I don't think you'd have a body at all."

He gave a deep chuckle. "That'd be nice. But you don't really know, do you? Not really."

"Not really, Paul."

"So, I think it's safer here."

"Safe isn't everything."

"If I go and I don't like it, could I come back?"

"I don't know."

"You're as useless as I am."

"Of course. That's why we're friends."

We lay on the bed and chuckled, the easy laughter of old pals.

"Maybe once I get there, I'll come back and tell you what it's like."

"I'd really appreciate that."

"I'm scared."

"It's okay to be scared. But you're a brave guy."

His eyes set with determination. "I am. I've always been brave. You have to be brave to wake up every morning."

"Go for it, Paul."

"I'll see you over there."

"Yeah."

And he was gone.

I lay on the suddenly empty bed, full of elation. Energy. My soul felt three hundred pounds lighter. He was gone from me. I'd miss him, it was true, but all the new room inside me felt luxurious. I bounced off the walls inside myself, glorying in the space.

But it was more than being free from him. I'd found my calling. I was a composer sitting at the piano for the first time. An artist picking up his first brush. A writer sharpening his first pencil. If this was being special, for once it didn't seem scary at all. It seemed invigorating. Validating. A reason for being.

Of course, as soon as I felt all this, the warning voice sounded in my ear, bringing me down to earth. Telling me to be careful and not to get too excited. After all, I still didn't know what I was doing. All sorts of things could go wrong. I shouldn't get too full of myself.

I turned and saw a middle-aged woman with a hatchet face at my side, continuing her monologue, telling me not to get my hopes up, that something was bound to go wrong, it always did.

So, there she is, I thought, the face that goes with that voice.

"Shut up," I told her. She went silent, shocked, offended. "I'll feel good if I want to," I went on.

"You're just setting yourself up for disappointment," she told me.

"I'll worry about that when it happens," I said.

"You'll see. You'll see I'm right." She wandered away. I'd have to deal with her hatchet face later.

I felt a stirring at my side, down low. I looked; nothing there.

Then, I felt a little hand slip into mine.

NINETEEN

The little hand, as it touched me, was soft as a feather, smooth as cream, cold as seaweed. I saw her now, standing at my feet.

"Hi," Jellica said. Her short hair was wet and plastered to her face; her clothes were dripping a puddle onto the floor. I was in another room now. A barren room, painted all in black.

"Hi," I croaked, managing a feeble smile. The confidence and elation of moments before faded. This was the trouble that the middle-aged lady had been talking about. I hated that she'd been right.

"You don' like me, do you?" the little girl asked.

I shook my head. "I don't know you."

"I don' like you." Her face was stern and solemn. I figured she meant what she said.

"Why not?"

"I don' like the way you play with Kat'leen."

"Kathleen's my friend."

"I don' think so."

"Do you like Maggie?"

"Maggie's nice. She plays with me. She says I'm like Casper. You rumember Casper?"

"Sure."

"He had a friend who was a fox in one of 'em. You

rumember that one?"

"I think so."

"I like that one."

She sat on the floor in front of me, her chubby legs folded underneath her. "Are you gonna keep playing with Kat'leen?"

"It doesn't look like it."

"You don' like her?"

"I like her very much. But I...don't think she wants to play with me anymore."

"I don' blame her. You were bad."

"When was I bad, Jellica?"

"You did that thing. You touched her. Down there."

"You saw that?"

"I see everything Kat'leen does. She's my friend. She doesun' like to play that game."

"Look, that's a grown-up thing. It's not something kids can understand."

"Mommy said that's the worse sin ever. Even worse than me talking to the people in the dark."

"Your mother was wrong about that."

"Mommy was *stupid*. She said I musta done that with people in the dark and that's how I got so bad. I woodun do that. It's gross."

"You mother was confused about a lot of things."

"I hate her."

"I understand that. But you have to let it go, Jellica. You can't keep hanging onto it."

"You made Kat'leen scream when you played that game."

"I know."

"That means she didun' like it."

"Jellica, listen to me. You have to let all this go." I faltered, not having a clue what to say next. "That lady over there," I pointed to the phantom figure of Mrs. Day, "she explained it to me. You need to cross over. Then, you can start again, and maybe it'll be better next time."

"You're not makin' any sense."

"I know. Jellica, you know you're not alive anymore, don't you?"

"O'course! I *said* I was like Casper."

"Okay. Then, why are you still here?"

"Where'm I s'posed to go?"

Well, there was an excellent question. "I don't know exactly." I glanced to Mrs. Day, feeling terribly ill-equipped for my task. Paul had at least had an idea of what I was talking about. This child didn't have a clue. What was I supposed to tell her to do? Follow the light? What if there was no light? Take Jesus's hand? What if the old boy didn't show? Follow the sweet, beatific smile of her grandmother? What if her grandmother was as crazy a bitch as her mother?

"I like bein' with Kat'leen," she said.

"I know you do."

"I take care of her."

"You do?"

"Yep. I watch her alla time and take care of her."

"That's nice. How come your clothes are all wet, Jellica?"

"I got drownded."

"You did?"

"Mommy tied me up and put me in the bathtub. Are you cold?"

She must have seen me shudder. "No. I was just wondering why she would do that."

"So the people in the dark wouldn't play with me anymore."

"Jesus."

"She said it was his idea."

"Whose idea?"

"Jesus. I don' like him."

"I don't think your mother was telling the truth when she said it was Jesus's idea."

She shrugged. "Don' really matter. How's come Kat'leen didun' keep me like she said she would?"

"She tried, she really tried. But she couldn't. You can't always do what you want."

"Why not?"

"I don't know. Are you mad at her for that?"

"I was. But that was when I was little. I thought she was big so she could do anything. The more I watch her, though, the more I think she's just really pretty silly. She couldun' help anybody. But I still like her. That's why I take care of her."

"How do you take care of her?"

"I keep her away from bad people."

"Who are bad people?"

"You're bad."

"Why?"

"You play that game. All the boys want to play that game."

"So you keep her away from boys?"

"That's one thing. That's why I brought her here."

"You brought her here?"

"Sure. I can make her do lots of things, and she doesn't even know." She giggled.

"How do you do that?"'

"I can talk to her, and she doesn't know it's me talkin'—she thinks it's her talking."

"Do you think that's fair?"

She frowned. "Why not?"

"You keep her alone, don't you?"

"No. I'm there."

"She doesn't have any friends."

"We don' need friends. We're just alike that way. Two peas in a pot, she used to say."

"You keep her alone."

"I just keep her away from bad people."

"Who's not bad, Jellica?"

"I'm not."

"I think she's lonely, Jellica. I don't think you're being fair to your friend."

She glared at me. "You just want to play that game with her."

"That game is a complicated thing."

"I'm not listenin' to you anymore. You're boring."

"Kathleen deserves the chance to live her own life."

"No, she don't. She's too silly. She'll just start getting stupid alla time again."

"When was she stupid?"

"She would drink that stuff to make her stupid. When I first started watchin' her, she was stupid alla time."

"But not anymore?"

"No. I got tired of it. I tol' her to stop."

I stared at the child, confused. "You told her to stop drinking?"

"A bunch a' times."

"And she did?"

"Yep."

"That was good. It was good that you did that."

"I tol' you I take care of her."

"You love her, don't you?"

"That's a stupid word."

"You want her to be happy?"

"Sure. She is happy. I'm gonna go."

"She can't be happy all alone, Jellica. People aren't happy when they're alone."

"That's stupid. That don' make no sense. I was always happy when Mommy left me alone."

"Not when the bad people came in. At night. Right? You didn't want to be alone then, did you?"

"Sure, I did. I wanted the people in the dark to leave me alone."

"Okay."

"You can't trick me. I'm not stupid, you're stupid."

"But you *did* want someone to play with."

"...sometimes."

"I think that's how Kathleen feels."

"She has me."

"She doesn't even know you're there."

"That's not true!" Jellica stood up, much bigger in her anger. "She knows! You better go away, that's all I'm sayin'."

"You can't keep her alone forever, Jellica. I won't let you."

"You can't stop me. I can stop you."

"Jellica, you're not even there. There's nothing you can do. You can't scare me."

She lowered her face and smiled up at me. "I haven't tried yet."

I felt a chill but tried not to show it. "Besides, you don't really want me to go away."

"Do too."

"Then why did you come to see me?"

"I didun'."

"Did too."

"I came to tell you to go away."

"I don't think so. You came because you want me to see you. It's nice to have somebody who can see you, isn't it?"

"No."

"Even Kathleen can't see you, can she?"

Her lower lip started to tremble just a little. "No."

"It's lonely, isn't it? Not having anybody see you?"

She pulled herself together with an adult toughness. "No. I like it. When people could see me they used to do stuff I didun' like."

"They did. That's true. But not Kathleen. You'd like her to see you, wouldn't you?"

"Yes." Tears. She looked around to hide them. "Can you make her see me?"

I hesitated. "No, I can't."

She gave me a long look. "I don' like you."

"But I can see you. And Maggie can, too. Do you like that?"

"Maggie's okay."

"And if we leave, if we go away like you say you want, then nobody will see you. What do you think of that?"

"I think you're stupid."

"Maybe I am. But why do you think I can see you, Jellica?"

"This is boring. I'm going."

"I can see you because you want me to help you, and you know I can."

"I know you're boring."

"You're tired of all this, Jellica. You want to rest."

"Blah, blah, blah. Stupid liar. I'm tellin' Kat'leen what a liar you are."

"Don't try to threaten me." Sometimes you have to be tough with a petulant child.

"Can if I want."

I tried to summon up some of my mother's sternness. "Jessica Delecourt, you are dead. You are a dead little girl. You are not even here. It's time for you to stop playing and go where you belong."

"You're mean."

"Fine. Hate me all you want. But you can't hurt me. You can't even touch me."

She screamed. A loud, harsh, screeching sound, like every temper tantrum you've ever thrown, to the tenth power. She jumped at me. I fell back from the impact of her wet little body—the sharp sting of her nails digging into my arm, her teeth biting my hand. I struggled against the rough hide of the sofa, tried to pry her off me, but she clung and kicked and hissed like a frenzied cat. I flung her away, and she was on me again; I shoved her down into the cushion, hearing the springs twang as she flailed, feeling her little shoes kicking my shins, my knees, my balls. I held her down with two hands, pressed my knee into her stomach. She stared up at me, terrible, terrified, spitting anger and fear. Eyes wide and staring at me with all the hate I'd ever seen.

They opened up and swallowed me whole.

I didn't even fight it; you can't when you don't know what you're fighting. The little girl brought her soul out and smeared it with mine, like a child playing with fingerpaint.

I was in her room. I was in the dark. A lonely dark, but not an empty one. A dark full of threat and promise.

All at once it bore down on me. The dark. The weight. I felt Jellica's fear. I was Jellica. I felt the crushing powerlessness of a child under the control, under the weight of a man. It was big fear, bigger than anything I'd ever felt, bigger even than the fear I'd felt in the cellar when I'd hidden my children from those evil men. Because it was a fear that held no hope. It was fear that said, "This is the way the world is. These are the rules you will always have to play by."

The body on top of me was huge and rugged. It pressed down on me with elephantine weight. It touched me with rough fingers, dug at me, shoved at me, split me open with tearing pain.

"I don' wanna play anymore, Daddy," I said, Jellica said.

Then the weight told me it loved me.

All at once, the door flew open, and light streamed across me, across us.

"Sammy?"

The weight clambered off me. I started crying, and it started crying, too.

"Are you okay, Sammy?"

Mommy was there now, screaming at me, slapping at me. The weight was gone. and Jellica and I both missed the dark.

"You whore," Jellica's mommy was screaming at me, at Jellica, "you little whore, why don't you leave your father alone!? You littleslutwhore!"

I curled into a ball and wished she'd go away, but she pulled at me, unwound me, dragged me into the bathroom, turned the hot water on again, and I screamed and fought and cried, and I felt so much more fear than I could contain that I prayed for it to burst out from me, to fly away like it did last night in the cellar. But it wouldn't go away, and it wouldn't stop building, not even when I felt the wires binding my arms and legs, not even when I felt the steam coming off the water.

It didn't leave me until she let it.

Until Jellica closed her eyes and released me. I fell back into myself with a wet thud, her fear, her despair, still clinging to my skin like rainfall, like a slug trail to a sidewalk.

I hadn't moved. My body was still sitting on the horsehair sofa. She was still sitting in her little yoga pose in front of me. Mrs. Day was still sitting across from me, but now she was talking to someone else. I could just make out the indistinct figure of Neil bending over her, looking at me with something like concern. *"Are you okay, Sammy?"* he was saying. But he was in a different world and didn't really matter to me now.

I felt Jellica's hand on mine again, and she spoke quietly, with sympathy. "You all right, Mister?"

"No," I just managed to say.

"It's lousy, isn't it?"

"Yeah, it's lousy."

"Now you're ascared of me."

"I'm not scared of you, Jellica."

Neil walked over to me. I could just make him out as he knelt in front of me in the same spot Jellica was sitting. Neither of them seemed to notice.

"Liar. I could do it to you again. I could do it and not stop it," Jellica said. "I could leave you there as long as I was there, what d'ya think of that?"

"I wouldn't like that."

"Then do what I say."

"You're not the boss of me, Jellica."

"Or I could do it to Maggie."

"You wouldn't do that."

"I could."

"She's your friend."

"She's *your* friend."

"Don't do that, Jellica. It wouldn't be fair."

"You know what my Mommy always says? She always says life's not fair. And she knows."

"For Christ's sake, why don't you haunt her?"

"I'm goin' now, this is boring."

I reached out to stop her, and her eyes caught mine again. I tried to look away, but she caught me, and she sent it at me again. Her fear, her pain, her smallness, her helplessness, her hate. It rushed through me and sent me reeling, toppling off the sofa and into Neil's arms.

"Jesus, Sammy, what's wrong?" he asked.

"I'm scared," I was just able to answer.

TWENTY

I stared at the lack of bite marks on my hand in dull amazement. I could still feel Jellica's little teeth biting me, but they'd left no trace, no wound at all.

I didn't speak, hadn't spoken since Neil picked me up off the floor. I looked up at my friend, but all I could see was his watch and the hairs on his broad wrist working their way through the metal band. Mrs. Day was next to him, but she was just the slightly bulging fold of the waistband of her jeans. My vision seemed to have narrowed to tiny details, and I couldn't find the power to zoom out and see the whole of anything.

"Atter. Am. Kay?" That was Neil's voice, but coming at me in fragmented half-words, like a cell phone in a drop zone.

I looked up at Neil's face, which was an odd collection of pores and hairs and lines and eyes. I opened my mouth, but that trick of being able to speak actual words seemed a distant memory.

"All. Ight." That was Mrs. Day's voice, saying something comforting to Neil. All. Ight. *Put it together*, I told my sluggish brain. *All right*, I guessed. Sure, she's telling Neil that I'll be all right. Well, that was good news. I wondered if she meant it.

Neil's shoes scudded on a carpet that was red and

swirly. The carpet separated itself from Neil's feet and jumped up, doing that little flying trick from an old Thief of Bagdad movie.

Now, where do I know that carpet from? I wondered as I watched it dance for me. Not in the barn; the barn had a rough wooden floor. I could still picture little Jellica sitting on it in her wet dress. Little Jellica I could see all of—she didn't break up into little Cubist bits and pieces and dance around like everything else; she stayed whole and complete and still in my mind. She was the only real person in the world.

But the carpet, Sammy, I told myself, *the carpet is real. You know it. You've seen it before. And that's where you really are. In some room with a red carpet.* Though it felt like an abstraction, I knew it was important for me to know where I actually was. There was a theory formulating in my foggy brain that this reality place was where I was supposed to spend most of my time.

"Atter. Ih. Im?" This was Neil, talking again. *Now, let's try and guess what those sounds mean,* I told myself, thinking it sounded like a fun way to pass the time. "Atter." *Matter. Of course.* "What's the matter with him?" *There.* And once I filled in the missing syllables, I could hear Neil say the whole sentence. This was very good news. It meant I could follow conversations, even though it might be at a several-minute delay. My future was looking much brighter.

Now there's the matter of answering, I thought, remembering that this was a pretty important part of the conversation deal. I opened my mouth. Nothing came out, but only partly because I couldn't remember how to speak and mostly because Neil and Mrs. Day were looking at me in such surprise. I wondered how long I'd been sitting there, silent, motionless. Had years passed? Had the new century come? Was one of George Bush's children President?

"Am? Ah. I-it?" This was Neil again. His brow was wrinkled and the one eye of his I could see looked full of concern. *Put the words together,* I told myself. *And pull back so you can see the guy's whole face.* I concentrated, feeling my features distort with the effort, as if I was trying to solve Fermat's Theorem or paint the Sistine Chapel. Neil's round, red, worried face started to put itself together before my eyes. "Sam? What is it?" I heard the words he'd spoken seconds or minutes before; I saw his complete face. Seeing that face, hearing his voice; it was such a miracle, such a simple wonder that it brought tears coursing down my face.

I blinked, feeling embarrassed at the whole scene. *Neil can't see me cry,* I thought. Crying and Neil just don't go together.

"Jesus, what the hell's the matter with him?" Neil was saying to Mrs. Day, clear and loud and coherent. Her face was all put together, too, but it didn't look nearly as worried as Neil's. Even as I tried to suck back the tears I found that comforting. She was supposed to be the expert here, after all. If she wasn't so worried, why should I be?

I gasped, trying to stifle the sobs that came out of me with a body-shaking force I hadn't felt since childhood. "I'm...oh...kay...," I heard myself croak. It startled me to hear my own voice, so dull and stupid sounding, so broken by tears.

"What the fuck happened to you?" Neil asked. It was comforting to hear him swear; somehow it took the solemnity out of the situation.

I shut my eyes and held my breath, trying to kill the crying as if it were a bad case of hiccups. My chest settled itself, and I opened my eyes again. The forms and colors of the real world rushed in at me like oncoming traffic. *God, it's beautiful,* I thought, *so real, so living.* I felt the tears again; my heart burst with gratitude at being able to come back into this glorious place. I wasn't embarrassed at having Neil see me cry now; it was just so fucking wonderful to be part of this spook-less world. I searched for words to express the depth of my feelings.

"Hi, Neil," I said. And I meant every word.

Neil looked even more appalled than before. "What the hell has he been doing?" He was talking to Mrs. Day again, clearly blaming her for the fact that his good friend was suddenly weeping and grinning and talking like Forrest Gump.

"He'll be all right, Neil," Mrs. Day said, and she sounded so sincere I just wanted to hug her and kiss her. God, she was beautiful when she said I would be all right.

"I'm okay, Neil," I said, my words still slurred and dopey. "It's just...I do, I do, I do believe in spooks." I said this in my best Bert Lahr, and it struck me as not just a little funny, but full-blown, gut-busting, Three Stooges funny. I laughed so hard, snot joined the tears flowing down my face.

"Jesus, Sam." Neil laughed a little when he said this. A slightly freaked out, frightened laugh, but a laugh all the same. One that said that whatever fucking strange thing had gone on was at least over now and thank God for that. Amen, Neil.

I tried to collect myself. (And it really felt like that; as if I was gathering scattered bits of myself from around the room.) "Neil," I said, and then paused as I wondered at the marvel that each face in the world had its own name attached to it; who came up with that miraculous concept? Some forgotten genius caveman. I promised to light a candle to him the next time I passed a church. I shook my head to try and pick up my train of thought, and the room squiggled like a digital effect in a jeans commercial. Putting my hands to my head, I held the universe steady and continued, "Neil, I need to talk to Mrs. Day."

Neil looked unhappy for a moment, but his politeness got the better of his worry, and he stood up and moved to the door.

"No!" I said. "Don't go. You can stay." From the worried look on Neil's face, I knew I sounded too urgent, but I really didn't want him to leave. I remembered reading in one of the many child development books I devoured when you were first born that babies believe that when someone leaves their field of vision, that person ceases to exist—in my heart I was back at that stage, and I wasn't sure that if Neil left the room I'd ever see him again.

"I mean, you don't have to go. I just want to ask her a question." I congratulated myself that my voice sounded so calm and rational now. "Then, I'll ask you a question. Then, you can ask me a question. And we'll all answer them." God, I was thinking clearly, I noticed. I should write a book about this whole question thing. Why hadn't anyone thought of it before?

Neil gave Mrs. Day a dubious glance, but went ahead and sat down. Neil was a good friend.

"Mrs. Day," I said, "why did I go into other rooms and yet never leave this room?"

Mrs. Day nodded. "The spirits build homes for themselves. Rooms."

"They build them in my mind?"

"Or in theirs. It doesn't make much difference. The rooms are the places they reside. For the spirits, their room is the whole world. The universe. They carry it with them wherever they go. Like hermit crabs. It's their protective shell."

"Okay," I said. I rubbed my eyes. There was only one thing I really wanted to know. "Will I get over this?"

Mrs. Day smiled. A bright sunlight, birds chirping, Mary Poppins smile. I didn't even have to hear her words to feel relieved. "Of course," she said. "You've done something very brave, very new. You've allowed yourself to go somewhere you've never been. To enter a new flow state. It's not easy to come back. To travel back and forth. I find rituals help. I think that explains all the séance rigmarole you see in the movies. Some people find rituals help their bodies through these transitions. But it doesn't have to be dark lights, candles, and crystal balls. A nice cup of peppermint tea works for me. You'll find something that's right. And it'll get easier every time. You'll learn to navigate from room to room."

She stopped when I started laughing so hard.

"Is something funny, Sam?"

Well, it was funny. It was funny that somebody, especially somebody as smart as she, could miss the point so entirely. "You think I'm ever going to do that again?" I said, between gasps.

"Sam, it's never easy the first time. It gets better."

This was like doing brain surgery on yourself. It isn't easy the first time, and then the next time it's impossible because you're a drooling, lobotomized idiot. "I'm not going back there, Emily. I felt like I lost my fucking mind. Like I had a stroke. If I ever put myself back together again and remember how to tie my shoes, I'm never going to even think about another spook. I'll leave well enough the fuck alone."

She came over and sat next to me, and only then did I notice that I was sitting on her sofa, in her living room, with George Strait playing on her radio. The real world was still coming back to me in dribs and drabs.

"I understand how you feel."

"Good. Enough said. Now, I'm going to talk to my friend Neil, who thinks I'm a certified maniac, thanks to you."

"Not thanks to me."

"No, you're right. That was unfair. You did what I asked you to do. Thank you very much. End of story."

"It's not over, Sam. This is a part of you. You have to learn to control it."

"No, I don't have to learn anything. I was curious, okay? I tried it, I'm not curious anymore. Hi, Neil, what did you want to see me about? You came here to see me, didn't you?"

"It'll keep."

"No, Neil. You were looking for me, you came all this way, talk to me."

He glanced at Mrs. Day.

"Don't worry about her," I said. "You can talk in front of her. She knows all about me. She knows all about everything. She's in touch with the Other Side and she loves it; she thinks it's cool. I do not. It is not for me. And she sees that, don't you, Mrs. Day? You accept that?"

She looked at me evenly. "If you don't learn to control it, it will keep on controlling you."

"I am talking to my friend Neil. You had your turn, now it's Neil's turn. That's the way conversation works. So, Neil, what did you want to tell me?"

"Really, it's nothing."

"Now you're embarrassed. You see what you've done, Mrs. Day? You've embarrassed Neil. I've never seen Neil embarrassed before."

"I'm gonna go and talk to you later," Neil said.

"No! Neil, stay. I'm okay. I know I sound like I'm crazy, but I'm not. I had a little breakdown is all. I wish I'd done it the way you guys on the island do it, you know? Something healthy, like drinking too much or beating my wife. I went another way altogether. I started talking to ghosts. You believe in ghosts, Neil?"

"No."

"Damn right. You cling to that, Neil. 'Cause you give those fuckers an inch, they'll take the whole damn mile. But I'm over it; I'm putting it behind me. Now, what did you have to say to me?"

"Not now, Sam."

"Why not?"

"Not here."

"Right. Damn straight. We'll walk out of here, we'll go to Boongies Grocery Store and buy ourselves a six-pack of Rolling Rock and a hard pack of Camels and sit on the dock and throw rocks at the gulls and talk about things the way men are supposed to."

"You oughta sleep this off, whatever this is, Sam."

"You don't sleep this shit off, Neil. You exorcize it, isn't that right, Mrs. Day? But what's your topic, Neil? We're on your topic now. Is it about me? Is it about Kathleen? Is it about Charlotte?"

"I'm goin', Sam."

"It's about Charlotte. I can tell. What about her? She okay?"

"She's great, Sam."

"You can tell me, Neil. I'm your pal."

"Forget it, okay? Another time."

"Now's the time, Neil. I'm all yours. The weirdness is over."

"All right. I'm thinking about asking her marry me, Sam."

"See?" I turned to Mrs. Day. "That's the kind of problems people are *supposed* to be dealing with. My best friend wants to marry my sister. How do I feel about that? What do I do? What advice do I give? That's reality, Emily."

She didn't answer, so I walked out. Just walked right out without even looking back at her, or at Jellica, who was sitting on top of the pine china cupboard, her wet hair dripping onto the blond wood and staining it black.

TWENTY-ONE

Viscous phlegm built up in my throat before I'd finished the first cigarette. I coughed it up and swallowed it down, reveling in the goopy reality of it.

"Don't you think marriage is moving a little fast, Neil?" The smell of rotting fish bait wafted over the harbor; they should bottle it and sell it to people in the Midwest. "Shouldn't you, like, ask her out first, or try to sleep with her, or something?"

Neil skipped a stone across the water; five quick jumps and a long arc. How *did* he do it? "That's the thing. I'm really in love with her, you know?"

"So?"

"See, I've never been good at landing girls I'm in love with. The only girls I can ever nail are ones I don't really care about."

"That's normal."

Neil shook his head. "What's that about, anyway?"

"C'mon, you know. When you don't care, that's when you can be cool and say all the right things. But when you're in love, then you start worrying and messing up and acting like an idiot."

Neil shifted on his butt, leaning back on a tarry pylon. "But what's that *about*? Don't women want guys who love them?"

"Theoretically."

"I mean, I know when they're young, they don't know any better, but by the time they're our age, haven't they figured out how men act? So, shouldn't they be out looking for the guys who act like idiots and run like hell from the ones who say the right thing?"

"I don't think it's that simple. For one thing, some guys who act like idiots are just idiots."

"That's true."

I thought back on Anne and Bill Zacharias. "For another thing, I'm not so sure about your whole premise. Do people really want people who are in love with them? I mean, love's exciting and all, but it's an awful lot of work. I think people end up just wanting someone who's comfortable. Someone who'll make life easier. Someone from the right gene pool. Someone who can help them build a stable life. I think love only fits into that incidentally."

"That's depressing."

"I don't know. Love's kind of a disaster, isn't it? A disaster that comes into your life now and then, like those hurricanes that hit Florida every other year. Love comes in and wipes out the trailer park of your life."

"You could write a country song out of that," Neil said.

"I may. And the person you settle down with is the nice stable insurance adjuster who gives you the check to build your new house."

Neil twisted open another bottle. "Thing is, Sam, there's no point in me trying to act cool with Charlie. I'll just fuck it up. That only leaves me being honest with her and telling her how I feel."

A grim prospect. We sat in silence for a moment—the noisy silence of the bustling harbor: water lapping on the hulls of a hundred boats, the fluty gossip of fishermen calling from boat to boat, the screams of the gulls, the tight-throated whining of the summer teenagers stranded around the ice cream stand, the slamming doors of the cars waiting in the ferry line, the AM radio songs mixing in the sea air and blending into a medley of Spice Girls and Beastie Boys and Dixie Chicks.

A grim prospect because we both knew your mother and recognized that there was nothing more sure to scare her off than sincerity. A casual and unlooked-for leap into love might be possible for her. But to see it in front of her and deliberately take the plunge? It was like asking her to take a fifty-foot bungee jump with a sixty-foot cord.

"Look, it's not that she doesn't like you, Neil. She does. And I really think it could work out with you two. God knows, that would make me happy. But...she's been burned so many times, Neil. If you could just take it easy for a while—"

"Don't you think I know that? But I can't. I don't know how."

"So, what are you going to do?"

"I'm gonna propose to her."

"See, I'm thinking right now that would be a disaster."

"I know that, too. But I'm gonna do it. I can't help myself. I mean, even if I don't say it, she's gonna see it in my face."

That much was true. Neil's face was an open book.

"Isn't it better for me to just come out with it than to have her, I don't know, guess it and just slink away and reject me without my even taking a shot at it?"

Better to be rejected to your face than behind your back. Love leaves men such humiliating options, Maggie.

"Let me talk to her," I said.

"Jeez, it's like we're back in junior high. 'Neil likes you, do you like him?' Jeez."

"No, I'm not gonna do that. I'm gonna pave the way. I'm gonna see if her mind's open to the idea. And if it's not, I'll open it, I swear I will." I looked over at Neil and said something to him I never thought I'd say. "I love you, Neil. She'd be lucky to have you. I'd like for you to be my brother."

Well, what could either of us say after that? We just sat in the crowded empty quiet and sipped our beers. I recognized, in some way I couldn't put my finger on, that if I hadn't gone off to that weird place and said good-bye to the Krispy Kreme Donut Man and felt those horrible things Jellica made me feel, I'd never have been able to say that to Neil. For a moment, I was glad it all had happened.

It was a brief moment, and it was over the second I saw Kathleen's car go by, loaded down with all her belongings, and park in the ferry line.

She didn't even look startled when I knocked on her window, just leaned over and opened the door so I could slide in.

"At least it's good to see that you're not avoiding me," I said.

"This is the only way off the island, Sam. I don't really have a choice."

"Look, all right, I came off like a nutcase, but—"

"Sam, no. I know in situations like this people always say 'it's not you,' but it really is not you. You're probably fine. This is probably something you just need to work through. Or maybe you really can talk to the spirits, whatever. The thing is...and this is me, it's all me...you're just too dramatic. I got enough drama in me for a lifetime. If I ever find a guy, he's going to have to be boring and normal and strong enough to put up with my shit, not add a mountain of his own."

"But I'm going to be boring from now on, that's the plan. I have it all worked out. Let me tell it to you, you'll fall asleep listening, I guarantee it."

She did laugh a little. "You couldn't be boring, Sam." She turned toward me now, looking at me with that frank tenderness women reserve for when they're saying good-bye. "You've given me a lot. Last night was beautiful. I never thought I'd feel that way again. Hell, I don't know if I've ever felt that way before. And you helped me find the courage to go back home, which again, I never thought I'd have. I only wish I could have given you as much."

"You've given me a lot."

"Then, that's good. So, this was good. I'm glad it happened. Good-bye, Sam."

"Okay, that's nice, but—"

"No. That was the good-bye. I said what I wanted to say. Now, the ferry is going to take ten minutes to load, and if we sit here all that time, one of us is bound to say something stupid and spoil the whole thing, so leave now."

Of course, she was right. My only hope was to wait for a long-term delay, like the ferry blowing up or something. But, up ahead, the boat was frustratingly intact. I got out onto the cracked pavement of the ferry landing.

"Okay, here's the stupid thing that's going to spoil everything," I said, leaning back into the open door. "She's dangerous, Kathleen."

"Who is?"

She knew. "She's in your life. She's haunting you. You'll never be happy, you'll never be safe, until we find a way to release her."

All trace of affection vanished from her face. "Shut up, Sam."

"You were right. They did kill her. They drowned her in the bathtub."

"They?"

"Her parents. And the doctor was wrong. She *was* molested. Her father used to abuse her. I saw it all."

She looked at me in pure disgust. "You don't know what the fuck you're talking about. Her father was dead before I even met her. You just make this shit up, don't you?"

"Kathleen, I *know*—"

"Let's try another good-bye—get the fuck out of here. I never want to see you again."

She slammed the door shut and locked it.

The ferry didn't blow up. It left right on schedule for the first time in years.

TWENTY-TWO

Watching the ferry clear Holborne Point, I ate a soft-serve chocolate ice cream fast enough to give myself a brain-freeze headache. The distraction was welcome.

"She wasn't good enough for you," Neil said, alternating puffs on his Marlboro with licks on his vanilla cone.

"Yeah, she was."

"Nope. She wasn't. I can't say you're right, 'cause you're wrong." We clambered back over the rocky shore to his truck.

"What if I told you it's not over," I said. "What if I told you I know she'll come back?"

"I'd say, of course, dumped guys always think that. My old high school girlfriend is my mail carrier. Every day she comes to my door, I expect her to open it, walk in, and fuck my brains out."

"Did it ever happen?"

"Once, but it was her substitute."

When I got home, Charlotte was at the kitchen table picking crab and you were out on the lawn setting free another kite.

"Neil didn't come in?" she asked.

Neil's truck was making dust down the driveway. He'd told me he was planning to drive Round-the-Island Road

twice and then come back. That gave me about forty minutes, so I could have hemmed and hawed for a while, but
instead I got right to the point. You'd never have known it
was me.

"He wanted me to talk to you first."

She looked up, apprehensive. "Things got weird,
didn't they?"

"No, they did not. I mean, it depends. He wants to ask
you to marry him, Charlotte."

She went back to picking.

"Well?"

She looked up again, clearly pissed. "So, what am
I supposed to say to that?"

"Yes or no, usually."

"Why is he having you ask me?"

"He's not. He wanted me to, you know, lay down the
groundwork."

"You didn't lay the groundwork, you just said it. You
said the whole thing."

"I'm sorry. I just thought it might take you a while to
get used to the idea. I mean, sometimes you lash out when
you're surprised, and I thought it would be better if...."

"Better if I lashed out at you?"

"Yeah, I'm used to it."

"So, am I supposed to act surprised when he asks me?"

"This is not a birthday party. He wants to marry you.
You're talking about everything but the point."

"I know." She went back to picking, angrily pulling the
flaky white meat out of the shell with an old metal pick.

"So?"

"So, I'm supposed to give the answer to you?"

"Well, I'd like to know what you're thinking. And I'd
like to know why you're mad."

She rested her head on the back of her hand. "It
wouldn't work out."

"Okay. Tell him that. Why are you so sure?"

She looked out the window at you running across the brown grass. "What's he going to do when he finds out about Maggie's dad?"

"He knows about Maggie's dad."

"I'm supposed to keep telling that story?"

"Okay, tell him the truth. Neil's a big boy, he can take it. Do you know how many babies on this island come from single mothers?"

"Are their fathers married?"

"Go ahead and make it sound as bad as you can. Neil loves you. He'll just get pissed at the asshole and love you more."

"He'll have to know everything about me."

"He wants to know everything about you."

"I mean everything."

"What is that? And why do you always talk that way? What have you ever done that was so awful? The only question is, do you want to marry him?"

She picked up a bit of crab and chewed on it thoughtfully. "I think, yes."

"Great!" I pounded the table; finally, something was working out.

"But I'll have to tell him everything."

I was hardly listening now. I was up on my feet pacing the room. "Fine, I know you always act like you have this big secret. Trust me, we all have one. So, you sold pot in high school, is that it? Big deal. Half the fishermen here smuggled the stuff in the eighties. And you tried cocaine in college. But you didn't get hooked did you? And you don't think Neil expects you to be a virgin, do you—"

"I made a movie once."

I stopped. That's never a phrase a man wants to hear his sister say. "A movie?"

"Remember when Maggie was about eighteen months

and you watched her while I went to LA for five days to visit my friend Gina Resnick?"

"Uh-huh?"

She pushed off from the table and walked out onto the porch. You (and no, you are never, never going to read this part, but I have to put it down now so I can cut it out later) were digging with your Pokémon shovel and pouring the dirt over your arms.

"Gina was doing this 'scene' and she wanted to know if I wanted to be in it. Paid five hundred dollars for an afternoon's work. That's a pretty good deal, huh?"

I came out and sat next to her.

"Okay. Okay. You've been carrying this around with you all this time like you committed murder. Well, I hear you. And it's not so bad. You didn't kill anybody."

She laughed.

"Okay, but you were young—"

"It was three years ago, Sam."

"You can do a lot of growing up in three years."

"I'm not making excuses. I did it because the money was good and I thought it would be fun."

"Fine. Fine. So, you had an adventure, and that's in the past."

"What's Neil going to think?"

"Well, you're not going to tell him."

"I am."

She went back inside and started picking at the crab again.

"Jesus Christ, why would you do that?"

"He has a right to know."

"No, he doesn't."

"What if he finds out?"

"How's he going to find out?"

"It's a video. It's out there."

"Come on. I work in a video store. The shelf life on

those movies is, like, two months. It's long gone by now."
I reached over and grabbed the crab claw from her. "Damn
it, I know what you're doing. You're using this as a way
to scare him off because you're afraid to take a risk at
being happy."

She slammed the pick down. "What do you know about
it, asshole? Have you ever faced anything in your life?"

"Why are you attacking me? And what does that mean,
'faced?' What are you even talking about?"

"Maybe I want Neil to know, okay? Maybe I want him
to know because I want to be able to talk to him about it
sometime, to talk to him about how it feels to have something like that in my past. Maybe I want him to know all
about me and what I've done and love me anyway."

We talked in circles for half an hour, but by the time
Neil walked in, she hadn't moved an inch. She's almost as
stubborn as you are.

(When I re-write this for you I'm going to have to
clean it up, I know. What will her secret be? Shoplifting.
A prison stint? Alcoholism? Maybe I'll ask you for advice.
Or is it possible that I will tell you the truth and it will
be okay? That honesty really is the best policy? No matter how old I may get, I'll never be grown-up enough to
believe that one.)

Charlotte walked right up to Neil and said, "I'm ready,"
and headed out to the truck, which was a little odd since
he hadn't even spoken yet.

Neil looked at me in surprise. "How'd it go?" he whispered, even though she was well out of earshot.

What could I say? I'd supposedly been getting her
ready for a shock, now I had to prepare him for one. "It's
kind of up to you now, Neil. Do you love her?"

"Oh, yes."

"A lot?"

"Sure."

"Then I don't see why it won't be all right."

I walked him out and told them both to be gone as long as they needed. Then they drove off and I went out to play with you. That's one thing I'm good at.

We dug a trench in the dirt and lined up your little plastic dinosaurs until you lost interest in that. Then, we played hide-and-seek and you never came to find me, so I had to start whistling, and you thought it was funny to walk right by me and not see me, so you did that for about twenty-five minutes. It was so funny we both just about wet our pants laughing. I made you a daisy chain of some island flowers that weren't daisies, and you scouted the shore for bits of sea glass and old bleach bottles.

By the time the sun was going down, I had to go in to pee, and you said you wanted to stay and dig for clams on our beach. I watched you from the upstairs window. Watched the sun setting over the Thorofare, a sight so beautiful it completely distracted me from the sound of my own urination. I wondered about Kathleen and where she was and what Jellica was doing with her.

I needn't have worried. Jellica was down on the shore with you.

I saw the two of you clearly. Like any other pair of kids running and laughing on any other shore. She was wet and dripping like before, but it didn't look so ominous here, by the seaside, where any little kid might get wet. I could hear your laughter through the windowpane. But I could hear hers louder, because the glass didn't block it out. It rang inside my head.

A boat went by and threw a set of angry waves at the rocks; Jellica let them lap over her feet and laughed louder as she pointed across the water to Brown's Head Island. You walked into the surf to see where she was pointing.

I was down the stairs in a second, hardly bothering to zip up. I banged open the screen door and ran out into the twilight air. You were alone at the water's edge, playing with seagull bones.

Out of breath, I plopped down next to you on the wet sand.

"You shouldn't play so near the water, you know. Not when it's getting dark."

"I'm not afraid of nothing. I have bravery."

"Who were you playing with a minute ago?"

"Jellica. She tole me her name, you know."

"I know. Where'd she go?"

"Dunno. You scared her off."

"Do you like playing with her?"

"Sometimes. Sometimes she can be kinda crabby. She was nice today."

"That's nice."

You leaned over to me, confidentially. "I don' think she's got a lotta friends."

"Do you have friends, Maggie?"

"Not so many."

"Doesn't it...doesn't it scare you to play with her?"

"Nope," you were very definite. "Mommy can't see Jellica, can she?"

"No. Only special people can see Jellica. Do you see a lot of people like her, honey?"

"Sometimes. Most of them are sad. Some of them are funny." You looked up at me, wet hair sticking to your face. "How come they scare you?"

"I'm scared of a lot of things." I pulled you onto my lap and we sat, watching the water turn darker. "Can you teach me bravery, Maggie?"

"Sure," you said. "Can you teach me how to write my name in scrip'?"

"Yes."

So, we had a deal.

TWENTY-THREE

You're still asleep in your hospital bed. Your IV is still doing its rhythmic drip. Are you resting? Are you at peace? God, I hope so. Sleep. Gather your strength. Come back stronger.

I got a Snickers bar from the vending machine. I'll get stronger, too.

The next morning, the morning after that ordeal with Mrs. Day, I woke up late. I mean, I actually woke up late; I didn't wake up early and lay there for hours in a sugary funk of half-dreaming masturbation. I said a prayer for the absent Krispy Kreme Donut Man, showered, and got dressed. I actually thought about whether my shirt went with my pants—I didn't know if it did or not, but I considered the question, which was very grown-up of me, I thought. I was coming along.

Walking downstairs, I heard dishes clinking in the sink and Trisha Yearwood singing her heartbreaker hit "The Song Remembers When" on the stereo. I didn't take that as an indication that things had gone well for Charlotte last night. Your mother doesn't mix housework and country music unless something has gotten seriously fucked up.

There was laundry neatly arranged on the kitchen ta-ble; a pile of socks and undies neatly folded and waiting to be tucked away for comfort. Coffee was brewing in the Braun, and strips of bacon were resting in their aura of grease on flowered paper towels while eggs spit in the frying pan.

"Mommy's makin' resa-rant breakfast!" you said, look-ing up from your Lite Brite.

"You act like Mommy never cooks, Baby Cakes." Charlie's forced cheerful tone was painful to hear. "You like yours over easy or sunny side?"

"Like they do at Denny's!"

"Fine, why don't you go get your Scooby Doo coloring books and crayons and you can pretend we're at Denny's and you have a Kid's Menu?"

"I like this game!"

You were gone in a thunder of bare feet. I poured myself a cup and sat down while Charlie switched off the stereo.

"Know what? I'm tired of sad songs. I think I'm going to go through all my CDs and throw out any of them that have sad songs. You want 'em?"

"Sure. That'll be pretty much the whole collection."

"No, I'll keep the instrumentals. From now on, that's all I'm buying. Maybe you can teach me to like that jazz crap you listen to. No words."

"What's wrong with words all of a sudden?"

"Oh, songs with words are always love songs. Love songs are full of shit." She flipped the eggs so hard they broke, splattering yolk onto her hand. Without a word, she dumped the eggs into the sink.

"I'd still have eaten those," I objected.

"You like sunny side, you're getting fucking sunny side." She smiled again, and the dreaded chipper voice re-turned. "You know, when we get back home, I'm going back to college, get a degree I can actually use. This temp thing, there's no future in it. It's temporary, right? That's why they call it that, right?" She laughed.

"What did he say?"

"He called me a whore."

She was standing with her back to the sink, still smiling. "Jesus, Charlie. What did you say?"

"Well, you know, I tried to argue with him, but the only real defense I could come up with was how little money I got for it. So really, the best I can say for myself is that I'm a poor businesswoman."

I stood up and put my arms around her. She put hers around me, too. Neither of us were all that comfortable about it, but we needed it.

"It's for the best," she said.

"The hell it is. I'm going to talk to Neil."

Her hug tightened into a vise grip. "You are not going to do that."

"I am."

She pulled away from me and gave me her best scary look. I'd been trained all my life to allow that look to turn my insides to tapioca.

I gave her a kiss on the cheek. "Sorry, Charlotte. After yesterday I don't scare so easy."

"Don't."

"Don't what?"

The Beachcomber was the closest thing to a bar on the Island. Ratty foosball and pool tables in the center of the room, white plastic tables by the window overlooking the harbor, a refrigerator stocked with Bud Lite hidden behind the counter. Sometimes somebody was there to take your money; sometimes you just dropped it into a Styrofoam cup and hoped it stayed there. Neil was on his second honor beer.

"Don't talk to me about this shit."

"Neil, goddamn it! You know her, you've known her all your life, you know what she is."

"Guess I don't."

"That's bullshit. What did you find out that's so important it cancels out years of knowing her?"

"You seriously asking that?"

"You never did anything wrong in your life?"

"Yeah. I took some lobsters over the size limit. I didn't..." He leaned forward and whispered in the empty room, "...I didn't sell my ass on fucking VHS."

"And you can't forgive her for that?"

He rested his head in his hands. "Sure, I can. Why not? People do lots of things." He looked up at me. "But if you're asking me do I want her to be my wife? I gotta say no."

"Okay...look, like you said, people do lots of things. But what they *do*, that's one thing. Who they *are*, that's something else. You know who Charlotte is."

He was listening, I'll give him that. But he shook his head in the end. "No. For the mother of my children? Sorry."

"Charlotte is a damn fine mother."

"I know she is." He spread his huge hands across the table, gripping the surface, as if he were about to pick it up. "I love Maggie. I see her with Maggie and I...but she had sex 'cause somebody paid her. Will you tell me how that doesn't make her a whore?"

I started shifting napkins around in the table.

"Look, Sam, I know she's your sister and I love you. Hell, I probably still love her. But I can't marry somebody who...can't we just pretend I never had this stupid idea?"

"I thought it was a pretty great idea."

"You're the only one."

"I thought it was a great idea, Neil."

We stopped talking then, with so much sadness hanging in the air I could see it gathering around us like mist. I might have left, but then the next time I saw Neil we'd have both been uncomfortable, might even have passed each other without speaking. I couldn't stand the thought of us behaving that way, so I figured if I just stayed with him until the discomfort passed, that would never happen. Maybe I'd have to stick around him for a few weeks, but, hell, I had no other plans.

Neil finished his beer. I finished my beer. He walked down Main Street to get a crab roll at the Harbor Gawker. I walked down Main Street to get a crab roll at the Harbor Gawker. We didn't feel the need to analyze whether I was doing this *with* him or just alongside him. It's this ability to ignore the obvious that makes men such wonderful companions for each other.

Deputy Beirko was sitting in his car at the curb under the stone eagle. Both doors were open, and I could hear him arguing with someone inside. "Goddamn it, what do you want me to do?"

"Something, Donny. Some damn thing."

Donny shifted in his seat, blocking my view of the woman he was arguing with, but I knew from her voice that it was Kathleen.

"I can't just go over there."

"Why the hell not, Donny?"

"I got no cause."

"I'm not asking for cause. I'm not asking you to do anything when you get there, I'm just asking you to knock on the *fucking door*."

Donny jumped out of the car like a scalded cat. "Goddamn it, Kathleen, you're pushing this too hard. Don't push this, okay? You are not a cop anymore, okay? I'm the cop here."

Kathleen leaned out the door and despite her anger I

saw that her eyes were red, as if she'd been crying not too long ago. "Then how come I'm the one in the patrol car?"

Beirko yanked the door open so hard, it swung back and slammed shut on him again. He fumbled with the handle and swung it open, slower this time. "Get out."

"Jesus, Donny."

"Get out of the car, ma'am."

She climbed out of the car and leveled her eyes at the deputy. "This is one of those times when you have the chance to do the right thing or act like an asshole, Donny. Don't you know they tally those up when you're trying to get into heaven?"

Donny was getting all official on her. "If you can give me some information to corroborate your belief that this individual is the individual you claim she is, and that she is suspected of some crime, I will be happy to follow up on this. Until then, I have no intention of harassing an innocent citizen. Now, I have my patrol to see to."

She stepped away from the car, hands open at her sides. "I had hopes for you, Donny. I really did."

"Just doing my job, Kathleen." He started the car and drove off.

I tossed my crab roll into the trash and walked up to her. "You okay?"

She gave me sad smile. "Sam." There was a noncommittal greeting if I ever heard one.

"I thought you were leaving."

"She wouldn't let me."

"Who?"

She turned to Neil and smiled. "He's a scary guy, your friend."

"Keeps me up at night," Neil said.

She turned to me again, her eyes raw and bloodshot and just beautiful. "I saw Jellica's mother on the ferry."

"What?"

"She lives out on Brown's Head Island. Turns out I was following her all along, I just didn't know it."

We went back with Kathleen to her house, and it was then that I realized how much she hadn't intended to come back. The place was shut up and cleaned out. No power, no water, no food. This woman doesn't do things by half measures, I thought.

We sat around the kitchen table with no coffee to warm our hands on. The sofa bed was pulled out, but there were no sheets on it. She must have camped out on it last night, but she hadn't done a thing to make herself more comfortable. She was making it clear to the house that she wasn't back to stay.

Neil can't sit in one place for long without something to drink or eat. He went out to his truck and brought in the only thing he had: a six-pack of Bud. He even offered one to Kathleen, and I was thoughtless enough not to stop him. She politely turned it down, though I saw her give the can a look of longing more poignant than any I'd seen her give me the night we'd made love. I wasn't jealous. We all have a soft spot in our hearts for our exes.

She leaned her chair back against a bare white wall and started to tell her story. Cold, simple, bare to the bones. A cop on the witness stand. When she started, she had a challenging glare in her eye, as if she was daring one of us to say she was crazy. Well, she had the wrong audience for that. Neil had too much island politeness to ever disagree with an ex-drunk, and me? I'd believe any shit anybody told me by now.

After our parting words on the ferry landing, she had driven her truck up the ramp and jockeyed herself a fine parking space. Dead in the middle of the boat and pointed right at the ramp. "Once the ferry docked, all I was going to have to do was hit the gas and I'd be on the road."

She sat in the truck for the first half of the trip, then she got out to use the facilities. While she was making her way to the starboard cabin, she saw the woman.

"White female, in her thirties, two hundred and ten pounds or so. Square build. Ruddy complexion. Short-cropped black hair. Fuzzy mustache." It was a description that fit half the women on the island. The woman was sitting in the back row of the cabin, next to an empty shopping cart. "I have no doubt that it was her." She said this calmly, making her report.

Kathleen went back to her truck and waited, not wanting to be seen by the woman. She watched the pedestrians disembark once they reached the mainland. Mrs. Delecourt left among them, pushing her shopping cart up the ramp.

Once off the boat, Kathleen parked her truck in the long-term lot and followed the woman on foot. Catching up with her was no problem. The problem was moving slow enough to stay behind her as she rolled that shopping cart up the long hill to Main Street, then down the asphalt sidewalk to the A & P.

Kathleen waited outside for an hour and a half before the woman came back out, her cart piled high with provisions.

"Weren't you cold?" I asked.

Kathleen looked at me like I was nuts. "What?"

"Waiting outside all that time in this weather?"

"Yeah, I was fucking freezing to death, can I go on?" Then, after a moment, she said, only a little softer, "Thanks for asking."

She followed the lady and her cart back to the ferry. It took the woman twice as long to get down the hill as it had to go up it, since the cart was now so full that she had to hold it back to stop it from careening away with itself.

Now and then, a box or a bag would topple off onto the pavement, and she'd have to brace the cart with a foot against one of the wobbly wheels and stretch out her body to reach the fallen item. Once or twice, passersby offered to help her, and she brushed them off. Eventually, she rolled the cart back onto the ferry.

Kathleen got her truck back onto the ferry, but stood on the deck the whole trip, watching Mrs. Delecourt through the little window in the cabin door. I didn't bother to comment on how the wind must have bit at her on the open deck.

When they docked at Fox Island, Kathleen again watched her roll the cart up the ramp. Again, items dropped. Again, the woman refused all help. Slowly, she pushed that top-heavy cart through the parking lot and down the road to Carver's Harbor. She rolled it all the way to the Municipal Dock where an old, beat-up Boston Whaler was moored. Methodically, she loaded her groceries and the cart into the boat until it was piled high, then she yanked the sputtering motor to life and pushed off. Kathleen watched the woman thread her little open boat through the crowded harbor, watched her round Norton's Point and enter the Thorofare.

"I couldn't follow her after that."

She asked around the dock if anyone knew who the woman was. Tommy Ireland said sure, she was Jake Moseby's daughter, Nancy. Didn't she know the Mosebys? They'd lived on Brown's Head Island as long as anybody could remember. Nancy had run away or something years ago. But she'd come back. Island people always came back.

"I wanted Donny to take me over there," Kathleen concluded. "Just to see. Just to find out...."

She let the sentence hang. Once she had the story out, none of us seemed to know quite what to do next. The energy she'd used to tell it seemed to be all she had in her.

She looked around in something like surprise to see herself back here in the house she'd moved out of, with a guy she'd broken up with (if you could say we'd ever been "together"). The answers to the questions that had tormented her for years were close by, just over the choppy water, and it ought to have been clear what to do next. Instead, the thought seemed to exhaust her. And it left me totally at a loss.

If Kathleen had been some other woman, she'd have burst into tears now, and I'd have held her close and maybe we would have gotten somewhere. If I'd been another man, I'd have gone ahead and held her close whether she cried or not. But we were stuck being who we were, so instead we sat in the silent white room and looked very sad and very uncomfortable and didn't say a word.

It was Neil who spoke with his usual wisdom.

"Anybody want a pizza?" he said.

How did he always know the right thing to say? We agreed that a cheese pizza from the Pizza Pit would be a good first step on the journey of the rest of our lives. Neil gestured for me to go with him. I hesitated, but Kathleen rolled over on her bed and told me to go ahead. She was going to nap anyway. The whole damn thing had exhausted her.

I supposed I should have objected, but I'm ashamed to say that the prospect of being left alone with Kathleen right then filled me with discomfort. I couldn't imagine saying a thing that wouldn't be wrong; I couldn't imagine that she'd want to hear my voice or see my face. But, I reproached myself as we walked out to Neil's truck, I couldn't leave her alone, not feeling the way she did. I might not have been the best company for her, but I had to be better than nothing. And "nothing" wasn't what she'd be alone with, anyway, I remembered with dread.

I was about to tell Neil to take off. To turn and head back in and just lay down in the bed next to her and be all

strong and silent and masculine and comforting. But then
Neil asked if we maybe ought to go talk to Nancy Moseby.
Sort of on the way to getting the pizza, you know?

"What?" I asked.

"Well, I don't know what Kathleen's business is with
her, but it sounds pretty serious. You know she's gonna go
over and talk to them eventually. I thought maybe you'd
want to talk to 'em first. The Mosebys can be pretty touchy
about strangers."

"You know them?"

"Sure. You remember Jake Moseby. Lives across the
Thorofare. The house with the green roof. You know the
one. You can see it from your beach."

A cold bead of water ran down my back and I knew
Jellica had dropped it there.

TWENTY-FOUR

It started to snow just as we rounded the Point. Big, sloppy snowflakes that splatted on the fiberglass surface of Neil's boat and glittered on his eyebrows as he leaned out over the gray, churning water. That same snow is falling outside the hospital window as I write this. Is this really only yesterday that I'm telling you about now?

Neither of us spoke as the boat crossed the Thorofare; I'd done enough talking on the way to the dock, telling Neil about Kathleen and Jellica and doing a pretty poor job of it, leaving out my part of the story, leaving out Jellica's ghost. Despite my omissions, the story was awful enough to make an impact, to leave a grim scowl on Neil's normally cheerful face. "That's the first time I ever heard a story about why somebody started drinking where I understand why they started drinking," was all he said.

I tried to get a little more out of him, to ask him whether he believed the Moseby girl could be capable of doing these things. All he said was, "Brown's Head Island folks can be pretty strange."

Brown's Head Island and its strange folks were drawing closer as we corkscrewed in the frigid water. Maybe it was on account of the leaden sky, but as we approached, that bright green roof that had always looked so vivid from our beach took on a dingier cast, and the house beneath it seemed less like a summer cottage than a white-trash hovel.

Why were we going there, just the two of us? What were we hoping to accomplish? Why hadn't we brought Kathleen with us, or even told her we were going?

I don't know, I don't know, I don't know, and I don't know. I only knew that I couldn't go back to Kathleen in that empty white house with nothing to say and nothing to offer her but a rubbery cheese pizza. I had to have something for her—some news. Proof that Nancy Moseby was Jellica's mother. Proof that she wasn't. In the best and most impossible of all worlds, proof that Jellica was alive and well and playing happily on Brown's Head Island. (Sure, the cloud in that silver lining would be that I'd have to have been insane all along, but I'd have happily taken that on.) Even bad news would be better than nothing. Bad news might at least lead to that mythical thing they discuss on the afternoon talk shows—closure. It would be a way to help Kathleen without actually being in the same room with her. So, yeah, I was taking the coward's way out, even if it led me straight into the home of the enemy.

Neil pulled the boat up to Moseby's dock, jumped out to tie her up, and promptly fell on his ass. The wooden ramp was sheeted in ice. I tossed Neil the rope, and he tied it up with red, chapped hands. I climbed carefully onto the ramp, and we walked toward shore, shifting our feet over the planks as if we were on roller blades. Another time we would have laughed.

As our feet finally reached frozen soil, the door to the house with the green roof swung open, and Jake Moseby came out to greet us. Neil had been right. I did know him, by sight at least. His was one of the faces I'd seen on the is-land all my life, though I'd never learned his name. Always old, from the time I was a kid, he was the one your mother and I used to call Yellow Beard. (Because he had a beard

and it was yellow. Not blond, mind you, but yellow. An unhealthy wash of jaundice over white, like pissed-on snow.)

"Eh, Amudsen, you crazy fuck," he said to Neil. "What
you doing out in ugly weather like this? You as dumb as
you look?"

"Can't say I am, 'cause I ain't. Blame this fucker." Who
was me. "He heard you were thinking of selling your piss
pot boat and he wanted to check it out before it sank."

That was our hastily pre-arranged cover story. It was
safe to assume that any fisherman on the islands was considering selling his boat at any given time, and there was
no better way for Neil to express interest in the craft than
to load on the insults.

Moseby looked me up and down with the expression
of a displeased Old Testament prophet. "You thinkin' of
takin' up lobstering?"

"God, no," I said hastily. Then I added, even more
quickly, "I'll leave that to the experts. I just want to do
some tooling around."

The Prophet squinted at me. "Tooling, eh? You want to
cheat the ferryman out of his money?"

For a moment, I thought he was making an allusion
to death and Greek mythology (ah, the curse of being
an English professor's son), then I realized he was just
talking about the Maine State Ferry system, so I laughed
and nodded.

"Come on. Check her out," Yellow Beard said.

So, we climbed into Moseby's stinking dingy and
rowed over choppy water to Moseby's stinking lobster
boat. We spent the next hour going over it from reeking
stem to reeking stern, while the wind got colder and the
water rougher. I knew when the sales job was over, I'd
have to find some way to stay and talk to this man, to
delve into his past, to find out if his daughter was here and
if she was the monster Kathleen suspected her to be, so I

was in no hurry to conclude things and asked all manner
of perceptive and foolish questions about the boat and the
waters around the islands. All this persuaded him of my
sincere interest in the boat, if not of its future safety under
my command. In time, though, the wind and water got so
bad I knew I had to get to solid ground, even if it meant
facing the reason I'd come here in the first place. So, in the
middle of his discussion of the bilge system, I told him I
thought I'd heard enough and that I'd give him my answer
as soon as I'd talked it over with a wife I made up on the
spot. The old man gave me a Book of Genesis glare, and I
guessed that discussing financial matters with a wife was
suspect in Moseby's world.

We climbed back into the bucking dingy, and I saw
that in the hour we'd spent on Moseby's boat, the snow
had transformed Brown's Head Island into a Rankin/Bass
Christmas TV special. Powdery white and preciously beautiful. I could almost appreciate it as I swallowed my bile
and gripped the side of the lurching boat. For a moment,
I thought Moseby would just drop us off at the dock and
wave us good-bye, but Neil hitched at his pants and said
he could sure use a piss and a beer, so Moseby invited us
in. No diplomat was more expert at the niceties of cultural
interaction than Neil.

The house smelled of wet dog, moldy wool, and stale
urine. The fire in the woodstove was blazing, so we quickly
added the scent of our sweat to the potpourri. Moseby
pulled off his sweater, giving me more of a glimpse of his
mottled gut than I was prepared for, and hollered, "Nan!
We got company! Bring some beer!" He threw his sweater
onto an aging recliner, then dropped on top of it himself.
"Lazy bitch probably sleeping."

Neil stripped off his jacket and took a spot on a stained
brown sofa. Despite the sweltering heat, I kept all my
clothes on, wanting as little of myself exposed as possible.

Moseby offered us smokes from a pack of Kools and let us know how much he hated Clinton, while two huge, square-headed dogs trotted in and started digging at what was left of the carpet. The bigger of the two rubbed a sore spot on his back against a stack of newspapers that lined the back wall. We took the cigarettes to be polite, and Neil and Moseby discussed how bad the lobsters off the Brown's Head shoal had been last summer (apparently, the Democrats were to blame) while I kept quiet, sucking in the chemical cold of the cigarette and studying a laughing Jesus torn from an old magazine. It was pinned to the wall next to a framed print of that old chestnut of the two kids crossing the bridge under the white-winged pin-up girl angel. I started to cough, and the dogs gave me a growl to shut me up.

"Nan, get your lazy ass in here! These boys want beers!" He started to haul himself, red-faced, out of his chair.

"I'm here, Daddy." Nan came in, carrying three Rolling Rocks on a TV tray in a show of hospitality that struck me as more sad than welcoming. But then, everything about this woman struck me as sad. As square-headed as one of her father's dogs, squat and burly, with a face like a clenched fist, not even true love or last call could have made her attractive. Her drooping eyes were downcast and runny. Her mouth was set in a fish-like, Edward G. Robinson frown. I remembered my father quoting George Orwell something to the effect that "after forty, a man has the face he deserves." I had an idea what Nancy Moseby had done to deserve this face, but my heart went out to her anyway.

"Where the hell have you been?" barked Moseby. "Sleeping again?"

"I'm still not feeling good," she said.

Moseby snorted. "Flu!" He tossed us two cans of beer. "I'm surprised we got any of these left. That's what's keeping her in bed."

She sat down heavily on a duct-taped vinyl chair. "Dr. Hopley says it's Epstein-Barr."

"Something from the bar, anyway." He laughed like it was the funniest thing he'd ever said, which it probably was. "You got any kids, Neil?"

Neil shook his head, but I piped up, even though I hadn't been asked. "I have a daughter. Four years old. Little blond girl," my eyes were fixed on Nan. "Blue eyes. Cutest thing you ever saw." Oh, I was clever. Moseby's daughter didn't respond in the least.

Moseby shook his head like one of his dogs. "Yeah, when they're little you think that shit. You got some use for 'em then. Wait till they grow up. You can't get rid of 'em."

"I thought I heard you moved off island, Nan?" Neil gave her a quiet smile. There wasn't a tense muscle in his body.

Nan opened her mouth to respond, but Moseby started laughing even harder than before. "Oh, she moved off all right. But she came back. I told her she'd come back and she come back. Her man run off on her."

"He died, Daddy." She didn't say it angrily, exactly. More like a little petulant, a tired shot in an argument that had been going on for months.

"So you say! I got my own ideas on that one."

"You ever have any kids, Nan?" It was my turn to ask a leading question, but unlike Neil, when I spoke, you could have bounced a quarter off every one of my nerve endings.

She looked down at her hands and shook her head. Moseby was laughing again. "No. She come back with nothing to show for it but three fucking heavy suitcases and these Jesus pictures she's got stuck up everywhere. Gimme the goddamn creeps."

"Where did you go when you moved off?" I kept going, taking a quick sip to dry my cotton mouth.

Nan again opened her mouth to speak, but Moseby was always too fast for her. "New York City."

"I think Nan can speak for herself." I meant it to sound encouraging but I'm afraid it came off cross and bitchy. She didn't like it any better than Moseby did. Father and daughter looked at me like I'd grown horns and a tail.

"Well, you tell him, Nan. You tell the gentleman. You got such a way with words."

She spoke quietly, her gaze again fixed on her pudgy hands. "New York City. But we didn't like it much."

Moseby couldn't let her run on like that. "Her husband was one of those sidewalk preachers. You know, those crazy bastards who stand on the corner screaming about how everybody but them is going to Hell."

"He wasn't," her voice was firmer now. "He was just saved."

"Saved from *you*. Wonder where he is now? Sponging off some other poor retard, I guess."

"He's dead, Daddy."

"Right, right. So, is he in heaven right away now or does he have to wait for the Rapture?" Moseby turned to me. "You want to hear her talk, you get her talking about the fucking Rapture. When she came back here, she wouldn't shut up about it. Tell your new friends about the Rapture, Honey."

"It's coming, Daddy. Laughing at it won't stop it."

"End of the world," he nodded to us. "She can't wait for it."

She was looking up at him now, and I saw the first flash of anger in her eyes. "It's not the end. You're just gonna wish it was. All the saved people are going to be taken up and you'll be left behind."

"A world without Christians," Moseby chuckled. "Now we're talking! Anything I can do to hurry that along?"

"You better listen to me before it's too late."

"Like she cares! She can't wait to go floating up to heaven and look down at all of us poor sons of bitches. Her and Jesus and the heavenly choir are all gonna be singing, 'I told you so!'"

Nan looked down at her hands again, but the anger wasn't gone, just shoved back inside.

"You've done all you can," I said to her. "He's got to come to it on his own."

She looked up at me in surprise and, I think, some disbelief. I wasn't sure I could pull it off myself, but I watched a lot of Christian independent films in the cult section of the video store (I highly recommend *Thief in the Night*, Mark IV Productions, 1972, five stars on the Kehoe Scale for creepy insanity), so at least I knew the Mark of the Beast from the Four Horsemen of the Apocalypse.

"Holy shit, Neil, we got ourselves a couple of fellow lodge members!" Moseby drained his beer. "You go ahead and do your secret handshake, you two. We ain't peeking."

Nan sprang to her feet and started clearing away the empties. When I got up to help her, she skittered out of the room, head bowed. I followed, offering to help and ignoring Moseby's coughing laugh.

In the dingy kitchen, she kept her back to me as she did the dishes, not looking up, not speaking. If she ignored me, maybe I wasn't there. I picked up a threadbare dish rag and started drying.

"I know what you're going through," I said. "My parents didn't accept it when I found Christ either. At least, not at first." *Sam*, I told myself, *you're really going to hell for this one. But then*, I thought, *if half of what Kathleen has said about this woman is true and God sides with her, I wouldn't want to be saved by Him anyway.*

She shook her head. "He's a sinner."

"We're all sinners, Nan."

"He's a bigger one."

"All he's got to do is open his heart to Jesus. You've paved the way; it's up to him now. It's like they say, you've just got to keep acting 'as if.'"

She looked up at me from the scummy water. "As if what?"

"As if it'll happen." I became uncomfortably aware that I was mixing Alcoholics Anonymous doctrine with born-again Christianity, but she was looking at me like I'd said something profound, so I guess it fit.

"You think?" she asked.

"I know. Tell me about your husband. What was his name?"

She looked back to the sink, thrusting her hands into the hot, greasy water. "Bill."

"Bill what?"

"Why do you want to know?"

"Just because. Never mind."

"Delecourt."

"So, you're Nancy Delecourt. That's a nice name."

"He was evil," she said.

"Pardon?"

"He thought he wasn't, but he was."

"Was he saved?"

"Oh, yes." She turned her blank, sagging eyes to mine. "You can be evil and still be saved. That's how powerful Jesus is." There was nothing behind those eyes.

She went back to work, her hands turning redder in the steaming water. I thought of Jellica in that tub and shuddered under my skin. Was she here with me? I almost glanced around the room to find her, but I shook off the temptation. *You're doing this on your own, Sam, with no spook interference.* I was pretty sure that was my own voice talking to me.

"Still, it's hard to lose someone you love. You must miss him."

"I do."

"I remember when my mother died," (forgive me, Mom, for involving you in this—but if you were right about the cosmos, you don't know a thing about this, and if you were wrong then you'll know I'm doing it for a good cause). "I thought I'd give anything just to talk to her one more time. Do you think that's possible? Do you think the dead can come back to us?"

She looked up at me, startled. "But that's wrong. That's evil. That's sinful."

"Well, I know, but it's one of the ways we're tempted, isn't it?"

She stepped away from the sink, still facing me, blank eyes wide, her wet hands dripping on the dirty linoleum floor. "You're one of them, aren't you?"

I could hear my own pulse throbbing in my ears. "No, I'm just saying. You wish you had something to remember him by. A child or something."

She turned away and trotted across the floor. "No, I don't want a child. I don't want a child."

"Really? 'Cause you strike me as the motherly type. I can see you holding a little girl in your arms. Washing her in a tub."

Suddenly, she kicked the door open and screamed out into the living room. "Daddy! It's one of them! It's a devil! He's saying things to me!"

Moseby was on his feet, hollering back at her. "For fuck's sake, shut the fuck up!"

"He's Satan, Daddy!"

He moved toward her, fast as lightning despite his bulk. "I am sick of you acting crazy! When did you get so goddamned crazy!? You're worse than your mother!"

"I swear he's the devil! He's saying things!"

"Everybody's the devil! The goddamn fuel man's afraid to come fill the tanks 'cause you keep howling at him that he's the devil!"

"Daddy—," she was pleading now.

"You stop! You stop right now, or I'll throw you out on your fat ass, and then where the hell will you go? Who's going to put up with your shit if I don't?"

She bolted through the room, banging open the door and running out into the snow.

The room fell silent except for the sound of my breathing, heavy and fast, as if I'd run a marathon. Moseby stepped into the kitchen and I flinched. "Sorry," I said.

He brushed past me with an angry wave of his hand. "Don't apologize for the lunatic." He opened the fridge and yanked a Bud from its plastic collar. "I shoulda cut my dick off before I fucked her mother. Never had a day's peace since. Crazy bitches, both of 'em."

"Shouldn't we go after her?"

Moseby snorted. "She'll be back." He walked past the open door on the way to his chair and hollered out into the snow, "When her ass gets too cold, she'll be back!" He kicked the door shut, dropped into the recliner, and turned to Neil. "Now you see why I don't get any goddamned company."

Neil shrugged. "We all got family."

"What was her husband like?" I asked.

Moseby shot me a dirty look for staying on this distasteful topic. "Hell if I know. She run off when her mother died. Met him later."

"I'm sorry."

"Why? Because she run away? I wasn't. Finally had some fucking peace. Every now and then I'd get a letter from her. Lying about how good she's doing. Saying she found Jesus. She met this great man. Christ knows what he coulda seen in her. I'd'a thought he was after her money if she had any. From the sound of the guy, just a bed to sleep in and three square might've been all he was after.

And somebody to listen to his shit. I wrote back and told her that. Then I didn't hear from her for a couple of years."

"Were you worried about her?"

Moseby shrugged and thumped a dog. "I figure, she's alive or dead, you know, one or the other. Then she calls me, all snot-nosed and crying. She's at Rockland. Ain't even got the price of a ferry ride. So, I head over, and there she is, with her suitcases, a bible, the clothes she's standing up in, and fuck all else. Oh, she showed me, didn't she? Running off. She did damn well for herself, didn't she? Well, I drug her and her shit back here, and she took over the back room and that's been, what, three years, four years? I can't fucking get rid of her."

He glanced at the window. The snow was heavier and the wind was gusting. He scratched a dog's head. "Blowing pretty bad out there," he said and fell back into silence. Then, he hauled himself out of his chair, swearing under his breath, "Freeze my balls off looking for her, damn it, that's just what the crazy bitch wants me to do." But he pulled on his sweater and coat and swung open the door. The dogs bounded out into the storm. "Go find her! Hold her down for me!" He glanced at me as if to let me know this was a joke, then started out after the dogs. Neil went with him. I offered to stay behind in case she came back on her own. At this, Moseby gave me a dark look and slammed the door, muffling the howling of the wind and leaving me alone in the quiet house.

It was odd to sit alone in a strange house. No music on. No TV. No task to perform. Nothing to do but sit and wait. It was unnerving. I tried to make the best of it. To close my eyes and think about the best way to use this unexpected moment of idleness. Perhaps there was nothing I needed to do. I had proved that this was Kathleen's Mrs. Delecourt; my task here was completed. But here I was, in her house, alone. Wasn't there something more I could do?

I could ask Jellica.

I could use the skills Mrs. Day had tried to teach me and bring Jellica here—hell, she was never too far away, was she? I could ask her what it would take to let her move on. Ask her if punishing her mother would set her spirit free.

Fuck that. I was no more ready to bring that little creature back into my brain than I would have been to shave my head in a garbage disposal. Who needed her, anyway? The world was full of people who dealt with trouble without ever seeing or even thinking about ghosts and shit. *From this day on, Sammy, you're one of the great, un-psychic unwashed. The normal dull ones. Hallelujah to me.*

I got up and went into the kitchen. Coffee would warm me up; better yet, making coffee would give me something to do. All I found was a jar of freeze-dried instant. Being a good man of my generation, it had been years since I'd had anything other than fresh roasted. *Well, you're in the wilderness*, I told myself, *you'll have to learn to rough it.* I put the kettle on and waited for it to whistle.

I never really decided to search the house. I started gradually, glancing in cabinets to check cereal and soup preferences (generic, heavy on sugar, bought in bulk) and progressed to a quest for the bathroom, which had me opening doors and finding bedrooms.

I guessed that Moseby's room was the one with the dog beds in one corner and the broken lobster traps stacked in the other. I guessed hers was the one with the Bible and Chick Publications cartoon pamphlets on the bedside table. I picked up one of the little comic books—I remembered the things from high school. Drawn and written with all the subtlety of a *Tales from the Crypt*, their goal was to scare the shit out of kids until they accepted Jesus and hated Catholics, Jews, and Muslims. This one told the touching tale of a teenaged prostitute who had been gorily blinded by two thugs who somehow looked Semitic, black, and gay all at once. In the end, she found Christ, so it all turned out all right. I put the pamphlet down with a shudder. There were more, explaining why we'll never have peace in the Middle East and why Mohammed and the Pope were the anti-Christ, and why *The X-Files* will turn your children into Satanists. Another time, I probably would have laughed at the things and felt smugly superior to their message. But in that room what struck me was their utter sincerity. The stupid, fear-ridden, simplistic, hateful message of those drawings came from a place so rooted in belief that they pulsated with power and fire. And in Nan they had an audience who would work to bring their world to life.

I opened her closet. Hers and her father's were indistinguishable; flannel shirts and jeans on the hangers, muddy boots on the floor. I picked up one boot and shook it—it was only then that I realized I was searching the room. The idea scared me a little and confused me more—what did I think I was going to find?—but I was in for a pound, so I decided to keep going.

A large chest of drawers sat next to the bed. There was an empty frame mounted on top of it; a few shards of mirrored glass still reflected gray light around the edges. Beneath that, a plastic hairbrush, a box of Tampons, more comic books. Opening the drawers felt like a further step in the violation of Nancy's privacy, so I had to take a breath first, but I did it. T-shirts. Underwear. I reached my hand among them, looking for what, I don't know.

The second drawer was empty. I thought about a life so empty it could only fill one drawer, then moved on to the last one. I couldn't open it at first. It was jammed up to the top with socks. I had to pull with all my strength, and I almost gave up before it shot open, socks popping out at me. The drawer tipped over from the weight and slanted down onto the floor. Why the hell had she stuffed this drawer so full and left the upper one empty? I rummaged around to see what made it so heavy. There was a layer of bubble wrap underneath the socks. I pushed them aside and saw a large object all wrapped up in the shiny plastic, like an old forgotten UPS package. I scooped up an armful of socks and tried to look through the overlapped layers of bubble wrap—it was like peering through the icy surface of a frozen lake.

At first I thought it was a doll. Blond hair swirled around her face like a mermaid's; her arms were twisted around her body, the left one flung awkwardly behind her, the right draped across the collar of her flowered dress. But the face was drawn and tight and withered and not like a doll's at all. I recognized her. I'd know Jellica anywhere.

"Do you know where my dad went?"

I turned to see Nancy Delecourt in the doorway behind me, melting snow dripping from her clothes and puddling on the floor.

TWENTY-FIVE

She walked to my side and looked down at the open drawer. "I know I should do something with that," Nancy said. "But there was this whole problem with the police back in New York, and I was afraid somebody would make a big deal about it."

I didn't respond.

"I thought when I got home here, I'd find a place to put it, but I didn't want Daddy to see. You know him; I'd never hear the end of it. And then, you know how it is when you stick something somewhere and just kind of forget about it and hope it goes away?"

"Who is she?" I asked.

"Well, she was supposed to be my daughter, but something happened, some kind of mix-up, you know, and she changed."

"When did she change?"

"Oh, early on. When she started crawling. I didn't see it at first, but Bill did. That's my husband. He started talking all 'oh, she's so pretty,' and 'doesn't she look so grown up?' And he started spending all his time with her. I was like nothing. The cook. The clean-up lady. Wiping up her shit, that's what I was good for. Pretty soon, he's spending every night with her. But it wasn't his fault, you know. It was her. What she'd turned into. It turned him, too.

Turned him against me. That's when he went all evil.

"One time I came in real late, 'cause, like, I'm still working, I'm the one with a job, and I switch on the lights and she was...they were...he was all on top of her like she was a whore. You shoulda heard that little bitch, the way she was screaming. I lost it. Screamed right back at her. And he, he took her side. Started beating on me. Oh, we'd had fights before, but this was different. He wasn't holding back. And she was sitting on the bed just all screaming like something that wasn't even human.

"It blew over, you know, like stuff like that does. But it wasn't the same. Went on like that for, I don't know. Years. And I'd been so happy when he loved me. Now, it was all...he stopped even trying to get work. All he'd do was drink and do stuff with her. Then he got sick and he died."

Neither us had moved since she started talking.

"I wanted to kill her then. But that's a sin, so I thought maybe if I could change her back. Like she was when she was first born. Before the bad stuff started. But she just stayed evil. She talked to demons. She brought 'em right into the room with her. So they could do things to her. That's how evil she was. Then Bill came back."

"Your husband? Your husband who had died?"

She looked up at me, challenging. "You don't believe me?"

"I believe you."

"He came back. But only for her. Only to see her. Wouldn't even look at me. That's how much she'd taken him away from me."

"How did she die?"

"Oh, she just did that on purpose. Just to get me in trouble. That's all she ever wanted was to see me sad. I was just giving her a bath, and she made herself look like that. We were in a hotel, and I knew if I left her there I'd get in trouble, so I put her in my suitcase and brought her

here." She looked down at the clumsily wrapped parcel.
"She looks all quiet, but don't let her fool you. She's just
pretending. I hear her screaming some nights. I don't even
sleep good anymore."

I heard the front door open and Moseby's voice calling
out, "Nan?"

She looked at me with worried eyes. "You won't tell
him, will you?"

"I think I'm going to have to."

"Do you think he'll make fun of me?" she asked.

TWENTY-SIX

There are places where bad things happen every day. Where cleaning up after death and disaster is a commonplace task. Fox Island isn't one of them. So, the discovery of Jessica Delecourt's body wasn't something that could be easily slotted into anyone's routine. Certainly not Donny Beirko's. He stood looking at Jellica's mummified body in the drawer with a mixture of disgust and irritation, refusing to accept that it was what it so clearly was.

"You sure this is her?" he asked. He'd heard the story from Kathleen, he'd rejected it, and it clearly pissed him off to find himself in the middle of it.

I told him I didn't know for sure if it was her. But it was somebody dead in a drawer, so he probably ought to do something about it.

Donny grunted unhappily. Doing something could only mean calling the mainland police in and then standing around like a helpless small-town cop while they did all their mainland police shit. It must have been a humiliating prospect.

"Are you sure it's even a body?" He squatted next to it for a closer look. "I saw something like this in a carnival in Bangor once. Turned out to be a dead monkey." He reached out as if he might unwrap her, and I reminded him that this was probably what they called a crime scene.

He nodded and stood up; I wasn't sure if it was on account of my advice or queasiness at the prospect of touching the thing.

When the mainland cops arrived, they were every bit as officious as Donny must have feared. Bustling into the place, skeptical at first that anything a Barney Fife–type like Beirko could say would possibly hold water, then pushing him aside at the sight of the body and asking, "What happened here?" as if there could be a simple or even comprehensible answer to that question.

I told them the story as well as I could while leaving out everything that actually mattered. I had come here because a friend had recognized Nancy Delecourt from a child endangerment case in New York, and this friend wanted me to check to see if Mrs. Delecourt's daughter was all right.

"And is this the daughter?"

Well, I couldn't really say, could I? After all, I'd never seen Jessica Delecourt. In life. I looked down at Jellica, still wrapped in her plastic shroud, looking so much like the withered monkey from Donny's freak show. It was her. The structure of her face, the color of her hair, the faded pattern of her dress. If I opened my mind, I knew she'd be there with me, watching this scene with wide, glittering eyes. Was she happy that she'd been found? Did it matter to her that her mother might finally be brought to account for killing her? That her little body would now be laid to rest with whatever honors this sorry world could give her? I wasn't going to find out. That was a door that was going to remain resolutely closed.

So, all I could say was that she matched the description my friend had given of the little girl in question. The cops went to Nancy Delecourt, but she simply denied that there was anything human in the drawer. She'd had a daughter once, she explained, but she'd been replaced by that thing, and she didn't know where her real daughter was now. She was glad, though, that the cops were here, because they could take that thing away now, couldn't they? Wasn't that their job? It made too much noise at night, she told them, and she was sick of having it around.

Moseby was no help either. He just sat in the kitchen with a beer and cursed his dead wife whenever anyone asked him anything. It was the forgotten man, Donny Beirko, who came up with the name of the one person on the islands who could identify this body as Jessica Delecourt's.

So, it was Donny's fault that Kathleen was already gone by the time they let me and Neil head back over to Fox Island. Not that I'd been dying to break the news to her, to be the one to confirm her worst fears. But to not be with her when she heard, to be out of touch with her while she went through the ordeal of identifying Jellica's body, seemed more than wrong. It seemed impossible. There had to be a way I could be with her or talk to her. But no one in the Rockland County Police Department could tell me anything about where Kathleen was or where Jellica's body had been taken. All I could do was sit in the living room of our house on the Thorofare, watch the snowdrifts pile up in the moonlight outside, and not be with Kathleen. "She's bound to come back, Sam. Or at least call. She's bound to call." Your mother said that every now and then, just to break the silence. I felt sorry for her; the news of the little dead girl being found on Brown's Head Island had horrified her, and now she felt confused and vulnerable because there was obviously a lot more to the story that no one was telling her. I didn't have the heart to explain it now. I wasn't sure I ever would.

More silence. She looked over at Neil, but he had

dropped off to sleep, or at least pretended to. They hadn't spoken since we'd come back from Brown's Head. I hadn't been sure Neil would even want to come back to the house with me, but as little as he fully understood what had just happened, he knew I didn't want to be alone. We walked into the kitchen and sat down, drinking coffee instead of beer, since beer seemed only to remind us of Moseby. Over the baby monitor, I could hear Charlotte telling you a bedtime story. I dipped the volume for Neil's sake. One crisis at a time, I thought.

When your mother came down and saw Neil, she stopped dead still. A whole lot of stuff would probably have happened right then. Maybe Charlotte would have run back upstairs. Maybe she would have started crying. Maybe she would have thrown a punch at Neil. Maybe they would have run into each other's arms and made up right then and saved us all a lot of trouble.

I'll never know. Because I headed it off, launching into the story of how we'd found the body of a child in Moseby's house and how the police had taken Moseby and his daughter in for questioning. A story like that puts everyday heartache on hold. That's why I told her. I thought if I shook her world up enough, she might see what really mattered and try to make things up with Neil. I had the same hopes for him. Instead, they just sat in silence, and all I'd achieved was a truce in their current cold war. I started to think it might have been better if I'd just let them fight and get it over with. The snow fell heavier outside.

Neil's fake sleep breathing slowly shifted into real sleep. Your mother curled up on the sofa and began to snore. I was left alone with my thoughts. Never good company.

I must have nodded off myself, because the sound of Kathleen's truck struggling down the road startled me awake. The wind whipped the snow sideways through the beams from her headlights as she lumbered to a stop in the driveway. I left Neil and your mother sleeping and hurried to the kitchen door.

She had on a sweater but no coat, and I knew she must be freezing. She didn't seem to care.

"I didn't think you'd make it back tonight," I said.

"They didn't keep me long." I got her a coffee. She stood at the window, melting snow dripping from her sweater onto the floor. "I don't think they could figure out what to ask me. I told them I'd be back tomorrow. I just had to come back to the island to get my things."

"I thought you already packed your things."

She gave a half-smile. "I did."

Did that mean she'd come back for me? I felt slightly ashamed of myself for letting selfish hope intrude on this conversation, so I quickly changed the subject. I tried small talk. I asked her if the cops had brought her back. She said she'd taken her boat back and forth. She loved that boat, she said. She was going to miss it.

"It was her?" I asked, finally.

"You know it was," Kathleen said.

I nodded, getting ready to tell her everything that had happened.

"Is she all right?" Kathleen asked before I could start.

"What do you mean?"

She looked impatient. "Jellica. How is she?"

I couldn't answer right away. It was a question I'd never expected from her.

"Kathleen...."

"Just tell me, Sam," she said, quiet, urgent.

I leaned back against the sink. "I thought we both decided I was crazy."

"Come on, Sam."

I shut my eyes. "I haven't...." I hadn't what? Heard from her? Contacted her? Christ, I didn't even have terminology to use with this shit that didn't make me sound like

Madame Arcati. "I don't know how she is."

"They hadn't examined—they hadn't cut her open yet, but the pathologist thought she'd probably been drowned. Like you said. Did Jellica tell you that?"

It was so hard to explain. "More like showed me."

"You said she was dangerous. Why would she be dangerous?"

"She's just a kid, Kathleen. She's scared. Angry. Possessive. She doesn't really mean any harm. But she wants you...to herself. She's so alone."

Kathleen flinched. "Is she still alone?"

I looked away from her.

"I mean, it can't be," she said. "It can't be that all this shit we feel when we're alive, we can't keep feeling that after we die. Then there's no escape. There's no peace. There's no way out."

I didn't have any comfort to offer her. It seemed like a hellish prospect to me, too. I could deal with the absence of heaven. The idea of a big fat nothing after death didn't scare me. To be honest, it sounded pretty relaxing. But the idea of carrying the baggage of our lives throughout eternity seemed horribly unfair and bleakly exhausting.

"She was haunting me," Kathleen said.

I nodded. "Her father haunted her when she was alive. That's why her mother was so jealous."

"I don't think she's haunting me anymore."

It was quiet in the room. Only your steady breathing over the baby monitor eased the stillness.

"When I saw her in the morgue, I felt...quiet. Like there'd been some electrical charge humming through my body for years and somebody just switched it off. This big knot of anxiety I'd had stuck in my throat for as long as I can remember was suddenly unwound. I felt relaxed. Peaceful. And I knew; it's because she's gone." Kathleen laughed. "Jesus, am I just going to think I'm crazy tomorrow morning? Maybe this is all just relief at finding out what really happened to her. Maybe it's my biochemistry finally getting used to being sober. Maybe I'm coming out of a depression I've been in for so long I don't remember what it feels like to feel good." She gave a humorless laugh. "Well, I might buy that tomorrow morning, but right now I know it's bullshit. She's been with me ever since she died and now she's not. I want to know why."

She was looking at me. God help her, she was looking at me for answers.

"We found her body," I tried to explain. "She can rest now."

Kathleen shook her head. "I used to think, if she was dead, as least she wouldn't be suffering anymore. Now I know it wasn't true. And I don't see why lying in a cooler in the morgue would give her any peace. I need to know if she's okay. I need to know that she's not hurting anymore."

I took a breath. "I would think, if you can't sense her presence—"

"Sam. Do...whatever it is you do. Talk to her. Or see if she's even here. If she's not, if she's really gone, then I guess that would be good, right? That would mean she's crossed over or whatever you call it."

"I don't call it anything, Kathleen. I don't know any more about this than you do. I can't turn this thing on and off. I don't even know how it happens. And I don't want to know. You have to understand, I can't ever do it again."

"Sam. Please."

I sat down across from her. "Kathleen, my whole life's been screwed up by this...power or whatever the hell it is. And nothing I do makes it any better. Denial, acceptance, it's all the fucking same."

"You have a...." I could see her start to say *gift* and stop herself. I'll give her credit for being that smart. "An ability."

"Yeah. An ability no one wants. And one that I don't

have a clue what to do with. I'm like...did you ever read *A Christmas Carol*?"

"What, Tiny Tim, Scrooge?" she asked, irritated.

"Uh-huh. Remember Marley's Ghost? His curse was he could see the suffering of the living, but he'd lost the power to do anything about it. I'm like the opposite of that. I see all these spooks and I know what's hurting them, but I can't help. So, what's the point? It's like I'm watching a closed-circuit TV of some torture chamber, but I can't stop the pain. I can't affect anything."

"When I was a cop I felt that way a lot of the time."

"Yeah. And isn't that why you quit?"

That shut her up for a second. But only a second.

"I know why you don't want to do it anymore," she said. "But this one time you *can* help. You can help me. If you can tell me she's gone...well, I won't know if she's in heaven or if she's just disappeared, but at least I'll know she's not still stuck in place. Still in that bedroom with the windows painted black."

I wanted to help her, God knows I did. But it was like I was an alcoholic and she was asking me to take just one drink. I knew if the door opened, I'd never be able to shut it again.

Telling her no was the hardest thing I'd ever done in my life. Was it hard because I was hurting someone I cared about? Or because I knew if I at least tried to help her, I might see that affection and caring in her eyes that had been there when we kissed the first time? Was it hard because I was resisting temptation and doing the right thing? Or was it hard because I knew it was stupid and cowardly *not* to help her? How was I to know which was the right impulse? Which voice in my ear was the devil and which was the angel?

I felt her hand touch mine and looked up at her. There it was. That look of affection I'd been hoping for. Not quite

the same as before, of course. Then, it had been mixed
with excitement and hope; now, it was tempered with sadness and grief. But the core of it was the same. "Look," she
said, "I don't know what it takes to...I don't even know
what I'm asking you to do. If it's too much...."

Dear God, she was letting me off the hook. It was up to
me now. I could decide on my own whether to act or not.
Jesus, I hate that.

"Fuck you!"

I was yanked from the precipice of decision by
Charlotte's yell from the living room.

Kathleen and I sprung from our chairs as Neil
stomped into the room, heading for the door. I blocked
his way—it wasn't as hard for me to take action in other
peoples' dramas.

"What the hell's going on?" I asked.

Neil's a big guy; I'd never seen him mad before, so I'd
never realized how big he really is. "Out of my way, Sam."

"I'm not letting you go like this."

"Yeah, you are."

"Let him go," Charlotte called out behind me.

"Damn it, nobody's going anywhere," I shouted at them
both. "Jesus Christ, how can you look at what happened
today and think that you have problems?! You're two people who've known each other for years and you love each
other. The rest is shit, the rest is details! Let it go!"

If I thought my words of wisdom would chasten them,
I was as far off as I usually am.

"What the fuck do you know about it?" Charlotte said.

"Just shut up and stay out of this," Neil said. At least
they could agree on something.

"He asked me when I was going to tell Maggie about
that video—"

"I didn't say that!" Neil protested. "Do you *want* me to
get pissed at you, is that it?"

"I just want to know what you really think!"

I made small bleating noises to quiet them down. Not surprisingly, they went unheeded.

"We were talking about the little girl on the island," Neil explained, but he was talking to Kathleen, not me. I was clearly on both their shit lists. "About how hard it would be to explain something like that to Maggie. But she thought she ought to. She said she didn't think kids should be left in the dark about important things. So I asked if, *if* she was going to explain to Maggie about her video—"

"Like that's a reasonable question," she was in his face now. "Are you saying that's a reasonable question?"

"I don't know, maybe not. But are you ever going to tell her?"

"No, I'm not. Of course not. I care about what she thinks of me. Why the hell would I tell her?"

"Then why did you tell me?" The anger suddenly fell out of Neil. "I didn't want to know that." Weariness, vulnerability, and bone-deep disappointment filled his eyes.

Charlotte saw it. Her voice softened. "I *wanted* you to know. I wanted you to know and still be okay with me."

"I wish I was the guy who could do that," he said, quietly.

I watched them, my heart pounding in my throat. They were so close. Why didn't one of them take the step? The right word from either of them and they could start mending this. But I didn't know what that word might be, and I don't imagine they did either.

"Sam?" Kathleen was tugging at my sleeve. I glanced over quickly, not wanting to take my eyes off Neil and Charlotte. Kathleen was looking toward the stairs. "Where's that snow coming from?" she asked.

I followed her gaze. Snow was drifting down the stairs. A breeze caught it, whirling in the stairway, twisting it into a little spiral, like a storm seen from a long way off.

The house groaned from a gust of wind. The snow puffed into the room and dusted us. There was no sound except wind and creaking wood. Sometimes a parent can hear silence more clearly than any noise. Charlotte snatched up the baby monitor and held it to her ear. Your breathing had stopped.

We both dashed up the steep staircase, running with controlled panic. In your room, the covers were thrown back on your empty bed. Snow from the open window was collecting in the creases of your pillow and drifting on the wind.

Your mother ran from room to room calling your name, but I knew you weren't going to answer. Through the open window, I saw footprints on the snowy roof.

There was only one set of prints, but I knew you hadn't left alone.

TWENTY-SEVEN

just went into the hospital room to make sure you were still there. That you hadn't jumped out of the window and rappelled down the steep incline of building. No worries. You were still there, tucked into your bed. At least your body was.

Where the rest of you is, I can't say.

The howling wind cut through my shirt, burned my fingers, and stung my eyes. The four of us gathered around the scuffed depression in the snow where you'd dropped from the roof to the ground. From the look of things, you'd made a good landing then taken off toward the shore. Toward the water.

We raced down the slope, slipping on the powdery snow, trying to track your footprints even as the wind whipped them away. When had you left? I tried to place the last time I'd heard your breathing over the monitor, but it was useless. I was sure that Charlotte and Neil were blaming themselves, thinking that it was their fight that had woken you up and driven you out of the house. I knew better.

Neil stopped when we got to the well. I'd had that horrible thought myself, but I kept on running. Neil would stop me if he saw signs that you moved the lid and dropped in, like those damned kids in TV newscasts were forever doing. I followed what I hoped were the faint traces of your footprints further onto the beach. The tide was high, so any sign you might have left in the sand was under the cold, choppy foam that lapped at my feet. Neil was beside me now, panting heavy clouds into the night air.

"The well's okay."

We both looked across the water. We couldn't see the green roof of the Moseby house, but we knew it was there.

"Why would she do this?" Neil asked, plaintively.

I could hear Charlotte and Kathleen calling your name. I turned to see them racing aimlessly across the snow, hands cupped to their faces, screaming into the wind.

"Go help Charlotte," I told Neil. He went off without questioning. I moved fast, racing along the shore toward the woods. There were no footprints to follow, no sounds to lead me forward, but I wasn't going to any particular place. I just needed to be alone. I couldn't do what I had to do in front of the others.

The crowded trees make a thick wall at the edge of our property, a tangle of gnarled trees and new growth fighting jealously to reach the sunlight. I hit that wall of branches without breaking my stride, raising my elbows to protect my face, drained parchment-dry from the cold. Welts stung my hands as I broke through the brambles and tripped over a fallen trunk, tumbling onto the frozen ground. Back there on the lawn, the moonlight and the reflecting snow had given the night a twilight glow. Here, everything was pitch black, dark as the inside of Jellica's windowless room must have been. I struggled onto my knees without thinking, in an instinctive imitation of prayer.

"All right, you little bitch," I whispered, more in my mind than through my cracked lips, "I'm here. Talk to me." My fingers entwined, smearing blood on the back of my hands. I opened my mind. Or tried to. There was nothing there but the cold wind, the ragged pain in my hands, and the aching of my knees on the frozen ground.

Damn it. Why did I have to be so useless? I grabbed a handful of grit and snow and rubbed it on my face, gasping. "It's all right, Jellica," I mumbled, trying to calm myself. "I'm not mad at you, I just...The hell I'm not mad! I'm furious!" I was shouting against the wind now, and I felt my dry lips split open, "You're hurting Maggie. Don't you know that? Don't you care?"

The laughter came from someplace far away, though whether it was a distance inside my head or outside it, I couldn't say. The tinkling laugh of a child delighting in a new game. I sprang to my feet, running at the sound. It seemed to have no source, but it led me forward, pulling me with its mocking glee. I slipped over slick granite slabs, tumbled into frozen ditches, ran at icy branches that tore my face and stabbed at my eyes. I ran until my lungs ached and my breath gave out, and then I ran farther, but no matter how much ground I covered, the laughter never grew louder or softer, closer or farther away.

I burst into a clearing and stopped, my body drenched in sweat despite the cold, my eyes blinded by the moonlight, which was dazzlingly bright after the darkness of the woods. The wind, even colder now, swept up at me from below. I stood on a ledge ten feet above dark water. Black Granite Quarry. One of the many long-abandoned stone quarries on the island, filled with freezing water from underground springs. Some of the quarries were used as swimming holes or for skinny dipping, but this one was too small, too off the beaten track, so it had become overgrown and forgotten. I stared around in the colorless moonlight. The laughter stopped. Had Jellica led me here, or had I been running blindly from something inside my own mind?

Below me, the dark water reflected the stars, a circle of night sky planted in the earth. But the scattering of stars was incomplete; in its center was one spot of pure blackness. Something dark and motionless floating in the quarry.

Something shaped like you, Maggie.

I jumped. Feet first, without thought, without grace. Ten feet of freezing air, and then the water hit me, stabbing me with needles. I sank into the murky darkness. I knew I wouldn't hit bottom; the quarries were deeper than I could imagine, so I forced my arms and legs to move, to slow this fall and carry me the impossible distance to the surface. I swam upward, my wet clothes weighing me down, pulling me toward the cold vastness beneath. My mind fought against me, recalling in involuntary flashes every childhood story I'd ever heard of the mysteries hidden in the bottomless deeps of the island quarries. Large, vicious eels; lost cars full of forgotten tourist skeletons; unpredictable undertows that snatched innocent swimmers and sucked them through hidden channels to the sea. *If your mind is fighting you,* I told myself, *then shut it up. What good has it ever done you anyway?* Who I was talking to at that moment, if not my own mind, I couldn't guess. A multitude of voices argued inside me, but none of them seemed to bring me any nearer to the surface.

All at once, I burst out into the night air. I gasped for breath too soon, sucking water into my lungs, so that I had to cough and spew it out again. I twisted in the water, looking for you. I spotted you, still floating, still motionless. I splashed toward you, the cold sapping my energy, seeping into my joints, making every movement an agony. I pushed past the pain, threw myself like a seal through the water, stretched out my hand as far as I could reach. My fingers grabbed your leg. My grip was weak, but I pulled you toward me, straining to see your face. Your eyes were shut, your expression relaxed and much too calm.

"Maggie!" I yelled, feeling myself sinking. No response.

I wrapped my right arm around your waist and fought to pull you toward the shore. I spotted a ledge level with the water a million miles away on the far side of the quarry. I wasn't sure I could have reached it even on my own, but pulling you with me? I told myself that would only make it easier; I could give up on myself, but never on you.

Should I rest for a moment and regain my strength? But no, the effort of keeping us both afloat was exhausting in itself. Rest, and I'd only use up the tiny resources I had left. I took in a breath, snow caking my split lips, and pumped my legs, pivoting my free arm, dragging us both slowly, unforgivably slowly, toward the ledge.

I kicked off my waterlogged shoes, trying to use the stinging pain of the cold to keep me awake, to keep me moving. Something brushed against my stocking feet. I kicked hard, forcing from my mind the image of quarry eels slithering around my legs. There it was again. Tendrils fluttering against my feet, my calves. I thrust my aching body forward, pulling away from whatever it was—algae, seaweed, or nothing at all but a manifestation of my panic and the frozen state of my limbs.

But again, it was there, stroking my leg, feathering the soles of my feet. Playing with me. And as soon as that thought entered my numb brain, the thing grabbed hold of my leg. Gripped me tight and strong and yanked me under the water. I lost my hold on you as I sank into the darkness. Flailing, I kicked my leg free of the icy grip. I struggled to the surface and grabbed you again, pushing you now, shoving you with what feeble strength I had left. We were almost there. Another thrust with my legs. Another. My muscles burning and freezing, aching and numb all at once.

We reached the ledge.

I felt you bump against the granite lip, allowing myself

to hope that you might react to this, that you might reach out and grab the rough stone. But you simply bobbed against it, limp and unaware, like a bundle of clothing someone had dumped into the water. I got underneath you and pushed, lifting you onto the ledge, shoving your awkward limbs onto the cold, snowy granite. You rolled over. I winced as your head cracked on the stone and you lay still. Dead weight. The phrase came unbidden into my head, and I shoved it away. I hugged the ledge, treading water, staring at your face. Your mouth was open, and water drained from your lips, just the way spittle used to when you were a baby sleeping on my shoulder.

Then, I felt it again. From under the water, something grabbed my leg, seizing me tight. The cold grip of tiny fingers. I scratched at the slippery surface of the ledge, fighting to hold on, but the grip was too strong, or I was too weak. It pulled me down into the cold water, and even as it flooded my mouth and nose and ears I could hear Jellica laughing.

The night sky rushed away from me. The pressure of the water bore down on me, crushing me until I was small, tiny. Until I disappeared altogether.

Breathing was no longer a struggle. No longer necessary at all. Time slowed or sped up, was extended or compressed. It became meaningless, like breathing, like the beating of my heart or the throbbing of my pulse....

Water drained from my body, pattering into a puddle on the wood floor beneath my feet. Wood? Why should there be wood underneath me?

I could see the wood, examine every whirl of the grain, but I couldn't feel it. The soles of my feet rested on it, but did not touch it. I wondered, again, why it was there. Then, I remembered Mrs. Day's teachings. I was entering a spirit room. Some spook's home. I braced myself. I took a deep breath.

The air was so hot and humid that the freezing water of the quarry evaporated from me in a cloud, leaving
my flesh painfully sensitive. Every hair on my body stood
on end, antennae straining for reception. But I could feel
nothing, come into contact with nothing. I could see a
room around me, but I was not in it.

I could smell it, though. This room stank of New York
summer heat. It was dark, but I didn't need light to see.
I knew the room; I'd been here before. This was Jellica's
room. Whether it was in my head or her head, the dis-
tinction made little difference. I couldn't see a door, and
even if I had, I couldn't move to use it. I was here, and
all I could do was stand and look at the bare room with
the windows painted black, listening to the tiny scratching
sound that came from inside the upended playpen in the
center of the room with the crumbling cinder block holding it down. Jellica's fort.

The scratching was constant, purposeful, like rats in
the walls, building paths unseen all around me. Fingernails
digging an escape route or trying to signal to the world
from under the plastic lip of the playpen that rested on the
scuffed wooden floor. Then, I saw the plastic lip bend, bow
outward, pushed by something from within. A tiny hand
with broken dirty nails worked its way out, still scratching
at the floor.

"Mommy?" The voice was small and frightened.
"Mommy, can I come out? I'll be good. Please?"

I tried to open my mouth to answer, but I couldn't.

"I said please, Mommy. I sorry. I made a potty in here,
can you please lemme out?"

I watched the little hand retract, pulling itself back
into the playpen. The air grew thick and foul all around
me. I felt a nauseating wave of claustrophobia and anxiety,
like the worst morning terrors of my life. Every moment
of depression I'd ever felt filled my heart and weighed me

down, as if this room were the black heart of my soul. The world was bleak and hopeless, and as bad as things were, they were only going to get worse.

The lip of the playpen bowed out again. Two hands crept out this time, extending from beneath the plastic wall. Shoulders came now, pressed to the floor, bones flattening like a rat's when it squeezes through an opening no bigger than its head. A mass of hair flowed out next, like spilled ink, then the head of a little girl twisting and rolling as she dragged herself forward, her ribs collapsing flat, forcing herself through the tiny opening. She lifted her head to look at me. Jellica's dark, gleaming eyes, devoid of fear now. She pulled herself free, rising to her feet with slow, easy grace, and looked at me through greasy, matted hair. Her body was shining, slick with blood and filth, but as she moved toward me, the muck evaporated from her in a fetid cloud so that by the time she stood next to me she was clean and perfect in her little flowered dress. She smiled at me, then turned back to look at her playpen cage.

The scratching started from inside it again.

A tiny hand crept out from underneath the plastic lip and scraped at the floor. Next to me, Jellica gave a little laugh and slipped her hand in mine. The touch of her fingers was like sandpaper on my raw skin.

"I hate being in there alone," she said.

"Then come out," I said. I could speak now, at least to her.

"You're stupid. You say stupid things." She looked up at me. "Will you come in there with me?"

"No. You have to come out."

"That's where I live," she said, simply, as if that decided everything. "I leave, but I always have to go back there."

"Why?"

"I jus' do." She was irritated now. "Maggie said she'll stay with me."

The fingers scratched harder on the wood.

"What do you mean?" I asked.

"You're stupid. Why are you always so stupid?"

"Mommy?" It was your voice now, coming from inside the playpen. Your little nails scrabbling on the wooden floor. "Unca Sam?"

"Maggie?" I tried to keep my voice steady.

"She can't hear you," Jellica said. "She can't hear you 'less you're inside there. She's such a crybaby. She said she'd stay with me, but she doesun' like it. You wanna go in?"

The room reeked of fear, sweat, and shit. It was the worst place I could imagine, but there was no way to leave. I tried to picture the universe around it, but it was no use. This room was all there was. It was reality, and every other place I'd ever been was a dream. This room was all that life had to offer me or Jellica. Or you.

"If I go in, will you let Maggie go?"

Jellica thought it over. "I guess so. She's kinda boring right now."

I wanted to move. I wanted to say "yes, I'll go in. Just let her go." But where would you go? How could there be a hope of escaping this room if this room was the whole universe?

Something moved, flashing quickly past the corner of my eye. Something white in the dark edges of the room. I felt a rush of fear. Who could it be? How could there be anyone else in this world of a room that contained just the three of us? I forced myself to look closer, but the white blur eluded me. The fear shook me, and I hugged it close. Fear was better than the despair I'd felt seconds before. Fear wasn't emptiness. Fear meant that something in this bleak world could change, even if for the worse. Fear meant there could be a way to run or fight.

"Yes," I told Jellica. "I'll go in with you."

The world of Jellica's room didn't behave like that other world, the one I only vaguely remembered, the one I used to live in. In that world, you moved in some way I couldn't recall to get from one place to another. Here in the real world things simply shifted and flowed to Jellica's will. The playpen was all at once around me, and I was small, insignificantly small, trapped inside its sweating walls. There was no air in the cramped, humid space. The world had shrunk down to this. Even fear and the cold comfort that had offered me was gone.

"Unca Sam?"

I reached out my hand and touched your matted hair.

"Maggie. You're not supposed to be here. You have to go."

"I don' know the way."

I held you to me and told you there was a way out. There had to be.

I turned to Jellica, who sat against the corner of the pen, and demanded that she show you the way. Jellica shrugged. "If she's too dumb to figger it out, that's her problem."

I tried to control my anger. "You said if I came in here, Maggie could go."

You held on to me tighter. "I don' wanna go by myself," you whimpered.

I was suddenly weak and powerless. A child whining at the world's injustice. "It's not fair!" I cried.

Jellica's eyes flashed in anger. As I watched, she grew in front of me, Alice in Wonderland after eating the mushroom. Her voice boomed with authority. "Who told you life was fair, you little shit! You sinned. You're damned. Be grateful. You could be in hell."

You started to cry, and as I turned to you, I saw another figure flitting past the corner of my eye, a dark figure this time. I looked up to see it, but as soon as I tried to focus on it, it vanished. I understood at once that the voice I'd just heard hadn't been Jellica's. It belonged to the dark figure who wanted to stay hidden. I felt a rush of fury. Who was it? Why was it watching, playing with us? Were we entertainment for it?

I used that anger to push me forward, grabbing Jellica by her hair and dragging her down, making her small in front of me. Making her a child again. She wasn't the only one who could control this world.

"I don't believe in hell," I told her, or whoever she was. I felt power surge through me. I heard a voice clear and loud in my head.

You can do anything you want to a child, it said. I hated that voice, wherever it came from.

Jellica looked up at me, a frightened little girl, all too used to the anger of adults. I let her go, and she retreated to her corner. I felt ashamed, polluted, invaded. The voice that had spoken through Jellica was in my head now. I tried to find it inside me, but it dashed away, like a cockroach in a flash of light.

Jellica was crying now. "It's not my fault," she said. "We're in his house, we play by his rules."

"Whose house? Who told you that?"

"Daddy. He pays the rent. What he says goes."

I rose to my feet. I had to confront him. "Delecourt!" I yelled. "Let me see you!" The white figure darted past in the corner of my eye, but I ignored it. It was the dark one I wanted. Jellica's father. "I'm not some kid you can scare," I yelled, hoping it was true. "I'm not some puny civilian! I'm a medium!"

The playpen and the bleak room surrounding it flew away.

It was replaced by another room altogether. A white room. Sunshine through Venetian blinds making blinding slashes of light on the walls. A boy sat on a twin bed under a Molly Hatchet poster, his face turned down, his eyes red from crying. Did I really have the power to move from room to room? Or did they just drag me along?

I looked around for you and for Jellica. I couldn't see you, but I knew you were there. That Jellica's room was somehow within reach.

I was sitting on the bed now, without even moving. "Why are you crying?" I asked the boy.

"I'm not," he said quickly, wiping his nose. "I'm okay."

"What's your name?"

The boy turned to me. I tried to guess his age, but it kept changing from boy to teen to adult as the clouds moved across the blinding sun, shifting those slashes of light like semaphore signals. "Billy Delecourt," he said.

"Is this your room?"

"Sometimes." He looked away. "You better go."

"Why?"

"You just better."

He was scared now. I could smell fear in every corner of the room.

The sun washed the room again and Delecourt grew up. Suddenly, he was tall and rail-thin, with black, glaring eyes and the patchy, stringy beard of a teenager trying to look like a man. He glared at me, his unwashed body stinking like those homeless panhandlers you cross the street to avoid. "You better go," he growled.

I kept my voice even. "You go. You don't have to be here, Delecourt. You can leave. You can let all this go. You can cross over."

He shook his head, defiant, certain. "I never hurt her. My Jellica. It was that bitch of a wife of mine. She kept trying to keep us apart. She couldn't do it, though. We're together now. Always."

"This isn't always," I said, calmly. "This is just a trap

you've built, and you're both in it."

Delecourt smiled. "You don't even understand. You don't know what I've done for her."

What he'd done for her? I wanted to knock his teeth in for what he'd done for her. For the hell he'd put her through. For the hell he was keeping her in. But I knew anger wouldn't work. I couldn't get mad. I had to get smart.

"I know you're keeping her here," I said.

"Yes. Yes, that's the point," he said. "She's safe here. It's the best I can do."

He opened his hands and looked down at them, empty and helpless. They were little boy's hands and he was a child again.

Behind us, the door opened. Billy looked up, eyes wide, welling up with tears.

An ogre strode into the room.

"Who the fuck are you talking to?" it said to the boy.

"Nobody," Billy answered, with the quick habit of habitual apology.

The ogre walked to the bed, ignoring me as if I wasn't there. Which I suppose I wasn't.

He took his huge hand and placed it on the boy's head. He was a monstrous man; his body hairy, bulging, distorted; his gray face covered with a sandpaper five o'clock shadow; his eyebrows wild and bushy; his knuckles swollen and knobby. He stank of shit and sweat and urine. He was a giant out of a fairy tale. Popeye's Bluto. A child's nightmare of the awful power of the grown-up.

"Have you thought about what I said?" His voice was a low rumble in my rib cage, like the bass beat at a rock concert.

"Kind of, but—" The boy started to speak. The ogre twisted Billy's head upward, wrenching his neck.

"Are you going to whine again?"

"I'm sorry."

The man's breath smelled like beer and onions and rotting meat. "Have you thought about how sick you are? Have you figured out what's wrong with you?"

"Yes, I have."

He smacked Billy with his hammer of a hand. "Don't lie to me! You think you can fool me like I'm some kind of retard? You're not leaving this room until you give me an answer. Do you hear me!?"

"Yes."

"You're not leaving this room!"

The boy nodded rapidly, hoping that a wordless reply wouldn't provoke him.

It didn't work. The boy's head rocketed back from the ogre's slap.

"You sick little fuck!" the ogre cried. "You're making it happen again. Look at what you're doing to me." He bent down and kissed the boy with his blistered lips.

A hand gripped my shoulder and pulled me away, yanking me out of this room and back into Jellica's windowless prison. I turned to see the grown-up Delecourt holding me, keeping me there.

"You like to watch?" he asked me. "Is that what gets you off?"

In anger, I seized Delecourt by the hand that held me, prying it off my shoulder. He looked startled, surprised that I could do that.

He still hadn't accepted that I wasn't helpless in front of him. It was then, I think, that he realized what a mistake he'd made inviting me in. I was learning. I was learning how to navigate in this world.

I swung him around, but not through the room, not through space. I swung him through time, back to that other room. I can't explain how I did it; it was as if I'd found a new muscle, a new limb I'd never known I had.

I could work this world as if it was a part of me. I had learned so much.

Delecourt wrenched himself away.

"You touched her," I shouted at him, spewing hate.

"I *had* to. She's like me. She's got so much sin in her. I had to find a way to let it out. To release the lust from her."

He wasn't lying. Feeling nauseated, I realized that he'd made his sin her own and convinced himself that all he'd done had been done to save her. "You thought you were protecting her?" I asked.

"I am. You saw what happened to her when I left. What my wife did to her. God, that was my fault. I'll never let anything happen to her again. I have to keep her safe."

"Let her go, Delecourt. Nothing can hurt her if you let her go. She needs to pass over."

"No! She's sinned. She's evil. If I let her go, she goes to hell."

"She won't. She's innocent, she'll—"

"Nobody's innocent, you stupid fuck. We're all corrupt."

"We're not," I said. "We don't have to be." I took Delecourt by the wrist.

"What do you want to do to me?" He tried to pull away, but I held him still. I had the power to do that, and this was why it had been given to me.

I turned to the ogre, calling, "You!"

The ogre stopped moving, his back hunched over. But he didn't turn to look. He tried to ignore me.

"You heard me!" I cried.

The ogre twisted around, black slime dripping from his broken teeth. "You're next," he growled.

"Show me *your* room," I said.

He tilted his shaggy head, puzzled.

"Show it to me," I repeated, my voice calm, steady.

It seemed he was used to being told what to do—the sudden wash of fear looked absurd on his heavy brow.

I reached forward, pulling Delecourt along with me. Before the ogre could back away, I'd pressed my hand against his greasy chest, pushing it wrist deep between his huge ribs, plunging inside of him.

The world twisted and rippled again. We found ourselves in a new room. A tree house made of splintered planks and knotty branches. A group of boys were huddled in the center of an uneven floor, spitting on something, laughing at it, punching it with their hard little fists, kicking it with their Keds-clad feet.

I craned my neck, though I knew what I would see. A small boy curled up in the center of their huddle, wet with spit and tears.

"Look at the pussy cry," the boys said. "You know what we do with pussies?" And they started to piss on him.

"Who is that poor boy?" I asked Delecourt.

Delecourt yanked at my hand, trying to turn us both away. "I hate this place," he screamed.

But then I understood. The little boy was the ogre as a child. And he grew up to be Billy Delecourt's father.

"This is where he comes from, isn't it?" I said. "Your monster. This is his room."

The rooms were like Russian nesting dolls, I told him. One resting inside the other. Delecourt's father's room in this tree house, Delecourt's room inside that, and Jellica's room inside that. And outside of those rooms, there were others, on and on. There was no telling how far back it went. It was a legacy, passed from generation to generation.

"Original sin," Delecourt whispered.

"No," I told him. "It started somewhere. It can end somewhere. It can end with you."

He looked at me, terrified. "No. This is the way things are. I can't change this...."

"Take us back," I told him. "I want you to take us back

to Jellica's room."

He couldn't meet my eye. "You do it."

"No," I said. "It has to be you. I can't do it."

Delecourt shut his eyes, tears streaking the dirt on his face. And he did it.

He made it be Jellica's room again. You and Jellica sat in the playpen, but we could see you. We could do anything we wanted, if only we knew it.

"Let her go," I said to Delecourt.

His breath caught in his throat. "I can't."

"Don't you see? She's trying to pass it on to Maggie. Even though she's dead, she's still trying to pass this pain on. That's how strong it is."

"Too strong."

"But you can break the chain. You're the one who's holding her here. You can let her go."

"No. She's safe here. She's not hurting anyone."

"You know that's not true. She's not like you, not like the others. She's too powerful. Power like hers, combined with this kind of pain, is too strong. It can't be contained. She's killing Maggie. She's killing me. She'll take Kathleen next, and she won't stop there. She's too powerful to be trapped between worlds like this. You have to let Jellica go."

"But what will happen to her?"

"I don't know. Nobody knows. But it's what has to happen."

He turned in my grasp, twisting, writhing, changing from man to boy and back again. "Won't he be mad?" the boy asked me.

"Who?"

"The monster?"

"He won't know," I told him. "Not if you go, too."

His eyes opened wide with fear. "I can't. If I leave here, I'll go to hell."

"This is hell," I told him. "There's no hell unless you build it. You put up these walls and you can tear them down."

He shut his eyes. The color drained from him. I felt him trying to disappear, but it was a trick he couldn't play with me. Not anymore.

I heard the patter of dripping water on the floor next to me and turned to see Jellica at my side, looking up.

"Daddy?" she asked. "What's wrong?"

He shut his eyes tighter, turning away from her. Fading from her view.

"Where are you going, Daddy? Where are you going?"

The color drained from the room around us. I felt the walls grow less substantial, as if they were beginning to stop being walls. The white figure was there again, flitting past my peripheral vision like a flat stone skipping on water. It was sharper and more defined than before. Growing more real as the room began to fade.

"I'm not going anywhere," Delecourt told her. "You are."

Jellica blinked her eyes in confusion. The white figure was swirling behind her now. "I don't want to go anywhere, Daddy. Are you mad at me?"

The white figure was wrapping itself around her. It was a woman, I could see that now. Its smoky gown fluttered to wrap itself around Jellica.

"I'm not mad at you, Jessica," Delecourt said, his eyes still closed, his shape flickering and dimming. "I love you. Go with her."

The white figure bent low, her hair flowing around her face. She looked up at me now, eyes piercing and brilliant. I knew the face. I'd seen through those eyes. It was the Good Mother, her expression filled with compassion and hope. Jellica's little face tilted up toward hers, and for the first time, I saw peace on the little girl's features.

Their arms flowed into each other until they were the same figure, and then they were gone.

I looked around for you, but I couldn't see you anywhere. It was getting harder and harder to see anything here. The place was disappearing from the world, and everything in it was flowing away.

I could hear Delecourt sobbing. A faint sound, from a great distance.

"Go with her!" I called to him. "Go!"

From a long way off I could just glimpse him, just make him out shaking his head, small, tiny, helpless. "I live here," I heard him say.

And then water burst through the windows, though the windows themselves were gone, and crushed the walls, though they weren't walls anymore. Freezing water engulfed me. I resisted it, shaking it off me like a dog.

I was in the kitchen at our house. On the Thorofare.

I heaved a sigh of relief. Everything was normal now. The way it was supposed to be. There was Mom and Dad and George at the table playing cards. I pulled up a chair and joined them, happy, relaxed for the first time in years.

But I wondered if I'd done something wrong. They were looking at me, surprised and maybe a little irritated, as if I'd committed some obvious faux pas.

"Can I play?" I asked.

Dad laughed, good-natured. "No."

"Not yet, little brother," George said, shaking his head.

"Wait for the next hand," Mom said, reasonable as ever.

Then the room filled with water, and they were gone.

Cold air and moonlight hit me with a sudden shock. I was struggling on the surface of the quarry, my lungs and arms and legs blazing with pain. My hand slapped against stone. I grabbed the granite ledge and pulled myself toward it. I saw you stretched out on the gray rock, foam drooling from your open lips.

I don't know where I found the strength to pull myself out of that water. It came from some deep reserve I never knew I had and that I'll never be able to refill. I'll die a month earlier because of that effort, but at least it'll be some month in the future. The distant future, I hope.

I hauled myself up onto the rock and crawled to your pale, still body. I pushed on your little stomach, trying to pump water out of you. I opened your lips and blew my breath into you, filling your chest. Again. Again. I wanted to give you all my breath, every breath I'd ever taken and would ever take. I gave you as much as I could, and between my breaths I heard myself repeating the same nonsense words, over and over.

"Knock-knock. Who's there? Banana. Knock-knock. Who's there? Banana. Knock-knock. Who's there...."

You still hadn't told me the rest of your joke, Maggie. You couldn't die without delivering the punch line. You couldn't leave work that important unfinished.

Your jaw clenched, and you spit up water and phlegm. I scooped the spit and vomit from your lips and breathed into you again.

You breathed back at me, feebly.

Orange, I thought, remembering the joke from when I was four. *Orange you glad I didn't say banana?*

My eyes drifted shut, and I fell back toward the water. Someone caught me. My eyes opened, and I saw Neil and your mother standing over your shivering body. Someone asked me if I was all right. I looked up and saw that it was Kathleen holding me in her arms.

I laughed. They looked worried, like I was acting crazy or something. But they just didn't get the joke.

I'd never been better in my life.

❄

I don't know that Neil and your mother ever made up, exactly. They just spent the next twenty or so hours hovering over you, caring for you. Comforting each other. Bringing each other food, taking shifts sleeping and eating. They became a unit, a team. A couple. So, I don't think they have a choice. They're going to have to work out their shit, whether they want to or not.

With me and Kathleen, it's a little less clear. She showed up at the hospital after we were airlifted to the mainland. She's brought me coffee four times and Chinese food once. She hasn't left town. And I think she's genuinely glad I'm not dead. More than that, we'll just have to wait and see.

Waiting is the main thing we do now. Waiting for you to wake up, to open your eyes, to laugh. They won't tell us if you will. They act as if they're protecting us, holding back information that might disturb us, but I think that's just an act. They don't know either. And they're so foolish, they don't even know that they don't know. They ask me how long you were in the water, but how can I give them an answer they'd understand? We'd spent a lifetime in that quarry, you and me.

The Good Mother isn't trapped here like the other spooks. She's not here because of fear or denial or pain. She's not looking for her missing children, not the way I thought. She's here for the same reason I am. For the same reason I think you are, Maggie. She's here to help the lost ones, the trapped ones. We can help them from this side; she can help them from the other.

She's here now, standing in the hospital corridor, looking at me as I write. If I were a religious man (and how is it that after all this, I'm still not?), I'd say she was an angel watching over us. To my mind, she's something better than that. A human soul trying to do good.

But she's gone now.

A nurse is there, standing in the space the Good Mother had occupied a second ago. I'd write more, but the nurse is talking to me.

She tells me you're awake.

ABOUT THE AUTHOR

Phoef Sutton is a *New York Times*–bestselling author whose work has won two Emmys, a Peabody, a Writers Guild Award, a GLAAD Award, and a Television Academy Honors Award. The first novel in the Crush series, titled *Crush*, was a *Kirkus* Best Mystery of 2015 and a *Los Angeles Times* "Summer Reading Page-Turner"; the next two, *Heart Attack & Vine* and *Colorado Boulevard*, were also *Kirkus* Best Mysteries.

Sutton has been an executive producer of *Cheers*, a writer/producer for *Boston Legal, NewsRadio,* and *Terriers*, and the creator of several TV shows, including the cult favorite *Thanks*. He is also the co-author, with Janet Evanovich, of the *New York Times* bestsellers *Curious Minds* and *Wicked Charms*. His other novels include the romantic thriller *15 Minutes to Live*.

He lives with his wife and family in South Pasadena, California, and Vinalhaven, Maine. Learn more at www.phoefsutton.com.